Frances Wells

Hap

Love,

SISTERS Chris & Marcia

Also in the River of Freedom Series by Tim Stafford
The Stamp of Glory

SISTERS

A Novel of the Woman Suffrage Movement

Tim Stafford

THOMAS NELSON PUBLISHERS®
Nashville

Published in Nashville, Tennessee, by Thomas Nelson, Inc.

Scripture quotations are from THE KING JAMES VERSION of the Bible.

Library of Congress Cataloging-in-Publication Data
Stafford, Tim.
   Sisters : a novel of the women suffrage movement / Tim Stafford.
      p. cm. — (River of freedom series)
    ISBN 0-7852-6906-1 (pbk.)
     1. Women—Suffrage—Fiction. 2. Women's rights—Fiction.
   3. Suffragists—Fiction. I. Title.

PS3569.T25 S57 2000
813'.54—dc21
                                                      00-034876
                                                      CIP

Printed in the United States of America.
1 2 3 4 5 6 — 05 04 03 02 01 00

Contents

Book I
Twin Sisters

Chapter 1
1890: Out of the West Pole

Santa Rosa was such a quiet and remote farming town, cut off from San Francisco by forty miles of bad roads and the body of water known as the Golden Gate, that a departure for the East was a rare event. By the time the driver had carried the Nethertons' trunks downstairs and strapped them on the carriage, a small crowd of spectators had gathered on D Street to see them go. Some of the Nethertons' neighbors had come out, along with boarders who evidently had no business to conduct so early in the day, two staring Indian children, and Mayor Brooke, a garrulous man who had happened by and went around the group shaking hands indiscriminately. A brilliant morning sun glinted off puddles in the macadam road and drew the green of winter lawns through their masking of frost.

Rebecca Netherton paused at the top of the porch stairs, an impressive figure in her embroidered traveling gown, her large feathered hat, and her cape. She was a woman of medium height, but she stood up so straight that people often thought of her as tall—not leggy like a dancer, but monumental, like a general. Her trunk did not flex—had not even done so when she was a younger woman. Now she was in her fifties and a speech maker by nature, who tended to see her neighbors as a mass rather than as individuals. If she had not been born a woman, a political career would have been natural.

"Friends," she announced in a full and fruity diction, "we will miss you. We will carry the people of Santa Rosa in our hearts. My daughter and I go as your representatives in a great historical moment. Remember this day. I believe it will develop as the beginning of the end of a terrible mistake."

Rebecca paused, as though expecting some token of approval, perhaps applause. Her daughter Susan, a grown woman who had stood patiently by, took the opportunity for moving past and down the stairs. "Come, Mother, we'll miss our train," she said. She did not mean it to be funny, but some of the neighbors laughed.

"She'll be making speeches on the cars," their silver-haired neighbor Robert Adams said, loud enough to be heard. "To the conductor, I imagine."

"Wait, I must take a photograph," Rebecca said. "Where is the Kodak?" She fumbled in her bag to find the black oblong box she had ordered for the trip, and lined up her neighbors in the viewfinder. The Kodak had recently been offered as the world's first portable camera, and Rebecca loved few things more than a new invention, the epitome of progress.

They said their last farewells. Mayor Brooke shook hands vigorously, saying he was always happy to have every respectable point of view represented in the town. Flora, a pretty, dark young woman who would take care of the boardinghouse in their absence, kept cheerfully reminding them of their departure. "You don't want to miss that train!" Finally they were in the carriage and wheeling down Fourth Street toward the depot.

For a few minutes they ran alongside McDonald's streetcar. The streetcar driver tipped his hat and gave his horse a flip of the reins. A druggist who had gone to high school with Susan was seated in the car. When he saw them, he raised his fedora and shouted happily, "Give it to them, ladies!" Then the car fell behind. The street was flanked by brick buildings, two or even three stories high, stores and banks and offices. At the courthouse square some of the idlers shouted out to them or waved; one group broke into loud laughter when they were past.

"How glad I am to be escaping these rubes for a few weeks," Rebecca said. "Every time I travel I ask myself why I settled in such a backward zone."

"It must have been the climate," Susan said dryly. "You often say so. Look, there is Mr. Burbank!"

The neatly dressed but absentminded figure of Luther Burbank, the plant wizard, was making his way along the boarded sidewalk of the street. When Rebecca called out greetings, he tipped his hat, although it did not seem to Susan that he had recognized them.

"I wonder whether he is with our cause," Susan mused.

"Of course he is," Rebecca said. "Luther Burbank is a genius. A man of that stripe is always with us. It is the illiterate fools and the corrupt drunkards who won't support us."

At the train station they found two women from the Woman's Club, nearly identically dressed in large black hats and heavy dresses, looking as though they were attending an affair of state. Rebecca immediately unstrapped her Kodak to take pictures. The women marveled; they had never seen a portable camera. Susan had to extricate herself from their flurry of talk to get the trunks into the hands of a porter.

They kept talking while Susan glanced between her mother's face and the door of the train. Mrs. Henry and Mrs. Anderson gabbled on. Would they really see Susan B. Anthony and Mrs. Stanton and Lucy Stone? Would they really be received at the White House by President Harrison? Would his wife preside at the meeting? Yes, yes, they would see all these people.

The conductor called. They climbed aboard the half-filled car and waved to Mrs. Henry and Mrs. Anderson. The train jerked and began to roll. In less than a minute they were across the creek on the iron bridge, out of the town, and into the country.

Susan took a breath and leaned her cheek against the window. Only rarely had she been on the cars, a few times to Petaluma, twice to San Francisco for great meetings. Only once had she crossed the country, and that was when she was five years old, coming west with her father. To their left, paralleling their route, she could see the road-side scruff of the Petaluma Road. A single wagon pulled by a single mule approached the town by that route. Otherwise, the landscape was empty of people. Susan saw pasturelands sprinkled with the mush-roomed heads of valley oaks.

Rebecca was staring ahead into space, disinterested in her sur-roundings. She was a handsome woman with a strong, square mouth and close-set eyes. She noticed her daughter. "This will be the greatest experience of your young life," she said and smiled, patting her hand.

Susan responded while keeping her eyes on the streaming country-side. "Greater than what, my high school graduation? Or the agricultural fair? I can't decide."

Rebecca ignored her sarcasm. "Years from now, when they write the history of this century, they will remember this convention. You are extraordinarily blessed as a very young woman to be an eyewitness to the greatest reform movement of the age. Half the world will gain their free-dom. Think of it."

"It's an American movement, Mother. The world comes later."

"It will spread through the entire world. The spirit of liberty and democracy, when it breaks out from this chosen nation, will spring up everywhere. Susan, I feel that the time is come. We threw off the monar-chy of England a hundred years ago. Now the greatest monarchy is in its last gasp, the monarchy of men. We will win our freedom."

Rebecca turned suddenly to her daughter. "Susan, I want you to remember this. Promise me."

"Promise what?"

"That you will remember this moment, when I made the prediction that this will be the greatest experience of your life."

"I'm sure I will remember it without any special effort," Susan said and thought that it might be a very long trip to Washington if her mother kept making speeches.

———————

While the train climbed Petaluma Hill, Rebecca closed her eyes and drifted off, her mouth falling open and her head collapsing onto her bosom. Ordinarily she did not awaken so early; she allowed Charles, the Chinese cook, to feed the boarders and bring breakfast to her room.

Susan was glad to be left alone. She wanted to take in every tree, every shack, every fence that the window would reveal to her. The train had a view like God's. She had never moved so fast, high above everything.

From this perspective, flying away from it, the dreariness of her life brought just tolerable pain, like a toothache one only occasionally notices. She was a twenty-five-year-old woman with long red hair and appallingly white skin, coloring that made her seem unearthly and frail, she knew, though she did not feel that it told the truth about her. She felt quite the opposite: as ordinary and as durable as dirt. She had no prospects of marrying. It was worse than that—she had no desire for such prospects. She was as sunk in her surroundings as a rock bound in the roots of a heavy oak stump. She didn't care if a man came along. She couldn't foresee caring.

Her mother, at least, was notorious; everybody knew Mrs. Netherton and her high-toned, speechifying, woman-woman-woman drumbeat. People laughed at her, they avoided her and patronized her, but she at least had a part to play. Mrs. Netherton was a suffragist, every inch of her. If Susan were identified at all, it would be in the same way. Why, however, should Susan be identified?

Susan did not like her own thoughts. She could almost hear herself drone, like a state senator she had once heard who had a cold and spoke in such a slow, nasal drawl he seemed likely to drift off in the middle of his own sentence. She was a twenty-five-year-old woman who ran a boardinghouse. No, even that was not true. Susan did most of the running, but her mother always spoke as though she did everything herself. People called it Mrs. Netherton's boardinghouse. Susan didn't care. She took no pride in it, no interest. She ran the house because she didn't want to teach and she couldn't stand to sew, and they needed to live. What could she do that no one else could do? She could keep score for the town baseball team.

For just a moment she smiled at herself. Truthfully it gave her a spark of life. Such a tiny, useless spark of life. She liked it, though: the way the ball bounded up the middle, eluding everyone; the authority with which she could sweetly record 6–4–3 to make an event a fact.

Susan shifted her cheek against the window. She liked to feel its cold. The train had cleared the top of Petaluma Hill and was grinding downhill again, preparing to stop in Penn's Grove. A cluster of eucalyptus broke up the sunlight. She tried to catch the smell of the leaves. *It is winter*, she reminded herself. When the spring burst out of the trees, their scent would blow on the breeze for miles.

Already she felt better, even thinking such depressing thoughts. She was far from the place of her droning. She was like that bright ball bounding up the middle.

Rebecca's face had relaxed, her skin sunk into deep, soft wrinkles around her neck, with the texture of fine leather. Her head waggled slightly with the rocking of the car. If she were to hear what Susan was thinking, she would reprove her. There is nothing wrong with your life, she would say, and she would interpret the misery entirely in political terms. She blamed men, in short. And Susan was not of a mind to disagree. She had grown up on her mother's thoughts. She had read (or listened as her mother read) the recorded essays and speeches of Elizabeth Cady Stanton and Susan B. Anthony and all the rest, and they spoke perfect sense to her. She ought to have the vote. If the loungers at the Occidental Hotel got it, she certainly should. Susan knew her mother would say that her feelings of pointlessness started and ended with the fact that she had been made a noncitizen in a democracy. Her mother would say that a mind like hers should be properly engaged in the issues of the day. That was, no doubt, what her mother thought when she said that this would be the greatest time of her life—for this suffrage convention would feature oratory on the great issues. She would meet women who did not keep score for the town baseball team, but who spoke on matters of philosophy and politics, even science, who made their living speaking on the Chautauqua circuit, women who were doctors and ministers and authors.

It did not stir her the way it did her mother, but possibly that was only because she had never been with such women.

Really, she wanted most to see her twin sister. That was the single hope she could dwell on, day in, day out. They had not seen each other for seven long years, and Susan had missed her sister every single day of those years. Once they had been twins in the deepest spiritual sense, utterly different in appearance and outlook, yet snug in their shared location in the world, their complete, detailed understanding of each other's mind. That had been the real intellectual challenge of her growing years—to understand every knob, every bump of her sister's head.

Certainly they were different. Elizabeth had never seemed to have a doubt, never conceived of a room where they would not be welcomed. She had made it easy for Susan. Susan had only to trust her sister, only to do as she said, and be led into battle with the world. In high school Elizabeth had insisted that they join the debate team, though no girl had ever debated in Sonoma County. She had made Susan practice and prepare, and then go before the Board of Education demanding their right to participate. When they won the county contest, defeating Petaluma, the newspaper had taken their pictures and written an editorial of backhanded congratulations. Still Elizabeth had insisted that they would not present the trophy to the school unless the principal issued an apology. Which he did! Elizabeth had challenged and triumphed—and they had always done it together, the twins. In public her beautiful sister led, but in private they were equals and intimates. They had poured out thoughts to each other like a fountain.

And then that terrible treason—Elizabeth left for the East. She married.

They wrote, of course. Susan wrote constantly—wrote in her mind, when she was not sitting at the table and writing sheet after sheet. She wrote until her mind was emptied out, not just of news from what she called the West Pole, but even of feeling. She wrote down every living thought that flared, however briefly, in her brain. It was a habit now, but not a satisfied one. Elizabeth, the independent one, wrote back rarely and seldom at much length. When Susan finished her sister's letter, she would read it again, searching for what surely was missing—the brains, the heart of her sister. She did not complain, for what did she have to offer back? Left alone, without her sister's daring, she was a grub. Her sister had more than enough life without Susan. She even had a daughter, whose name she had never bothered to mention, though Susan had asked it several times.

They would see each other, surely. Susan thought about it desperately and not only because she loved her sister. She hoped that somehow her sister's daring would again help her to find herself. For when she had known her sister's mind so clearly, she had seemed to know her own mind, too, and to have a real existence.

———————————

The approach to Tiburon ran by the bay, easing sideways along hills that ran steeply down to deep, faceless water. Only a few shacks littered the waterfront, with boats tethered to graying docks. Susan could hardly breathe, knowing she would soon be suspended on that water, what, a hundred yards deep? She had seen the bay before and seen the ocean, she had been over the water to San Francisco and back, but this was truly her jumping-off place on a voyage that would take her unfathomably far.

She and her mother sat on benches in the station house, watching a crush of passengers embark on the busy ferry to San Francisco. Heading for Oakland and its railway terminal, they would take a smaller boat.

Rebecca had brought lunch in her purse. She now produced it, wrapped in Charles's neat newspaper bundles, tied with twine. The knots were all but impossible: fine, hard-bitten knobs of fiber. "I don't see why he couldn't tie a bow," Rebecca fussed as she picked at one. "Only a Chinaman could undo this." She worked assiduously with no luck. Then she went into her bag and came out with a pair of sewing scissors. With one quick click she cut the knot in two. She undid the other packages in similar fashion. There were chicken sandwiches and boiled eggs (with salt twisted separately into a triangle of newsprint) and apples, their skins just beginning to wrinkle over softening flesh. Rebecca spread a handkerchief in her lap and ate hungrily. It was not yet noon.

"You should eat," she said to Susan. "When you travel, you must eat as you have the opportunity."

"No thank you," Susan said.

"Why is it that anything I suggest is exactly what you refuse to do?"

My whole life is as you suggest, Susan thought.

———

Susan remembered the day she had come home to find her mother crying. Neither could say a word: her mother because of tears, Susan because of perplexity. Her mother never wept.

Hurrying into the parlor, Susan saw a man seated on the sofa, and then her dark sister, prettily perched on the edge of her chair. Elizabeth was teaching school in Fulton; she boarded out; they saw her only on Sundays. Why had she come home? Elizabeth got up happily, making a gesture in the direction of the man. She seemed to glow with delight: her skin flushed, her eyes bright, her deep auburn hair lustrous.

The man was middle-aged, of a small, light build, with fine red hair that hung straight over his collar. "Susan," he said, "my Susan." He stood up and extended his hand. Then she realized who he was, and she felt herself stiffen, as though her limbs were filled with drying cement.

"It's our father!" Elizabeth said. "Don't you know him?" She got out of her seat and almost pranced over to the man, putting one arm around him.

"Don't worry her, Elizabeth, my dear," their father said. "It's a shock to see her old dad after such a long time. Sit down, my dear, sit down. There's no hurry. I'm not going anywhere. We can talk and catch up on old times now, if you like, or do it tomorrow or the next day." He smiled. His face was burned red from the sun, but she saw that his fingernails were perfectly groomed and he wore a good suit. He looked much smaller than she remembered him—a short, limber, well-groomed man with the manners of a gentleman. His eyes were webbed with fine wrinkles now, but otherwise his face looked just as she remembered it.

"Where have you been?" she asked. She meant it as a time-passing question, but as soon as she said it she felt its accusing tone.

"My dear, I've been here and there and everywhere. You know that the stock market has collapsed? Out here I sometimes wonder whether anybody knows anything about the rest of the world. I had a lot of my money tied up there, and I've been trying to regroup. For a time I was in Chicago. Then I went down to Albuquerque, doing some business for a fellow I know in Pittsburgh. Very wild country there. Did you know the Apaches are still on the warpath? I was nearly captured myself. I met their chief, Geronimo, the ugliest fellow I ever saw. He told me that when he was a child, a dog attacked him and left the scar of its bite across his cheek."

"You met Geronimo, Daddy? Really, did you?" Elizabeth asked.

"That's how he introduced himself," their father said. "I didn't question him. You don't question a man like that."

"You have the most interesting life," said Elizabeth. "Not like us, moldering away. Did I tell you that I am a schoolteacher now?" She made a face.

"Oh, yes, I know. Mother told me," he said. "I want to discuss some serious matters with both of you. Matters of your future. But not now." He waved the subject away. "This is not the time for dreary matters. The prodigal father is returned! Kill the fatted calf!" He laughed and pushed his red hair behind his ears.

He talked along in that way. He told stories no one could pin down, with details as fair and ephemeral as moonlight. Elizabeth responded just the way she always had—she was entranced, as though he were a Merlin. And, Susan realized, she responded in the traditional way. She turned into stone.

Their father had always been more symbol than human being for them. He was the original sin shadowing their lives, Man the Tempter responsible for whatever misery they endured. He would appear occasionally, always without warning, always without substance, as though to renew the power of his symbolism. This was the fairness one could never kiss; this was the flooring that had rotted away and would drop one into the cellar, however strong its surface might appear. From her father and his sporadic forays into her life Susan got her fear and her resentment, and for this, too, her conservative character, she found him responsible. He had always let her down.

Elizabeth took just the opposite turn. Her father was the Prince of Escape, promising something elegant outside the boardinghouse and outside their mother. Elizabeth collected in her mind the stories their father let fall; she picked them up and embroidered them, making him into her hope. So her eyes were bright when he appeared. Their father was the Other Possibility that could wound their mother and change the subject. Elizabeth used him as a sharp stick to keep her mother at a distance. Susan had analyzed these reactions from the time she was a teenager, but as her father danced about and played his hand, she saw them and felt them, just as helplessly as ever.

———

Susan stayed on the ferry deck; she didn't like the close, oily feel of the cabin, noisy with the reverberations of the engine. The water frightened her, but it also exhilarated her. The sky had a light skim of cloud filtering its blue, but the bay water lurching heavily against the boat captured none of the light: it was a fearful gray-green mass, a liquid sledgehammer. Susan thought she could watch its weight smash and rebound forever. Still her eyes were pulled upward to the soft gray mountains surrounding the bay, and the gray furze at the base of the hills that, as they drew closer to Oakland, resolved itself into trees and buildings. The dock rose out of the water, then its pilings and human figures took on shape, and finally the fine definition of wood and rope.

With their luggage they crossed a huge paved plaza, full of wagons and carriages and porters with their two-wheeled carts. The railway terminal was massive, a cathedral that echoed to the hubbub of travel. When Susan read the chalkboard postings, she found that their train was already prepared for boarding.

They had not afforded Pullmans, so their seats would be their home for four days and nights to Chicago. Fortunately the seats were padded with a corduroy cushion. Looking around at the car, Susan approved its polished wooden racks with their brass fittings and the clean-swept wooden flooring. She felt she could settle in here.

Rebecca got out a newspaper—the *Woman's Journal*. Other passengers were arriving and stowing their luggage. One family had four little boys, speaking an unknown language and wearing clothes that were unmistakably foreign—little caps, embroidered vests. A sprinkling of well-dressed men came on without luggage, carefully pulling up the creases of their trousers before they sat down. A farmer wearing jeans rolled down the aisle, throwing his straw hat up onto the luggage rack. The only woman was the foreign wife. She had a red face and a kerchief on her head. Irish? Susan was really quite ignorant of foreigners—they were rare in Santa Rosa.

They settled and waited, as placid as cows ready for the barn. The little boys made a shrill racket until their mother gave one a cuff and spoke sharply—then they were still except for stifled weeping. Up ahead Susan could hear the chuff of the engine. The train lurched, seemed to hesitate, then lurched again with a slow shriek of metal wheels. The town of Oakland came into view as they emerged from the station: brick warehouses, storefronts, canneries, then frame houses, laundry hung out on lines, dogs and milk cows and, in an alley, five skinny boys, as tall as men, running effortlessly to some business. Soon the train was into the hills again, gray harp-shaped hills with an underlayer of brilliant green just showing under last summer's dead grass.

Chapter 2
1883: The Separation of Twins

Ordinarily Rebecca Netherton presided over the boarders' dining room, but on the evening when her husband arrived out of nowhere, the family ate in the kitchen, so the boarders were only a distant rumble. Susan would remember for the rest of her life that cozy evening, sitting around a small table, with the rich, moist aromas of the meal radiating from the stove.

Her mother began the meal on edge, flaring up at her husband's words, using her sharp tongue. It was not long, however, before she showed signs of enjoying herself. Paul Netherton was a storyteller, and Rebecca loved talk of every kind. He did not directly address her very much, except to compliment her on the meal and the quality of the boardinghouse. He aimed his talk at his daughters, telling them their mother's history in the years before they were born. Of course they knew it from their mother's angle, but it was interesting to hear what their father remembered. Susan, though she tried to keep aloof, could not help being drawn to the image she saw around the table of a complete family. She felt herself softening toward the man she distrusted, all the more so as she saw her sister treat him with such yearning and fondness.

"Your grandfather Nichols was a very brave man," he said. "I knew him well. Everybody in New York knew of him, and most admired him, unless they were part of the slavocracy. I'm sure you know he was a very staunch abolitionist. He worked closely with the Tappan brothers, who were wonderfully successful men of business, absolutely tremendous in the support they gave to the fight against slavery. You know all that, don't you? You don't know about your grandfather? Well, I would say that your mother got her convictions about suffrage directly from him. You don't agree, my dear? Yes, because all the abolitionists favored woman's rights. This is a point that many people confuse. They might not have favored a woman holding office in the antislavery societies, but that was because it would cause such a scandal. They put the slave's cause first, but they always respected woman and her rights."

Rebecca began to object, but he waved her off. "I know what you want to say, my dear, and you're right about their lack of consistency, but it's very hard for these young girls to imagine how shocking it was for a woman to even speak or pray, yes, pray, in public in those days. People were outraged at it. Your grandfather was a friend to the great Angelina Grimké, who was the first woman to speak to mixed audiences, men and women. They called them promiscuous assemblies. Isn't that charming? Promiscuous assemblies. She was the very first. It was such a scandal, the Boston Ministers' Association wrote a public letter condemning her for it. She was speaking against slavery, incidentally, not about woman's rights. But a woman could not speak at all in public. Your grandfather knew her and supported her. I believe he may have introduced her to her husband, the famous Theodore Weld. Can you think of that? And Mrs. Weld was one of the first women to meet Elizabeth Cady Stanton when she was just married and didn't have any idea about woman's rights. Mrs. Weld set her going in that direction. You see, all those first women were abolitionists. That's where they got their ideas about liberty. They spoke up for the slave, and then they thought, *What about us?*

"Rebecca," he said reproachfully, "you haven't taught these angels about their grandfather? He was a great man. I admired him tremendously. But then, everybody in New York admired him. He made a lot of money in his business."

"I wish we had some of it," Rebecca scoffed, but she was smiling, swaying slightly with the breeze of memories.

"Did you know those ladies, Daddy?" Elizabeth asked. "Mrs. Stanton, and that Mrs. Grimké, and Aunt Susan?"

"Of course I did, as well as your mother did. We were always a suffrage family, right from the beginning."

"You, suffrage?" Rebecca asked. "Be honest and say that you had other interests."

"Other interests, yes. I was struggling to make a living. They were hard times after the war. I couldn't donate my time to a newspaper that was going out of business, the way you could." He held up a hand. "Stop. My dear, let's stop there. We do not need to quarrel again. These lovely girls deserve better."

"They could have deserved a father to support them."

"Oh, Rebecca, my dear, let's focus on the good. We have, after all, a great supply of it here! Girls, do you know that Aunt Susan would sometimes rock your cradle? Right in our little parlor, Susan B. Anthony would have one foot on the cradle and her hands on a piece for the *Revolution* she wanted your mother to edit. We had a double-size cradle that I had made for you to share. An old black man built it to my specifications, and he asked me what I wanted it for. I said it was for my beautiful twin daughters. He said, 'Oh, master, don't put them in there together. They'll suck the wind out of each other!'"

Rebecca's face softened as she laughed; she seemed genuinely to enjoy her husband's charm. Susan watched this with confusion. Her mother's tears that afternoon had shocked her, but she understood them. That her mother might still enjoy the company of this man who had done so much against her, Susan could not comprehend.

"Do you remember that cradle, Rebecca?" their father was asking. "It was a beautiful piece, and I don't know what became of it."

"Of course I remember it. I'm sure I left it with my mother." Rebecca turned to Elizabeth. "Oh, you two were such a terrible burden of work. You would both be crying, and I couldn't feed you both or hold you. I pray you never have twins, either one of you. I think the Indians must be right, to kill them both as a curse from God. Now that you are grown up, it is all right, but then!"

Their father had alluded several times to an important subject he wanted to discuss. *Probably,* Susan thought, *he wants money.* They had nothing to give him; they lived just comfortably. A woman could not earn like a man, and her mother was forever getting cheated by some peddler who could not pay his bills. She complained about it, but would turn around and extend credit to the next one. For such an imperious character, she had a surprisingly sentimental side.

Susan wondered where her father would sleep that night. Had her mother given him a room under their own roof? Then she thought, *Surely he will not sleep in Mother's bed.* Merely the thought caused her to burn with embarrassment. Surely not. But she would have thought it impossible for them to talk so fondly of old times.

———

Paul Netherton had brought apricots. The Chinese cook, who had a name they could not pronounce, carried them to the table in the large blue Dutch bowl, perfect fuzzed orbs that had swallowed the glow of a rising sun, soft, perfumed fruit that fell from its stone. Even the stones were beautiful. Plump, ridged, walnut in color, they collected on the table like lopsided marbles. Netherton said he had bought the fruit in San Jose that morning as he got on the train.

"Now I want to talk seriously about the future," their father said grandly while brandishing an apricot, holding it up by his thumb and forefinger. "Rebecca, these girls of ours are grown. I don't want them marrying farmers and spending the rest of their lives washing and cooking. I want them to go to college."

"Neither of them has much interest in that, Paul," Rebecca responded. "Elizabeth started a course at the college and didn't go on."

"I don't mean the Methodist college, my dear," their father said with elegant disdain. "I mean for them to go away, to meet cultured people and people of means."

"We meet cultured people already," Susan interjected. "You don't realize how Santa Rosa has grown. We have an orchestra and a theater and a library. Between San Francisco and Portland you wouldn't find another such place."

"My dear, you have no idea. When you speak of San Francisco and Portland, I want to laugh. That you would think these a standard. San Francisco itself is a wasteland. I mean the East. In the East you will meet people of lineage and of learning. It's not the schooling I'm after. It's the exposure to a world you can never find in the West."

"But that is so far, Daddy," Elizabeth said. "How would we ever get so far?"

"I would take you, of course."

At that Rebecca stood up so abruptly, her chair fell over backward. She held herself up like a queen and said, "No. You will *not* take them away from me a second time. I will not allow it."

"My lovely, I don't want to steal them from you. If you would go with them, I am content. Who accompanies them is not the point. I feel they need to escape this wilderness. A few years at a college in the East, and they will know an entirely different side of life."

"No, I won't stand for it. You stole them once and once only."

"Sit down, please, Rebecca. You are quite melodramatic. They are eighteen years old. They have to decide for themselves. Sit down."

"Sit down, Mama," Elizabeth said. She picked up the chair and guided her mother into it.

Susan thought she saw where her father's plan would go. "Where would we get the money?" she asked. "We don't have any money here."

"I realize that fully, Susan, my dear. Nor have I, nor have I, I regret to say. This is my plan: I would accompany you to the East where you could visit your uncle Lewis. You know he is a minister."

"Lewis has nothing to do with me," Rebecca said.

"It has been many years, my dear, and I hope he has softened. And these are his own nieces. I saw Lewis last year. I don't think I have mentioned that fact. Yes, I went to see him, and I think he would welcome his nieces very gladly if I were to bring them along. And I am hopeful that he would agree to pay their fees. For him it would not be too much! They might go to Vassar or Swarthmore or Cornell. All those colleges and several more now take women students. I intend to consult Henry Ward Beecher, and I am even hopeful that he can put us in the way of a scholarship."

"Beecher? That snake! I want nothing to do with him!"

"I understand that you do not remember him fondly, but he is one of the most influential men in the nation. Many young women would be very grateful to him for his attention."

"Oh, quite, like poor Libby Tilton, whom he seduced and ruined. That man is a snake, and I don't want him near my girls."

Their father almost got up and danced, smiling so broadly. "Reverend Beecher is seventy years old now! I think he is safe. Oh, my dear!" He threw himself back in his chair.

Rebecca stood up again. "Paul, you have done cruel things to me for so long that I expect nothing else. But this you shall not do. You shall not steal my girls again. You will not introduce them to a brother who despises me and would welcome them only without me."

Elizabeth had a crooked smile on her face. "Mother," she said, "I'm not stealable."

"That is what they said in 1870!" she said. "Look what he did to me!"

After Susan had assigned Elizabeth to put her father up in a guest bedroom, she went to her mother's room upstairs. Only one light had been lit, and her mother faced away from it, looking into the shadows.

"A woman is helpless before a man," Rebecca said in a low voice. "He took you away once before, when you were just five years old. You came from my womb. I had raised you, but in the eyes of the law you belonged to him. I could do nothing! No, not nothing, I could cry and tear my hair. He took you away in broad daylight."

Susan had taken a chair. "How did you know where to find us?" Her mother had never discussed these events in any detail, though Susan knew something dreadful had occurred.

"Oh, he made no secret about his plans. He saw no shame in it. He had stolen my life. It seemed as though he had ripped out my own heart. I came and found you here. As soon as I had settled and made you a home, he was off. He never intended to keep you."

"Then why did he steal us away?"

"God only knows what a man thinks. A man can do anything he wants. He doesn't need reasons."

"But surely he had some explanation."

"He said it was the land of opportunity. He wanted you to have the opportunity you could never have in the worn-out East. Now he will steal you back because *that* is the land of opportunity. I will not follow you this time, though."

"Mother, we are too old to be stolen."

"You don't know. A woman is helpless. He will twist you into his way. My brother Lewis, indeed. That man is so pious, he would put you into a prayer meeting for a year. You might as well join a convent and swear allegiance to the pope. Beware of religion, my darling, beware! And Henry Ward Beecher, that adulterer and liar. 'He is seventy. My girls will be safe.' No woman is safe with that man."

After a while Susan drew a kind of comfort from her mother's stubborn ranting. This was the woman she knew. She told her mother that her father would be off as soon as he realized they had no money for him.

"He knows we have no money, my darling. That is why he wants to steal you away. He thinks he can use you to get money from my brother."

When Susan left her mother and went to her room, she found Elizabeth brushing her hair in front of a mirror. "Look at my eyes," Elizabeth said immediately. "Look." She turned to face Susan, a thick queue of hair still clenched in her two hands. She insisted that Susan stare at her.

"You look happy," Susan said. "You are excited."

"Yes, wildly excited. Susan, I know you will say it's folly, but I want to go with Father."

"Why? You don't want to go to college."

"I know I don't want to teach. I can't make a farmer's wife. Susan, there's more in the East than we know. He's telling the truth. There are cities and museums and culture."

"Mother says he just wants Uncle Lewis to give him money."

"Well, if Uncle Lewis wants to give him money, is that so bad? I want to see something, Susan. If I don't like it, I can come back. And I don't believe he is a bad man. Mother says a lot of things that aren't true. Did you see how charming he was tonight?"

She had no heart to argue. Susan did not speak the argument that screamed inside her: *Don't leave me.*

Susan knew by all the inexorable laws of her existence that she could not go. For whatever reason or none, she was stuck where she was until something in her life ripened and could be released. No strong force held her, but she was not ready to go. The only strong force, one that ripped at her like strong gusts of wind, was the urgent fear of seeing her sister leave. *Don't go,* she thought.

Chapter 3
1890: At Cape Horn

An hour and four stops after leaving Oakland the train emerged from the hills into flat, marshy land. A low fog clung to the sloughs, and the sun emerged intermittently as an orange disk. Not a ripple, not a rise showed in the level ground. A picture would appear for an instant: perhaps a fisherman throwing out a net from his boat or a cat creeping paw by paw beneath a bush—and then the fog would throw a shadow over it and the train would rush away.

By now their fellow passengers had unlimbered, spreading out with papers and packets of food. The immigrant parents were involved in a heartfelt discussion, both of them making points with their hands and voices. Their children, quite ignored, made up games together, crawling under the seats or popping their heads up over the seat backs. They were different ages and sizes, but they all had the same dark and deep-set eyes.

Several rows ahead a young man got up, took his hat off the luggage rack, and walked back to the seats immediately before theirs. He carefully placed his black hat on the aisle seat, lifted the creases of his brown trousers, and sat down by the window. Susan caught a scent of pomade. His hair, directly in her view, swirled around his part, dark, clean, and shining.

"I'm not bothering you, am I?" he asked, turning his face to look at her. He had the ghost of an accent, something European. His face was young, clean-shaven, and his nose was snub, which gave him a cheerful look.

"No, that's all right," Susan said.

"I like kids," the man said, "but those are a little noisy. I hope you don't mind."

"No," Susan said, though she did regret an interruption to her reverie.

"Are you going to Sacramento?" he asked in a friendly way. "That's where I'm headed. Ever been there?"

"No."

"Are you from San Francisco, by any chance?"

"We come from Santa Rosa."

"Oh," he said. "Up north, isn't it? I've been in Frisco for a few days. I had a little work." He swallowed his *rs* so that *work* came out *wuk*.

Susan smiled and said nothing. She turned her head to look out the window.

"I guess I'm bothering you," the man said. "That's okay. I've got a newspaper to read."

Rebecca glanced over at Susan, a look of knowing approval. This irritated Susan more than the man's interruption.

"Oh," Rebecca said ten minutes later, throwing down her newspaper, "I do hate that Lucy Stone. Why Susan felt obliged to invite her to the convention I can't imagine. I feel sure that she will do something mean."

"Mother," Susan said, "the convention is to unite the two organizations. They couldn't very well leave Mrs. Stone out."

"Why not? She could send a letter. Between her and that husband of hers, and now their daughter who acts so very nice . . ." Rebecca groped for words. "It is a dangerous combination, and I wouldn't have them there."

"What harm could they do?" Susan could not help herself asking.

"Do you know what they did? How Lucy Stone had the gall to question whether Susan was stealing from the National? Stealing? When she had raised every penny herself? They tried to break the movement, criticizing Susan and Mrs. Stanton for their association with George Train, when he did nothing but give them money to make a newspaper. Lucy Stone went out and started . . ." Rebecca picked up the *Woman's Journal* and smacked it with the back of her hand. "She started *this* just to wreck the *Revolution*. Which she did, and left our Susan with all the debts to pay."

Susan was not anxious to rehearse this history, which she knew from many tellings. "The thought is," she said in a level voice, "to put that ancient history behind us. I would think it necessary, or at the least desirable, for the former rivals to be present."

"Yes, I agree," Rebecca said, "and you know I never like to quarrel. I am always the first to extend my hand in peace. You ask what I fear. I fear that Mrs. Stone's narrow principles are going to become the rule for our entire cause. Everybody will have to sign a creed to do everything in the approved Boston way. They will probably try to line us up with the ministers and the mission societies. They are so afraid of offending anybody! I am sure that I and Mrs. Duniway and Mrs. Stanton and others like-minded will find no room in such a movement. They will ride us right out. They fear a strong woman."

Susan looked out the window, pondering why nothing more up-to-date had replaced these ghosts in her mother's brain. Did a person's youngest years thoroughly stock her cupboard of goblins?

At that moment the man in front of them turned full around. "Pardon me," he interrupted. "I couldn't help hearing you. Are you ladies headed for Washington? For the woman's rights convention?"

"We are," Rebecca said, always pleased to be recognized. She changed her tone at once. "The National Woman Suffrage Association convention. We are delegates from California. Do you know it?"

"Ma'am, I was reading about it in the newspaper. To be honest, I'm surprised ladies like you take part in that." He grinned, a mischievous humor flickering over his amiable features.

"Why," Rebecca asked in a grave manner, "why would you find it surprising?"

"Begging your pardon, ma'am, I would think a woman who wanted a political career was out of her proper sphere. It's not a ladylike thing. And you seem like real ladies."

Susan cringed. She was glad to be rescued from her mother's speech making, but she shrank away from arguments.

"You don't need to beg anyone's pardon, Mr. . . ."

"Konicek. Fred Konicek."

"Mrs. Rebecca Netherton. And this is my daughter Susan." Rebecca extended her hand, and then Susan was obliged to do the same.

"I am glad you are speaking your mind," Rebecca said. (*She really is glad,* Susan thought woefully.) "I hope you will not mind if I tell you with equal frankness that it is always a mistake to speak about subjects that you know so little about. Unfortunately that tends to be a very *manly* thing to do. Since you speak about ladies and their business, let me ask you, do you have a wife, Mr. Konicek?"

He almost laughed. "No'm, but not because I'm not interested."

"Well, you have a mother then."

"Yes, ma'am. Back in the old country."

"Well, suppose you went back to the old country to see her. Wouldn't you expect that she would give you some advice? Most men admit that their mothers give them better counsel than any man ever did."

He said shyly, "Yes, no doubt."

"Well, then, if some wives and mothers think that they have advice to give the nation, wouldn't it be the wise course to let them say it? The question with me, Mr. Konicek, is what kind of a gentleman would silence his own mother and tell her she had no right to speak." Rebecca sat up a little taller and narrowed her eyes to slits.

Konicek seemed more serious now; he stopped grinning. "A woman says what she wants in the home," he said. "My mother did, anyway. She has influence on her men, and they are the ones who go out in the world."

"Why should the men speak for her?" Rebecca asked. "Do you think that men have shown themselves to be peculiarly apt in spreading their mothers' wisdom?"

"No, I guess not, but it's a rough world, Mrs. Netherton, not at all suited for the gentleness of females. I know I wouldn't like my mother to have to go to the places I go and see the things I see. Or my wife either, if I had been able to get one." He gave a slow wink to Susan.

Rebecca sniffed. "I have seen things I would not want anyone, male or female, to see, Mr. Konicek, but most of them happened inside a home, not outside. Do you think a mother ought to see her husband come home drunk, having spent the rent money? I have seen that. I think you know that a lot of women have seen that. My opinion is that such women will want to say something about the laws that license the liquor interests. She won't be very well able tell her husband what to say on her behalf, do you think?"

Konicek started to speak several times, but made no sound. Suddenly his grin grew so large, he broke out into a little fit of laughter. He could not stop, though he tried several times. Eventually he got his mouth to stay straight, and they stared at each other in silence.

"Mrs. Netherton," he said at last, "I guess you have me there. Pardon for the laughter."

Rebecca raised her eyebrows and said nothing. Konicek gave a slight shrug, and his face grew red. "I hope you aren't offended. It struck me as funny that you have so easily outargued me. Especially when our argument had to do with the fitness of women to make public arguments." He could not help himself. He showed all his teeth again. He wanted to laugh and barely restrained himself.

Continuing to stare icily at him, Rebecca finally said, "I am afraid I do not see the humor, Mr. Konicek. You have never known what it is to have your voice silenced. You are here in this country for a few years, and your voice and your vote are welcome. I was born here and am told to speak through my husband."

Rebecca pointedly went back to her newspaper, and Konicek was forced to turn around and find something for himself to do.

The mention of her father—for he was the drunken husband her mother had in mind, certainly—always turned Susan toward sadness. She would have liked never to think of him at all. He appeared at moments when he was not wanted and disturbed what little peace they had. Always playing the benefactor, always speaking fondly, when he had no right to a place in their lives. The thought that such a man and millions like him were appointed—by their own like—to rule over women, to instruct the nation in what they called a democracy, to attend to all the public business, to act as women's benefactors and protectors—such men!

Susan stared at the back of Konicek's head with its slick, smooth, dark whorl, feeling both angry and regretful. She had liked the man's friendly talkativeness, and his relaxed stand-up way with her mother, until he laughed.

Water had encroached on both sides of the train—shallow, muddy water, with rafts of debris lodged against broken trees. An egret perched on one such raft, moving its long legs daintily, extruding its snow-white neck slowly as it searched for food. Snow-white, amid such filth—the sight amazed her. From where had all this water come? They were not on a bridge, but on a causeway, in a sea stretching to the dim edge of sight in the fog.

Then, a bank of trees, hip-deep in the flood. Then, an iron bridge, spanning a racing spume of brown water. Then, a solid bank, with a boy and a black-and-white dog like toy figures. Susan realized that they had passed over the Sacramento River. Pressing her head against the window, she strained to see ahead. Sacramento City would be near. A new place. She wanted to see new places.

At the station Konicek bid them good-bye, wishing them well on their journey. "You made good points," he said to Rebecca politely. "You've given me something to think on."

Rebecca extended her hand. All was forgiven. Konicek grabbed his hat, pulled on his belt, and went down the aisle. At the door he looked back and waved.

Already gathering her papers together, Rebecca said, "A very nice young man. I don't suppose he had ever actually talked to a woman who had political views. If we could only get more such men to listen, they would give us the vote."

———

As the train ascended the Sierra foothills, the murky sky grew slowly brighter. At first Susan thought that she imagined the change, but then she saw the color of the clouds grow pink. What had been a solid cap of gray broke into distinct puffs of cloud, with purplish sky between. Then they broke out of the clouds altogether and saw the sun, glowing orange near the horizon. The clouds were below them now, a bed of gray as level and endless as the sea.

A few miles farther up the train stopped. They had been winding up the side of a canyon, and now the conductor came through the cars announcing that they could step out to see the view if they liked. "Where are we?" Susan asked. "What are we looking at?"

"They call it Cape Horn," he said. "It's the point of no return when you're leaving California. That's the American River down there."

Rebecca chose to stay in her seat, but she persuaded Susan to take the Kodak out for a picture. The camera had film for one hundred pictures. They had to use them up before they could send the box back to the manufacturer to be reloaded.

Susan walked over the rocky grade to a rickety wooden platform overlooking the precipice. A handful of passengers lounged there, looking into the soupy purple canyon. The air was still and cold, a relief from the cigar smoke and coal exhaust they breathed in the cars. Somewhere in the west the sun had disappeared, and the bright spot of Venus had come out just over the fiery horizon. Susan's eyes were drawn into the dark folds of the mountains. They seemed to spread out into eternity, wave upon wave, quite empty of people and purpose.

The passengers talked very little as they loitered and only in low tones. *Why,* Susan wondered, *are they all so somber? Do passengers traveling in the other direction feel the same mood?* She could not think so. Surely the first sight of California must fill travelers with excitement at its bursting potential. But to go back East was a soberer thing. It forced the traveler to think of what he or she had done with the vast openness of the West.

Later that night, when the train was thumping over the rails somewhere in the pooled blackness of the desert night, when Susan had awakened for the hundredth time to stare out the glass into a void, she thought again of that view and the quiet mood accompanying it. She had no real knowledge of the East. Her life had been formed in

California, cut off from the rest of America. The West Pole, truly. Yet even for her, going east meant a revisiting, a reassessment of where she had been and where her ancestors, too, had lived. She was raised a suffragist. Very well, now she would meet the suffragists from whom she had sprung, and there would be a kind of reckoning on her part and perhaps on theirs. Her mother made so much of her connection with Aunt Susan and the rest, but did it occur to her that those linkages might have broken from disuse? Might she be as cut off from the main body of suffrage as California from the country?

These possibilities were all wrapped up in Susan's mind with the reencounter with her sister, Elizabeth, who seemed to have formed such a solid and comfortable life, unlike Susan's own stranded, solitary existence. Sometimes Susan thought that she had made a mistake at eighteen not going east along with Elizabeth. She had never really considered it. She had clung to the life she knew.

Chapter 4
1890: Meeting Aunt Susan

The lobby of the Hotel Gallanty was an elaborate affair, decorated like a tiered, frosted wedding cake. It had white marble busts set in niches over the vast carpeted stairway, and a white marble fountain spurting quietly under a gigantic gaslit chandelier, with mazes of mezzanine opening onto private dining rooms, and the walls painted in bright pastel murals of the capital monuments. Elaborate hats and heavy embroidered dresses moved about this ornamented space, worn by women who clustered and promenaded, breaking and reforming ranks, gliding over the carpet. It was almost too much for Susan Netherton to take in, following her mother as she zigzagged about the room with her Kodak.

"Oh! Mrs. Butler! There she is. Lavinia Butler, I am sure!" Rebecca took her daughter's elbow and steered her to a grouping of ladies, who looked up at them and smiled the bland smiles of nonrecognition. It was, indeed, Lavinia Butler. She said, "Of course, of course," when Rebecca introduced herself and her daughter, "From Santa Rosa, California, but I used to know you, Mrs. Butler, during the days long ago when I worked at the *Revolution*." Mrs. Butler introduced the other ladies, but Susan was not sure that Mrs. Butler really remembered her mother.

Mrs. Butler agreed to pose for a photograph, however, which Susan took after protesting to her mother that it was far too dim indoors for pictures. "I think I know something about cameras," Rebecca said firmly.

"Now look, those ladies over there"—Rebecca indicated a cluster of hats following a cart full of luggage—"they are all from the Boston group. You see how they are looking down their noses at others?" Susan saw no such thing, but before she could say so, Rebecca veered in the direction of a woman who wore a huge lavender hat topped with netting and silk lavender roses. "Mrs. Babcock, this is my daughter Miss Susan Netherton. You may remember her from when she was very small."

Mrs. Babcock had a kind, serene expression. She did seem to remember and asked hesitantly, "Do I recall correctly that Susan had a sister?"

"Oh, yes! Quite, Mrs. Babcock. A twin sister, as dark as Susan is fair. They were named for the famous pair, this one being for Aunt Susan, and the other after Mrs. Stanton."

"And where is the Stanton counterpart? I hope she is still a part of our cause!"

"Yes, yes, but like her namesake, she does not always come to conventions. Elizabeth has a child and cannot escape."

"Just like Mrs. Stanton when she was young, then."

"Just."

"And where have you been, Mrs. Netherton? You used to be at every convention, years ago."

"Yes, many years ago, but living in California, I find it difficult to travel so far."

"Oh, yes, California! What an extraordinary place, I am told. I had no idea there were any suffragists there. I thought it was all miners and grizzly bears."

"Heavens no, we have strong suffragists. I came this year because of the joining of the two organizations. I could not bear to leave my Susan—the original Susan, that is—in the lurch."

"Oh, yes." Mrs. Babcock smiled serenely and said she must go.

"That was a strange response, didn't you think?" Rebecca said to her daughter when Mrs. Babcock moved on. "I wonder whether she has gone over to Lucy Stone."

———————

Susan found that the ladies' dresses and hats put her in mind of her father, strangely enough. She could imagine him here, with his New England manners and his neat high collars. A few men were present, mostly young, all well tailored. She tried to think what people in Santa Rosa would make of suffragist men. Of course they would expect effeminate monsters, but these polite, grave young men were not vivid enough to inspire alarm. Monsters seemed better represented by the ladies' hats, large enough and live enough to be swallowing ladies whole, beginning from the head.

Looking at a face under a gorgeous scarlet hat, Susan realized with a golden shock that she was seeing her sister. Elizabeth was turned halfway away, talking animatedly. Susan cried her name. Elizabeth looked up, searching. Susan waved, crying her name again. Elizabeth smiled brilliantly. They met, kissing, the scarlet hat crushing against Susan's brow.

Susan pulled back and gazed at her sister's lustrous hair, so beautifully tumbling in rings from under her hat. Her olive skin was shining, her eyes darting with amusement as she gushed over Susan. Marriage and childbearing had added depth to Elizabeth's features—she looked strong and knowing, beautiful and alive, more than Susan had remembered. Susan reached her hand out and squeezed Elizabeth's fingers. She had written so many letters, trying through ink and paper to accomplish what took one gesture in the flesh.

"Did you bring your little girl?" was the first question Susan could ask.

"No, Lucy is at home."

"Lucy!" Susan laughed. "I hoped I could see her."

"She is too young to travel. Not yet three!"

"I do not care for the name," Rebecca Netherton said as she joined them. "Why did you choose it?"

Elizabeth smiled. "I thought it a pretty name, Mother. I know its associations are unpleasant to you, but surely you agree that is all past and gone."

"I will be glad to know a real Lucy," Susan said. "What about Mr. Phillips?"

"I will tell you all about Mr. Phillips," Elizabeth said. "Let us go and have some coffee together. We have so much to talk about."

Rebecca let her daughters go without her. She was glad to see Elizabeth but far more interested in the assemblage of ladies. "I want to see who is here," she said. "I want to find Susan and Mrs. Stanton if I can." She gave Elizabeth a peck and moved off, veering toward a group of ladies seated in a corner of the lobby, then moving past them when she failed to recognize anybody.

"She is happy," Elizabeth said as she watched her go. "Do you realize this is what we heard of nonstop when we were growing up?"

"She doesn't get much of this in California," Susan said.

"She certainly shows no interest in me. Do you know she's never written me? Not once."

"I suppose," Susan said slowly, "that she thought I was doing enough writing for us both." She hesitated to go on, feeling that they verged on a subject full of emotional pitfalls. "We didn't hear from you as much as we wished."

"You are such a writer, Susan. I adore your letters, with all the details about home. You really should write for the magazines. I wish I could find time to write like that. With a husband and a child to raise, it's just impossible."

They found a table in the tearoom. Such luxury, with the snowy tablecloths and silent waiters. The air seemed to have all the sound ironed out of it, like wrinkles smoothed from a garment. Susan had been discomfited by the snatch of conversation about letter writing, but now she tried to fix herself on the moment. How long had she dreamed of this, to have her sister alone? She longed for the two of them to open their minds and unload seven years into each other's brain.

"How *is* Mr. Phillips?" Susan asked. It was incredible to her that she knew next to nothing about her sister's mate, only that he was tall and well off and from a large family. She did not even know how he looked, let alone the shape of his mind.

"Mr. Phillips is very active and well, thank you. *Extremely* active. I sometimes wonder whether he knows his daughter's name. He remembers *my* name, I think." Elizabeth gave a laugh.

"He is taking care of Lucy, then."

She laughed again. "Oh, no, we have servants to do that. Lucy has a governess. Can you imagine, Susan? After my upbringing, a governess."

They ordered coffee, and when the waiter left, Susan realized that Elizabeth was staring hard at her, her brow furrowed. It was a look she had forgotten, and Susan felt disturbed by it, without remembering why.

"You have a lovely face, Susan. I wish I had your skin. I had forgotten how pale you are. And not a freckle! Remember how your freckles came in when we were girls?"

"I always envied you."

"Me! I remember you said that, but I never believed you. I would get as dark as a Mexican, and Mother would not keep me in or put a bonnet on me. You know, I don't see why you don't marry, Susan."

"I can't marry if no one asks me," she said. She remembered why the look agitated her: it always preceded one of Elizabeth's plans.

"Oh, Susan, that's just a detail. If you came with me to New Jersey, I could get you a dozen offers in a week. But you had better not wait too long."

Susan looked up and smiled at her sister. "A dozen offers? By actual count? Would these be men with two arms and two legs?"

"Yes, whole specimens."

"Just what makes these New Jersey men such a malleable lot compared with the men of California?"

Elizabeth cocked her head sideways, looking at Susan as though wondering whether to tell her something. "If you were a man," she said finally, "would you come courting into that house?"

"What do you mean?"

"I mean our mother. I think most men would call her a hellcat." Elizabeth said it with a slight smile.

Susan disliked the crude word, and she must have shown it on her face. "I know I shouldn't talk like that," Elizabeth continued. "I don't see how you tolerate her, Susan. In just a few minutes standing in the lobby I felt it all wash over me again. I would think by now you should be out of that home."

Perversely Susan felt herself rise to her mother's defense. "I don't find her so bad. You always fretted more than I did."

"I'm sure she's been cutting down Lucy Stone every minute she's been here, hasn't she? Do you know, they set back the cause of suffrage fifty years with that silly fight of theirs. Men look at that and think they are dealing with spoiled children. Why should they let them vote?"

"Men, I believe, have their own silly quarrels," Susan said.

"That doesn't make them eager to bring in more warring parties. I think women will have to show themselves better than men to get the vote."

Susan was irritated, not that she had never heard such a line of thinking, but that it came from her own sister. "And you think that is right?" she asked.

"Oh, dear," Elizabeth said. "I'm just describing the facts. If the American and the National hadn't spent thirty years fighting each other tooth and nail over some squabble no one can even remember, women might have the vote already."

An elderly man appeared at Elizabeth's elbow. He had a grizzled beard wrapped around a tiny, shriveled head. *He has a build exactly like a monkey's*, Susan thought. The man's rounded shoulders extended into long, stringy arms.

"Mr. Blackwell!" Elizabeth exclaimed gladly when she noticed him, and she did the introductions. Susan involuntarily stopped breathing as she put the name and face together. This aged monkey was Lucy Stone's husband.

"Mr. Blackwell," Elizabeth said, "you may not know that my sister and I were actually named for the famous pair. My mother hopes that Susan will meet her namesake here."

Blackwell gave a little bow. His graying hair suggested that he must be quite old, but he carried himself as spry as an elf, all bone and gristle. "Those are wonderful names in the history of woman suffrage," he said. "Your mother has given you something to live up to."

"Have you always thought so well of them, Mr. Blackwell?" Elizabeth asked teasingly. "I had thought that there was some criticism."

He gave a little cough. "There have been differences. Friends and comrades will have differences."

"Has Mrs. Stone come?" Susan asked eagerly. "It would be a pleasure to meet her."

"No, she is not well. She has sent a letter to read to the gathering, but she could not manage the trip. I am afraid that we are all feeling the effects of age."

"It has been a long struggle," Susan said, feeling unexpected sympathy for the man. He seemed decorous and kindly in his manners, sad and gentle, a completely unexpected appearance to her.

"Too long, too long," he said. "When we were young as you are, we never thought we would grow old fighting these battles."

He excused himself, and Elizabeth signaled the waiter for more coffee. "Lucy Stone is not well," she said. "I believe she has the Susan sickness. She gets the chills to think of having to speak to her old enemies."

"Her husband seems very kind."

"Are you surprised?"

"I suppose that I am. He is not what I would have guessed, hearing Mother rail against him and his tribe for twenty years. Besides, I had no idea that you knew him. No wonder you named your child Lucy."

"He is quite nice." Elizabeth put on a wicked smile; Susan knew she would say something juicy. "So is Mrs. Stone in her way, but she is a suspicious old lady. I think she was once a suspicious young lady. I hear that she does not even trust her Henry to take care of her investments, but demands that he put her rents in her account promptly. In her name."

"Why did she not take his name?"

"He had to talk and talk, people say, to convince her to marry him at all. She thought she would be lost to the great cause if she became his appendix. He finally convinced her that they could work together for woman suffrage. Some people say *he* became *her* appendix. She wouldn't ever trust him completely, though, and so she kept her name."

"And he did not object?"

"I think not. He is a very amiable man, as you observed."

"Still, I think Mrs. Stone had a very reasonable point. Marriage often ends the useful career of a woman."

Elizabeth seemed to scoff at that. "That may be so, if you consider that a wife and a mother do not have a useful career. Most women, however, think differently. The simple truth, my dear sister, is that women would much rather have a husband than the vote any day."

Susan was stunned by the remark. "You seem to be determined to offend me," she said. "I don't regard marriage as the highest achievement of a human being. You once didn't either."

"Nor do I now. I'm just being frank. Women want to marry. Don't you, Susan? The cause had better take that into account."

———

"There you are," Rebecca Netherton said to Susan. "Come quickly. I have found her."

Susan had been sitting blankly in the tearoom, trying to put together her thoughts. She had been startled, after Elizabeth hurried off, to find that she was left to pay. They were counting pennies, and her sister was rich. How could she be so thoughtless? And then, beneath the anger over a careless act, Susan felt shapeless disappointment over an encounter she had longed for.

When she thought over the words they had exchanged over coffee, words she had expected to treasure, she was amazed at how many ways her sister had found to prick her. At every turn of the conversation Elizabeth had managed to be contrary. It was as though she confused Susan with their mother, pushing away in a streak of independence. Susan recognized the contrariness, the pert, knowing snapping, but always she had seen it used on others. Never had her sister pushed against her.

She and her sister had grown up as close as twins could, isolated from the town by their mother's eccentricity. They were the only ones in Santa Rosa known to disbelieve, the only Protestants who attended neither Sunday services nor Christian Endeavor. Consequently they weren't invited to parties by other girls, nor later on did the right kind of boys ask them to dance. They might very easily have grown up misshapen and resentful, but Elizabeth's natural zest had never let them sink into isolation. The Netherton twins were too smart, too active, too forward; they won respect and admiration, if little love. They made their own society, independent to a fault, leaning only on each other.

Now, it seemed, Elizabeth wanted independence from Susan too. She had a family of her own and did not need a sister from the other side of the continent. Susan felt as though she had been hurrying down a corridor and, coming to the sudden, darkened end, found there was no door. The sister whose life Susan had charted like a navigator—no more. For months she had been rushing to this place, and suddenly she was stopped, befuddled.

Elizabeth seemed satisfied with marriage. In fact, she pitied her sister who had not married. Poor spinster sister. Had that been an invitation, to come to New Jersey and receive a dozen proposals? Just half an hour ago the idea of going with her sister, of meeting her friends, of being introduced to eligible men, would have been pleasant beyond all bounds—but that had soured in one conversation.

Trying to keep up, Susan followed her mother, who no longer zigzagged but moved purposefully toward the elevator. As they ascended, Rebecca Netherton looked over Susan, critically appraising her from foot to head. "Remember to speak up," she said. "Miss Anthony appreciates those who have their own minds."

Susan thought that she wanted only to get into her room and write a long letter, pinpointing her feeling. That was her habit, to find relief in a letter to her sister. She would no longer write such a letter. The sister she had written was no more. Was she being melodramatic in thinking so? No, Susan thought. The conversation was all of a piece, white marble without a crack. She could have been drinking coffee with a stranger.

Engrossed in such thoughts she stood with her mother in a hotel hallway. A young woman with her hair piled up on top of her head came to the door and looked carefully at them.

"We've come to see Miss Anthony," Rebecca Netherton said.

"She is occupied," the young woman said. Her eyes were small and hard as buttons.

"She will want to see me," Rebecca said. "We worked together on the *Revolution*. She will want to see Rebecca Netherton and her daughter Susan, named after Miss Anthony," she added. "Aunt Susan rocked her in her cradle."

The woman stared at Rebecca for an instant, as though looking her over for a job that five thousand had applied for. She gave Susan a glance and then shut the door. A minute later she returned to usher them into a simply furnished sitting room, with a fire blazing and rows of chairs surrounding it. The room was loosely filled with women, a few of whom glanced up at them but quickly decided they were of no interest. Attention centered on a figure seated on a saffron-colored sofa before the fire, her back to them. She was speaking, but Susan did not immediately attend to her words. She was occupied with looking about the room at the women, some seated and some standing. Most were young, well dressed, sophisticated. They all wore a curious expression on their faces. They listened intently to the speaker but at the same time seemed to want to appear casual and disengaged. One of the women was surreptitiously taking notes in a notebook hidden in her lap, and the rest of them had a way of leaning forward and holding their heads that suggested mental notes were being stored.

From behind the speaker Susan could see only straight pepper-gray hair pulled back into a bun, and thin, sturdy shoulders in a plain black dress. The voice was low and conversational. Susan saw that her mother, her face intent, had begun to work her way through the crowd like a stalking cat.

"People often say that it was a personal quarrel that split our movement, something between me and Mrs. Stone," Susan B. Anthony was saying. "That was not so. Mrs. Stone and I would have had no important differences if not for the great travesty that was brought on us when the Negroes were given the right to vote, while women were denied. The key to our differences," Anthony said, "was the Fourteenth Amendment."

One of her listeners commented that the Negro vote had put a great burden on the southern states.

"I was very much for their suffrage," Anthony said, "so long as it was not at the cost of ours. We sought suffrage for every citizen. That, we believed, was the meaning of democracy. However, it was nonsensical to begin the extension of democracy with men who had no education and no property, who had been abused by their masters so that they were unable to use their suffrage intelligently. It was rank injustice to give such men the vote and deny it to women who had graduated from college, who were doctors such as Elizabeth Blackwell or philosophers such as Mrs. Stanton. Mrs. Stanton and I believed that we could not support such a cause. There were others, like Lucy Stone, who believed that the Negro's hour had come and we should stand back. I have not been willing, nor am I willing now, to stand back. Somehow the opinion has been spread that it is more ladylike to stand back and wait for rights to be given to us. I have never wanted to imitate that version of a lady."

A small ripple of murmuring passed through the room. The note taker pursed her lips and scribbled. No one spoke until a girl in the back asked about George Francis Train.

"Our principle," Miss Anthony said, "was very simple. Anyone who would back us was most welcome to back us. We had so few allies, our cause was so disreputable, that we could not be particular. Or so Mrs. Stanton and I believed. Others maintained that they must have nothing to do with those whom they considered disreputable. You can see where that policy has brought us. In how many states can a woman vote today, twenty years later?"

"In one state."

"Yes, and that state is Wyoming. I never saw Mr. Train act as anything but a gentleman. He made it clear that he was not in favor of the Negro's advancement. Well, I did not agree with him. Neither did Mrs. Stanton. But he offered us money to start a newspaper, something that our cause sorely needed. We had no money for such a thing, and when he offered us what we had long dreamed to have, we took it. I regret only that the *Revolution* could not endure. I have no regret that it existed for a time.

"It was nearly the same with Victoria Woodhull. Mrs. Woodhull came to my attention right here in the city of Washington, making a stirring appeal for women to be given their right of suffrage. She was a beautiful and winsome speaker. At the same time, she held very controversial views on certain topics—notably on the sanctity of marriage. Mrs. Woodhull was an advocate of free love. But I have never thought that we ought to accept support only from those who held perfectly acceptable opinions on all subjects. After all, *our* cause is not regarded as an acceptable opinion in many circles."

Another ripple passed through the room. Susan, who listened with fascination, put a word to the gathering. This was an *audience*.

"Victoria Woodhull's skewering of that sanctimonious windbag Beecher was the best thing she ever did." Susan did not need to look to see who was speaking. Her mother had found her way to the front. "I was glad when Victoria exposed him as a hypocrite, and I am still glad."

Looking from behind, Susan could see that Miss Anthony sat up straighter. Already she was as straight as a ladderback chair, but her head rose. "Who is that?" she asked. "Will you remind me of your name, please?"

"Rebecca Netherton." And as though she was not certain she would be remembered by name, she added, "I was with you on the *Revolution*."

"Mr. Nichols's daughter!" Anthony said. "Rebecca Nichols!"

"Yes. And I have brought my daughter Susan. Named in your favor, do you remember? She is a grown girl now."

"Where are you? Where have you been?"

"I am in California, where I have been all these years."

"For twenty years? What have you done?"

"I have raised two daughters. I am active in the suffrage movement there."

"I remember you had children. Now twenty years have passed. You have not attended a convention in twenty years, have you?"

Susan had never before seen her mother blush. She cringed to watch her, standing straight and queenly before twenty young women. She had thought to be embraced by Aunt Susan, and instead she was reminded of her absences.

"Where is this Susan?" Anthony asked as if she realized Rebecca's embarrassment and wanted to change the subject. It was Susan's turn to blush when her mother pointed her out. "Come here, Miss Netherton," Anthony commanded. "It is Miss? Or have you also married?"

"No, ma'am," Susan said as she found her way to the space between Susan B. Anthony and the fire. It was an uncanny feeling, perhaps the most embarrassing of her life, to stand there under inspection from this famous woman.

"And are you working for the cause?"

"Some, Miss Anthony. It is not a large affair in our little town. But my mother and I try."

"What town is that? And where is your sister? I remember you had a sister."

"Yes, Miss Anthony, she is here at the convention also. She lives in New Jersey."

"Is she active in the cause there? I have not heard of her."

"I do not think so, ma'am. She is married."

At this, unexpectedly the group broke into laughter. Susan had not intended to say anything funny, but she could not help grinning. Aunt Susan, however, did not smile.

"I know that people think it amusing for a spinster to advise others regarding marriage," she said. "I would remind you all that I am a spinster with considerable experience. From the earliest days of our movement I would visit Mrs. Stanton and find her consumed with the needs of her children. That great intellect had no time to write or think because she had to do mending. She had to wipe noses. Perhaps I never did anything greater for our cause than when I visited her in that little village of Seneca Falls and insisted that she write a speech while I wiped noses in her place.

"So you see," she said directly to Susan, "I welcome the news that you have not married. I want you to spend yourself on the cause of woman. We have an excellent chance in South Dakota this year. Since you are unmarried, you can join me there and work for the cause. Will you do that?"

"I don't think I have the money," Susan said.

"Fiddlesticks, Miss Netherton. I have never had any money of my own, but do you think that has ever stopped me?"

To Susan's great relief, Anthony turned to other matters, allowing Susan to back away from the center of attention. Susan's mother found her way to her side and gave her hand a significant squeeze. "South Dakota," she whispered in her ear. "That is wonderful."

Shaking her off and wandering into the farthest corner of the room, Susan felt hot and in need of air. There she discovered, on a small sofa in a window alcove, the sleeping form of a short, round woman, covered with a yellow shawl. This was so unexpected that she studied the woman for some time, wondering who she was and why she was sleeping through Susan B. Anthony's audience. Occasionally the form stirred, and the woman pulled the shawl up toward her chin or shifted her weight.

Susan was the only one to see the woman awaken, slowly sit up, and look around her. She was very fat, a short, gray-haired, motherly figure with round, brilliantly blue eyes. She shook the shawl off her, wiggled her face, and looked around with exactly the bright, innocent curiosity of a small child. With her bright eyes surrounded by curls, she looked very much like a toddler that had, by some accident, prematurely aged.

The woman listened intently to Susan Anthony, as though trying to hear birds sing. Unexpectedly she interrupted.

"You are speaking of superficial barriers, Susan," she said in a strong, deep voice. "Our cause has not been stymied because women have married and had children. I do not think you will eradicate the survival instinct that makes a woman want to bring children into the world and raise them.

"We must go deeper and confront the forces that men use to keep women in thrall. They are not maternal feelings, but the superstitious religion that draws on a thousand years of woman's oppression to justify a thousand years more."

This speech was followed by a brief (and shocked, Susan thought) silence. Then the unmistakable voice rang out. "You are right, Mrs. Stanton." It was Susan's mother. "They use a big Bible to beat us down."

Susan was amazed even more: this fat little woman with the baby's eyes was the famous Elizabeth Cady Stanton! Mrs. Stanton looked around her with smiling curiosity, as though she had never seen a hotel room filled with women before.

"I don't agree," Anthony said. "Where are these great church armies that you seem to imagine opposing us? What holds woman back is woman. If the women in this room would put all their energies into the cause, we could break through. But too many of them are like you: they have a hundred interests; they have families; they want to read a book; they want to go with their husbands to hear the new Gilbert and Sullivan. They will work for woman suffrage when they can manage it. As a result, we wait."

"Why do you fault me, Susan?" Mrs. Stanton asked with a happy smile. "Have I not worked enough for the cause?"

"No, you have not, Mrs. Stanton. If I had not badgered you, I think you would have stayed at home and read novels. And now you want to take us off on another rabbit trail, fighting against the churches. Don't you realize that will only put off more women from giving themselves to the cause? You are not going to separate them from their faith."

Chapter 5
1890: South Dakota Summer

A clutter of footprints trailed across the plank floor of the Hotel Paradise lounge, scuffed out of a skim of colorless dust. Dust drifted in the corners of the room and coated the windowsills. Through the thick, hot air, flies cruised lazily in and out of unscreened windows thrown open to catch any breeze.

The room was furnished with miscellaneous plain, unpadded wooden chairs scattered at random, mainly against the wall. A couple of heavy plank tables had been set near the center of the room, with nothing on them and no chairs near them. Susan Netherton was alone here; hardly anyone had invaded the lounge all day. Those staying at the Paradise apparently remained tightly shut in their rooms or left on business very early in the day.

A room at the Paradise cost two dollars, she had discovered on arrival that morning after three days of a scorching, filthy train ride. Susan's mother had found the money to send her here; Susan had a return ticket but only eight dollars and twenty-five cents to live on. "Aunt Susan will take care of you, if we can only get you there," her mother promised.

Well, she was here. The hotel clerk confirmed that Miss Anthony had a room. He did not know when she would return.

Pierre, South Dakota, wore a harder face than any town Susan had seen yet. If California was the West Pole, what was this? *The No Pole,* she thought. Here were no flowers on hats. Women wore plain bonnets, leaving only a dark hole for their faces. They walked purposefully, their eyes on the ground. Susan found their seriousness slightly fearful.

She had taken a leap in coming. She had no idea what Anthony would say to her (assuming she ever arrived) or what kind of work she could do in such a place. Deliberately Susan steered her mind clear of such questions. Waiting in the filthy lounge was all her frayed nerves could take for the moment.

Everything depended on that very brief moment in Washington when she had stood on exhibit before Miss Anthony, when Anthony had invited her to come to South Dakota. That had been their only interaction, but her mother said that was Aunt Susan's way of taking on young women. This was a don't-miss opportunity, Rebecca said. On Susan's behalf she had cabled the National American Woman Suffrage Association (as they now called the united groups) and received this reply: "Meet July 16 Hotel Paradise Pierre SBA."

Susan had come because of her mother's assurance and because she had nothing else left to hope for. During the long train trip home from the Washington convention, Susan had played and replayed her encounters with her sister, Elizabeth. She had tried to put a kind construction on her sister's behavior, but had felt only an emptiness, as though she had pried up a loose board in a closet to find no treasure at all but only the dank, moldy earth smell of the cellar. What does a Christian do when she has lost her God? Some continue to pray from useless habit or perhaps from dread of doing nothing. Susan was temperamentally unsuited to carry on, however. She could not write her letters as though nothing had changed. She could not continue to throw hope in that direction.

She had thought of that all the way home, while she stared out the window at an empty continent streaming away behind, and then during the long, aching spring. The boardinghouse mocked her: full of men, full of noise, full of business, but with nothing to meet her mind, nothing to waste her soul and blood and spit on. She felt dead there, or like the one live creature in a universe that is dead. She could not talk to her mother about this; she might as well address one of the drummers. Once she tried to write Elizabeth, but it was no good. She wrote half the letter and then wept.

Susan had come to South Dakota in a calculated way. She was trying to dare something, the way her sister always had. Susan hoped to find in suffrage something or someone to staunch her loneliness. She took the telegram as a summons.

As she reviewed this, Susan could not help smiling at herself. Could she imagine a more unlikely hope in the whole world to be fulfilled in this dust-blown, orphaned, rickety frontier hotel?

———————

Miss Anthony arrived near nine o'clock, when the light was nearly gone. Susan introduced herself and was momentarily overcome with relief that Anthony recognized her. Anthony was entirely alone, and her face set in weariness. Susan saw the pale dust clinging to Anthony's eyelashes, etching the corners of her eyes as Anthony faced toward the last light flooding in at the uncurtained lobby window. The heat of the day seemed to radiate from the walls and the ceiling, as though a fire burned just behind the partitions.

Anthony appraised Susan a moment before shaking hands. "Welcome to the prairie," she said. "Where are your bags?"

Susan gestured toward her trunk.

"That is too large. You would be better served with two or even three smaller bags that you could manage yourself." Then she seemed to think better of her asperity and softened. "We can have someone bring it up. Come along. You will want to wash."

Anthony spoke matter-of-factly as they slowly climbed the stairs, reporting as though to a colleague. "I went out to Blunt today. Some women had arranged for me to speak, but when I arrived, no one was prepared. They had waited to see me before making any plans. I told them that I could not remain overnight, so they arranged a meeting for six o'clock, probably the hottest time of the day. I nearly fainted. We had only about twenty people, and all but one of them women who can't vote."

They arrived on the second story. "Tomorrow we leave very early for Marshall. It is a small place, but they have two families that are quite enthusiastic. I hope we will get a good gathering of voters. We will stay the night. You can put a few things into my bag."

The room, when Anthony flung the door open, held a single iron bed, a tin washbasin, a desk and chair, and four neat stacks of papers on the floor against one wall. "We can get a cot for you," Anthony said as she stripped off her black bonnet and ran her fingers through her gray hair. "What have you eaten?"

"Nothing," Susan said truthfully. "I had some breakfast," she added. She had felt ravenous all afternoon but now momentarily forgot it in the strange excitement of being alone with this famous, exacting woman.

"They will feed us at Marshall tomorrow," Anthony said. "You can't count on much in this state, but you can be sure they will feed you whatever they have." She paused. "I have some cheese and a box of crackers," she added thoughtfully. "It will get us through until tomorrow, I think. You're a young woman."

After they had used the basin to wash, Anthony pulled the desk over next to her bed and on it untied a small piece of cheese. Though dry, the cheese had wept a film of oil on the paper. Susan's stomach turned over when she caught the musty smell. Taking a small knife from her bag, Anthony carefully pared away the rind, then sliced narrow strips from the cheese. She laid these out on the paper, all in a line, then got up and found a tin box of Swift's Crackers. She set out two stacks of three crackers next to the cheese, then closed the box and put it away. "Why don't you bring that chair over?" she said. "Do you pray?"

"Not usually," Susan said.

"Neither do I. But if you want to, you may."

The meal was over before it began, almost. It left Susan more hungry, if anything. Anthony carefully wiped her fingers with a large white handkerchief, offered it to Susan, and then ran her fingers through her hair again. "And how is your mother?" she asked.

"She was well when I left her," Susan answered.

"She was a very excitable young woman," Anthony said. "Are you excitable?"

"I don't think so."

"Good. There is a time and a place for that, but I am far more interested in someone who can work steadily. Perhaps that is because it is the only thing I have been able to offer this cause."

"Ma'am?"

"Steady work. I am not a brilliant woman like Mrs. Stanton. But I never will stop until I have done what I set out to do. I am a worker for the cause. I hope you will be too."

———

They were on the train already when they saw the sun come up. It made a fiery entrance but immediately went about its business, for there were no hills, no buildings, no shadows of any kind to cast over the level, ashen horizon.

Presently Anthony put away her diary. She asked Susan whether her mother had told her much about the history of woman suffrage.

"Yes, ma'am. She talks about the early days. And we have your book."

"*The History of Woman Suffrage.* You've read it."

"Yes, again and again."

"I hope you will live to see the last volume written."

Anthony began to talk about her memories. "I began as a teacher because that was the only way a young woman could earn a living. Of course I didn't make half what young men made who were far poorer teachers than I."

It was not hard to imagine Anthony addressing a class in her even, clear tone, laying out the logic of a subject while watching her students carefully to see that they paid proper attention.

"I always thought I could make more of myself than a teacher, and so I became active in the temperance movement. It was the most obvious place. The men drink and their wives and children suffer.

"Through temperance I discovered suffrage. Or, I should say, I discovered politics and the fact that women had no voice in them. Women needed better laws to protect them from drunken husbands, but because women couldn't vote, the legislators wouldn't listen to them. It was true fifty years ago and it's true today, though the laws have improved in most places. At least a woman can have title to a business she's built up or a house she's bought with her own money, in most places. It wasn't so at all in 1850. Her husband or her father had all the rights, and she had none.

"And then, too, I learned that we would never get rid of drunkenness unless we got rid of alcohol, but the laws to license liquor were all made by men.

"The temperance organizations themselves wouldn't permit a woman to speak. Women did nine-tenths of the temperance work, but when temperance conventions were held, they gagged us.

"So I decided that the first order was to get women a voice and a vote. Soon enough I discovered a marvelous woman with more brains in her little finger than I have in my whole body. That's Mrs. Stanton. She had held a convention for woman's rights a few years before I met her. That was the Seneca Falls convention with its marvelous Declaration. Seneca Falls is not too far from Rochester, where I was raised, but I didn't hear of the convention until later on. I met Mrs. Stanton, however. Her husband left her nine months of the year—he was doing politics with the other men, and doing it badly—and she was raising this immense crowd of children all alone. She had no time to use that brain for something worthwhile. Mr. Stanton came home occasionally to impregnate her with another child. She had a great weakness for that.

"I began to rehabilitate her. I took her great mind and gave it hands and feet. I watched her children while she wrote speeches. I insisted that she come to conventions and speak—though she usually sent a letter or wrote a speech for me to give and stayed home."

"I thought Mrs. Stanton *was* a speaker," Susan said. "I thought she went to Chautauquas all over."

"That was later on, when her children were grown up. Even then I could rarely get her to attend our conventions. She did the Chautauquas for money, you see."

Anthony began probing Susan for information about California. She knew a few names, for she had visited the state years ago. Anthony was exacting in her questions, even after she ought to have realized that Susan knew very little. Eventually she asked Susan whether she thought a suffrage amendment could win the popular vote in California.

"I wouldn't think so," Susan said, after trying several times to get off with an "I don't know." "My mother has been at it almost as long as you, but people in our town don't take her seriously. They can't see the difference it would make. They don't see how it hurts women that they can't vote. And for every one of those Don't Cares, there is some Dutchman or Chinaman or ignoramus who doesn't want a woman to show she has any brains at all. He'll vote no every time."

Anthony said nothing immediately. She had a severe face when she looked unhappy. Susan could imagine that she had scared schoolchildren.

"You may be right," Anthony said, "but we must not allow ourselves to think so. It is too discouraging. We can never give up. Never."

Marshall was a ghost town in the making, a huddle of sad buildings on a single street. To Susan's eye, the gritty dust seemed to be in the process of burying the town and its people, blowing in from the fields where it smothered skeletal wrecks of row crops, filling pockmarks and ruts, throwing a skim of lime over all that stood still to hold it. At the train station they were met by a Dr. Deeds, who pointed out a wagon parked across from the station, piled with faded lumber. "They're taking the buildings down," he said. "They send the lumber on to someplace, I don't know where." Coming from Wisconsin by train, wood was scarce and expensive.

"I don't see where they're getting the lumber," Susan said. "Those buildings look all right."

"They work from the back side, so no one can see what they've done," the doctor said. "I don't know why. Everybody knows." He was a short, neatly dressed man who looked down at his feet while he spoke, as though he had done something wrong. "They take down the front on the last day, and it's as though it never was. You see the gaps between buildings? It was solid all down the street. I don't know how many people will be living in Marshall by the election."

"Where do people go?" Anthony asked.

"Anywhere they can. Some back to their folks in the East. If they have anything left, they go to another homestead someplace. This place was beautiful five years ago, when a lot of us came. We had good rains and the crops came up. I'm moving on as soon as I can. There are plenty of sick people here, but they don't have anything to pay me with, so I can't stay."

He asked whether they had seen the Russians when they came in. "You might not have noticed their places. They hardly look like houses. They're all dugouts and they have skin roofs. Those people will be all that's left here, and they don't want a doctor. I went down to their settlement this winter because I saw they were burying a lot of children, but they wouldn't have me. One big man who speaks some English told me, 'If God wants His children to live, He will do it.' Those are our new Americans. They'll starve their way through. I think they eat only potatoes. I haven't seen a cow or any animal there."

"But they will have the vote," Anthony said. "No cow, but the right to make laws for us all. They may let their children suffer and die, but they will vote because they are men."

"I doubt those ones will vote," the doctor said. "They don't have much to do with the rest of the world."

They had planned the meeting for two o'clock in the afternoon, so that those who came in from the surrounding country might have time to return home before dark. There were no roads in the district; the first settlers had plowed a furrow to their neighbors' and to the school and to the edge of town. That way they could not be lost in a blizzard or a dust storm; they could follow the furrow home. The furrows had become pathways from use.

After one o'clock they began to see lone figures appear on the horizon, barely visible because they were so far off. The land was so bleak and unmarked that the slightest wavering flaw in the visible surface of the cobalt blue sky was sure to be a human being. Families came, the children on foot even if they were barely up to a knee, babies carried in arms. The women had put on their one good dress of calico, and if the men had a dark suit, they wore it. All the children were barefoot but not even the smallest child failed to have a hat on. To go bareheaded under this staring sun was to entertain death, so their faces were hidden deep in shadow. Susan and Miss Anthony stood at the door to the schoolhouse shaking hands as the people arrived, seeing the sunken eyes glittering out of puddles of darkness. Some of the faces looked sick, emaciated, fevered. Susan wondered what could have driven them to come.

They were too many for the schoolhouse. The doctor said it was the biggest building in town, but it was barely bigger than a corncrib: a dugout about three feet deep, with sod stacked up to make walls and an open-frame shingled roof. The stove took up space so they got some of the men to detach its pipe and move it into the corner. The people who came were very quiet; they would lean down and peek through the doorway, then back out again because every bench was full and the children occupied every inch of the floor. Somebody said the children ought to go out, but somebody else said that the children would have more years to make use of whatever they learned, so let them stay.

Anthony eventually made a solution. "I will stand in the doorway," she said, "so some can be on the ground outside and still hear me. I believe my voice will carry."

She stood so straight and still in her severe black dress that she looked not like an old woman, but like some kind of immovable pillar—*Lot's Spinster,* Susan thought. Out the open door was a swathe of brilliant sunshine crowded with swatches of faded calicoes and dark hats. Surely at least fifty were seated in the dust. Anthony began her lecture in a clear and ringing voice, perhaps too loud for the inside crowd but probably necessary to reach those outside through the wind. She would take turns between speaking to the schoolroom and stepping over the threshold into the open air.

The room grew unbearably close. A baby began to cry lustily, and then as if in sympathy, another joined it, and then more until they heard a raging chorus of babies. Some of Anthony's words got swallowed up, and Susan found it hard to keep her mind on the logic of a woman's rights. She began to note how Anthony flinched at the noise; each scream caused an almost indiscernible hitch in her voice. She went on, but Susan felt—and perhaps every other woman felt the same—a growing tension. At every caterwaul they would flinch with her.

Anthony suddenly stopped—the babies did not—and they listened to the continuous, loud, high-pitched clamor of a half dozen angry voices.

"Poor things," Anthony said. "All women feel that way sometimes, I think."

They laughed. It was such a funny image: unhappy, red-faced women, bawling until their eyes might pop from their heads. After the laughs and the coughs died down, Anthony went on with her speech. The babies continued to cry, but the atmosphere relaxed. Despite the heat, despite the noise and discomfort, a kind of pleasure extended itself. They had come not so much because of the woman's cause, but because a woman whose name had been in the newspapers had come to Marshall, of all places. Here she stood in their own dugout schoolhouse; she made a joke over their babies; she joined them. The children might someday tell their children about hearing this famous woman.

When the talk was finished, they all came to shake hands with Anthony and with Susan too. It was a relief to stand out in the open air. Susan could feel perspiration trickling off her back. She wondered how the dust would look streaked onto her face. She had done nothing, of course. Yet the people, both men and women, seemed so pleased with what they had heard that they wanted someone to thank. One of the men told her to be sure to tell Miss Anthony that he was won over and would vote for her in November.

The sun seemed to bear down more intensely, as though someone had opened the door on an unseen furnace. When they turned toward it, the heat pushed on their faces like a bright fire; and when they turned away, they could feel it working hard on their shoulder blades.

———

They stayed over with a family by the name of Rodgers at a homestead a short walk out of town. The house was made of grayed sawed lumber, a single room with a loft where the children slept. Mr. Rodgers had dug a well, and that was it—no other outbuildings, no trees, not even a feeding trough to break the unaltered line of earth between here and eternity. There were five Rodgers children, the oldest of whom was eight—four girls and one tiny boy, who all stared silently at their guests.

Mrs. Rodgers had a large face with oversize features, which gave her an accidentally vivid expression of tragedy. Her mouth was double the size of Miss Anthony's trim lips and looked always about to open in a sob. Her eyes were wide set and dark, and her jaw looked big enough for a barnyard animal. Yet she was a very quiet and gentle hostess, complementing her silent, staring children and her red-faced, stuttering, gentlemanly husband. Mrs. Rodgers seated the two Susans in her only two chairs and proceeded to make johnnycake for supper. The fire made the room even hotter. They tried to make conversation with Mr. Rodgers, but he seemed too embarrassed to do more than stutter out an occasional yes or no. They could not even get that from the children, whom they would have thought stone-deaf if not for their periodic gales of giggling.

Eventually Anthony hit on the brilliant suggestion of asking Mr. Rodgers to show them around the homestead. There was little to see, only the clean horizon making a circle around. Mr. Rodgers led them south, trailed by all the children, to where his trees were planted. They were tiny saplings hardly waist-high, set out in rows to the limits of their vision. Rodgers broke one off at the root to show them—it had dried out and died completely. The soil around its broken stem was cracked and brittle. "I'd have to replant," he said shyly. "I don't have money for that, so we're going on."

It was the first moment that Susan realized the Rodgerses were desolate and would leave their homestead.

"We tried to take water from the well for them," Rodgers said, "but it just poured through the soil." He kicked at the stub of tree he had broken off. "I might have planted at the wrong time. I don't know."

When they were returning to the cabin, they saw a wooden cross in the ground, two thick sticks tied together with twine, standing almost in the shadow of the house. Rodgers explained that they had lost a child in the winter. "I couldn't dig to bury him either," he said. "Ground was frozen. We had to wait until it thawed out this spring, and then it was all mud."

He seemed worn out by the effort he had put into explanation. When they went back into the cabin, Mrs. Rodgers served the johnnycake in a bowl, and they ate with the intense awareness of the children's eyes following every bite. Their mother had given each of them a bowl, too, but whatever little she put inside was gone in an instant. Susan had the distinct impression that she was eating their food.

"We are sorry you lost your little one," Anthony said. "We noticed the grave."

"I want to get some rocks to put on that," Mrs. Rodgers said. "The wolves want to dig him up. They've been howling around, and twice Mr. Rodgers has had to go out and fire his gun at them to make them leave." She had come over from the stove and sat in a crouch on the ground near them. Three of the children found her, to sit on her knee or lean against her.

"I think it's the worst of being in this land," she said. "That howling sets me on edge. Mr. Rodgers sleeps through it, but I can't."

"Did they howl before?" Susan asked cautiously.

"Before what?"

"I mean, before you lost your child?"

"I don't remember they did. There wasn't anything to howl over, you know. We haven't had any meat since I can't remember."

"Autumntime," Mr. Rodgers put in. "When I shot the goose."

"Oh, yes, wasn't that a feast. I wish we had some of that to feed our guests, don't you, children?"

The two Susans had finished their meal and sat holding the bowls awkwardly in their laps. Mrs. Rodgers noticed and asked them if they wanted any more. They both said no, and a light shot through the faces of the children. More! They could eat more! They never made a sound. Mrs. Rodgers went and scooped food into their bowls, and a smile lit her large features as she did. She came back to them and settled down into the same hunched posture. The children found their niches on and against her, and Mr. Rodgers rocked back and forth in his squat, his arms around his knees.

"Now tell me, ladies," Mrs. Rodgers said, and then stopped short. She seemed torn as to whether to go ahead with her question.

"Go ahead, Mrs. Rodgers," Anthony said. "You have fed us a good meal, and we want you to ask anything you like."

That seemed to encourage her. "I hope I'm not prying. You're both handsome women with a lot of good schooling, and I guess you had your pick of the men, so why did you not want to marry and have babies? I mean that as a compliment. You could have married, I'm sure."

Susan glanced at Anthony and saw her composed, steady face. "I've been asked such a question a great many times," Anthony answered matter-of-factly, "sometimes right out and sometimes going around the edge. I don't mind a direct question, like the one you've given me. I did get some requests for marriage when I was a young lady, but I never thought of them seriously because I had seen I had a work to do, and marriage was only going to take me away from that work. Perhaps others make other choices, but I have not regretted mine. I know a few ladies who have chosen otherwise and do regret it, very much!"

Mrs. Rodgers seemed to swish this around in her mouth for a while, thinking it over. Then she said, "It's a great work you're doing, Miss Anthony, going around the world making speeches. I don't blame you for wanting it. You have seen a world that I'll never see. But if I had to do without my babies, I couldn't do it. Not for the finest things." She said it ruefully.

"And you?" Mrs. Rodgers asked, turning to Susan. "You're still a very young lady. Don't you ever want to get your own children?"

Susan had been thinking furiously. She fell back on her mother's lines. "There are a great many children in the world," she said, "but only one suffrage amendment. As a mother I can give to a few children, but as a suffragist I may give to half the world." In honesty she added, "That is what my mother taught me, and I have followed her."

"Your mother had her children, though. At least she had you. Do you have brothers and sisters?"

"I have a sister. Yes, my mother married, but she was one of those who lived to regret her choice."

"Why, what was wrong with your father?"

Anthony glanced at Susan but gave no clue how she should answer. Her look seemed almost a challenge, like "work it out yourself."

"My father was a drunkard, who tried to steal my sister and me away from my mother when we were young. Then he went off and abandoned us."

"A ne'er-do-well," Mrs. Rodgers said with a sigh.

"A very charming ne'er-do-well," Susan confirmed.

"I can see why you're skittish then," Mrs. Rodgers said. "I'm grateful that Mr. Rodgers is an honest man." He nodded, confirming the compliment, without even looking up.

———

They had nothing to eat in the morning. Mrs. Rodgers admitted the fact with great sorrow when they came down from the loft, where they had slept beside the children. She had sent the oldest girl to the neighbor's for milk, she said, but they lacked any.

"What will you eat for yourselves?" Susan blurted out.

"Mr. Rodgers has gone out to see about finding some work in town," she said with dignified simplicity. "We hope he will bring us something before the day is over."

They walked together to the train station, a little troupe of children who had shed their silence and now wanted to hold their guests' hands, quarreling over who would do it. Their mother seemed sunk in worry. In the cool of the day the prairie looked more hopeful: the straw was yellow and looked alive, and birds sang their penny notes from the thickets along the path. Susan held to the tiny paw of the smallest girl, who gripped her fingers fiercely. She tried to work out in her mind what would happen to this family. If they had no wagon, how could they move on? If they stayed on, how could they help but starve? She dared not ask.

It was a sober farewell, with few words. When the train was away, Susan watched the small group until they were out of sight; then she watched to see the dugouts of the Russians that Dr. Deeds had told them of. All she saw were two low mounds, more like the dwellings of prairie dogs than human habitation. Her eyes were just accustomed to their shape, she had just begun to make out other such shapes more distant from the track, when the train carried her away. The prairie fell away into its pale oblivion.

"What will happen to that family, Miss Anthony?" she asked.

"Please call me Aunt Susan, if you will. All my young women do so." She said it in a businesslike way, kindly, though not inviting intimacies. "Mr. Rodgers will have to get work."

"And what if he can't?"

Anthony paused to ponder it. "Perhaps they have some relatives or friends who can help them."

"And if not?"

She paused again. "The parents may be all right, but children can be carried off very quickly. Especially if they are weak."

The thought of those tiny, birdlike frames brought tears to Susan's eyes. "Oh, Miss Anthony, Aunt Susan, doesn't it break your heart to see it?"

"Yes, but you see a great many things when you travel the world as I have. Some of them do break your heart if you let them."

Anthony went back to her diary, while Susan thought of what she had seen. Amid such suffering she found it hard to imagine much importance for the cause that had brought her here.

"How do you go on?" Susan asked, breaking in on Anthony again.

"How can you keep on with the suffrage business when you know the people you're speaking with are hungry?"

Anthony put down her book and focused her eyes patiently on Susan. "Dear one, it tears your heart, but you must simply continue to do what is given you to do. The poor are always with us. I know, I have been poor beyond measure myself. You don't know how I have had to scrimp and do without. But my motto has been, do the work. If I get distracted by people's troubles and fail to do what I am able to do for the cause, woe is me. It is fatally easy to get distracted. Remember that."

She stared at Susan a moment, as though trying to judge whether her words had achieved their purpose. Then she said, to make things easier, "When we have the vote, we can do a thousand other things. Until we have it, we can do comparatively nothing. You see that, don't you?"

Book II
A Charming Man

Chapter 6
1895: Fred Konicek

Rebecca Netherton ran a strict temperance house. She was liberal minded when it came to morals displayed somewhere else, over the hill in Petaluma, or even across town, but in her own house she tolerated no latitude. Whereas her reputation as an atheist and a suffragist would have otherwise killed the business, this surprising moral conservatism made the boardinghouse a popular place for families to board their young men. She got a steady clientele of tradesmen of the better kind, supplemented by boys who came from outlying farms to attend the new high school on Humboldt Street, Sweet's Business College, or the Methodist college.

She declined female applicants. Even when a family who had boarded three of their sons asked for an exemption, she said no. She ran a kind of informal finishing school for young men, insisting that they dress for dinner, stand when she entered the room, and follow the regular conventions of civilized behavior. For some of the farm boys, doing this required considerable concentration. She was not above ordering them from the room when they displeased her and making them do without supper.

One result of this policy was that Susan, just as much as her mother, was treated in a queenly way. Over the years untold numbers of raw country boys had gawked at her as though they had never seen a lady before, as indeed some of them had not, at least not to notice. A regular series of them fell in love, simply because she represented their first encounter with the fair sex in its garb of manner and chivalry. They had seen only sisters and mothers and aunts with red hands and a practical walk, never a real dressed-up decorous lady.

Susan had grown up with this attention, as though it were entirely natural for a girl to have young men staring at her and smuggling notes to her. No one can help enjoying the admiration of the opposite sex, even if it comes from gaping country boys, but at the age of thirty Susan was quite beyond thinking of it. A few times when she was younger she had reciprocated a young man's admiration, but it had never come to anything. By now if a red-faced boy hung around on the front porch waiting for the slightest chance to see her walk in or out the door, she glanced at him and kept moving. That explains why she did not at first notice Fred Konicek's attentions.

He was, as she would come to realize, the same young man she and her mother had met on the train to Sacramento five years before. He sold blankets for a St. Louis manufacturer, traveling all over the northern logging camps and the Sacramento Valley as far as Redding. His rounds brought him to Santa Rosa six or eight times a year, where he would lodge for a week and call on customers throughout the county. Of course Susan knew his name: she answered his letters when he wrote to reserve a room. Otherwise, she had not distinguished him from any other male.

That began to change in April of 1895, when he came to a Santa Rosa baseball game. Susan always sat in the very top row of the stands, and she wore what she thought of as her scorer's outfit, a red polka-dot dress and a wide straw hat. She sat alone. This was partly because keeping score required her full attention, and mostly because she was generally the only woman present.

Susan enjoyed the faintly lawless male atmosphere, though she never let on. Here, a woman could not enforce good manners. She was a neat and careful scribe, whom the men had come to depend on and hardly notice.

Konicek climbed up next to her while she was filling in the lineups. He tipped his hat to her; she said hello, but barely looked up. She had to work fast to get the batting order down before the first pitch.

"What are you doing?" Konicek asked, leaning over to look in her book.

"Keeping score."

He pointed at the scoreboard in center field. "There is no score," he said.

She looked over at him. "You don't know much baseball," she said.

"I love baseball," he protested cheerfully. "There's nothing I like better."

"Keeping score means writing down everything that happens."

Konicek watched the game and watched her. Two batters had made outs in the bottom of the first inning before he spoke again. "Can you explain those symbols to me?"

She showed him how to read her hieroglyphics.

"Do you remember me?" he asked suddenly.

It seemed like an odd question. "Of course I remember you. You've been our guest what, half a dozen times?"

"I mean from somewhere else, a long time ago. I wonder if you remember our first meeting."

She had to record a fastball fouled off out of play, and then she looked over at him again. He was quite young, of medium height, with a snub nose and a cheerful, clean-shaven face. It was not a face anybody would remember. He was dressed well in an understated blue suit and a bowler hat.

"At a suffrage meeting?" she asked, though doubtful.

"No," he said. "Think. Have you never been in Sacramento?"

"No," she said and turned back to the game. But she could not help thinking about Sacramento. "I have never been in Sacramento, except once passing through by train."

"And I was on that train with you. Do you remember?"

"Were you the man who laughed? Who couldn't stop laughing?"

"Yes!" He seemed pleased.

"I thought you were very rude then," she said. "That's why I remember."

He stayed around for the whole game, interrupting her concentration and asking questions about the players. He made many observations about their play, some insightful, many mistaken. He did not know much about baseball, but he seemed genuinely interested. When the game was over, he offered to escort her home, but she told him to go ahead, she had to finish her totals.

"I can wait," he said. "I've nothing to do."

"Thank you," she said firmly. "I would rather you didn't wait for me."

He came to another game on Wednesday, sitting by Susan once again and leaning toward her to study her scorekeeping. He even asked if he could try an inning, with her to coach him. She said she would rather not, but this did not seem to offend him. He liked to talk. He talked about the towns he visited to sell his blankets, little coastal towns where the tall timber grew down to the shoreline, or inland hamlets that had only the railroad to communicate with the outside world. A few such places she had seen for herself, when she went to deliver a suffrage lecture; most she had not. She found it interesting to listen to him, though it was difficult to keep score. He distracted her.

He did not ask permission to walk home with her this time; he simply did it. The ball field was west of town, on Sebastopol Road just beyond the railroad tracks. They were crossing the railroad grade when he stopped and peered up the track going north. "Don't you think it would be quicker to go here?" he asked. "And less muddy too." It had rained the night before, and they had to pick their way along the edge of the road, littered with puddles and mired tracks.

"There's no way to go through there," she said. She always followed the Sebastopol Road up to Main Street and crossed the creek on the iron bridge.

"Sure there is," he said. "You can cross on the railroad bridge. I bet it's quicker. Have you ever tried it?"

"No," she said. "What if a train comes?"

"You can see a train coming a mile away," he said. "Haven't you ever walked on a railroad track?"

Against her better judgment she followed him. It was certainly out of character for her, but she found herself making the long, awkward strides from cross tie to cross tie. Konicek walked ahead with a little skip in his step, and then stood smiling back at her while she caught up. Meanwhile he kept talking: about his work, and what he learned about Sonoma County as he made his rounds. When they came to the bridge, Susan was nervous that a train would come, but Konicek cajoled her on. Once she had started across the span she walked as quickly as she could, keeping her eyes on her feet and trying not to see through the gaps to the sand of the creek bed below. It had never occurred to her how high a bridge was. She had to concentrate on her step, for she dreaded falling into the gaps. She could not lift her eyes to see whether a train might be bearing down on her.

When she finally got over, she took a deep breath and looked around. The town spread strangely before her: there was the courthouse, there the theater, unfamiliar from this angle. Beside the railroad grade were small houses of workingmen, where children played in a yard, and laundry flapped on a line. It was almost like entering a strange town.

She suddenly wondered who might see her. Ladies did not cross the creek on the railroad bridge. Yet by the time she scrambled off the grade and back onto the street, she felt oddly pleased that she had done it. It had been years out of memory since she had tried anything physically brave.

Not that she thought too much of it, but she was aware later that day that somehow her center of gravity had shifted toward the man who had coaxed her to do it, that she had begun watching him to see what he might do next.

Susan's life had changed very little in the five years since her great adventures in Washington, D.C., and South Dakota. She was still bound into the small-town life of Santa Rosa; she still ran the boardinghouse and kept score for the town baseball team. The only difference lay in her suffrage work and the seriousness with which she treated it now. Her sister, Elizabeth, had all but disappeared from her life since that year, had certainly disappeared as a North Star guiding her life. Susan had tried to replace that loss with the only higher cause she knew and believed in.

She had come back from her summer in South Dakota determined to follow a career in suffrage. If she could become a speaker, it would pull her out of Santa Rosa. It would give her life direction.

Susan B. Anthony had given her opportunities to speak while they toured around the state, and after one effort had offered advice: "Talk about something you know. Don't try to talk like a book you've read." Susan had not immediately understood this. What did she know? She knew how to run a boardinghouse, nothing more.

Once a week for a year after coming back from South Dakota she took the train and the ferry to see a professor of rhetoric at Berkeley.

One day after her lesson she asked whether baseball could be a suitable subject. "Of course, yes," he said. "Baseball is a very good subject. I have been in America for twenty-three years, and I do not understand it." The professor was Italian.

Her talk spoke about the need for two well-matched sides for every baseball game. It spoke of the need for symmetry; the rules must be the same for both teams. It spoke of the woman's struggle like a nine-inning game, and predicted that women would have the last at bat. Susan was not really proud of the talk, but it was quite popular and she received invitations. She enjoyed escaping Santa Rosa to visit other places. Once she had been as far as Monterey. She had met women in many parts of the state and kept up a correspondence with several of them.

She did not understand why she wanted to keep this secret from Konicek. Perhaps, she felt, the subject connected by hidden channels to the chambers of her inmost being, which she as yet had not fully explored.

He claimed to be a believer in woman suffrage, dating his conversion to their first meeting on the train to Sacramento. He said with a smile that he had never forgotten the woodshedding her mother had given him. Susan wondered whether he said it only because he thought she would like it. The subject was serious to her, so she kept her distance from it with him. She could throw out opinions about other topics, but she made sure she did not draw him out on the subject of woman. Several times in the spring she went off to another town to lecture at a Political Equality or a Woman's Christian Temperance Union (WCTU) club, but she did not mention it to Konicek. He asked where she had been, but she said only that she had business.

Through the spring Konicek found reasons to do his own business in Santa Rosa, and he became a quite regular spectator at baseball games. He never announced his plans to attend. He appeared, beautifully dressed, and sat down by Susan.

She could not pretend to herself that she remained disinterested. When he ascended the stands and stood beside her for a moment before plucking the crease of his pants to sit down, she felt a happy leap of the heart. She was often nettled after they parted, however. He seemed like such a friendly ninny. Perhaps he believed that women could not think, that the way to their affections was to blather on.

Konicek talked customers, horses, stories he heard in his travels. He talked over the news he read in the paper. He discussed the baseball team, the boarders, the gossip of the town. He was careful to let her get the lineups written down—he must have seen that she needed quiet to do that—but after she looked up from that, he could not contain himself any longer; he had to talk.

Susan might have ignored him. She had heard plenty of talkative salesmen at the boardinghouse and had the trick of nodding at them but not listening. To her consternation, however, she found Konicek interesting. He was not particularly clever or self-consciously eloquent, and he never talked about important ideas, but he observed the world carefully and had a knack for summing up an event or a person. She found herself listening even after she had made up her mind not to.

One Friday at breakfast Konicek stopped at Susan's table and asked whether he could stay through until Monday. His manner, beaming and leaning his weight back while he pulled on his lapels, suggested that he had some idea behind this request.

She said of course; they generally had extra room over Sundays, and they were not about to turn away business. He then asked whether he could offer her a ride to the baseball game in Petaluma; he had read in the newspaper that the town team was playing Saturday.

"You're not staying over for that," she said.

"No, I have some other business, but I understand this is a big game."

"Yes," she said. "I was planning on taking the train."

"You'll save the fare if you come with me."

He had a one-horse carriage with a cab in back where he kept his samples. Susan felt quite conspicuous riding with him through town and south on the Petaluma Road. Would someone notice? She reminded herself that no one cared whether she rode in a carriage with a man, but nonetheless she sat rigid and uncommunicative, as if all Santa Rosa watched. Konicek seemed to respect her feelings by keeping silent, but once they were into the country he began telling stories about the roads of Sonoma County, which he reckoned to be the worst in the state. He told one story after another of mud pits and landslides and holes big enough to lose a wagon in. He told Susan that he loved to be out on the road, and his pleasure was obvious. She felt herself relax—partly.

On the Petaluma downgrade they saw another carriage far ahead down the hill. Konicek stood up to peer ahead, then sat down and with a grin slapped the reins. His horse began to trot; Konicek shook up the reins again, and the horse went into a canter. The road was rutted and rough, so the carriage bounced wildly. Susan looked at Konicek and saw his face frozen in a smile, his attention riveted ahead. "Can you slow down, please?" she asked, but he seemed not to hear her. She clamped the seat with her hands and hung on. Once the ruts they followed ran out and it seemed the carriage would spin over the edge, but Konicek never slowed—he seemed to thoroughly enjoy the speed. The dust flew and Susan's teeth chattered as they bounced. At the bottom of the hill they caught up with the other carriage and passed it wheel to wheel. Konicek leaned over and waved at the other driver, then promptly slowed the horse to a trot.

"Was that a friend?" Susan asked. Her heart was racing, but she was loath to admit it.

"Not a friend or an enemy either," Konicek said. "I never saw the fellow before. I just can't stand to follow somebody's dust." He looked over and grinned apologetically. His dark, gleaming hair had fallen onto his forehead. "When you drive on these roads as much as I do, you can get a little lopsided," he said. "I hope you don't mind."

Did she mind? She had been frightened, but she almost liked it. It occurred to her that her sister had similarly dragged her into terrifying escapades.

He asked Susan what church she belonged to; she said she didn't. "Not any church?" he said. "I'm a Methodist, so when I go to any town, I look up the Methodist preacher. If they don't have a Methodist, I try the Presbyterian or even the Baptist."

"What about the Unitarian?" she asked. Many of the suffrage women she knew were Unitarians.

"Not the Unitarians," he said. "I wouldn't be interested in a church that doesn't have any beliefs. Why, are you one?"

"No," she said. "I told you. I don't have a church."

She was surprised, when they arrived home, that he brought up church again. He wanted to know whether she would go to church with him the next morning. "We can ride if you like." He grinned; it was only a few blocks.

"I don't attend any church, Mr. Konicek." She said it stiffly.

"You told me that, so I thought you might like to try it out. What else do you do on a bright Sunday morning?" He was smiling, almost as though he intended to mock her. He had hazel eyes, she noticed for the first time.

She did not want to be rude, so she paused for a moment's thought before responding. "Religion is not something I want to try," she said firmly. "I have no desire to attack your sincere beliefs, but I am a suffragist."

"They don't allow you to go to church?" he said.

"Mr. Konicek, the churches have stood against women more than any other force in our world. Perhaps that is not important to you, but it matters tremendously to me. There may be a religion that truly stands for the dignity of woman, but I do not believe it can be found within the walls of any established faith."

"Well," he said, "most of the churches I see have more women than men inside. The ladies appear satisfied to me, but maybe I'm missing something."

Konicek did not press the argument. He thanked her for her company and left to put his horse and carriage into the livery. Susan brooded on what he said, however. He was a serious Christian apparently, and she felt oddly deflated by this discovery.

It did seem odd that women were known as the most religious members of the community, while unfailingly oppressed by the religious teachings of the churches they followed. Susan knew the argument, chapter and verse, because she had heard it so often from her mother. Women had been blamed and silenced since Eve. She could not help thinking, however, that this argument somehow unfairly had kept her from other women. The newspaper often mentioned their doings in the churches.

One evening after supper, Susan's mother called her into her room. This she rarely did; Rebecca's room was a private sanctum.

"Would you like me to light another lamp?" Susan asked. "You're likely to stumble over something and break your head."

"No, thank you, Susan. We need not waste kerosene just to illumine our conversation. I will come to the point. Mr. Konicek."

Susan had an idea what her mother would think of Konicek, and her first impulse was to provide her mother with relief, to assure her that she had made up her mind to put him off. Before she could respond, however, her mother went on.

"Do you think you are behaving wisely?" Rebecca asked.

The question raised her hackles. "I don't know whether I understand 'wisely,'" she said.

"I mean," Rebecca said, cutting her syllables very finely, "is it wise to encourage him?"

It would have been easy to put her mother at rest, but for some reason, to Susan's surprise, she found herself suddenly unwilling to do that. Perhaps it was rebelliousness. "Mother, what is your concern? Do you think your spinster daughter will run off with a man?"

"Where you 'run off' to is no concern of mine, my dear. You are a grown woman."

"Quite."

"I want you to think of what you have made of your life. Ever since you met Miss Anthony, you have been moving steadily upward. You have calls to lecture throughout the state. You might easily gain a chance to make a national reputation. Do not throw it all away lightly." Rebecca sat up straight and regal, looking into the distance. After a pause she said, "I feel concern that you will think of marriage as such an escape from the difficulties of life that you give up a wonderful future."

"Excuse me, Mother, has Mr. Konicek come and asked you for my hand?"

Mrs. Netherton raised her eyebrows. "What a man speaks of and what he is thinking are two very different things. I am surprised you do not already know that. Promise me that when he speaks to you—I say *when*, not *if*—you will come directly to me before you make any answer."

Susan declared she was making no promises of any kind.

"Well," her mother said, "I see you have decided."

Susan considered the possibility of flying into a rage. Instead she said, "Good night, Mother," and walked out.

"Think, my dear, only think," Rebecca called after her.

She did think, and at great length, about why she had found it impossible to reassure her mother. She liked the man. Being quiet herself, she did not object to a man who liked to talk. Konicek was disarmingly friendly, he had a self-disparaging sense of humor, and when he talked, he filled the air with interesting pictures. He was not handsome, but he had a simplicity and neatness to his looks that gave pleasure. She enjoyed the sense of danger that sometimes came from being with him, too—for he would try things that she would never do, left to herself.

She could not imagine marrying him, however. He was not a thinker, while she spent most of life inside the confines of her skull. She had given up on the prospect of marriage years ago, and this man gave her no reason to reconsider. Besides, there was the detail that he had said nothing direct at all.

She told her thoughts to Flora, her younger friend. Flora was talkative, saying exactly what she thought the moment she thought it. Sometimes she helped at the boardinghouse when the work was overwhelming. Working side by side scrubbing the stairs with Flora, Susan felt freedom to talk.

"I know who you're talking about," Flora said. "I saw you with him. Susan, if he's courting you, I wouldn't be too quick to say no. Unless you mean to tell me that suffrage means so much to you that you would give up a chance to get married."

Put that baldly, Susan was not sure.

On June 14 she went to Sonoma to do an oration for the Bear Flag Republic celebration. On the plaza the Suffrage Club had set up tables for a chicken dinner. The men clustered around one table discussing horses. The children ran on the grass, playing some brand of tag. Sweet, warm sunshine filtered through the trees while crowds of spectators wandered over the grass. The club president sat Susan down at one of the tables and brought her a plate, but she could hardly eat for the interruptions. She was nervous, as always before she spoke.

Susan sat with a tribe of others on the bandstand, which was decorated with a huge bear flag. The club president made the expected references to the brave, outnumbered men who had raised the flag, seizing their freedom as Americans. In that same spirit, she said, women demanded the rights of their citizenship. She was a short, broad woman whose voice carried well over the benches full of suffrage women and their families. Behind the benches an audience came and went, listening to a bit, circulating, murmuring.

Susan, when she began, made no mention of the Bear Flag Republic, but went straight into her regular talk. Speaking about the principles of baseball was always a risk. She could sense the puzzlement of the audience: Where was she going? She spoke of the sheer pleasure to be found in a well-played game, and of the rivalries between Sonoma and its neighboring towns. Men listened because it was unusual to hear a woman talk of baseball; women listened because they did not understand her point. A critical question of timing concerned when to change to principles: how fairness, equality, and mutual respect undergirded the game. Susan spoke without any text, having learned from watching Anna Shaw, the greatest of the woman orators, that she must match the temper of her audience by looking at them and feeling with them.

She began to speak of the rules, how critical it was for the base path to be precisely ninety feet, and the pitcher's rubber sixty feet six inches from home plate. And it went without saying, both teams must follow the same rules. It would not make a game if one team could only play the field and never hit.

Just as she warmed to her subject she saw Fred Konicek. He had a seat on the farthest bench; he was dressed casually in a loose blue jacket. She had no idea when he had come. Certainly she had not expected him—he had left Santa Rosa a week ago and made no plans to return.

Seeing him made her nervous, but she took extra energy from his presence, raising her voice and her energies. Her own reaction surprised her. She had not even wanted him to hear her, fearing that he would laugh or misunderstand. Instead she felt unexpectedly glad and excited, and she aimed her speech at him. She thought, when she finished, that it was perhaps the best speech she had ever given.

Afterward, well-wishers surrounded Susan. The president of the club stuck to her side, taking congratulations with her. When Susan had a moment to scan around her, she saw Konicek still sitting on the farthest bench. Everyone else had left the seats, but he sat calmly, with one leg up on the bench ahead of him, smoking a pipe. Eventually he got up and strolled over to her, standing six feet behind the last, enthusiastic admirer. She caught his eye; he looked at her and smiled.

He was unusually quiet as they rode toward Santa Rosa in his buggy. Holding out a small basket of cherries, he said he had bought them for her.

"I can't eat those, Mr. Konicek. They'll stain my dress."

He merely shrugged and volunteered nothing more even after they had cleared town and headed through the tall oaks on the way to the springs resorts. Susan mentioned that she had never known that he smoked a pipe.

"I don't usually," he said. "Only when I'm agitated."

She waited, but he said no more. Susan's reaction was irritation. She was not going to worm it out of him. If he wanted to be silent and mysterious, let him be.

He kept silence for several miles, until they passed Boyes Hot Springs. The road ran under some giant oaks there; the sunlight was almost eliminated. Susan found that she could not enjoy the beauty because she felt the tension of his silence. He started to speak once, then throttled the thought and fell silent.

Finally he said, "Why does it have to be a contest?"

She let that hang until it was clear he was not going to explain himself. "Go on," she said.

"Go on with what?" he said brusquely. "It's a question. Why does it have to be a contest?"

"Why does what have to be a contest?"

"Men and women. That was what you said, isn't it? That men and women are in a contest to see which one gets the upper hand, and it has to be fair. I want to know why you think it should be a contest."

"I don't know that it should be, but it is, Mr. Konicek. Not a fair contest—women are hardly given a chance to hold their own. I do not think women made it a contest, but they know when they are being cheated."

He did not answer immediately, but hunched over in his seat, concentrating on guiding the horse. "If you said just that," he said eventually, "I could agree. The baseball angle is something different. You play the game to win. You've got to take advantage of the other side's weakness. Somebody must lose, not just in the end but with every play of the game."

Susan would not allow that the metaphor was wrong. It went to instinct with her. The antisuffragists talked of harmony and cooperation, but they meant the harmony of a clinging vine attached to a strong oak—in fact, they used that very analogy. They meant domination, strength controlling weakness. She knew nothing about cooperation; she wanted only fairness.

Konicek would not yield either. "Actually I don't believe human beings are contestants at all," he said. "I don't see that it's the survival of the fittest. Mr. Darwin might be right about sea creatures but not people. I think we owe a lot to each other."

She thought he was finished, but he went on as though he had something in his throat he had to get out. "For you it's like that picture in the dining room."

"What picture?"

"There's only one. 'These cannot vote.'"

She understood. The chromolith was, indeed, the dining room's only decoration. It showed a well-dressed, motherly woman flanked by a convict, an idiot, a maniac, and a ferocious Indian in full battle dress. The caption read, "These cannot vote."

"I don't see what's wrong with that," Susan said.

"You give me the feeling that you'd be happy to vote and leave those other poor souls to their proper misery. There doesn't seem to be any concern for anyone else."

"Women spend their lives in concern for others. That is why they are never accorded any dignity. We have to agitate for ourselves. Nobody else will."

For most of the ride, which required more than an hour from that point, neither one talked at all. "I wish you well," was all Konicek said when he walked her to her door.

She could not sleep that night, even though her body was heavy with fatigue. She got out of bed and lit a lamp; she found stationery and began a letter to her sister. That was unsatisfactory, however. She did not know what to write. She got back into bed and all night heard the clock chime. She doubted she slept at all. In the early morning she got up and looked at her pale, wan face in her small dresser mirror. The eyes looked back, sad and secretive. Susan washed and dressed even though it was Sunday. Then she went out walking. She walked from one extreme of the town to the other, and even out into the country past the iron bridge. She was hungry, but she did not want to go home.

Susan passed by the Methodist church just at the hour that people were arriving for services. Ordinarily she saw churchgoers with a feeling like contempt. It had to do with the fact that she had excluded herself. Today, she wondered whether he was there. On impulse, she went in and sat down.

When she got home, her mother met her at the door. She looked as though she were under terrible strain, as a person may look who hears news of death or desperate sickness. "Where have you been?" she asked in a tone that was half accusation, half care.

"All over town," Susan said, "just walking." She decided to go ahead and tell the whole truth. "I ended up at the Methodist church."

Rebecca caught her daughter's sleeve. "I know he is a handsome man," she said in a heavy voice. "A charming man."

Susan pulled her arm back. "Mother, I went alone, and it had nothing to do with him."

Rebecca clutched at her hand. "Darling, I know. Believe me, I know. It all seems very innocent."

"What seems innocent, Mother? What?"

"To go to church. If you compromise there, you'll soon find yourself without any soul of your own. I know about charm. I do. Please listen." She pulled Susan down into a chair. "Listen."

Chapter 7
1865: The Charm

Susan's mother rarely told stories. Any day, she would pick an argument over something she read in the newspaper rather than drift into reveries of her past. True, for her a quarrel lived forever; and she took status from her days with Aunt Susan as though they had worked together just down the street, and only yesterday. The details, however, were sketchy. She lacked the patience to explain step-by-step how things had happened because she lived so vividly in the present and had no real interest in the past except for its impact on today. That was why Susan, for all that her whole sense of identity had grown up out of her father's dissolution, knew very little detail about the past—about who her parents were, and how exactly they had come to make such a wreck washed up on the western shore.

Now, though, with a strange, quiet way of holding herself straight, almost as if she could tremble, Rebecca sat down in the parlor and began to tell her grown daughter of the way Paul Netherton had, long ago, charmed her and destroyed her.

She had been Rebecca Nichols then, the only daughter of Thomas Nichols, New York manufacturer and abolitionist. She first met Paul Netherton at the Orange Springs water cure where she accompanied her father in his deep slough of despond, when his arms were paralyzed from the despair of John Brown's slaughter at Harper's Ferry. Rebecca had noticed the young man's eyes following her, but she had been mute and unable to respond. They spoke a little, very little. She wanted to wake up and seize her chance, but before she could move, he disappeared without warning and without explanation. They had never exchanged a word of love. She knew nothing of him, except that he was the nephew of the famous evangelist Asahel Netherton.

Four years she lived with that regret. She turned thirty. The Nicholses and their friends lived well in Brooklyn, guilty for their luxury while young men struggled and suffered and stank and died, not so far away. The war overshadowed them all.

Then one day the maid brought a card to the kitchen. At first Rebecca had no memory of the name, she had so completely put aside that lost chance. Then she grew hot and jumped up. "What?" her mother asked. "What is it?" She laughed when she understood. She was glad enough to go out in her kitchen smock to keep the man occupied while Rebecca ran up the back stairs and dressed.

He wore an officer's blue uniform. He had been wounded in battle, though he showed no scars, no limp, no visible weakness. Four years before he had been a decorous, quiet young man. Now he seemed enlarged. He spoke in stories, and his smiles alone were sweet enough to catch Rebecca. This time she did not repeat her mistake. She spoke; she smiled.

His charm covered everything, obscured everything. How he loved to talk, and how they loved to listen to his vivid stories of Bull Run and Antietam, charmed names, and especially Gettysburg. With the sweep of a palm he showed the lay of the battle land. Story after story: if only they had written them down, they could have made a fortune.

She asked why he had left her at Orange, not to blame him but to recapture the agony of that disappearance, the sweet pain that had led to this bliss. "Oh," he said, "did your heart dry up? Mine did when I had to leave without a word of good-bye. I swore I would see you again."

When Rebecca remembered herself as that young, green thing, she saw only a shadow. Voices rang around her while she made no sound; she was a fragment of a human personality. Paul Netherton returned to her in 1864, and it was as though a ghost had taken solid flesh (hers as well as his). He gave her substance.

She asked what had drawn him away—what urgent matter. He said it was a summons from his uncle, which could not delay a moment, but he never told what it was precisely. She ought to have been warned by his vagueness.

He claimed a good position with the New York Port Authority, where Henry Stanton himself had worked. Rebecca's father looked into it; it seemed that Netherton had a good chance. So they married. Later she would ask herself a hundred times why. The answer was, he was a very charming man.

———————

The twins came a year later, in a fine June. The war was over, Lincoln was dead, and the city was full of bearded, sunburned men come back from the fighting. Rebecca and Paul Netherton lived in a small house in the village of Harlem, far from the noise of New York. They had an acre to grow vegetables, songbirds in an old apple tree, a horse and carriage. Netherton had modern ideas. He did not send Rebecca to bed to wait for the child, nor did she go to her mother's. She stayed with her household routines until the very last weeks, and then he took her to Elizabeth Blackwell's hospital in the city, where she would give birth in a scientific manner. Rebecca was frightened by the prospect of birth, but she drew courage from this modern approach.

The hospital was a large and rambling house on Bleecker Street, populated, along with patients, by members of the Blackwell tribe. They were all dead serious, no-nonsense people of great determination. Henry, who had married Lucy Stone, was perhaps the kindliest of them all. (Rebecca reminded Susan that she had met this Henry Blackwell, Lucy Stone's husband, at the woman's rights convention in 1890.)

The hospital made a fascinating place, absolutely opposite to the serene, unintellectual home where Rebecca had been raised. The two spinster sisters, Elizabeth and Emily, ran the place with a stony asceticism. They were among the very first woman doctors, graduates of medical school who had overcome all that men could afflict them with. Somebody was always contending sharply for something among the Blackwells. Rebecca watched and listened with fascinated delight while waiting for her baby to be born.

The twins came at night, in the long, silent darkness. Dr. Blackwell was straight, tight, and thin; she spoke of babies as though they were unavoidable parasites, and she wasted no sympathy on prospective mothers. The house seemed to listen to Rebecca's cries, to absorb them thoughtfully but make no reply. She liked to say ever after that childbirth was a simple, natural thing—like passing a watermelon. Then to discover, in the exhaustion and confusion, that another had to be passed! She lost consciousness in the process. Perhaps Dr. Blackwell gave her laudanum. All she remembered were the howls, which must have come from her own lips—where else?

When she awoke, the nurse brought two weak, scrawny things. One had a wet mop of black hair, the other no hair at all. Her mother had always described the rapture of motherhood, so she expected to feel that—but when she examined her feelings for these two creatures, she found an emptiness that chilled and frightened her.

She wanted her husband's confidence and charm to assure her. Dr. Blackwell said bluntly that he hadn't been seen and would be no use to her anyway. Did she want to see her mother? No, not her mother. She could not confess the lack of love for those two worms, which she mentally referred to as Black and Tan.

He finally came when she had been there a week. As soon as he opened his mouth she smelled the sickly sweet aroma. She had lived a sheltered life, but she recognized it as the scent seeping from the saloons. He leaned over and kissed her; the smell was insidious. "You've done double duty, my love," he said. "How are you getting on?"

Tears came into her eyes. She could only look at him.

"Now, don't, love," he said. His voice was slurred. "Don't cry. My heart is too full for that. They're lovely girls, a healthy pair. Who would have expected two at once? You've done a great thing. What shall we call them?" He took a seat on the bed beside her. "It's a beautiful day, so lovely I thought of remembering this season. What if we called them Rose and June?"

She broke in a sob.

"But why aren't you speaking, my dear? Are you too weak? It's all right. I can do the talking for both of us." He leaned over to kiss her, but she pulled away and he staggered before regaining his balance and pulling himself erect.

He looked at her with full blue eyes. "I'll tell you what, Rebecca. I've lost my job. I've been fighting them nonstop. That's why you haven't seen me. I wanted to be here like all the earth, but it seemed I had a slim chance to get out the truth, and I went to work to do my best. You don't blame me, do you? But the greater powers were too much for me. I tell you, dear, in all sadness I must say that it looks evil for our country. We have won the war, but I fear we have lost our souls. There is darkness such as I had never imagined. And I have been crushed." He took her hand.

He talked on in this manner. He was sad not for himself (his life meant nothing), but for the avarice he had seen in men he once trusted.

He would do anything, see anyone, to preserve the honor of his country. He had little hope, but he would continue. Would she pray for him?

How could she resist such a plea? He was weak, but who was not?

———————

She had a picture in her mind of babies in white dresses on fine summer days, perhaps dawdling peacefully beneath the apple tree. Her father took her to Harlem in a cabriolet and arranged for a neighbor to look in twice a day. He had no sooner left than the two were wailing, their little mouths as round as an *O*, their faces red as blood.

On the third day her mother came. Rebecca had not slept: if it was not one twin, it was the other. She was glad to resign from responsibility for an hour, for however long. Her mother had her sit in a rocking chair, holding the dark baby asleep, while she circled with the other bouncing between her two small shoulders. "What do you call them?" she asked.

"Mr. Netherton wants to call them Rose and June, for the season."

"Which one is this?"

"I haven't thought."

"Call this one Rose. She will be a redhead like your father. Yours will be a dark rose, I predict. Where is Mr. Netherton?"

Rebecca was filled with confusion and embarrassment. "Did you know that he has lost his position?" she said.

"Yes, your father told me," her mother said kindly. "What does he intend to do?"

This seemed to Rebecca the worst anyone could say about her: she did not know where her husband might be. *Yet,* she thought, *I should keep faith with him and believe that he is in the right.*

Two days later a man came to the door and handed her a paper. It seemed to be a legal notice, but the dark baby was hiccuping and threatening to cry, and she could not concentrate to read a whole sheet. The man, who wore a dirty brown wool jacket and a beaten three-cornered hat, looked on pensively, as though he planned to stand there until he moldered into dust.

"What is it?" she asked him. "Can it wait for my husband to come?"

"It's a notice, ma'am," he said. "It's for anybody that has the money, you or your husband or your uncle Harry."

"I don't follow you," she said. "What kind of notice?"

"An eviction. Pay up by tomorrow or you have to get out." He said it without any evident attempt to speak harshly—it was just a fact of life to him.

"What are you waiting for?" she asked with trepidation. "I don't have any money to give you."

"Any messages?" he said. "I can take you to the landlord if you like."

"No," she said, "I'll have to talk to Mr. Netherton. Can I keep this sheet for him?"

"It's no use to me," he said, and without another word turned and left her.

Rebecca could make no sense of the notice. The words were written in a fine, legible hand, but they seemed no more connected together than fish in the sea. She had lived entirely protected from such events as evictions.

She had the dark baby crooked in one arm; she was worn out with crying and had subsided to a whimper, while her sister shouted in outrage from her crib in the kitchen. Rebecca looked down at the little face in her arm and for the first time felt love—love sponsored by pity, that this child must be thrown out of her only home. Where could they go? She started in to the kitchen, then stopped short. Why should she go to the other one's cries? She did not know how to relieve them. She took a chair. The little one in her arms fell asleep. Rebecca listened to the strangling sobs of her child in the next room.

Abruptly the cries stopped, as suddenly as if the child had been lifted away by the angels. Rebecca listened to the quiet—she could actually hear a bird sing, and it frightened her. She stood, careful not to disturb the baby she held, and went quietly into the kitchen. The hairless one lay motionless in her crib. Terrified, Rebecca reached out one hand for the child—and just before she seized her, the baby stirred in her sleep, and she felt the warm, limp body move against her hand.

Rebecca set the dark one down beside her sister. Poor things, they had given up their troubles and fallen into rest.

She let go and cried for her children as she had not been able to cry for herself. She went back into the parlor and held the paper that would expel them. She wished with all her heart that Paul would please come. She did not know what to do.

Then she realized that he was not going to come. Not in time. He had disappeared as surely as he had in Orange—just disappeared.

She went to the neighbor's house to ask if the lady there could come to watch the babies. The sun was bright and warm, it was a drowsy day outside, and she found her neighbor hanging clothes in the yard. It was laundry day, Rebecca was startled to realize. She had lost track of days. She heard a dog bark somewhere off in the distance under the lazy-making sun.

"Can't you have your girl watch them?" the neighbor lady asked. Her flabby mouth was full of pins.

"I haven't got a girl." Rebecca did not want to admit that the maid had left while she was in the hospital.

"Would you mind if I sent Frances over, then?" Frances was her maid, a quiet girl with a large, dull face. "I have so much to do. If she has any troubles, I can be right there."

The whole matter seemed ordinary. This simple girl would watch the babies. Rebecca would go off to see her father, who would know what to do. In the kitchen she showed Frances the sleeping babies.

"What about food?" Frances said. "I don't suppose they can eat bread yet."

"No, I provide the milk to them." It sounded strange, coming out of her mouth that way. "I hope to be back before they are hungry, but you can spoon them a little cow's milk." She blushed. "I haven't got any, but your mistress might."

Just as she was locking up the door she felt herself gripped tightly from behind. She screamed, just a small, breathless shriek. "No need to scream, ma'am." It was Paul's voice, alive with that fine, tuneful electricity he always carried with him. She whipped around, grabbed his waist, and broke into hysterical sobs.

"What's the matter? What's the matter?" he asked. She could not speak, but seized his hands and led him into the house. She rounded the room, looking but not seeing, until she found the notice on a chair.

"My dear, my dear, is that all?" he asked, smiling. "Nobody died, did he? The babies are well?" He laughed at her with the charming, confident look that put her soul at rest.

"They are fine. They are sleeping." She gestured toward the kitchen.

"Come, I want to see them," he said, taking her hand. Frances was sitting on the kitchen floor, her back against the wall, and she stood quickly as though caught in the sugar. "Who is this?" Paul asked. "Did you hire a new girl?" Before Rebecca could explain he was standing over the babies, then plunging his hands down into their bed and lifting the dark one to his face. Rebecca's protests that he would wake them, he quite ignored—surely he could work his charm on their tiny forms! He picked up one and then the other, and very soon both were wailing piteously.

He put them back into their crib and tucked their blankets over them, even though they were making a chorus like cats. "What are you naming them?" he asked.

"But you named them," she said in astonishment. "Rose and June, don't you remember?"

He smiled his beguiling smile, full of sun and confidence. "I do remember. Aren't they beautiful names in a lovely season? Come, let's get away from this noise so we can talk. Is there any food? I am famished."

She was ashamed to admit that she had no food, except half a loaf of bread that she had bought yesterday. When she went to get it from the bread box, she found that chunks had been torn from it. She held up the moth-eaten corpse, distressed and puzzled, and immediately Frances began to protest that she had been hungry.

"So," Paul said calmly, taking the bread from her hand. "So much for the maid."

"You were here no more than ten minutes, Frances!" Rebecca said. Frances put up her hands as though to ward off a blow.

"Go on home, girl, we won't be needing you," Paul said. He had put the bread down on the table and was cutting it into slices. "Any butter?" The babies continued to cry.

He could do that. He could interrupt her solitary panic, walk in and disrupt everything, making life from silence. She always yielded to his confidence. He had business of a hundred kinds, with real estate opportunities, someone's invention, a merchandising scheme. He was vague on the details, and vague on when amounts of money would come, always vague on where he would be and when he would return. Yet the enchantment of his tongue! And his smile, his eyes blazing with the sun of conviction!

They lived in Harlem for another month—Rebecca never understood how, but Paul talked to the landlord and an arrangement was made—then moved to an apartment block near the Hudson River. That winter they had no coal during November. Paul airily encouraged her to burn scraps of wood from the construction sites on nearby lots. One day she put blankets over the window in the parlor and inspected the brick walls for any pinprick of light, sure that she would find some source of polar wind. The pitiful fires she managed made a heat that the walls sucked into their arctic core. She thought of warmth every waking hour; she even dreamed of a coal fire and its potent heat.

She had stopped expecting Paul to come. When her mother visited, she pretended that all was well, feeling afraid of disapproval and interference. Rebecca worked out routines for locking the children in a bedroom while she went out to buy food. She thought that her mind was deteriorating; at times she wondered whether she was still capable of speaking English. She talked to the children just to have the pretense of conversation. It occurred to her that she would have to break this habit someday, when she met adults again, but this seemed so distant as to be impossible—a theory from another era.

The week before Christmas he came home with a bucket of coal, and that was bliss—to build the fire so hot that the walls themselves grew warm to the touch. He brought eggs too. She went out and bought a loaf of bread and a pat of butter, and scrambled the eggs with bits of toast. The little ones crawled at her feet, looking distracted and whimpering—they knew that something good was in the making, though they had never tasted solid food. When she held Rose in her lap and fed her a dab of egg, she made the funniest expression—repulsion and curiosity and surprise, all mixed. Then she wanted to eat it all! Rebecca had to stop her, for fear her stomach would rebel.

Paul stayed put most of the week. When he talked, he would raise up warmth and volubility, putting on that sun-filled smile and chucking the babies on his knee. Left to himself, though, he seemed to sink down into silence. He sat by the stove, leaning close and thinking. The babies made no impact on him then, even when they cried. Initially Rebecca took this on herself, trying to raise him from the doldrums with questions, but after the first day it became harder to capture his attention.

At suppertime at the end of the week he grew vexed with her. Why had she not cooked his meal? She felt the injustice deeply, felt it as shame. They had no food, she told him.

"Why didn't you tell me?" he said. "Are you out of money too?"

"Pretty well," she said.

"Then I have to get something. That is for me, but I can't do it, woman, if you don't tell me of the situation." He went out and did not return. She expected him any minute, but at nine o'clock she took the three pennies she had left and bought some bread from the Dutch woman who said to knock at any hour. While she ate and fed some to the babies, she hoped he would not come in and find her betraying him. It was a new feeling: to hope that he would not come.

He arrived in the middle of the night, banging on the door until she opened it. When she let him in, he clutched her. She smelled the sweet musk on his breath; he was leaning against her and wavering on his feet as though he had been hurt. Rebecca lit a lamp and saw a soft, stunned stupidity on his face.

"Did you bring some food?" she asked. She could see that he had nothing in his hands.

He started toward the bedroom. "Don't wake them!" she cried, but he pushed ahead like a rutting boar and proceeded to pick up both babies, one in each arm. Rose slipped out of his grasp. In catching her he pinned her body against his side with his elbow, and slowly let her down to the floor. By then Rose was awake and wailing. Rebecca caught her as she slid down his leg to the floor, and Rebecca's head and Paul's met, hard. Seeing stars, she dropped the child so she clunked on the floor and stopped crying.

"You've killed her," Rebecca shouted.

"I didn't," he said. "You dropped her." They were the first words out of his mouth, and they sounded strangely distorted. Rebecca scooped up the child and took her loose form in tight to her body. Rose stirred, then struggled, then began to cry angrily.

"You're a drunkard," Rebecca said, horrifying words.

"I had to go into a saloon to gain something to eat," he said. "No food at home from my beloved wife."

———————————

The next morning he slept late, and when he did get up, he did not speak. About midmorning he left. She asked him where he was going but got no answer. She ran to the door. "When are you coming back?" she shouted, but he did not respond.

Misery swamped her all that day, but at the nut of her misery was a new, hard feeling. He knew they had no food; if he came after suppertime, he would not find them. It was simple logic: they had to eat. Yet the feeling was more than a calculation of necessity. She was afraid, and she was also learning to hate him.

At the six o'clock church bells she began to dress the girls. She had not worked out how to transport them, but somehow she would do it. The twins whimpered in their unfamiliar clothes. She took a chair and waited in the darkness. The twins crawled to her legs and pushed against them, but she did not pick them up. They were hungry, but she had nothing for them. The single bell rang, her signal. She stood up. No fire to bank, no lights to extinguish. The room was terribly, numbingly cold.

She could hold them both at once, one on each arm, if they did not squirm. Down two flights of stairs she went. Under the streetlight she could see a thin shell of ice in the gutters. Fortunately the air was still. She set off toward her mother's house carrying her burdens.

Rebecca had the idea that someone would see her struggles and offer help. Surely she was a piteous sight! The street was fairly quiet; only occasionally did a carriage pass with a rumble. No one slowed; no one stopped. When her arms could bear no more, she sat on a set of stairs, holding the twins between her knees. She could go only a long block before rest became necessary. After half a mile she could not manage even a block. Her arms were as heavy as dough.

She began to doubt whether she should go back. Sitting in a doorway where she had a bit of shelter, she thought that she might never get to Brooklyn—she lacked fare for the ferry. A man could go and come; somehow he could get money. How could a woman ever get money?

Getting up, she walked on another block. She had never paid attention to distances, but she began to see, from a few landmarks that she recognized, that the journey would be much longer than she had guessed. However, she was determined that she would not turn back. Going back home would mean waiting for a husband who never came.

Then a woman came alongside her from behind and said, in a dry voice, "That seems to be a heavy load. Could I help you carry one of those children?"

Rebecca did not hesitate to hand one of the twins to her. The woman wore simple black. She had spoken without any womanly pity, but as though it was an ordinary thing to carry a woman's child on a cold night.

She asked where Rebecca was going, and then, tactfully but directly, what she was doing in such a condition. Rebecca met this spirit exactly, explaining her situation as though it were quite ordinary for her to be strolling over miles of New York in search of a meal. The woman suggested that her apartment was nearby. Would she stop over for a cup of tea? Perhaps they could send a note to her family.

Rebecca asked for the woman's name, as a decent propriety, and mentioned her own. The woman said her name was Susan Anthony. It was a name unfamiliar to Rebecca, as was her own to Susan Anthony.

They arrived at a large stone building, four stories high. Anthony led her up the stairs to the third floor. Before going in the massive glass door, she turned to Rebecca. "I should explain that while I reside here, it is not my domicile. It belongs to Mrs. Stanton. I do not know whether you will see her."

"Mrs. Henry Stanton? But my father knows her husband."

Her father came for her the next day. He was obviously disturbed by the situation, though his good manners stood him well. The babies had slept in the drawer of a dresser, and they were crawling on the red carpet in Mrs. Stanton's parlor. The bitter smell of bacon was in the air—they had eaten a good breakfast.

Seeing his face drawn tight was enough to make Rebecca fear. She recognized that this was a step not lightly taken, to leave her husband's home.

She found it very strange, when Netherton arrived three days later, that they fell nearly back into the old days of courtship, sitting in the Nicholses' parlor, talking of everything but the questions truly on their minds. Paul's life remained as mysterious to her as it had been before their marriage. He always dressed beautifully. Where did he get his clothes? How did he live? What had he done, absent from their lives for a week? Yet he was as charming as ever, warming her heart like a coal fire, radiant, strong, and life giving.

She would have gone back if he wanted her to. But he did not ask her to return. He came to see the girls, who were soon tottering around the old house. Sometimes he would accept an invitation from Rebecca's mother to stay for the night. More often he came and went like a breeze, as though living in separate households was completely natural for him.

Only once did Rebecca go with him. That happened in the autumn of 1867, mainly because Rebecca's mother insisted on it. She said it was unnatural for the two of them to live apart. "I don't see that your lives can ever grow mutually dependent under these circumstances," she told Paul, with Rebecca standing by so embarrassed she wanted to cry.

Paul had taken another apartment in Manhattan, near the Broadway Tabernacle. The twins, who were two years old, went out to play, and Rebecca was appalled by their companions. It was a rough neighborhood. Paul had a position selling reference libraries into homes—a medical book, a dictionary, an atlas, and a two-volume encyclopedia complete with pictures. He might be gone into New Jersey or Pennsylvania for several nights, but his habits were predictable and he brought money for food and coal. Rebecca was glad to tell her mother that she was well provided now. She felt tender excitement in beginning again.

In December, however, the money stopped, and the drinking began—or at least, became visible to her. Twice Paul announced that he was going off for several days of work, and then returned on that same night with the smell of liquor on his breath and no explanation. He sold the dining room table. The first she knew of it was the arrival of two workingmen to take it away. Of course it was her husband's to sell; he was the head of the house. Yet Rebecca could not help feeling it as a great indignity. Her father had given them the table. That evening she set out dinner on the floor, with the chairs in their usual places surrounding the plates.

"What is this?" Paul asked when he came home.

"I have no table," Rebecca said. "We sold it today."

"Oh, my dearest," he said, "we'll get another. I never liked that one too much; it was far too ornate for a simple pair like ourselves, and I met a man who had a real taste for such things. I thought, why shouldn't he enjoy it rather than leave it with us not appreciating it? Look, here is the money." He held out some coins. "Why don't we get a joint of beef and cook a supper to make the neighbors jealous?"

She picked the coins out of his hand. "Shall I buy a pint of whiskey for you too?" she asked coldly.

"Don't speak about what you don't know," he said. "You know nothing at all of what I do."

"And who is responsible for that? Do you tell me anything more than half-truths? But I can see, and I can smell."

"What do you know of a man's life?"

"I know that a man should not come home to his children drunk! And if you sell more of our things for your liquor, I will leave you to get your own dinners."

"Back to Mama," he mocked.

In less than a week she found her silver gone, taken from the mahogany case where she kept it under lock and key. He must have picked it. Had her threat provoked him? She was inflamed with rage. She felt that she had to keep her promise.

Her father's reaction, when she came home, was to purse his lips and keep silent. He looked deeply pained, but he took his sorrow in silence. Rebecca kissed him and cried for him.

She was not prepared for her mother's response: vehement opposition.

"What is some silver or some furniture?" she asked. "What do you know of finances? You are to support the man you have married."

"Mother, he drinks." That point, she thought, trumped any other.

"You should have thought of that before you married," her mother said.

"How could I think of it before I married when I didn't know it? Do you think he told me he was a drunkard?"

"'Wives, submit yourselves unto your own husbands, as it is fit in the Lord,'" her mother quoted the Bible. "'Ye wives, be in subjection to your own husbands; that, if any obey not the word, they also may without the word be won by the conversation of the wives.'" Ruth Nichols had her fierce determination turned up high; her mild face seemed to burn.

"Mother, do you mean that I should obey him if he tells me to do what is wrong?"

"Of course not, but we are talking about the sale of some cutlery."

"I cannot raise my children in the home of a drunkard."

When Paul came around the next day, he did not seem terribly distressed over her course. If he did not care, it was hard for Rebecca's mother to care. So, they settled back into the mode of living that had already come to seem normal.

It took Rebecca a week to realize that she was deeply hurt. She had sought to provoke him by leaving; his mild response said, in so many words, that he would just as soon live without her. What other meaning could she draw from the facts?

She decided then to change the girls' names to Susan and Elizabeth.

Ever since her night rescue by Susan Anthony, she had maintained contact with that wonderful woman and her cause. That May she had attended, right in New York, the first woman's rights convention since the war. Since then she had gone to meetings whenever her mother would watch the children. She had known, through her father's abolitionist connections, a general sense of the right of a woman to speak. These reformers, however, brought a far stronger sensibility to the cause. Rebecca admired their nerve and their brains. Their sense of woman's injury resonated with her own situation.

It seemed a brilliant stroke to hit at her husband by taking away the names he had given the twins—and what did he care about them?—and substitute the names of these brilliant women. Rebecca announced the plan first to her mother, who was more confused than horror-struck. Her mother said she had never liked the name of Rose; it sounded too Irish. Susan and Elizabeth were more proper English names, she said.

Her father understood her and asked whether she had discussed the change with her husband. "I haven't seen my husband," she said, which was approximately true. He was dealing in real estate again and always moving around to see another piece of property.

"You cannot change the names of your children without his agreement," her father said. He spoke as though from deep sadness; his eyes were sunk deep and surrounded in folds of skin like a turtle's.

"When he acts like a father, he will have the prerogatives of a father," she said with fire in her eye. "I am not his slave."

———

Paul didn't blink at the changed names. When Rebecca thought it over, she realized he had never really used their names. Functionally it made no difference to him because he called them by pet names— Beauty and Morning Glory and Sweetheart and Kitten. He adored the girls. The maid would let him in, and he would dash up and down stairs looking for them. He liked to take them out to the stores. They made a touching sight, holding hands in a chain. He asked Rebecca to come, too, but she never did. His bouncing into the room always affected her the same way. She burned with anger, but his charming ways kept her off balance. He got the best of her every time; and the girls treated him with such love, one would have thought he brought them pearls, not stick candies.

Her father offered Paul a place in his firm. Rebecca knew it because Paul told her freely—but he said he could not be distracted from speculating in properties. There was money to be made, he claimed. "When I get rich," he would tell the twins, "we'll live in a mansion and you'll have ducks and swans on a pond with lily pads."

Rebecca became increasingly involved in the American Equal Rights Association. That was the organization the women had joined with, promoting rights for women and Negroes. They seemed to do nothing but quarrel, however. The Republicans promoted a federal amendment that would give the vote to blacks but not to women; and Susan B. Anthony hated it. Frederick Douglass told her in front of the assembly that women must wait, since the cause was urgent for black men, who were being lynched and mobbed because of the color of their skin. Wendell Phillips backed him. Lucy Stone protested that she wanted it to be otherwise, but she would go along. Better that some get freedom than none. But Anthony and Stanton would never bend, not an inch. They would oppose giving the vote to black men since it meant adding more male oppressors to the list. Why should women be glad that their black lords could vote? These arguments were the most thrilling Rebecca had ever heard. She had been attracted to Anthony because of her kindness, and because of the frank and rigorous discussions she heard at Mrs. Stanton's house. As she joined in the fight, the women became heroes, like the abolitionists her father had known, standing against mobs of humanity and clinging only to the most uncompromised truths. When Mrs. Stone launched her American Woman Suffrage Association just to undercut Anthony's and Stanton's

National, that only added to the wallop. Now they had traitors and spies and all the excitement of war between sisters.

Anthony always had something for Rebecca to do: some document to locate at the New York library, some letter to write or petition to collect, some meeting to attend. Rebecca's mother gladly watched the twins while the *Revolution,* Anthony's newspaper, kept Rebecca busy.

Try filling up just one page with small type some day, let alone sixteen! Anthony was tireless, but she went here and there to give her speeches, and she needed help. They placed a small cot in the offices, where sometimes Anthony slept, and sometimes Rebecca slept when there was late work to do. After Mrs. Stone began the *Woman's Journal,* they had to juggle funds to pay the printers and typesetters, try to collect from subscribers, and generally run themselves like steam engines. When a small apartment became available at the rear of the offices, Rebecca all but moved in. She lived for the day the newspaper came from the press, still wet and black. It seemed like a miracle, as strange as a hen laying bright green eggs: women publishing a newspaper.

If Rebecca had been regularly with women whose marriages were rewarding, she might have thought of Paul more. But Anthony had never married, and one could hardly imagine her married, so singular and self-reliant was she. Mrs. Stanton rarely saw her husband and, as far as Rebecca could see, might as well not have been married at all. Rumor had it that even Mrs. Stone, that virtuous example, did not always have the happiest relations with dear Henry Blackwell. They said, cattily, he had other interests.

———————

Rebecca's father came into the *Revolution* looking ruffled and aged, like a sheaf of papers worn by use. "The girls are gone," he said. "Your husband took them this morning with all their clothing. Not far, not far, my dear, they are going to his apartment for tonight. In the morning, however, he indicates that he will take them to California. Do you know anything at all of this?"

She did and she didn't. Paul had made threats, but she had thought it was just his usual nonsense, like his plans to make money in property. She still thought so. He was a charming man—she could predict the charm like the phases of the moon—but not a serious man.

Paul had asked her how often she saw the twins, how much time she spent with the newspaper. She had turned the questions back on him and asked him how many millions he had made in rents.

"I'm talking about our daughters, Rebecca. I don't want them raised by their grandmother. A child should have a mother."

"They have a mother. They have a mother with a mind. They are in no doubt of who their mother is."

The scene when they arrived at Paul's apartment was dreadful beyond any measure. Rebecca screamed and wept, which upset the twins. She ranted at Netherton that he would be arrested.

"For what would I be arrested?" he asked. "For taking my children with me?"

"When have they been *your* children?" she screamed.

He said that in the eyes of the law they were his children, his alone, and he could take them anywhere he liked.

Chapter 8

1896: *The Woman's Bible*

The letter awaited Susan Netherton when she checked in at the Hotel Gallanty, exhausted and greasy from the five-day trip across the country. Her face sagged, her shoulders ached from the effort of holding her skull aloft, and her skin itched for the bath. Glancing at the neat, scrolled handwriting on the envelope, she recognized it as Fred Konicek's and thrust the letter into her purse. She had conflicting feelings about his writing. That he could follow her here, through the mail, rubbed on her.

At the same time, irrepressible gladness leaked in. Who, having traveled three thousand miles, would not want to hear from a friend? He was thinking of her, and she could not help feeling grateful.

Susan was confounded by her reactions to Fred. His persistence both pleased and alarmed her: she felt like a cat that rubs up against someone's leg and then bites the hand that strokes it. Grieved with herself for the pleasure she got from being courted, nervous and jumpy about the claims of a man on her soul, unsure of what this man might mean to her ambitions, she grew sick to death of her own inner argument. She tried to heed her mother's warnings and let him go, but the man kept coming back, even after their quarrel, and she let him.

When he invited her to church, she said no, but then changed her mind and attended with him. This she did partly to spite her mother. She could not bear to follow Rebecca in every particular. Then she discovered, to her surprise, that she enjoyed attending with him; a kindly normalcy surrounded the church meetings. They were not fanatical at all, in fact, the very opposite of fanatical. Afterward she kept asking herself why she was there, however. Was it because of the man?

She liked to be with him, but she did not trust her reactions. Oh, certainly, he appeared to be pursuing a conventional courtship, but what did that mean? Why with her, who was thirty years old and plain? When Susan tried to imagine the future this courtship might lead to, she could not manage the trick. And yet conventional possibilities allured her. She sometimes let her mind drift into images of children, of her own home, and then she had to shake her head to clear it of such ideas.

At the bottom of it all was her sense that he could not possibly like her just for herself. He must have some other motive. Her self-doubts combined with her mother's lifelong training in the distrust of male motives. All the patterns of her mind were set up to reject him. Yet she liked him. She liked to talk with him. Susan even liked looking at him.

Susan came to the suffrage convention in Washington on her mother's behalf because Elizabeth Cady Stanton had published *The Woman's Bible*, a scholarly diatribe against all the injury done to woman by the literal words of Scripture. It caused a storm of protest from conservatives, who had suspected all along that woman suffrage was a mere cover for atheism and infidelity. The issue, Rebecca heard, threatened to surface at the next convention of the National American Woman Suffrage Association. Mrs. Stanton would be censured, Rebecca heard to her horror. She wanted to go and defend her hero, but she was not in good health. She spoke of sending Susan in her place.

Susan could not take seriously the thought that Mrs. Stanton could be censured for such a thing by the very organization she had founded. Surely Susan's mother was overreacting, as she so often did. Yet Susan was quite willing to entertain the possibility of being sent. If she were to advance her suffrage career, she ought to go and meet the leaders of the national organization. She liked the idea of seeing the East again, and her sister. When she first thought of meeting Elizabeth, she broke into tears.

Most fundamentally, however, Susan wanted to get away from Fred Konicek to gain enough space to think. She knew that she approached a fork in the road. If she could only be alone, completely alone, in a still, clean, quiet place where no one knew her or thought of her, surely then she would know her own mind. And so she had come here, to the Hotel Gallanty. And so Fred's letter had pursued her.

———————

The letter, which Susan opened in the secrecy of her room, read as follows:

Dear Susan,

I have only just returned from putting you on the train, but I hope this letter may cross the country ahead of you and be waiting at the hotel when you arrive. I know it is nice to have mail waiting on arrival. I have, as you imagine, arrived at many strange places with nothing and no one to greet me! Therefore I write without allowing for a decent interval. May this letter find you well after your long journey; such is my hope and my prayer.

Writing within the hour of your departure prevents me from using the usual social devices, such as describing the weather or mentioning people I might have seen. The weather is the same as when you left. I haven't seen anybody to mention except your mother, who is holding up well. I guess she is cheered to think that you are out of my clutches and that you are doing your darndest to beat back the devil from her idols Mrs. Stanton and Miss Anthony. Except she would not say beat back the devil, as she doubts the existence of same.

Now I have managed to spend ten or twelve lines on useless talk, and I want to come to the point. I think you have made of me a greater difficulty than I really am. Point one, it is far easier to be an effective worker for any cause if you have some financial independence. You fear that I would drag you away from the cause of woman, but I claim that plain old embarrassment, money, has kept you and will keep you out of the field of battle. I am never going to be rich, but I can give you the comforts of home and the freedom to go out and make your crusade without worrying whether you will get enough to eat or have a roof to sleep under. Point two, I don't want to take you away from your cause. I am anxious to back you in it, and I think it is easier to do any job at all if you have got somebody who cares about you and is helping you. Two are stronger than one. Point three, religion as I know it is a help to woman, and I think most women will back me in that. Your mother has given you a mistaken picture of that based on her own bitterness. If you think about it logically, however, did your father's faults have anything to do with his religion? Or was it more his lack of it that contributed to his drinking? You know I don't drink and never will. I would credit faith with about nine-tenths of whatever is good in this world. This may be arguable by philosophers, but I think ordinary people know it pretty well. At any rate I know that for myself it does not contribute to whatever faults I may show, but helps me with them.

Take your time while you are away from everything and think

it over. I miss seeing you, but there is no hurry in your coming
home. I can make sure your mother stays well. You know very well
what I want, but more than my own selfish desires I want for you
to make the right decision, one that can bring you a lifetime of sat-
isfaction. I can take whatever comes of that. Take your time so that
you can reach a quiet certainty that you are doing the right thing.
You know what I believe that to be, so I will not repeat myself
except to declare myself

> *your devoted friend,*
> *Fred*

Susan showed his letter to her sister the next day, seated in the
sumptuous cream-and-gold dining room of the hotel. She did it without premeditation: the impulse came to her, and she took the envelope
out of her purse and pushed it across the table.

She had not forgotten her disappointment in her sister, six years
before in this same hotel. It was, in fact, her chief memory of that convention. She remembered the ladies' hats, and her mother's electric
excitement at meeting Susan B. Anthony, and most of all her own dismay as the petted image of a dear sister melted into that of a snobbish,
stylish society woman.

It had proved a blessing, of course, because that disappointment had
launched Susan into South Dakota, into a serious investment in woman
suffrage. It had been the end of her innocent sisterly romance and the
beginning of her ambition to make something of her life.

Yet Susan was not "over" Elizabeth, she knew. Despite everything,
she still leaned toward her sister for love. Perhaps that was how a drunkard felt reaching for his bottle.

Elizabeth had brought along her nine-year-old daughter, Lucy. Susan had longed to feast her eyes on this niece, who turned out to be blonde and full of curls, a pretty, teasing, too-soon-old little sunflower. She was sitting at the table with them, looking brightly around at the room, wearing a pink silk dress with muttonchop sleeves, the latest and most ridiculous fashion.

"So you have a proposal!" Elizabeth said with a smile when she had finished reading. "What does he do?"

"He sells blankets all over the northern part of the state. When he comes to Sonoma County, he stays in our boardinghouse."

"A drummer, then."

Susan felt annoyed by this term, accurate as it might be.

"He writes well," Elizabeth commented as she read through the letter again. "Is he handsome?"

"Not particularly," Susan said.

"You don't have a picture?" Elizabeth leaned toward her, lovely and beautiful. She seemed genuinely interested, and Susan felt relieved that she did not make fun.

Susan wished that she did have a picture. As soon as she left Fred on the train out of Santa Rosa, he seemed to disappear from her mind.

"Why does he go on about religion?" Elizabeth asked as she looked over the letter again. "It sounds as though you're discouraging him."

"I have been discouraging him. He's a very good man, Elizabeth, but I don't think that our minds are compatible. He's a very strict Methodist."

"How strict? Does he preach at you? Does he hand out tracts on Fourth Street? I think some religious sense is a good thing in a man as long as he doesn't go too far. Does he?"

"Not too far in the way you're asking it. But he's very serious about it. He's the kind who never misses a service."

"And he doesn't drink. What's wrong with that? Why don't you go to church with him? I go to church now, you know, with Mr. Phillips. I don't think it has hurt me a bit."

"I have been going with him." This was part of Susan's confusion: she could not reconcile the Methodist church with her image of herself. Susan was surprised to hear that her sister went to church too.

"And you can't stand it?"

"I can stand it readily enough, I think. But with our upbringing I don't suppose either of us could ever be Christians, do you? Other people find it all easy to believe, but I'm always doubting and disbelieving. I don't like to be there under false pretenses."

Elizabeth smiled mockingly. "Susan, you are too sincere. Don't you know almost everybody is in church under false pretenses?"

Susan could not return the smile. "I don't think Fred is. He's very determined."

"And so are you. You've taken up our mother's religion, but the children who get raised in church never feel quite the way the converts do, do they? Do you really have the same feeling for suffrage that Mother does? I can't believe you do; your eyes have always been too wide open. How does Mother feel about this Fred?"

Now Susan could not help smiling. She knew she could count on her sister to understand her mother, as no one else could. "I think you can imagine, Elizabeth. When I started going to church with him, I thought she would die of apoplexy. But I do care about suffrage, whatever you think. Of course I don't feel the same way that Mother does, but I don't suppose I could ever feel about anything the way she does. I want the vote, though. I'll work for it."

"Well, I will, too, to a point. I'm not as awful as you think, Susan. It sounds as though Fred will back you. Or don't you believe him?"

She had to think about that. She knew that he meant what he said—he wasn't the type to pretend. The problem was subtler.

"I believe him. I don't know whether he understands what marriage does to a woman. Look at you. You changed completely."

Elizabeth seemed to pull back into a cooler mode. "Did I? I don't know that I did." She made a face, pursing her lips. "Anyway, Susan, I'm not the only possible model. Look at Mrs. Catt. As far as I can see, she is the only one of the new generation with any idea how to get something done. She's married, isn't she? And to go back to the arch she-devil, Lucy Stone didn't do so badly, did she?"

"No, but Mrs. Catt has no children, and Lucy Stone had just one. And she edited a paper, so she didn't have to travel."

Her sister laughed, showing her teeth. "So it isn't marriage. It's children! And how many do you want, Susan?"

As soon as her sister said it, Susan saw that it hit on the key. She would want children, lots of them. Then what would become of suffrage? She suddenly understood more accurately her mother's hysterical resistance to Fred.

"I could do without any if you would let me take my niece with me back home." Susan had happened to glance at Lucy, who had her blonde head tipped back and was immersed in studying the muraled ceiling. Susan felt an unaccountable urge to seize and hold on to her. "Really. Please? Why don't you let me take her to California? Then you can come and get her in a month. You could see Mother. She might not live forever."

Elizabeth laughed, her dark eyes merrily dancing as in the olden days. "You don't fool me. Just like Father, you want to steal the child away. She's mine, I tell you, and you're not dragging me after you to California."

Another letter came from Fred:

My dearest Susan,

I fully intended to press my case in this letter, but now that I sit down to write I find that I do not have the heart for it. If I heard from you and got your objections freshly stated, I probably would respond, but as it is I think I have said everything about as well as I know how. What I want to tell you now is simply that I miss seeing you. I miss the cool way you look up at me when I annoyingly interrupt you at your books. I miss the all-business way you get where you are going. I miss hearing you contradict your mother like nobody else dares to do. I miss the honest way you respond to events. I miss looking at your beautiful red (yes, I said beautiful) hair.

The rest of the letter went on to bring news of the town, reassurances about the boardinghouse and its business, news of her mother's health. But it was this first paragraph that Susan read again and again. She felt ashamed of how greedily she gulped it down.

———————

Miss Anthony summoned Susan to her room. Susan had not seen or heard from Anthony since South Dakota and would not have bet money that Anthony even remembered her. Being summoned made her heart beat faster. Every woman at the convention would beg to be so called. Anthony had not a single piece of fluff in her soul, and that made her the very ideal of women who were dogged by the fear that they were not serious enough, that they cared about clothes and love and household goods too much to be true advocates for woman. That, at least, was how Susan saw it. If she could live like Anthony, she would not be pulled in so many directions, especially by a man.

Susan was escorted to the very same hotel room where she had first encountered Anthony six years before. Aunt Susan did not seem to have moved since then or changed a single hair. She was seated by the fire, dictating to a mule-faced young woman who got up and gave her chair to Susan.

"How is your mother?" Anthony asked. "I thought I might see her this year."

"Mother is pretty well, thank you," Susan replied. "Though her health doesn't allow her to travel anymore, or she would surely have come. She loaded me down with instructions on answering the Calvinists."

Anthony let only a small flicker of a smile cross her face. "How have you done at following her instructions?" she asked dryly.

Susan remembered that cool, uninflected tone; it brought back to her the withering oven heat of South Dakota. For an instant she wondered what Miss Anthony would think if she knew her thoughts about Fred.

"Not very well, I'm afraid," she said in answer to Aunt Susan's question. "I really thought she was overreacting. I couldn't imagine there could be a censure of Mrs. Stanton."

She had found that the issue was serious, indeed. The women at the convention talked of little else than *The Woman's Bible*. Susan knew more about it than most of them because her mother had ordered a copy of the book and took great delight in reading it aloud to the boarders over dinner. The book was a bore, all theological meandering, but apparently it scandalized some—or they pretended to be scandalized.

Technically no censure was at stake, but a motion to distance the organization from the opinions of *The Woman's Bible*. The motion would state what all knew: Mrs. Stanton's opinions on religion were Mrs. Stanton's opinions. The National American Woman Suffrage Association had nothing to do with them.

"And do you judge that the motion will pass?" Anthony asked.

Susan hesitated. It was very flattering to be asked her opinion, but she doubted whether Anthony would like to hear it. "Very likely, from what I hear women say," Susan said. "Many women want our movement to be a very different one from what Mrs. Stanton seems to desire."

A flash of annoyance raced through Anthony's eyes. "Yes. Mrs. Stanton is an intellect. Her interests are wide ranging, and she wants to get to the bottom of things. She reckons that religion *is* at the bottom of things. For myself, I don't think we can afford to go that deep. If we stay with practical matters, we may work together; if we deal in philosophy, we will have a movement of philosophers and never get anything accomplished."

"Nevertheless, we cannot have a movement that drums out people for divergent opinions. Especially not *such* a woman. Mrs. Stanton is not going to talk about her *Woman's Bible* on our platform; therefore, her *Woman's Bible* has no place on our platform. I want this campaign against Mrs. Stanton to be stopped."

"Yes, ma'am."

"I want you to make a speech against it when it comes up for a vote."

"Yes, ma'am." It had never crossed her mind. "But why me? I am unknown."

"You are a good speaker. Very few people know you, so they will not discount you before hearing you."

"Will you speak also?"

"I will. I hope these women will not reject their oldest leaders and friends."

Elizabeth laughed cruelly when Susan described this plea. "Well, that's pretty typical of those two. They think the movement is their personal property. You may remember that they were quick to throw Lucy Stone overboard when she took an opinion they didn't like."

Elizabeth took the view that Anthony must be desperate for support if she went pleading with Susan to give a speech. "Don't tell me that they wouldn't rather have Anna Shaw or Carrie Catt speak for them. The younger leaders know that this book is poison. Without the churches suffrage hasn't got a chance."

"But the churches stand against us!"

"No, they don't. For every minister who preaches that women should ask their husbands' opinion before buying a dress, there are a dozen who quietly say that women have better sense than men and ought to vote. Who do you think goes to church in this country? Mostly women. Take away the churches and the WCTU, and suffrage has only a little group of women who like to hear speeches and congratulate themselves on being smarter than their neighbors."

Elizabeth paused, smiled, and changed the subject, asking whether Susan had heard any more from her man. Already irritated by her sister's knowingness, Susan fired up. "He's not my man. I don't see that our minds are at all compatible."

They talked of other things, but Susan could hardly pay attention. A heavy sadness pulled on her, its current so strong she could not concentrate on the conversation. She had been proud to be asked to speak, and Elizabeth had skewered her vanity. She ought to have expected it from her sister, she knew, but did one ever, really? And there was something deeper: Elizabeth had made her doubt the depth and sincerity of Anthony's words.

Later on Susan thought what a fool she had been. She had thought speaking would give her an opportunity to show the entire association her ability. Invitations might follow, she had flattered herself to think. Her sister corrected that well enough. If the motion must pass by a wide margin, Susan would by speaking for it brand herself as an unwelcome fanatic. Rather than open up a national career, she would probably end any chance for it. For what noble principle? Only to buck up Miss Anthony in a cause that made no real difference to anyone, least of all to Susan.

Susan sat in her room trying to locate, by sheer concentrated effort, the deepest source of her gloomy irritation. It became appallingly clear. She missed him. She wished she could talk over everything with him to gain his sanity.

She tried, for most of the remainder of the day, to clear this out of her mind. She was only homesick, she told herself, living in this hotel without a friend or companion. Her sister, for all that she represented a sackful of memories, still remained far from her. Briefly she had felt the old longing, when she had given Elizabeth Fred's letter to read and had waited nervously for her judgment. Now she could see more clearly: the yearning for her sister was for a ghost of history. Her real sister was someone quite different. She had to get used to that, like it or not.

All this she told herself, but it didn't move the small and persistent pea under her mattress: she missed him. She had crossed some kind of continental divide. Even if Elizabeth were again the kindest and most understanding sister, Susan might never again care as she once had. She was leaning in a new direction, toward Fred.

Late that night she sat down at her desk and wrote,

Dear Fred,

I have been asked by Susan Anthony—Aunt Susan, to all the younger leaders—to give a speech in defense of Mrs. Stanton. It seems there really will be a censure motion, which I assumed was impossible. This request is a great honor—please do not mention it to Mother, she would have it all over town—but I am of two minds about it. My sister believes that the motion must be destined to pass, else they would not be so desperate as to ask me. Notice a sister's admiring opinion of her flesh and blood.

I would never mind supporting a doomed cause if it were truly my cause, but in this I am not so sure what to think. How do you take Mrs. Stanton's book? Get Mother's copy if you like—I'm sure she would loan it to you—and see whether you think it is scandalous enough to put Christian people off our movement forever. That is what the women fear, and I do not know whether I am a competent judge. I was not brought up to understand the mind of Christian people! I must say, Fred, that you are a source of sanity on such vexed questions. I do not know what I shall do about the speech, and I wish I had you here to give me your counsel.

You have been a patient friend to me in more ways than I have realized, until I could be alone to reflect. I must say that I no longer can conceive of you as hindering my work. On the contrary, I value your support and hope for a lifetime of it.

> *Sincerely,*
> *Susan*

She stared at the letter for a very long time, wondering whether she had been impetuous and forward. How much of her heart would he glimpse by reading carefully? She did not think he was a careful reader.

She sealed the letter, put a stamp on it, and walked it down into the deserted lobby. It was well past midnight, and the lobby seemed suspended in a dreamless, timeless condition, lit brilliantly as though for a party that no one would attend. She put the letter in the mail slot. She let the envelope go sliding down the polished brass channel and then walked away with a frightened sense that she had plunged into cool, deep ocean water.

Standing before the largest audience she had ever addressed and feeling a surprising lightness, Susan spoke for Mrs. Stanton. She said frankly that she was not the one to judge the religious controversy, but she urged the convention not to forget or forsake the women to whom they owed so much. She thought Mrs. Stanton a great woman, she said, and surely everyone in the world already knew that her original mind held many opinions that were no part of the woman's movement. Others had warned that they should not be diverted from their main subject by Mrs. Stanton's book, but Susan thought that this motion itself diverted their attention.

Susan had spoken often enough to know when an audience was against her. The vast hall was quiet and patiently grim, the women who listened unmistakably civil and yet determined not to be swayed. When Susan sat down, she was quite shaken. She had to stay seated on the dais for the rest of the evening, in full view of the room, like a moth on a pin.

Susan B. Anthony surely sensed that she had lost. Nonetheless every ounce of thought and emotion went into her appeal. Anthony was not a brilliant speaker, but she was as strong as a bulldog. One could not help being impressed by her refusal to bow. She had, Susan remembered, a lifetime of lost causes.

The vote was solidly against her and Mrs. Stanton. Mrs. Catt and Miss Shaw, leaders of the movement who owed everything to Miss Anthony, voted with the majority.

Then, in a rush, the convention ended, Susan said her good-byes, and she got on the train going west. She had come alone, but now she kept company with several California delegates. They ate in the dining car together, talking of their plans for a state referendum in November. The national organization had pledged its support for an all-out attempt at California.

Yet Susan was quietly miserable. It was not the failure of her speech—that misfortune seemed to fly away as soon as the convention concluded. No, it was the insecurity of her future. Having given in and admitted that she missed Fred Konicek, having written him a letter confessing her feelings, however obliquely, she had no sense of what would come next. It took all her concentration to endure the slow movement of time.

She had never felt this way before. All her life she had drifted along in the present, reacting as things came up. Now the present was a pure nuisance. She felt her life had stopped and could not lurch forward again until she saw him.

The desert seemed so vast. When they crossed the Mississippi, she had thought they were almost home, but the dead, dun sagebrush, the spats of snow in the ditches, the blue blinding sky ran endlessly and repetitively by her window. When they entered California, they crawled up the Sierra grade, into the deep snow and dark tunnels, and painfully eased their way over the summit and down through the dull, wintry foothills and onto the valley floor. Slowly, slowly, the train wound into Sacramento.

She would change here to a train going direct to Santa Rosa. As her car eased in, she saw Fred leaning against a pillar in the station. She did not recognize him on the first pass of her eyes, but something familiar made her look again. She looked directly into his eyes as her car passed him by, though he did not see her. She almost died. Her breath came in short bursts.

Getting out of the car almost before it stopped, Susan saw Fred strolling toward her, a bright, big grin on his face. He had a very ordinary face, she thought, a drummer's face, she supposed. She shook his hand, almost trembling.

"Is that all I get for coming all this way?" he asked, scooping her into his arms and kissing her.

"Why have you come?" she asked. "I didn't get any message to expect you."

"You didn't think I would share this moment with your mother, did you?" He winked. "I didn't think we ought to waste any time at our age."

She did not know what he meant.

"I'll get your bags," he said.

"There's no hurry," she said, not wanting him to leave her even for a minute. "I have two hours."

"No," he said, "we have no time to waste. Not if we are going to catch the train to San Diego."

"San Diego?"

"San Diego. I've got a room at a fancy hotel down there."

She felt a deep shriek of alarm in her brain. He had understood her letter, understood every inch, and taken it beyond what she had said or meant.

"I've got a Methodist preacher ready to marry us, and if you don't care for the Methodist, I've got a JP as a backup."

"Fred! What about my mother?" This was a stupid thing to say, but her mind had jammed.

"That's who I'm trying to avoid. I'll send her a wire. Signed Mr. and Mrs. Fred Konicek. Or any other name that you prefer, so it's Mr. and Mrs."

She looked at him. He was grinning broadly. "Just a minute," she said. "I need to clear my head."

But it did not take a minute. She realized with a leap of her mind, as though her brain flopped over on itself, that she had hoped for this, just this, without daring to think it. Why should they wait at their age? Why should they do the careful thing?

She looked at him again. He might dislocate his jaw with that grin. She thought of the worst thing she might possibly say, and she said it. "All right, Mr. Konicek. You're the boss."

Chapter 9
1896: Honeymoon

The train ran along the coast, parallel to toast-colored beaches, the deep glinting blue of the ocean stretching beyond. Susan curled herself into the corner of the seat, with no desire to talk. Her brain did all the talking; it whirled her about like the teacup ride at the fair, showing a repeating incomprehensible panorama of bright shapes and familiar faces, around and around, repeating.

Last night at the hotel in Los Angeles she had looked in the mirror, looked at her bright eyes as though into the stare of a wild creature. Here with a man, alone in a hotel, a man as unknown as a stranger. Yet she looked in those crazy eyes, and they said, *Yes, I am here. Count me in.*

She remembered standing with him before the preacher, a little man in a shiny black coat, holding a huge family Bible embossed with the portrait of his church in Berea, Kentucky. Her scalp itched; she was cold and greasy from days on the train, wearing a shirtwaist blouse that had grown heavy and soft with her own sweat, on her wedding day. Her wedding day.

Fred put his arms around her in the hotel and danced her softly. In the bed he lifted the cover to welcome her in, wrapped himself around her most quietly until she could feel warm and stop trembling. "I've dreamed of this," he said. "Have you dreamed of this?"

"No," she said.

But if not, why had it been so familiar? Why had she recognized the bidding of each step, as if an old friend in greeting? How did she know in the dead certainty of her heart that this was her moment? Why had it been so familiar?

She felt him against her now on the train, his hip against her leg, reading his newspaper. She had no wish to talk, though if he had talked or had read to her, she would have enjoyed listening to it as to music. Here was the strangeness again: she had no idea whether this man, her husband, wanted to talk. She had no idea what went on in his mind at all. If she studied him for a year, would she know?

The rounded green-gray hills ran by them, unconscious of the ocean or the train, though the engineer's cut sliced off a chord for the tracks to run through, and though the broad blue blade of ocean cut the land abruptly. They flashed over a dry wash, a narrow beach revealing itself, and saw three dark horses running along the edge of the waves.

"I want to ride horses," she said, the words coming out before she could calculate. "On the beach, can we ride horses?"

"If we can find some to rent," he said. "Sure, we can do anything. That's what a honeymoon is, I think."

He told her that in his village in the old country there had been no special treatment for the bride: a new wife was expected to make her man's breakfast the day after the wedding, to show herself a hard worker by lighting the fire before he arose to go to work. "How would you like that?" he asked, grinning. "Want to get up before dawn tomorrow?"

"I wouldn't mind," she said.

"I would," he said. "I want to wake up with you."

In San Diego they stayed in an elaborate white wooden ark with gables and red tiles, built by the railroad almost astride the beach. Their room, on the fourth floor just under the roof, was tiny. Rafters came down to the top of their one casement window, so Fred felt that he could hardly stand up straight. "Well, it was a bargain room," Fred said. "I should have known." He seemed bothered.

"It's cozy," she said. It was warm up under the roof. Some mornings she woke up with Fred already gone. Why was she so lazy? She watched the sun creep down the wall behind her, drifted off, and awakened with acute hunger pangs.

Fred sat in the garden with his book or his newspaper. He was reading some sort of religious work. She did not ask him about it, and he did not offer. They had a waiter who found it startling that they were so old, yet newly married. He laughed when she admired the flowers and asked for the names. All kinds of exotics flourished: frangipani, bougainvillea, bird-of-paradise. Some were blooming, though it was the dead of winter. Their meals were included with the room, so Susan ate greedily—she thought it made Fred happy to get his money's worth. In the afternoon they walked on the beach, leaving their shoes hidden in a sand dune, letting the icy water suck under their feet. Even then they talked sparingly, languidly. Susan laced her fingers into Fred's and listened to the sound of his voice. She liked to glance at his clean-shaven face. He had a new kind of razor, Gillette Safety, that he used every morning on himself.

Once she woke up from a nightmare. All she could remember was the accusing sound of her mother's voice, no, not even the sound, just the tone. It must have been about suffrage, though she retained no memory of her mother's complaint. Actually she was glad for the dream after she had shaken her head free from it, awakening enough to realize where she was and to identify the slow sighing next to her as Fred's. She realized she felt profoundly safe. Such voices could no longer reach her. *Not that Mother is so terrible,* Susan thought. But her mother's voice echoed in her own doubts and torments. She felt safe from herself.

Thinking of that troubled her. Yes, comfort came from Fred, but she did not like what this sense of safety said about herself. It made her angry to think that she was no suffragist, but only a girl who had wanted a man. And then it made her doubly sick because she thought to herself, *Why should it matter? If this is what makes me happy, shouldn't I be glad? Why should I preach to myself my mother's old diatribe?*

It occurred to her to wonder about her mother. Was she, too, just a woman unhappy for the lack of a man's attentions? Could she be cured of her complaints by a man who lifted the blankets and welcomed her into his arms? But when she tried to fit her mother to the description, it would not take. Rebecca was too complicated to fit.

And so am I, Susan knew. Only she was certainly not just what she had thought she was.

She wanted to talk to Fred about all this. While he read his paper, or while they walked with fingers interlaced, she wished to tell him all that she was wondering. She felt instinctively a willingness to trust him with such things. He was as straightforward as a stick, and in that she felt she could relax. But when she looked up at him and tried to put the words out into the air, she grew shy and afraid to speak. Afraid of what? That he would laugh at her? Or condescend? She thought it had more to do with the unfamiliarity of intimate speech. It had been so long since her sister left. And never, with a man, had she spoken so.

In bed, in the blindness of night amid the utter communication of skin and muscle, between the drug of sleep and the wakefulness of listening to the tune of breathing, she did not want to know a thing. She had no questions then and no need to talk or any fear. But in the day she had many questions.

Certainly she felt herself relax. She could live easily with this strange man, she told herself one day, and that almost scared her again, because it seemed too pat, too almost smug.

"Do you still want to ride horses on the beach?"

Susan wondered whether she was gaining her mother's habit of lying in bed until all hours. Fred had come into the room where she lay drowsy. She found the blankets like a drug as she curled into herself and listened to the sweeping of the ocean waves. Fred had been up some time, drinking his coffee.

"They're Mexican horses, but the man says he has one that is gentle. Don't look so vacant. Remember you said you wanted to ride horses on the beach?"

She did remember, though it seemed very long ago that she had dreamed and worried her way through that long train trip. She could see in her mind's eye the swept-back shape of the dark horses as they ran, but it seemed to be from someone else's memory, perhaps a chromolith she had seen in somebody's parlor.

"I can't ride in a dress," she said.

He stopped at that, looking so boyish and confused that she could not help smiling. She wanted to help him. "Did you go to a lot of trouble?" she asked. "I could wear your trousers."

He looked blindly uncomprehending, and then he laughed. "Yes," he said. "You can. If they fit. Let's try."

"Right now?"

"Right now."

It made her want to laugh, to think of wearing his clothes. It seemed to bring them closer together than she could fathom, like sisters sharing.

"But how will I get to the beach?"

"The way you always get to the beach."

"Right through the hotel? Somebody will see me."

"So? What's the difference between that and wearing bloomers?"

She looked at him and pressed her lips together. As though he didn't know the difference between bloomers and men's trousers. "All right. I wish I could see what I look like." The room had only a small mirror over the sink.

"You look divine," Fred said. He sidled up to her and put his arms around her. "Maybe you should wear these all the time."

"And you will wear my dresses?"

"Maybe," he said.

———

Far down the beach they saw a man's figure with two horses, walking them in the wrong direction. Fred let out a loud whistle, but it was caught in the sound of surf. They had to shuffle fast down the sand to catch him, a thin, dark-faced man with a pencil mustache and a wide, rakish hat. One of the horses, a gray, was dancing.

"Where's the other saddle?" Fred asked. He was out of breath.

"I have one saddle," the man said. He nodded at Susan. "For the lady."

"So what did you think I would use?"

The man shrugged.

"All right," Fred said. "I can ride bareback. But the price will have to come down."

The man with the horses went through his predictable argumentation, to which Susan did not listen. She watched the waves as they grew from swells far out in the rocking ocean.

Her horse was a small bay with a blaze over one ear. *It looks at me with tolerant amusement,* she thought. *How does it know? Can it smell fear, as dogs do?* Fred helped her into the saddle—she liked his steadying hand on her—and without a command the horse slouched easily into a walk, rocking her from side to side. She had no control. She had not even slapped the reins. To think she had seen men riding horses her whole life, and she had never had the slightest idea how difficult it felt, how lacking in control.

Fred came bouncing up alongside, his horse slewing sideways and kicking its hooves. "How is it? Is it all right?" he asked. "This one is a handful." He held the reins in one hand and a fistful of mane in the other. He was panting from the effort of holding the horse's head up while it made short whirling motions. "I ought to charge for breaking it." He looked over his shoulder, down the beach, to the horse's owner.

Susan's horse began prancing sympathetically. She grabbed at the saddle horn. "Don't lean over," Fred said. "Stand up and grab with your knees."

He shouted, "I'm afraid my horse is stirring yours up. Let me take a little starch out of him."

For just a moment horse and rider were frozen in place, and then they raced ahead on the beach, scattering sand. Susan's bay skittered and stood still while Susan watched the gray become rapidly distant. Overwhelmingly and suddenly the beauty struck her: sand and waves, piping birds pedaling over the reflecting beach, her own long shadow atop a horse. Fred and his mount veered into the shallows, exploding through a small wave in a flash of silver water.

"Come on," she said to her horse and kicked it as she had seen Fred do. The horse stayed still as though deep in thought.

"Come on," she said again, kicking and then slapping the reins. The horse wallowed forward.

The scene struck her as funny: her man racing off astride a wild animal while she waddled behind. Fred and his horse had become a mere squiggle down the beach. Even while she laughed she saw the gray squirt sideways, twist its neck, and pull its head low. Fred in slow, helpless motion continued forward like a trout leaping while the horse pulled up and let him dive over its neck. When she saw Fred hit the sand, Susan let out a cry. She watched him roll over and over, like a piece of whirling machinery. Then he was still. His horse wheeled and galloped back down the beach toward her, slowing and lifting its head as it came near. She was frightened for a moment that it would attack, and then realized that it only wanted the bay's companionship. Its violence had been innocent, merely incidental to its desire to be free. It nickered, nuzzled the bay's neck, then led it along companionably. Fred, Susan saw, had got to his feet.

"Are you all right?" she shouted when she was near enough to be heard. Fred stood with his fists on his hips. She could not yet see his face to read the expression; she was still too far.

"Knocked the breath out of me," he yelled. "Got sand in my teeth. Cut my eye. I'm fine."

Blood was blotched with fine white sand over Fred's right eyebrow. She looked at it and poked at the wound before she noticed his eyes. They were shining, bright as a bird of prey's.

"Are you sure you're not hurt?" she asked because she did not know what else to say. Plainly he felt no pain. "I saw it. You really tumbled."

"I'm fine. Help me catch the horse."

"Oh, Fred, let the man catch him. He didn't even give you a saddle."

"No," Fred said. "I want to ride him again."

Afterward they ate in a Mexican cafe, the entire establishment, including the chairs, painted blue. Fred had found it on his morning walk. They ate some kind of fiery stew and nibbled on thick tortillas.

Susan found it easy to talk after the morning's excitement. Fred was distracted. He had still a bright stare, as though his thoughts remained on the horse's back, as though he felt the jolt of the hooves. When he put his attention on her, it was in the wrong way: he worried that her horse had been worthless, that she had been bored and miserable and had hardly enjoyed the ride on the beach she had imagined.

"No, Fred, that was more than enough excitement for me," she told him, but he did not seem to understand.

She looked at his interesting face, with the dark angled eyes and the small mouth, and she wanted to kiss it. Instead she decided to tell him what she had been thinking. He would not understand her, but she wanted to plunge in anyway.

"Would you mind listening to me ramble about something?" she asked. He had his mouth full, but he nodded. "I am very confused about myself. I am finding myself to be a different type than I thought. I expected marriage would be difficult for me, an old maid set in her ways and a suffragist not too happy to give up her independence and serve a man. Didn't you expect that too?"

"And what are you discovering?" he asked, interested but reserved.

"All I want to do is lie in bed." She blushed when she thought of how that must sound. "No, that's not what I mean. I'm very peaceful, Fred. I thought that you would worry me all the time, that it would be quite a strain, and instead I feel more relaxed than I can ever remember. I feel safe. And here is what I don't understand, Fred. Safe from what? Nobody has ever threatened me. Nobody has ever noticed me enough to think about bothering me. So I was thinking this: I must have felt unsafe from myself. I must have been very unhappy with myself, very much at odds with myself."

He started to speak, but she put a finger to his lips to shush him. "No, listen for a minute longer. I want to try to say it all together. Here we have been married for one week, and everything in my life looks quite different from what I thought it would. I wonder whether I was a real suffragist at all. I'm not sure whether I even care about all that now. And since I don't know now, it makes me wonder whether I ever did care. I am worried about what I have been all these years. And even more I wonder whether I can go back and do the same things again. You know I hate it when people say that suffragists want only to get married and then they don't care, and it's sometimes true. I've seen it true. It was true of Elizabeth, my sister. Now I fear it's true for me."

Fred looked at her glumly, like a doctor thinking over his patient's symptoms. "But you said you are very peaceful," he said at last. "And happy? Did I hear happy?"

Susan forced out a smile. "Yes, happy. I must have been very unhappy before."

"How does that follow? If you were unhappy, you didn't let on to me."

"But for so long I didn't want to marry you. And I never thought that I would feel so peaceful."

"Susan," he said, "you worry too much. I think you were happy before. I'm glad you are happy now. I don't see why the two should be the same. Of course you worried. No sane woman would marry without worrying."

Fred put out a hand and caught hers. She pulled away, embarrassed to hold hands in a public place. He put out his hand again and held her firmly. "Susan, we are alone in this room," he said.

He looked at her and smiled. "Do you still want the vote?"

"I wouldn't turn it down."

"As much as ever?"

"I don't know."

"If you still want the vote, you're a suffragist. The way you feel about men is something else again, as far as I'm concerned. I can't see what that has to do with voting. You remember the day in Sonoma? You remember what I asked you?"

"Why does it have to be a competition?" She remembered that very well.

"You don't have to be a suffragist the same way your mother is a suffragist."

Chapter 10
1896: California Campaign

Susan Konicek went wherever the railroad went, down the broad valley that seemed to be a plain, to Modesto, Merced, Madera, Fresno, Hanford, Visalia. It had been dry so long—it was October—everything had died unless it was irrigated, even the weeds. From the train she saw a desolate landscape in which even trees and vineyards seemed half dead, coated with dust. It was hard to see this as fertile farm country. She would arrive in the little farm towns, clinging to their Midwestern respectability, shaded by ash and maple and sycamore with its patchy silver bark. The people were polite, quiet, impossible to read. Dogs lay unmoving on front porches with their heads between their paws. Lawns were brown and tufted with weeds. Overhead the sky lay relentlessly blue, nothing like Santa Rosa, where the dim gentleness of fog launched each morning.

The schedule Mary Hay had given Susan, when she assigned her to the speaking tour, turned out to be more imagination than reality. If someone met her train at all, the person might have no idea who she was or why she had come. Sometimes Susan came in on the night train to find the station deserted. She would locate a scabby hotel or a boardinghouse nearby, where the clerk would act as though he had never seen a lady traveling alone—as perhaps he had not. She felt scummy, vulnerable, small—like a green algae tail waving slowly in a stream. Yet she had to muster her energy to gin up a meeting and even to print up and tack up her own posters.

Mostly she spoke at women's meetings put on at a church, talking to ladies whom she could urge to speak to their husbands or brothers about the suffragist cause. She tried to arrange evening meetings to get to men, even if it was only a few men in a home parlor, and sometimes she managed them. Regardless of her audience, she felt that the speech was no good. It was her baseball talk. Susan delivered it well enough—she had given it so many times, after all—and her audiences responded well. It felt wrong, however. It seemed artificial, a decoration. She doubted the speech could move anybody to change. She doubted that it showed anything other than her cleverness.

Perhaps once it had made some skeptics lift their eyebrows and acknowledge the existence of a brain in a woman. She needed more than that now. She asked for a decision. The suffrage amendment was on the ballot in November, and it struck her forcefully that they might actually win. All these years of going to meetings and writing newspaper columns came down to this one great chance to win the vote.

———————

One good thing: she had plenty of time to think about her life and how it had changed since her marriage. This was the disturbance that lay at the back of her mind, whatever she did, wherever she went.

Susan was amazed at how easily Fred made up with her mother, once they came home married. Susan felt nervous all the way back from San Diego, worrying about it. Fred parked her at the Occidental Hotel by the railway station and went off to face the dragon. He came back forty-five minutes later, whistling. "She says, why don't we live in your old bedroom, if it suits us?"

"What did you say to her?" Susan had been unable to sit down the entire time he was gone.

"Not too much. I just said you would like to continue in your old job if we could live and board there together. If not, I would make arrangements to get your things."

"That's all? What did she say?"

"Oh, she scolded me for running off with her daughter, like I knew she would, but I pointed out that you had reached the age of accountability sometime back. 'I saved you a lot of trouble doing the job out of town, Mrs. Netherton,' I said, and she laughed. Your mother and I will get along. There's probably a reason that she takes in only men."

And so it had proved. He handled Rebecca as if he were a blue jay: saucy and quick, never sticking to any position long enough to get caught. Yet he made his points.

He had promised Susan that he would back her in suffrage, and he was as good as his word—maybe better because he nagged her into doing more than she would have, left alone. "The way you two are acting," he told Susan and Rebecca one night over corned beef and cabbage, "you must be ashamed to be associated with woman suffrage. You don't have any sign anywhere on the house. You haven't made your boarders sit through any canvassing. If I didn't know better, I'd think you would rather not let the world know where you stand."

He put a sign on his buggy, VOTES FOR WOMEN, and carried it all over his territory. "Right now people don't know there will be a ballot measure," he told Susan. "You have to get them thinking about it, even if they don't think very hard."

As a result of his badgering, Rebecca had one of the boarders construct a very large yellow sign with black letters, reading GIVE DEMOCRACY TO THE OTHER HALF OF AMERICA. The sign was on canvas stretched over a frame and stood almost head-high when they staked it in the front lawn. Nobody in Santa Rosa had ever made such a gaudy display. Susan hated the sight of it.

"For a woman who wants to vote, you don't seem to have paid much attention to what elections are like," Fred said.

Subtly her life changed, like a shift of the wind or a turn of the seasons. She still occupied the same house, did the same work, ate the same food, but to be married, to share not just a bed but her daily life with Fred, could absorb her thoughts from morning until night, even while she was working at the house. She thought of what she must remember to tell him, considered what he would like to eat, remembered their last conversations. When Fred was gone selling in the North, she thought a hundred times about how it would be when he returned. She had never expected marriage to do this. Everything else was not devalued, but a little sidetracked.

She had become a more substantial person in the town. She and Fred received dinner invitations from families in the church; and around Santa Rosa she fell into conversations that would never before have occurred. "How is Fred's business going, Mrs. Konicek?" the butcher asked her. For people in town marriage had made her real. She had a future they could understand. She resented this assumption, but she knew it partly reflected her inner sensibility. She liked being called Mrs. Konicek. It did feel more substantial.

And yet here she was, away from Fred, speaking for suffrage, on the greatest suffrage campaign of her life, and it was largely because of Fred. His insistence had made her take the election seriously. But it was also because of him, she felt, that she had no peace while she did it.

Susan knew her speech was no good. For some time, suffrage had been a respectable cause, one that educated people and reform-minded newspapers would support. She had always taken some pride in these good credentials, but Fred, to her surprise and confusion, argued that the cause was so respectable, it barely stirred the blood. "You have to give people a reason to vote with you," he said, and when Susan or her mother spoke of the contributions of women to science and education, he insisted that these did not constitute a reason. Certainly a cute analogy to baseball did not.

She remembered her sister's comment at the convention, that neither of them could believe in suffrage the way their mother did. Susan wondered whether her tepid speech reflected tepid belief. She could not give men reasons because she did not have reasons, not reasons as strong as a cry of Fire! in a crowded theater.

In Lemon Cove she threw out the speech. The town was tiny, and she had only a handful of listeners in a schoolhouse, lit by kerosene lamps that people brought from home. They sat on benches, nine women and four men, quiet people who probably came out of courtesy to their neighbors who invited them. The women wore flowered cotton shifts and had kerchiefs over their heads; the men had tried to clean up their shoes, but mostly failed because the leather was half gone. She looked them over and knew these people would not care to hear about baseball.

Otherwise she had no idea what she might say, until she heard herself telling the Lemon Cove farmers and housewives about her mother's life. She never mentioned Rebecca by name, but she told of a woman whose husband disappeared for weeks and left her with the children, and then reappeared drunk and sold her dining room table. Who left her to be evicted from her own house. Who came and took her children away from her, took them to another state, and the law would do nothing to protect the mother from that terrible fate.

"Now you may say that those laws, if they are wrong, can be changed by our present system. But what you cannot change in the current system of half-democracy is the rage of that mother when she realizes that she has no voice of her own—that she is not listened to, that neither she nor any other woman can speak in the house ordained to make or change laws, that she virtually does not exist by law because she exists only through her husband. In the eyes of the half-democracy, she is no better than a child. It is not just the injustices done by these laws that I would change. It is the bitterness of soul that afflicts anyone who finds herself done injustice while bound and gagged.

"You may say, and rightly, that I do not seem much like a woman who has been bound and gagged. But as far as our choice of leaders is concerned, as to who might best represent us, I am gagged. As far as deciding what laws are best, I am gagged. When it comes to the debate over how human beings should be treated, let alone how women should be treated, I am gagged. Marriage is regulated by laws, so is inheritance, and many aspects of child rearing, but I have no say in those things that concern me; I am gagged. In the voting booth, where a drunkard and an illiterate and a foreigner and even a semi-idiot are honored as citizens and their votes carefully guarded, I am excluded like a full idiot. I am telling you that this is an injustice, done every day in a country that claims to be a democracy and the best hope of an ignorant world. It is an injustice done not only to educated, refined women, but also to helpless women, who have no protection. What kind of man does such things to helpless women?"

She went on by proposing that women could bring their good minds and their knowledge of food and household cleanliness to the government of stinking slums in the cities, and to the regulation of food purity; that women could bring their knowledge of children to the questions of education and truancy laws and so on. When she thought of the speech that night on a train back up the valley toward the little town of Selma, these practical arguments were not the vein of gold she felt she had touched. Rather, she had finally found her own reasons for wanting the vote: that it was only fair, and fair was as important as anything in the universe. She did not know whether the men she appealed to would feel that way, but she knew she was giving reasons.

They were polite people in Lemon Cove, and they shook her hand and thanked her for coming. Certainly no one fell on the floor shaking with overwhelming conviction. Nonetheless, she began to feel optimistic. Surely they would win this election because it was right for them to win it.

Susan kept up this vein of speech until the election, and she gained in confidence as she did it. She felt a fierceness in her voice she had never heard before. She cared not merely to make a favorable impression now, but to turn voters to her side. She felt she had to track down their thoughts and convince them; she had to make them care. By the time October was over, she wanted to win the election something terrible.

Making her last speech the Monday afternoon before the election, she took the night train all the way to San Francisco. Her mother had taken rooms at the Gold Star, thinking to preside over a celebration. Susan arrived past midnight and wearily climbed to the rooms. To her surprise, she found Rebecca sitting up without a light.

Before Susan could ask why, her mother spoke with impeccable diction. "For all our work we may not see the victory tomorrow."

"Why not?" She lit a lamp so that she could see her mother's face.

"Because the liquor powers have come in. We were given a letter they distributed to the saloons in San Francisco and Oakland. They urge every saloonkeeper to make sure he influences his friends to keep us out."

On election day they watched polls on Howard Street, held in a grocery store back room. Susan had never guessed that the world could hold so many small, sunburned, sweat-stained men. They came in the door with suspicious looks, saying nothing, looking around the room like moral people entering a house of ill repute. They marked their ballots and left silently. Where did they come from?

Results were posted that night in a crowded, noisy, bewildering room at city hall where various candidates, their supporters, and the merely curious came and went, talked in noisy clusters, and shouted questions at the ratlike clerks who chalked numbers on blackboards. Most of the interest was in the presidency. Nobody but the ladies seemed to care about the suffrage amendment.

The chalked numbers showed that they trailed badly in the city. Rebecca pointed out that if they excluded San Francisco's vote, they might actually lead the state—and she thought perhaps the rural returns, which were slow, would prove favorable. But as the night grew late this trend never developed. Statewide they were only ten thousand votes behind, but they could not close the margin. At midnight Susan and her mother made the quiet walk back to the Gold Star.

"I may not live to see suffrage," Rebecca said, and Susan had no answer for her.

During the night Susan's emotions reverted to a natural optimism, and she awoke with a sharp sense of hope. In the lobby a vendor in a gold hotel uniform sold newspapers. She bought one, took a seat in a red leather chair, and could not for a time find the results on suffrage. McKinley had defeated Bryan—that was the great news. Senate and congressional totals were posted. Suffrage was buried in the inner pages, of small and secondary interest. The margin had not changed. They had lost.

All the rest of that day, as they made their way back to Santa Rosa on the ferry and train, Susan kept forgetting the permanency of a vote.

She would begin thinking of ways to address the liquor question. She would begin to develop more reasons. Then it would wash over her afresh that they were defeated, that her speeches had disappeared into thin air, unheeded, that she would have nothing to do for suffrage tomorrow.

She told Fred of her speech, how she was able to speak of fairness and find in it a reason to offer the men. "I thought often of what you told me, that we had to offer men reasons to vote with us. I think I found my reason. Simple justice. A woman shouldn't be denied the very privileges that a man awards himself. It's that clear to me."

"And to me," Fred said. "Though I admit it was not so before I met you and your mother. It took a while for the idea to get through my skull and into my brain. But I agree, it's simple."

They were up on McDonald Avenue, a wide, straight street where the wealthy were building their homes. Fred liked to come and look at the new construction, so they often took walks in this direction, to the end of the street where it ran into the rural cemetery and off into the hills thick with live oaks.

"Why is it not so simple to other men?" Susan felt her frustration rise up from where she had stowed it. "Women have been talking about these things for fifty years without making any headway."

"You've made some headway, I think," Fred said. "For a difference of thirteen thousand votes you would have the vote here in California."

"But, Fred, to lose a close one is still a flat loss. I often say that a team can lose a whole summer's games by one or two runs each. We never win."

He took a deep breath and blew it out. "It's not fate, Susan. It's votes. You have to change people's minds. You gave them a reason, but maybe you didn't reach enough of them. Look, I know this from selling blankets. You have to keep trying until you find out what will sell."

"All right," she said. "But I still don't understand why it's so hard when you say it's simple."

He shrugged. "There's a certain amount of fear, I think. Men think if women were like men, they wouldn't care two cents for men."

She laughed at that. "Really? They think that? When women think about their men all the time? Do you have any idea how foolish women are about men?"

"Yes," he said dryly. "That's it, foolish. Men are afraid that if women awoke from their foolishness, the nice, comfortable situation would end. That's why the vote scares them, and anything else that gives a woman a chance to think and act on her thinking."

"You don't sound very hopeful," Susan said.

"I don't know that I am," Fred replied. "But I believe in trying."

Book III
Ordinary Times

Chapter 11
1897: Family Life

Thomas Nichols Konicek was the first and last baby to be born in Rebecca Netherton's boardinghouse. He arrived during an October 1897 heat wave that cooled dramatically after supper when the wind blew in off the ocean. Susan began her long labor in stifling heat that was not improved by her mother's conviction that women in labor should be completely covered in blankets, as though to lubricate the baby's passage with perspiration. (The doctor said nothing; he was not ready to stand up to Rebecca Netherton over such a trivial thing.) After the child came out in the early morning hours, Susan would have given anything for those blankets. She shook uncontrollably in the bed, too exhausted to rise and close the window or fetch covers. Susan called for aid, but nobody heard her. Her mother had left her to follow the doctor and the tiny, shrunken baby to another room.

Rebecca never seemed so interested in Thomas after that; she let it be known that she would prefer a granddaughter. Her wish was granted in 1900 with the arrival of Rebecca Netherton Konicek. Grandmother Rebecca was so extremely pleased by this event that she made her namesake a quilt, talking almost constantly about its production, and showing it to anyone who came into the house, interested or not. Rebecca had never liked handwork, and they now discovered why: she did it badly. Susan had little use for the quilt and stuck it in the back of her closet. The result was that little Rebecca grew up with only one handwork item in perfect mint condition, the quilt her grandmother made with huge looping stitches and mismatched patterns. All the rest of her things were mauled by constant use and eventually turned back into rags. She always had that ugly quilt.

Before Rebecca's birth the Koniceks had moved into their own small house, a redwood cottage on Humboldt Avenue, with two bedrooms, a parlor, and a kitchen. The move was Fred's decision. He did not want to raise a family in a boardinghouse. For a time Susan continued to help her mother with the daily work there, but she had to give it up. They could afford no help, so she managed all the cooking, cleaning, and laundry at home, often with children hanging off her like leeches. Sometimes she remembered the suffrage referendum and the speeches she made across the state. That seemed to be from another life, in another world.

A third child, George Konicek, was born in 1902. The lack of a middle name reflected his mother's loss of steam. By the time George came, it was all Susan could do to find a first name.

She thought the whole quality of her life could be summed up in one question, "How did you sleep?" Sleep became sometimes like a god to her, a severe and unattainable idol. Nevertheless she found a grand movement of satisfaction under the daily exhaustion of her life, an ocean current that pushed her imperceptibly toward some good shore even while she feared that she would surely drown, choking and gasping. Her tormentors, the thankless children who pulled on her and puked on her and screamed at her or for her, who fought with each other and barely ever stayed content and happy for five minutes—they were for her as delectable as plum blossoms or as the slowly winding Russian River where twice Fred had taken her to swim. Susan did not miss the suffrage movement, which all but dried up in Santa Rosa after the election anyway. It was not that she did not care about its goals as surely as ever, but that she had found another cause far more engrossing. The study of her children took her entire energy and thought.

This peace—for peace it was, even when she became mindless and numb from endless chores—could never stop surprising her. Right in the middle of washing stinking diapers in the big tin tub she would feel a tingling gratefulness for this unforeseen joy of family. Amazing! Head down in the filthy slop she felt contentment. Sometimes she would break out in a silly grin at the sheer surprise of it.

For Fred, work seemed less satisfying. The new catalogs meant that people ordered direct from Sears or another supplier, and his business went steadily down. This had two unattractive results: Fred was gone more, trying to make a dollar, and when he was home, he fretted. Susan kept a garden, canned vegetables and fruits, made cucumber pickles, because money was scarce. She tried working in the canneries in season, but though the money was easy, it developed that Rebecca could not handle the children. She was too old and had no patience for them.

Fred talked of finding another job, but nothing obvious beckoned, and he was afraid to let go of what he knew. Once or twice he spoke of becoming a minister, and he even made an appointment to talk with their bishop about what that would require. But Fred didn't keep the appointment. When the time came, he thought of how strange it would be, and the way people would talk to him (or not talk, except behind his back), and he could not go through even the step of inquiring. Susan was relieved. The idea of being married to a minister sounded as strange as being married to a Chinaman.

He became increasingly devout, however. Fred had always been a very active Methodist, but now he carried a Bible with him wherever he traveled. Susan approved because his anger worried her, and she thought religion could only do him good. Also, she found herself drawn in the same direction, even though she could barely acknowledge this fact to herself. It was another great surprise to her, another glad descent into the ordinary.

———————————

They were late to baptize Thomas, perhaps because of an unspoken tradition that the mother of a child will be the one to show active concern for faith. In this case, Susan was not one to show such concern. She was not actually aware of the practical necessity of baptism until the preacher gently raised it with her after the child was more than a year old. Then she mentioned it to Fred, and he surprised her by taking it in such a fret.

"My goodness, Susan, I can't believe that we forgot," he said.

"I didn't forget," she said. "I never knew."

The ritual called for them to carry the infant to the front of the church, where they stood and took vows to raise him as a Christian. Then a little cold water was dipped on his head, the baby cried at the sudden shock, and the church people murmured and laughed fondly. It was as brief and homely a ritual as it was possible to devise, and yet Susan found that her interest grew with each of the children, until by the time George was ready for his she looked forward to the day.

She did not understand her interest. It seemed to her that she passed some important milestone when the baptism was complete, but that the milestone was in shadow and she could not read it. When the minister placed his hand on the baby's head, and the drops of water drizzled down his forehead, she watched with the greatest intensity, although what she hoped to see she could not say. With the sleepy, familiar congregation, and the happy, avuncular pastor, the ceremony was no more dramatic than grace over meals. She never had any grand sense that heaven had broken through, that the hand of God might be seen. Transcendence did not seem to be on offer.

Fred was no help. With his practical cast of mind, he could not say much about baptism other than that it was the normal thing, that it could do no harm, and that from the evidence of the families he knew, it provided no certain good. On the subject of religion, Susan and Fred had trouble making sense of each other. She had a mind to question the underlying reasons for doctrine, while Fred was an intuitive believer with no taste for metaphysics. When they talked about religion, one or both got rankled.

Therefore Susan went to the minister. It unnerved her to do so, even though she knew from two years of his preaching that Reverend Arkes was not a fearful figure. Susan felt the ghost of her upbringing, her mother's firm association of religion with repression, inquisition, and ignorance. To go for a private interview with a minister was as though to invite a witch doctor to examine your baby.

Nonetheless she persuaded herself that it was a sensible and harmless thing to do, visiting a pastor to discuss a matter where he was presumably expert. Why not satisfy her curiosity? She let the man know immediately where she stood to avoid any potential confusion.

"You know, Reverend Arkes, that I am not a genuine believer. I go to church because of Fred."

This was not precisely true. She had started going to church because of Fred, but she had found that she liked its comfortable rhythms, its normalcy. Other women would greet her, ask about her family, pick up Tommy and admire his growth. As the daughter of a woman who had spent her life avoiding anything ordinary, Susan felt this as a relief and a blessing. She was more than ready to sink down into the democracy of motherhood and church attendance.

Arkes was a thin, red-faced man, always dressed in the same black suit. The way he held his mouth, with the corners naturally slanting down, made him look grim—and they had some thunderers in the Methodist church, where the ministers generally changed every three years and were sometimes judged by the degree to which they put the fear of God into their congregation. But Arkes was a soft-spoken, genial man. "That's all right," he said to her disclaimer about church, and let it lie there.

"I came in to talk to you about baptism," Susan said, forced by the silence to come to her point. "All three of our children have been baptized in this church, but I find Fred doesn't understand baptism, except that it's the done thing among Methodists. I hope I'm not insulting you, but it seems to me it must be a holdover from a primitive superstition. Washing away sins, as though they are little black spots susceptible to soap and water."

She had put it crassly with some purpose. The pastor's study was a cubbyhole full of books and papers, a sympathetic mess. She liked it instinctively, and that aroused her defenses. She wanted to warn Arkes that she was not a candidate for salvation.

Arkes merely asked, in a mild, cheerful voice, "How do *you* think about sins, Mrs. Konicek?"

"I don't think about them, really," she said. "I'm not sure I believe in sin. Unless you mean ignorance and superstition. I believe in ignorance."

"I do too. There's a great deal of that." Reverend Arkes smiled softly, as though sweetly remembering.

"Then you should understand my question. I wonder whether a ritual like baptism perpetuates superstition and ignorance rather than doing away with them."

She was embarrassed for him as soon as she asked it. He simply stared for a few moments. "I wonder why you care," he asked.

She started to answer, then stopped and thought it over. Finally she said, "My husband is a good Methodist, and I want to cooperate with him in the raising of our children. But only insofar as it is actually good for our children."

"And you find baptism disturbing?"

It was not in Susan's nature to be deceptive; she wanted too much to have straightforward relations with others. Anyway, she had come with a mind to understand baptism. "Disturbing in a way," she said with difficulty. "But probably not in the way you are thinking. I feel very moved by my children's ritual, and it worries me because I do not know what lies behind it."

Thankfully Arkes did not crow over her admission. He did not even smile. "So you are concerned for yourself?"

"For my children. I don't want to support a ritual that will undermine their moral feeling. I want them to grow up knowing that the world needs something a great deal more than a little water sprinkled on it with some holy words."

Arkes cocked his head sideways, picked up some papers on his desk, and moved them over into another pile. "I'm not sure I understand. You find baptism moving, but you don't know why. Your mind tells you that it's just superstition and better left in the Dark Ages. But the fact that it moves you makes you hesitate."

"Yes, and it's important to my husband. He is a good Methodist."

Arkes leaned back. "Yes," he said. "It's interesting that you find the service attractive. I'd estimate most people don't have a great deal of feeling for a baptism." He paused and looked thoughtfully at Susan. "Do you have any idea what moves you?"

"No," she said.

He thought some more. "Then all I can do for you is explain baptism as best I can. You'll have to make the pieces fit for yourself. I'll try to explain it, but you understand it is a mystery. Nobody really understands it."

"Aren't there different beliefs?" she asked.

"Oh, yes," he said. "All kinds of different beliefs. Immersion, sprinkling, in the name of Jesus, in the name of the Holy Trinity. There are many differences, some big and some small. I suppose they're all big to somebody. The Catholics believe that in itself it saves you from hell, and that's opposed to every word of the Bible. I'll just tell you about the Methodists. We Methodists see it as a symbol. Here's this little infant, helpless before the cruelty of the world, and before the cruelty of his own heart. We believe even infants can be cruel, you know, or soon will be as they naturally grow. They are born to sin. And we say, God can save even the helpless. We put a sign of God's grace on the child. It shows that God's grace washes away sin, that the little one is welcome into the family of God's people who are so washed. That the cruelty of the world and the self can be overcome, not by the child but by God Himself."

"It doesn't really work, though, does it?" Susan asked. "There's hardly anybody in this town who isn't baptized, except reprobates like me and my mother. You're not claiming they've overcome cruelty and selfishness, are you?"

"It's a symbol," he said. "Symbols don't work. They point. The love of God certainly works—not on everybody who feels it, but on anybody who is willing to let it work. A person has to be willing.

"You could say baptism shows God's grace beginning to work on people, even before they know enough to be willing. If I had to guess, I would think that's what you find so troubling and so moving: that the love of God is poured out like water on babies."

"Poured out like water," she said.

"Yes," he said. "Does that help you at all?"

"I don't know," she said. "It's a mystery, as you say."

"Yes, but by that we don't mean incomprehensible. We mean bigger than our minds can hold. We're a little like blind men trying to get a grip on a redwood tree. There's more tree than we can handle."

Afterward Susan often thought of that conversation, particularly the minister's almost-last phrase. She felt, in many ways, like a blind woman trying to get a grip on a redwood tree. It was not an unhappy image.

Chapter 12
1905: Elizabeth Returns

In the spring of 1905 Susan received a letter from her sister, who said that she would visit Santa Rosa that summer on her way to the NAWSA convention in Portland. Furthermore, she would bring Lucy with her.

Susan gripped George in her arms and began to dance with him, whirling him about until he cried, "Mommy, stop!"

She held him tightly and kissed him. "Your aunt Elizabeth is coming," she said. "We'll all be dancing."

Susan walked with Becky and George to the boardinghouse, a ten-minute stroll that expanded to double the time with the children's toddling. All the way, despite her impatience to be moving faster, Susan felt overwhelming elation. *Why,* she wondered, *was Elizabeth coming at all? And Lucy!*

Charles came out on her mother's front porch to greet them. A series of Chinese men had cooked for Rebecca over the thirty-five years she had lived in Santa Rosa, but Charles had lasted by far the longest. Rebecca was extremely anxious that no one steal him away: Chinese were not so plentiful as they had been before the Exclusion Act.

"Are you looking for your mother?" Charles asked. "I will go and get her. She is upstairs, maybe sleeping."

"Swing me! Swing me!" Becky said to him—she was already crowding against his legs with her arms extended high.

168   *Ordinary Times*

"Just once," Charles said. "I have to get your granny."

Charles had lost in favor when he revealed, following the 1896 defeat, that he and every Chinaman he knew had voted against them. For a time Susan could hardly look at him without thinking of his betrayal as well as the principle behind it—that a Chinaman who could neither read nor write had the privilege of denying the vote to American women. Susan could barely imagine what her mother had thought or said to Charles. Perhaps with her exquisite ability to compartmentalize, Rebecca had hardly noticed. She needed Charles to run her boarding-house, however he voted.

Rebecca came down, a bloom on her cheeks (rouge, smeared on), straight and lucid, a grande dame even when awakened from an afternoon nap. She said she had taken an Aspirin, and it put her to sleep. She had always been attracted to patent medicines, as to all new inventions, and Susan automatically stopped listening when she began to speak of them. Aspirin was Rebecca's latest favorite, a miracle drug, she insisted, though nobody listened.

"Mother," Susan broke in, "I have a letter from Elizabeth. She says that she is coming to see us on her way to Portland, in June. She is bringing Lucy."

"Why do you say it is on the way to Portland? This is not the most efficient way to travel from New York to the state of Oregon."

It was absolutely characteristic of her mother to bluster an opposing position anytime she was unsure what to say.

"Of course not, Mother. Of course she wants to see you. It has been, what, fifteen years? And you have never seen Lucy, have you? I am sure that Elizabeth wants Lucy to meet her grandmother."

"Why should Portland be an excuse? It is a very important event. I would go myself if I were able."

No one but Mother could honestly think of Portland as significant, Susan thought. Undeniably, suffrage was in the doldrums, not just in California but throughout the nation. Susan B. Anthony had passed on her leadership in 1900—she was too old to push forward any longer—and then Elizabeth Cady Stanton, long an invalid, died. (Rebecca wrote long eulogies for the newspaper and was furious when the mayor declined to declare a city holiday.) A year ago Carrie Catt had resigned the presidency of the National American Woman Suffrage Association because of her husband's illness. Anna Shaw succeeded, but that woman was born to frustrate: she dithered over every decision and meddled in the other officers' work. She was a great orator but an ineffective executive.

No, Portland was no reason for her sister to come west. In her heart of hearts Susan doubted that Elizabeth even came to see her mother. Surely Elizabeth came for her; she was the twin. After this giddy thought crossed her mind, however, Susan had second thoughts about allowing herself to think it. Why should she extend her hopes toward her sister again? Just when she had achieved tranquillity, did she dare let herself be tempted toward something so unlikely as her sister's love?

She found that she could not help herself. Walking between her mother's house and her own, or on any errand, she would look over streets she would walk down with her sister, showing her how much had changed in the twenty-two years since she had left Santa Rosa. Susan wanted to point out her favorite flowers, the best houses, anything that she found pleasurable. When she met someone in town or at church, she would mentally check off whether this was someone Elizabeth should meet.

This despite her attempts to do just the opposite, to keep her expectations modest. When she married Fred, Susan had believed he replaced

Elizabeth in her heart. She had considered the NAWSA convention in 1896 her continental divide, crossing over from a mental world where everything flowed toward her sister, to another where every thought tended toward Fred.

She and her sister had corresponded only a little in the intervening years. She still knew next to nothing about Elizabeth's husband! She did not know what kind of house her sister inhabited, who she saw as friends, or what she thought about having just one daughter. Yet, Susan now found herself filling in all those blanks with the love they had known as children. *A husband,* she thought, *may be no substitute for a sister.*

They stood at the train station, she and Fred and her mother, plus the children. "There it is," Fred said, although she could not tell what he saw even when she strained her eyes. People on the shaded benches got up and stretched. Susan now could see the engine, not appearing to move but wavering in sight like the air over a tin roof on a hot day. Gradually it grew larger, a black beetle with strange protrusions, accompanied by a distant grumbling sound. Then the whistle, sweet and mournful, spread over them, and at just that moment Susan sensed the speed of the train, coming toward them full of violence. She grabbed at the children, to hold their hands tightly, and stood bracing herself while the engine blew past, followed by the rattling, groaning cars. The brakes squealed, the conductor called out, and in an instant people were everywhere, streaming purposefully. Among them Susan found her sister, as beautiful and as sparkling as ever. The years had deepened her beauty, so that while she lacked the stunning brilliance of her youth, her face was more interesting. She had cut her hair off fashionably to shoulder length, and she wore a tiny turquoise shell cradling her head. They reached each other and embraced.

The joy began to unravel a moment later when they clustered on the platform, and Fred extended his hand. "You must be the drummer," Elizabeth said with a smile.

She could not have known that she touched a sore spot, unless she had heard how the catalogs were affecting trade. Fred tried to smile it off, but he wasn't quite convincing. His face twisted as though someone had splashed vinegar in it. Elizabeth did not even pause to watch him. She was introducing everyone to Lucy.

Lucy stood tall, at least three inches over her mother, and she was as lovely as a dish of peaches. Of course everyone wanted to look at her, even little George. Lucy took in the attention as though it was entirely natural to her; probably it was. She seemed to be a quiet girl, polite but ready to let others take the lead in friendliness. She was dressed exquisitely in a heavy blue silk with puffed-out sleeves and a pattern of pleats down the front. She made everyone else look shabby; she made the train station look drab; she made the gorgeous blue sky hanging over Taylor Mountain look dingy.

Fred went to get the luggage while Susan occupied herself herding them all out to the street to Fred's buggy. They made small talk, mostly about the weather, while Fred brought the trunks and packed them onto the back of his vehicle. Then he handed Rebecca up into her seat and extended his hand for Elizabeth.

"But there isn't room!" she said. "We can't all go in that little buggy."

"The children and I will walk home," Susan said. "We live on Humboldt. It isn't far. We'll come up to Mother's house when you've had a chance to rest."

"Goodness, you can't walk," Elizabeth said. "I won't have it. You look exhausted already. What about those poor children?"

"It's all right," said Susan. "It's not half a mile." She was suddenly conscious of the children's appearance. She had dressed them, but

George had sat in the dirt and had a dark patch on the bottom of his trousers, not to mention a fringe of grime all around his mouth.

"Fred, my dear, go and hire another vehicle. I will gladly pay for it."

Susan looked at Fred wearing his worst hangdog look. Her mother was sitting in her seat staring straight ahead. Susan shut her eyes for a moment, then said, "All right." Fred went and got the cab—there was only one in Santa Rosa—and Elizabeth insisted that Susan accompany her and Lucy in it while the children rode with Fred and their mother.

Trying to make pleasant talk, Susan described the Santa Rosa that her sister could, she knew, hardly recognize from the time she had left it. Elizabeth, however, made only polite noises. Fortunately Lucy was extremely interested. "What a darling little town," she said. "What nice little houses." She took off her traveling bonnet to expose her fair skin to the glow of sunlight.

When they reached the boardinghouse, Elizabeth asked if Susan would mind paying the cab. "I'll pay you back, Sue, but I have my money packed away. Could you do it for me?"

"I'm sorry. I don't carry money with me," Susan said.

"Do you think he would come back later to collect? Or should we ask Mother to pay?"

"No," Susan said, and she felt the color rising in her face. "I do not think you should ask Mother. She is not very well off."

Susan did not hear what Elizabeth said to the driver, but he drove off without any fuss.

They had a horrible time together. Susan could cry over it; she did privately in her own room. She did not envy Elizabeth's wealth or her beauty—but she could not stand her sister's lack of love. What in heaven's name had made her come? Elizabeth too obviously thought that Fred was a rube, that their life was rural and poor, that she had been lucky to escape this obscure town, and that Susan was unlucky (or dim) to stay.

Every morning of the visit Susan determined to make a new day of it. Alone in her room, she felt the old hopeful feelings come crowding back in, and she was sure the coldness was simply a misunderstanding they could brush aside. They were sisters, after all, twin sisters, and surely a fresh start and a smile and a little effort could reclaim that. But it was never so. Each day began with hope and tumbled down quickly into stiff and angry boredom. Susan could hardly talk to her sister. Every word came out sticky and rigid.

It would have been far better if the visit had been for just a night, a fleeting exchange between two women who had little to say to each other. They had planned these weeks, however, and could not even talk truthfully to call off the visit. They had to act as though they loved each other to the very last breath. At times Susan wondered whether she could endure it, she seethed so with anger toward her sister and her niece. Day by day the time passed until she saw that soon the two weeks would be over.

Then she stared into a future quite dead of hope, for after she had endured this awful passage, and Elizabeth had gone, all the possibilities that had sustained her imagination for all these years of separation would be gutted and dried. Susan found that depressing beyond words, and yet it came on steadily with the end of the visit, and she was helpless to change it.

On the next to the last day of the visit, Susan planned a picnic excursion. Fred was gone. He said he had to work, but he obviously wanted to keep his distance from the little rat's nest of emotion at home. It would be a woman's affair—a day's excursion by train to the Russian

River, to see the giant redwoods. Susan had seen the trees just once—and she had never forgotten those astonishing living towers. *This,* she thought with a sense of righteousness, *cannot be topped in New York.*

She was up at dawn, making egg sandwiches with bakery bread. The morning was clear, the sky a pale, translucent blue. She could not help it. Her hope came rising again. They would eat plums from her tree—she had kept Thomas off all week to be sure the fruit survived. Besides, she had purchased a basket of strawberries from Mrs. Guilkin, who grew them in her garden. If they could have only one lovely day together.

When it was time for the household to awaken, just a touch was enough for the children to open their eyes and remember the nature of the day. They bounced into their clothes, the sooner to be on the way. Not a bit of fog had come in during the night. The air was still and clear; Susan could hear the sweet thrill of a meadowlark's voice from the pasture behind the college as together they walked to Grandmother's boardinghouse. There the boarders smoked on the porch while they waited for breakfast. One regular did push-ups and squats in the front garden. Susan sent the children to the back while she waited for Elizabeth and Lucy to appear.

After a few minutes she went to the kitchen. "Mrs. Phillips didn't mention any change in plans, did she?" Susan asked Charles. He was tying up brown paper packages, filled with unknown delectables.

"No, ma'am, she didn't."

"I'm afraid we'll miss our train."

The brewery whistle blew; it was seven o'clock. Susan climbed the stairs, noticing worn footprints on the treads, chipped paint on the spindles. *The house is showing its age,* she thought. She felt regretfully that her sister had probably marked every flaw. At the landing she turned down a bare, scuffed hallway and knocked on a door. Inside she thought she heard low voices, but no one answered. Susan knocked again. "Elizabeth," she called, not too loudly but with enough force to be heard. "Elizabeth, we should be going."

The door opened, and Lucy squeezed out, dressed in a rose-colored skirt and a white shirtwaist blouse with pearl buttons. She closed the door behind her. "I'm sorry, Aunt Susan, but my mother says to go without her. She won't be coming."

"Is she ill?"

"Only slightly." Lucy spoke in round tones of perfect, polite sadness. "She needs to rest for our trip. She asked me to give her regrets."

"Do you still want to go, Lucy?" Susan saw a look of uncertainty flash onto Lucy's face. *Good, let her stay.* Susan half wished to cancel the excursion and go home mad. The whole purpose of going had disappeared. The children would feel it as a terrible loss, though. She imagined Becky's large eyes and changed her mind. "Please do come. The children have fallen in love with you."

Lucy's face seemed to leap into a smile. "Oh, I'll come. I don't want to disappoint them."

"I think you will be glad to see the redwoods too."

"Yes, I love trees. They are very large, Uncle Fred said?"

"Yes, very large." *She has no idea,* Susan thought.

They took the horsecar down Fourth Street, the packets of food and little George in their laps. Tom held on to the arm of a seat and leaned out daringly, his little dark face lit up by a grin and his free hand fanning the faint breeze. Rebecca sat close to her cousin, staring up at her worshipfully. The horsecar followed the tracks down the middle of the road, by the courthouse, toward the railroad station. Susan looked ruefully over the dusty road and frowsy gardens of the houses along the street. For a month she had saved up all the small, delicious vistas that make a small town precious, had stored the characters and gossip and history, the close-grained texture of her environment, and her sister responded with conspicuous lack of interest. Everything in New York was better.

This opinion applied to suffrage too. Elizabeth barely seemed to know of the '96 election and thought of California's rejection as small and remote from the national heart. As though the stuffy Easterners had done one thing. Hadn't every suffrage success and near success come in the West? Susan thought that Elizabeth's interest in suffrage was fundamentally small. She went to the meetings to meet some excellent women. The cause was a club to her. Susan could not help wondering what her sister would have thought of her speeches about fairness. Would she even grasp the concept, this sister who had taken a rich world's wealth as her natural due?

And her daughter! Lucy made a living symbol of their differences. Lucy was beautiful, mannered, educated—exactly what the finishing school of Santa Rosa High School could not and never would produce. As the preacher had said, a symbol does nothing—it points. Lucy pointed to a vain life, rich, superior, and empty. Susan wanted to be generous to her niece, but she found herself tight and wooden.

The fundamental problem, Susan thought suddenly, *is that Elizabeth does not seem to love me.* That angered her and broke her heart. And what did her broken heart reveal about her life? Susan could not help thinking that despite her marriage to a good man, despite her beautiful children, despite the friends she had made in the Methodist church, she remained fundamentally lonely and took her loneliness out on others.

At the station they did not wait long for the train to arrive. For the children it was the great treat: to eschew animal power and rely on the miracle of steam to push them. They would talk of it for weeks. They would make the engine sound in their teeth; they would sit one behind another pretending to be in the neat, cushioned seats; they would recall the sense of flying in a noisy clatter above the surface of the earth.

The train's two cars complained their way to the Fulton station, only five miles. There they changed to a one-car wonder, painted gaily red, on the Guerneville spur. The car was old-fashioned and comfortless; they sat on wooden benches worn down and oiled by the seats of a hundred thousand passengers. Susan sat against the wall on one side of the car, with George on her lap; Lucy sat across from her, flanked by Rebecca and Thomas squeezed in tight against her. As soon as the train lurched into motion it was too noisy for them to talk across such a space, so Susan held on to George and let her eyes and thoughts wander.

Her niece had worn a white cotton shirtwaist blouse and a straw hat decked with brilliant wax strawberries. It was a simple, sincere composition that she filled out beautifully, an apparently artless outfit that attracted attention to its simplicity, its pure bleached white, and its touches of pink ribbon and red fruit.

It is a fraud, Susan complained silently. How long had Lucy labored to achieve that look? It was also expensive. She could only guess what Elizabeth had paid for that oh-so-simple straw hat. As Susan looked at her niece, this peach-colored bauble, she felt the whole two weeks of irritation stir in her. Her sister could not bear even to come, but had sent this representative with her blank and pleasant stare.

Then in the next moment Susan felt the weight of her sadness slump down on her. In another day her sister would be gone. Perhaps they would never see each other again.

Susan shifted her seat to one of the forward-facing benches, so she could look out of the window instead of gazing at her niece. She wearied of these thoughts; they traveled nowhere. They were near the Russian River now as it wagged its way across the broad plain, looking for a gap in the hills. Grapevines spread their fresh green foliage; hop vines dangled from their high arbors. There were orchards of plum trees marching in orderly lines for her review. Here and there across the valley she would see the crown of a palm tree rising above everything—a sure sign of a farmhouse, because new arrivals from the East liked to watch these aliens soar upward and think that they had arrived in California and could grow such monstrosities.

Soon the coastal hills squeezed them closer to the river. It was not a pretty stream. Already its summer flow had been reduced to a trickle, leaving a strip of puddles between wide, sandy banks. But Lucy was not even looking; she had closed her eyes, and her little cousins leaned against her from each side.

Susan tried to think what her attitude toward Lucy should be. Her mother would treat as she had been treated—she would react to disdain with disdain. How would Fred do it? Well—he might leave, to avoid a fight. He had done just that.

She admired her husband and knew there was something deeper in him than avoidance. He was thoroughly a Christian, somehow—by which she meant what? Susan knew that Fred would urge her to give her niece a chance. In fact, he had said that.

What had the preacher said when she had gone to talk to him—that God poured out love like water? Something in this she found enormously appealing, but at the same time doubtful. All right for God, but if human beings pour out love like water, will it not be wasted on the ground? Will it not be thrown back in your face?

Nine years ago, so far back she could barely remember, she had felt elation over what had seemed like a major discovery—that fairness was fundamental, and women should be, must be, treated fairly. How firmly she had grasped that, and how passionately she had appealed by it! But what made up fairness in this case of her niece? It came to her that fairness had two very different faces. There was the fairness of treating people as they deserved. That was her mother's principle. Yet Fred was an extremely fair person, and he had a very different version of fairness, one that presupposed the possibility of creating better relations rather than simply acting out the past. Fred was usually optimistic about the possibilities in people's nature, as though by his own friendliness and courtesy, he might awaken some hidden sweetness.

At Guerneville they got off in hot sunshine. The town was a single muddy street beside the river. The loggers had cut down everything—massive stumps near the tracks were head-high platforms ten feet across or more.

At the livery stable Susan rented a carriage to take them out to a property where the tall trees still stood. A wagon road wandered beside a creek for a few miles, dissipating into tracks before disappearing under what seemed, from a distance, an impenetrable dark wall. It was a canopy of enormous trees, unearthly in its scale. The tracks petered out as though intimidated, as though no living creature had dared go beyond into this forest. Still Susan could see well enough where to guide the horse, for as they entered the tall trees there was suddenly no brush, nothing to block their way except the massive trunks disappearing over-head. Unconsciously they fell silent in the cool gloom suffused with green. A little dappled sunshine reached the ground, but they could not see the sky when they leaned back their heads to follow the ruddy wooden towers in their steep stretch upward.

"Where shall we stop?" Susan asked. They had come perhaps a hundred yards into the forest, but they seemed already remote from any other world.

"Here," Lucy said. "Here is fine. I would like to walk."

They tied up the horse and spread a blanket on a duff-covered mound near the stream. The children clambered on a fallen tree, five feet through at least, its back broken into splinters on the stream bank. Lucy and Susan unwrapped the packages of food. No wind stirred, and no birds sang. The children's shrill voices made the only sound. It might have been eerie, Susan thought, but it was more like something enchanted.

After eating, they wandered up the bank of the creek, pointing out trees that had achieved, with the help of lightning, strange shapes hundreds of feet above them. At the base of one giant George toddled off from Susan's hand to explore, and before she could stop him, he disappeared completely in a hole at its roots. Susan sent Becky in after him, and she did not come out either. Susan could hear her muffled voice.

"There's a room in here," Becky said. "A nice, cozy room. Tom! Come down here!"

Susan poked her head down the hole with some alarm, but she could not make out much in the darkness. "Tommy?" she said. "Tommy, go in there and see if it is all right. I don't want them down there if it's not safe."

Tommy disappeared headfirst into the hole. She heard laughter.

"Tommy? Is it all right?"

Tommy assured her it was safe.

"Is it dry? Are you making a mess of yourselves?"

"No, Ma, it's nice. There's room for you. Come in!"

Becky laughed in delight. "Come in, Mama!"

"No, I don't think so." She smiled at Lucy. "I guess there is room for all of them in there."

"I'll go in," Lucy said.

"You'll get your dress all dirty."

"That's all right. I want to see."

"Then I'll come with you. If there's room."

After her eyes adjusted to the light, Susan found herself in a little room with a front and back entrance, and a flat, dry floor. The children could stand upright. She and Lucy had to stay on their knees.

"It's wonderful," Lucy said. "It's like a story. Can we get out the other way?"

Tommy said that they could and demonstrated. George and Becky followed him up and out. Susan's eyes adjusted so she could see Lucy's face now. Her hat was askew, and Susan straightened it for her. When she did, she saw that her palm was streaked with black. She rubbed at it, but it did not come off. Looking around her, she could see that the walls of the little room were charred black.

"Be careful not to touch anything," she said to Lucy. "It's charcoal, I think."

"I wonder when they had a fire."

They could hear the children's voices, laughing as they ran around the tree. Through the entrances they caught glimpses of their legs, dashing past. "Isn't this something?" Susan asked.

"Did you not know this was here?"

"Not at all. I've only been here once before myself."

"If I lived in Santa Rosa, I would want to come here often."

"You might want to. But if you had children to raise and a house to keep, you might not get here." She was tempted to mention the obstacle of money too.

After they climbed out, they sat on the bank of the languid stream, tearing up bay leaves, drawing in their heady smell, and throwing the fragments in the water to watch them bob away. Lucy had a black streak on her back, like a dark cloud on the extreme whiteness of the shirtwaist blouse. She said she didn't care—she wouldn't have traded the tree hole for anything.

They got to talking about Susan's girlhood and how Elizabeth had left to go to college when she was Lucy's age. "But Mother got married instead," Lucy said. "She thinks that will happen to me. I'm going to Vassar College in the fall, but Mother thinks it's a waste and hopes that I can meet a nice man. I think she means rich."

"What does your father say?"

"All Father thinks about is that I'll fall for some rotter and marry badly. He doesn't care if I go to college—he doesn't take my education seriously—but he insists that I go to a woman's college if I go at all. He thinks that's safer. My mother doesn't care, so long as the school is expensive. She thinks I might marry someone's brother if I go to a woman's college, and she wants to make sure that the brother is rolling in money."

Susan was amazed to be on the receiving end of this torrent of insight. The picture she got of Elizabeth and her husband was appalling, but she realized that it was not her business to say so to Lucy. "There's something to be said for a rich husband," Susan said. And then she laughed. "Though I wouldn't know for sure."

"I don't care about that," Lucy said seriously.

"Of course you don't," Susan said. "But you might if you married someone who wasn't rich."

"I don't know whether I'll marry," Lucy said. "I want to go to college, and I want to do something purposeful with my life. I don't know what." She had been looking up into the trees, but suddenly she turned toward Susan with a dreadful, hurt look on her face. "Don't laugh. It's important to me."

Susan was startled by this sudden assault. Her face, she realized, must reveal her skepticism. She could not take too seriously the thought that this beauty might not marry. "Would you want to do something for suffrage?" she asked, to move the subject to something less personal.

"I don't know," Lucy said dreamily. "Sometimes suffrage seems petty to me. Do you think you can really accomplish anything there?"

"I think it would make a difference if women could vote."

"For a lot of the women it seems to be a club activity. They don't act as though they plan to change anything."

"What do you mean?" Susan asked.

"Like my mother. Do you think she really cares to change anything?"

"I don't know. I can't make out your mother. I know that I wanted suffrage very much in '96, when we lost the referendum. I don't think I have recovered from that defeat."

"I would like to do something," Lucy said again. She suddenly laid her body down on the blanket, her hands folded under the side of her face, like a cat curling itself into a comfortable spot.

"Will you write me?" Susan said impetuously. She had suddenly been struck that this beautiful niece was not like Elizabeth, was not satisfied. "Perhaps we can exchange ideas. Old as I am, I want to do something, too, something beyond the children. Not that they are unimportant."

"No, of course not. Yes, I would like to write you, Aunt Susan. I have the feeling that you understand what I am trying to say."

Chapter 13
1906: The Earth Moves

Only a hint of silver dawn had unsealed the darkness when the Koniceks' house on Fulton Road began rocking with a motion so violent it threw Susan and Fred completely out of bed and into a tangle on top of each other. A heavy object was jumping against them like a large, boisterous dog, except the object was not flesh and fur, but something brutally hard and heavy. It threw itself against Susan's shoulder, knocking her down. Susan was fending it off with one weak arm; Fred was shouting imprecations.

"It's the bed, Fred! It's the bed!" Susan shouted. As if in response, the house's motion changed to a rapid trembling, a jerking, a sawing. Objects were falling. They heard crashing and hellish chattering, and the strain and wail of nails pulled out of timber. Underneath every sound was a deep roar as though the maw of the earth was clearing its throat. Out the window Susan caught a glimpse of their willow tree, forty feet tall, thrashing past on its way to the ground, traveling much faster than if it had fallen, and then a second later flying back the other way to upright, as though some giant shook it by the roots.

Susan scrambled toward the door, but the jumping began again and knocked her down. The children! She screamed out their names—Tommy, Becky, George—and thought she heard them cry in return, but with the pounding and screaming of the house she could not be sure what she heard, human or inhuman. She could not get to her feet. Fred did, and stumbled over her, kicking her hard in the side and falling full length into the hall, but scrambling forward immediately and out of sight. *He will help them*, Susan thought. *Fred will take care of them.*

The jumping and rolling suddenly stopped, though the earth continued to tremble and jerk as if in dying spasms. Susan was in tears and weak with fright. She had to see to her babies. When she got to her feet, something was wrong with her balance. She tipped backward and fell into the bed.

It was still now, unearthly still. Susan raised herself off the bed. Something was wrong. She could not walk straight. The whole house was tilted. Grasping the doorway with both hands, she made her way out of the room, then down the dark hallway bracing against the walls. Something blocked her way. She felt it and realized it was a bureau. Where had it come from?

Fred came out of the children's room, holding George tight against his chest. "They're all right. They're all right," he said. "Thank God."

Tommy and Becky wept uncontrollably. She took them to her, one in each arm, weeping herself.

"We need to get outside," Fred said. "Come now! Move quickly!"

He tugged on Susan's arm. *Stop it*, she thought, *stop it and let us be.* She looked at his medium torso, wrapped in his threadbare nightshirt, and she wanted to hold it, to feel him cradle her.

"Come," he said more gently. "We have to get outside. The quake may start again."

Was that what it was? A quake? She had felt them before, a gentle rolling, a brief swaying, or a jolt running through your feet. This had been something quite different: like the rat in a dog's teeth when he shakes it to death.

"Come on," Fred repeated.

Weeping all the more, she followed him down the stairway. The parlor looked as though someone had prepared to paint: all the furniture had migrated to one corner, tightly packed together, some of it turned on its side. The smell of kerosene was intense because the lamp had smashed.

Outside the air smelled of fog and new earth with just a hint of something dank and moldy. *Something stirred the swamp,* she thought, *not angels.*

"What's wrong with our house?" Tommy asked.

In the dawn light they could see that the front porch ran in a curving arc to the ground. The whole building stood at a rakish angle.

"Must have jumped the foundation," Fred said. "It's a wonder it didn't go farther. I thought I was riding the back of a bullfrog there." He laughed, and his dry, coughing chuckle seemed to come from some long-ago lost world. Susan reached out her hand to his and held it tightly as if it were the last handhold to safety in the universe.

They stood on their patch of earth until the sun came up. The land seemed peculiarly serene, considering what it had so recently witnessed. The chickens, silent as death, began to cackle hesitantly. After Fred inspected under the house and declared it safe, all of them went back in and got dressed. The children laughed at the tilted floor and tried to dance. George fell down, and when his brother laughed, fell down again. They could not cook breakfast until Fred fixed the stovepipe, but they had plenty to do cleaning up the mess. The kitchen was the worst: most of their dishes were broken, and pots and tin cups had all jingled off their hooks and bounced everywhere. For once Susan was grateful that they had so few things and not many of them precious.

After he put the stove back in its place and saw that it was safe to use again, Fred climbed under the house to take a better look at the damage. "I can't do anything," he said when he emerged covered with mud from crawling on his chest. "I'll have to jack it up and roll it back on." He seemed oddly satisfied with himself. "In the meantime we'll have to get used to living on the slant. I guess that will feel pretty normal."

Without explaining himself he hitched up the mule to take the wagon to town. He came back in to get a cup of coffee that Susan had managed to make. "Will you get a jack?" Susan asked.

"I might," he said. "Mostly I want to see how things are."

That was the first Susan thought of the damage others might have suffered. For some reason she considered the earthquake a local event, on their farm only.

"Let me go with you," she said. "I should see to Mother."

"I thought of that," he said. "But I'll go and see and come back. You watch the children."

"Why don't we all go?" Susan asked.

He shook his head. "I don't know what we'll find there. It might be better if children don't see it."

She had not thought that anybody could be hurt. If they were well, then everybody must be well. By midmorning she saw a smudge of smoke on the horizon in the direction of Santa Rosa. There must be fire.

They had moved to the farm over the winter, at Fred's insistence. He sold his horse and buggy to get the mule and wagon, and bought the land for promise to pay. He said there was no point in trying to sell blankets any longer. What little they had saved went into farm equipment. He had potatoes in mind. He thought the land would raise a good crop once it was drained. Susan had been doubtful: she did not want to live on a farm, and she hardly could imagine Fred as a farmer. He had been so weighed down, however, that she was willing to make an effort to adapt to farm life.

Trying to think how many breakables her mother had, Susan remembered so many plates, so many glasses. She went out of the house and looked to the horizon. The smudge of smoke had grown, rising up to the unclouded sky and spreading like a flatiron. Susan hoped the boardinghouse was not burning. She found herself growing inexplicably weepy occasionally through the day and wished to have Fred near.

Susan had cooked a pot of oatmeal for breakfast. Now she wondered what they could have for dinner. Or supper, when she presumed Fred would return. They had no meat, had not had meat for a week. She looked in the pantry at the sack of beans. Maybe Fred would bring some meat from town. At least some bacon. But it would be good to have beans ready. She took her pot out to the yard and pumped it full, then filled it up halfway with beans. She left it in the kitchen to soak, then got out her book. She was reading *Bleak House*.

For Christmas, her niece had sent a copy of *A Tale of Two Cities*. Susan was embarrassed to receive a gift when she could not reciprocate, but Lucy wrote that a friend at Vassar College had given the book to her and she liked it so much, she wanted to pass it on. Susan found she could not put the volume down. It was as real and as lively as a fire on a winter night. When a peddler came offering a complete set of Dickens, it seemed to her like too great a coincidence. She bought it with money she had saved in her jam jar, money meant for school clothes. The set came in eight massive volumes, tiny type composed three columns to the page.

Whenever she felt she wanted to cry or scream, she could go and look at those books, stacked in the corner of her bedroom. She read them slowly, looking up words in the dictionary. It did not matter to her that a book might take months. She wanted to get lost in Dickens and stay lost.

Fred came back near dusk. He was covered with a fine gray dust, his eyes the only color in his face, looking out as if from a mask. His brown hair looked gray, and when he took off his hat and struck it with his hand, a puff like smoke came out.

"I'll have to go back tomorrow," he said. "As soon as there is light. Susan, my love, you never saw such a thing. All the downtown buildings are gone. The courthouse collapsed; the dome is resting on the ground. The Athenaeum came down like a card house. Every brick building fell. I don't know one that's standing. And then the fire." He stopped short and pressed his lips together.

"Is Mother all right?"

"Yes, she came through. Her chimney came down, and the glass was broken, but she didn't catch fire." A glimmer of a smile passed over his face. "Mr. Adams lost his kitchen. Your mother seemed to think that it was the judgment of the Almighty." Adams was a next-door neighbor with whom Rebecca had feuded for thirty years.

"Was anybody killed?" she asked.

"More than I can count," he said. "I tell you, we are lucky to be out here in the country."

Susan made no reply, but she thought to herself that she would rather be in town, close to a hundred disasters, than alone on a farm.

Lucy Phillips looked into the wide-set, weak eyes of her friend Sarah Blackburn, seated across from her in the refectory. "Excuse me, Sarah, what did you say?"

Sarah was Lucy's roommate. She came from Brookline near Boston; she was very plain, with sallow skin, stooped shoulders, a long, thin jaw-line, and mousy hair. She had no money and dressed in very heavy, conservative clothes. Nevertheless, Lucy had already learned to love her in a deep and helpless way because she was a young woman without guile. Having been raised in good New York society, Lucy thought this the rarest gift in the world.

People commonly took Lucy to be pretty and shallow, with her brilliant blue eyes and luxurious ringlets of blonde hair. She was naturally quiet, which allowed others to fill in the blank of what a pretty girl should be thinking or not thinking. In reality, she had a strong and opinionated mind. Sarah had understood this early on, and it had made them friends.

"I said, you aren't listening to a word I say. What are you thinking of?"

Lucy was embarrassed. She took out a letter from a bag beside her chair. The handwriting was hasty, with scribblings and markouts all over the plain sheet. "I got this from my aunt in California. I've been worried about her ever since the earthquake."

More than a week ago they had read of a massive quake and fire in San Francisco, almost leveling the city. Brief reports from Oakland and San Jose made it obvious that the damage was widespread, but no one mentioned Santa Rosa.

"Is everyone all right?" Sarah asked.

"Yes, none of my relatives were hurt. My aunt says their house was jumping like a bullfrog and leaped right off its foundation, if you can imagine. Hundreds of people were killed in their little town."

Lucy would have liked to go to one of the men's universities that had opened to women, such as Cornell or Michigan, but her father had insisted that she go to a woman's institution. He wanted to keep her far from college men, whom he considered to be all dandies or anarchists. He was conservative that way. He would have been dismayed to know that the college was full of idealists, young women who had tremendous thoughts about reforming the world.

Yet it was not these reformers whom Lucy particularly liked. Sarah had captured her—Sarah, whose idea of radical thought was a missionary prayer meeting. Sarah was the only girl Lucy had ever known who did not care what others thought.

It struck Lucy that Aunt Susan attracted her in much the same way. With her copper hair and paper white skin, she might have been a beauty, but she did not think about that. She lived in a tiny house, deluged with children, wore plain cotton dresses and did nothing with her hair—and her mind was as straight and serious as a ruler. She had invited Lucy to write, which Lucy did, and received a torrent of words in response. Lucy sent a copy of Dickens and received in return five long letters commenting and speculating on the novel. Aunt Susan used not the distant prose of an aunt, but the intense, conscious, provoking words of a young friend. She wanted to know everything.

Lucy was not so interested in Dickens, but she felt extraordinarily fortunate to have found two friends who thought so freely and cared so passionately. It was, for her, a surprise that such women existed. She thought it must lead to something—must open up a pathway for her to do something. Lucy thought she had no genius, but needed to find a place where determination could tell. For the first time in her life she knew somebody who could understand what she was talking about.

———————

The boys were so quiet that Susan thought they were surely into devilry, torturing a frog or throwing stones at a cat. But she found them sitting on the front porch, both with fingers laced together in their laps. Tom's face was all shadows: he had dark skin and dark eyes that made him look pensive even when he was happy.

"Waiting for Dad?" she asked. She knew they were. "Have you done all your chores?"

"Mom! Please be quiet!" That was George, who was all of five now. "I want to concentrate."

Walking back into the kitchen, where she had *Pickwick Papers* open on the kitchen table, Susan sat down and dived back in. Sometimes Fred wondered why she read so much, why it absorbed her so completely. She could not help it, she told him. She needed it.

Susan had never been a sociable creature, but she had never been alone either, growing up in town, always with her sister to share every thought, and the boardinghouse to provide a familiar circle and a thousand diversions. Sometimes now she hated the silence; she hated Fred's view from every window unobstructed except by trees. Along with the deprivation of society she suffered from other shortages related to cash: rarely any meat to eat (the boardinghouse served meat every day), few new clothes. She spent hours at the mind-numbing task of mending old clothes that had grown so weak, the patches ripped out the first day the children wore them to school.

Fred felt some of the same crimping, but he could escape. The earthquake had been his salvation, as it turned out. He worked for six months in San Francisco, where any able-bodied man could get top dollar clearing debris and then constructing the new buildings going up everywhere. For six months the family saw him only every two weeks, when he came home as hungry as a wolf for the sight and touch of his family. Now he was working in Santa Rosa, and he had bought a Ford car to travel back and forth from the farm. Susan had questioned the expense, but he said the car would pay for itself in the amount he earned in town. She said he could as easily ride the mule or buy a horse, but he calculated that it would take so much oats and livery costs and even time—since when had time been so valuable?—that the Ford was better. Susan saw how much happier he was, and she knew how hard he worked. Often he could do nothing more than sit when he came home.

The farm was so quiet that the boys could hear the motor from a long way off, a soft buzz almost like a honeybee, and then while they listened, the close but distinct explosions—*puhpuhpuhpuhpuhpuh*. Sometimes, on a still day, they would catch the sound from a mile off or more. The sound would fade and disappear as the car went down into a shallow draw, suddenly bursting into their ears again as it strained uphill. And then the dust: they could see its spume across the field before they could see the black metal shape like a fast-crawling bug making its way. The dust grew bigger, the sound grew louder, and then Fred wheeled in the gate and was home. That was what the boys were concentrating on. They had not needed to explain. She understood. They were listening for the sound of the motor.

Susan read on. This book made her laugh. Sometimes she would laugh all by herself in the empty house while the children were at school, and she would shake so that she could not stop. That was a delicious feeling, but sad when her laughter ended and she had no one to share it with. Fred did not read, except for newspapers and religious books. He brought her the *Saturday Evening Post* but did not read it himself. She supposed there were women in town who liked to read, but she went to town only on Saturdays, to shop, and on Sundays, for church.

She heard the car clearly now. *What an amazing world*, she thought, *that enables people to buzz across the countryside, transported by mechanical magic.* Susan put down her book and went outside. The boys were already at the gate. Where was Rebecca? At the creek, probably. She was like a boy, the way she would explore. The car came slinging through the gate, always faster than she expected, always surprising the chickens that scattered before it. It stopped with a lurch and a pop. Fred got out, the boys came running, and he picked up George in his arms. Under his cap his hair was peppery, changing slowly from a sandy brown to a sandy gray. His mouth was the same: always with a pertinacious grin just budding, as though he had a funny remark on the tip of his tongue. He looked leaner than when they had first married. The farmwork and construction agreed with him bodily, though he said he found both intolerably boring.

He kissed her. "What's for dinner?" he asked.

"I was going to ask you."

"What d . . . ? Oh, Sue, can you believe it? I forgot again. I was in such a hurry. Did you make any bread? Can we make up something with what's on hand?"

"We have some bacon and eggs. No bread, but I can do biscuits pretty quick. What's the hurry?"

"There's a race," he said. "I thought we could go."

"Really?" she said. "Don't they usually wait for the fair?"

"Not a horse race, an automobile race. They're going to run up to Healdsburg from the square and back. They start at seven. I thought we might all go."

"You want to race?" she asked in dismay.

"No, no, silly, you can't race in the Ford. They'll have Packards and Oldsmobiles and I don't know what. Some of them are coming from Petaluma."

"But you can't see them all that distance."

"Of course not, but we'll see them start and finish, and the cars will be on display at the square."

By that time the boys were pleading. They had caught the fever from their father.

"I don't know where Rebecca is," Susan said.

"I know, I know," Tommy said. "I can go and get her."

"You don't have to watch the cars," Fred said. "You can go to see your mother if you like."

"Oh, all right," she said. "Boys, you see if you can find some eggs. No, Tommy, go and find your sister. George, you look for eggs. I'll see about biscuits. Do we have time for biscuits?"

———————

Lucy Phillips had put on her favorite dress for the occasion, a deep green with brocaded sleeves. She wore a wide-spreading hat in a matching green, trimmed with a silver ribbon and little silver bells that did not ring. She knew well enough that she could steal men's eyes, could even steal the eyes of women, but that was not why she dressed. She liked clothes. More important for the present situation, clothes made her feel protected. She did not know what might happen. They could even be arrested, and she would feel better if she were well dressed.

She was among fifty women processing from the Vassar chapel, led by a short, motherly figure with a round face and curls, who carried a large yellow banner on a standard. The woman had been introduced as Harriot Stanton Blatch, daughter of Elizabeth Cady Stanton. The banner read, COME, LET US REASON TOGETHER.

The day was steamy, the sky a crush of vague blue-and-gray shapes with silver seams. Later in the day those clouds might release their rain, but for now shadowless light seemed to illumine the trees from the underside. Lucy felt a thin bead of perspiration on her temples. How green and beautiful the world looked—all the more for her sharp sense of anticipation.

Mrs. Blatch was a Vassar graduate. She had looked around at the stone buildings and spreading trees. "Do they teach you anything besides deportment these days?" she asked Lucy with disdain.

They were marching to a small cemetery on the edge of campus, a place where presumably Vassar had no authority to keep them off. But who really knew? President Taylor had refused to let them meet, and nobody had ever doubted that he ruled Poughkeepsie.

As they walked in procession, Lucy kept her eye on Inez Milholland, who sauntered along just ahead, dressed in a flowing white gown, simple and yet somehow overstated. Lucy would not have been on this march if not for Inez, and neither, she thought, would most of the girls. Inez was a senior about to graduate, a wealthy, dramatic, persuasive, and glamorous young woman. She was the sort of girl who makes an unfair advantage even of her deficits. On another girl, Inez's features might be thought ugly, but she had made of them something sultry and tropical. Inez talked in a way that was hardly ladylike, being too loud and using her hands, laughing so that everyone in the room turned to see. But everyone in the room *did* turn to see, and Inez seemed to enjoy the publicity. Lucy had introduced Inez to her father once, when he came to visit, and he had referred to her later as a "rum punch."

From what Inez said—Inez knew all the leading suffrage women from New York City—Mrs. Blatch had come back from England determined to bring the style of the English suffragettes to America. Suffragettes—they were first called that as a gibe and had taken it for their own—threw rocks and marched and even got arrested. In jail they went on hunger strikes and had to be force-fed.

Mrs. Blatch did not look like such a radical. She looked more like a grandmother whose ambition was to make a superior apple pie. According to Inez, however, the woman was a force. Inez said this woman was waking suffrage from its slumber.

Behind Inez walked several middle-aged women. Charlotte Perkins Gilman—one of the famous Beechers, a genuine intellect who had written *Women and Economics*. She was a true author and not of novels. The woman next to her, Helen Hoy, was an attorney. Lucy found it difficult to imagine what a woman attorney might do, but the very fact of her existence seemed invigorating.

Next to them was the most amazing figure of all, Rose Schneiderman, the head of the cap-makers union in New York. She alone walked bareheaded, her auburn hair twisted into a simple bun up off her neck. It was unprecedented for a working-class woman, a trade union leader, to march with Vassar girls.

They reached the cemetery and poured through the gate. Inez Milholland was swooping around like a swallow, bucking them up, organizing their ranks. Her wide, frank face was overwhelmed by a huge smile; she was enjoying the scene, almost too much. Lucy could not help thinking of Sarah. She had invited her roommate to come along, but Sarah declined. Sarah said Inez made too much of herself.

She is too harsh, Lucy thought. Inez was a high-spirited woman, who could not help prancing any more than could a high-spirited horse. Sarah's ideal was self-sacrificial to the point of invisibility, while Inez's main idea was to grab, to cheerfully publicize herself and her cause. She wanted the attention. Woman suffrage might be a high-minded cause, but the end product would raise Inez, give her power, and turn eyes toward her. What was wrong with that? Why must a woman be self-effacing? A woman could stand for her rights and be extremely attractive, fascinating, and—Inez even said this with a smirk—pretty.

By the time Rose Schneiderman began to speak, Lucy's attention had wandered. The day was warm, and the speeches earnest and ordinary. They would not be arrested, she saw, which was both a relief and a disappointment. Miss Schneiderman's voice caught her up, however. It had a frank, almost manly quality, and an accent that was hard to place. A little German perhaps? It sounded flat and plain and matter-of-fact. The voice could not come from a Vassar girl, certainly.

"They tell us that if only a woman would stay home," Schneiderman was saying, "everything would be well. What they don't understand is that some women can't be at home. What should I say when a woman comes to me after her husband has lost his hand in the factory, and the company has sent him home with fifty dollars? She doesn't have the luxury of staying home."

The ideas were not new, but Schneiderman's plain speech seemed to conjure up real people, not theories.

"Now a fundamental principle with me is that, as the Bible says, a worker is worthy of his hire. I take that to mean that a woman who is supporting six children should get paid the same wage that a man supporting six children would get. What can be the excuse for paying her less? That her children eat less because she is a woman? It's hard enough for working people to survive in this world if they get paid a fair wage.

"And another thing: some of these employers take women over men just because they can pay them less. A man wouldn't accept such pay, but a woman who is trying to feed hungry mouths may not have a choice— she has to work at what they give her.

"They won't take advantage of a man the way they will take advantage of a woman, and do you know why? Because they know that he can vote, and that if things get too bad, the men will vote in some officials who will give them protection. You women who have tried to talk to our officials know just what I am saying. Why, I have men laugh at me when I try to talk to them, men who are sworn to serve the people. They don't consider us the people. Why? Because we don't vote.

"I know that a lot of very fine women—and some men, too, I have to give them the credit—are concerned for the poor, hungry children of the city. These good people want to give the children charity, and they want to use religion or other means to steer them in the right direction. That's all good, but I say there are reasons why the children are hungry. Sometimes it's drink. Sometimes it's ignorance. Sometimes it's a job that won't pay their mothers a decent wage. I say, give woman the vote and she may deal with drink, she may deal with ignorance, and I think I can say for certain that she will be treated with more respect. If you want to show respect for a poor mother, give her the vote."

Susan greedily began Lucy's letter while standing on the front porch. Not until the second page did she gather herself to sit down. It was such a pleasure to read these pages.

Savoring the moment, she set the letter in her lap and looked over the farm. Far down the road she could see a smudge of dust from the postman's buggy. Every morning her anticipation stretched out like a string, looking for him, looking for practically the only event of the day. She devoured the letters he sometimes brought before his dust was out of sight.

For a time, Susan stared across the front field, down the sandy strip of road to a distant line of eucalyptus. A breeze stirred the highest branches, where five or six turkey vultures patiently stood watch. Across the plain, beyond Santa Rosa, she saw the brown shoulders of the hills through a summer haze.

Life should be best in summertime when the children were free from school. But George and Tommy went with their father each day, crazy to ride that machine anywhere. Fred had all but given up on the farm: the potatoes were puny, and slugs had spoiled all the strawberries. That was all right. He was not cut out for farming. He had taken to buying up vegetables and fruits in small lots and selling them, mostly to the local grocers. Sometimes he would meet a train if he had some good fruits to sell. He hoped to get a regular contract with the railroad, but Susan thought that was probably a pipe dream. He was always most interested in the "almost."

Her thoughts depressed her. She meant to savor her niece's letter and instead sank down, as she often did, stewing over all the deficits in their lives. Fred was a good man, and she tried to remember it. Susan pushed herself to her feet, and Lucy's letter fluttered onto the floor. Bending over to pick it up, she thought of the energy that radiated from its pages. Lucy had been to a meeting called *outdoors*, despite the college president's opposition; and she had heard speeches about a new kind of suffrage activism.

When Susan sat at the kitchen table trying to compose an answer, however, she found that she had nothing coherent to say. Activism of any kind was beyond her. Her days of traveling and speech making seemed impossibly remote. So she began to write about the children, describing in detail what each one looked like, how they thought and acted, their reaction to the summer, and so on. She got through Tommy, but in the middle of describing Rebecca, who was naturally reticent and loved to go alone to the creek, Susan began to weep uncontrollably.

Why, she could not say. She wanted off this broken-down farm. She wanted some money to spend. She wanted to have somebody to talk to, even her mother. The letters were no substitute for a human voice.

The settlement house had been built as a residence for some minor business baron in the 1830s when the Lower East Side of Manhattan was still on the outskirts of settlement. It had been a bright clay-red brick in the beginning, but three-quarters of a century of coal smoke had stained it so it could pass for black. The house blended into its surroundings of warehouses and tenements, so that only a careful eye would notice its intended elegance, its strong, sweeping lines.

Inside the front door, this was much more obvious. A broad

mahogany staircase dominated the entryway, stairs that were perhaps not grand enough for Cinderella's ball, but would certainly impart a sense of distinction to anyone descending them in evening dress. Nowadays, the stairs were tramped by the peoples of the world, immigrants with holes in the soles of their shoes. The entryway had grown dingy, as if to suit its users: the elaborately figured baseboard unrepaired where some ancient blow had crushed it, the treads showing a lighter color of wood where shoes had sanded the finish from them. Most people came in and out of this entryway without noticing the grand brass chandelier (which needed dusting) or the darkened stained glass designs in the windows running around the top of the four walls.

Lucy Phillips liked to pause at the top of the stairs, however, just to look. Usually she was going out to visit one of the poor families that had attached themselves to the house. The entryway was a kind of metaphor for how she perceived these people, full of darkened grandeur. Further, it represented the way she thought of her calling to this place. She had been here since graduating from Vassar, looking for a kind of holy purpose where her own family, and many of her friends from college, saw only dinginess.

The settlement houses were a funny kind of business, difficult to explain. Jane Addams had started the first one twenty years ago in Chicago, and now they had spread to all the large cities, attracting an odd mixture of idealists and Christians and socialists. Sarah, who had come here before Lucy, said they were exactly like a mission station, an outpost of the gospel in inhospitable territory.

The people who ran the houses generally preferred the image of a pioneer settlement—an outpost of civilization. Settlement workers sat on city commissions, they worked up local clubs and cultural associations, they offered talks from eminent authorities, and so on. And one thing led to another.

Mrs. Pellegrini's building was five swarming blocks away, a four-story brownstone. Lucy went right in, past the tough young men and their hard-bitten English—she spoke to them but they did not respond—and up three dark and airless flights of stairs. She had visited Mrs. Pellegrini once before, but she had a hard time locating her door, for the hallway was so dark she could not read the numbers. She would have lit a match if she had one. Ultimately she verified the number by running her finger over it—it had been painted so thickly that she could feel its edges. Reading numbers by touch was a trick she had learned from one of the older residents of the house.

Opening the door a crack, Mrs. Pellegrini peered out and then silently let her in. She had the face of a mule, with large, hard eyes set wide apart. She wore a shapeless black dress that hung down between her knees and the floor. Not until she had shut the door did she say a word, and then, as soon as the door had cut her off from her neighbors, she began to burble.

"Thank you, Miss Phillips. Thank you a hundred thank-yous for coming. You are an angel, an angel of God. I knew you would come. You always keep your word. She is not a bad girl. You must believe me. She is not a bad girl."

Mrs. Pellegrini had first come to the settlement house for a lecture on the Italian Renaissance. In the question period she had asked, in halting English, about an establishment the lecturer had mentioned, the Metropolitan Museum. Was this in Italy? Mrs. Pellegrini expressed disbelief when told that it was in New York. Afterward Lucy discovered that she had been in America for almost ten years, but had not previously discovered that any Americans cared about paintings.

To Lucy's imagination, Mrs. Pellegrini was like the settlement house: a woman with a grand history and culture, begrimed with poverty. Who thought of the worn, empty faces in a sweatshop as music lovers and appreciators of paintings and flowers?

Mrs. Pellegrini had first brought her daughter, Lucia, to the Drama Club. Then she had brought her to the Garibaldi Club. Lucia was six inches taller than her mother and wore her hair cut off short in a straight, hard black line. She would come to the clubs only when her mother brought her, and then she would sit in the corner and refuse to say anything. She wanted nothing to do with culture. She wanted to be an American.

Lucy had learned to recognize these family civil wars, so common among the immigrant families. The settlement house had become, to an extent, neutral ground.

"What has happened, Mrs. Pellegrini?"

"I don't know what has happened. Ask her what has happened."

"She is here?"

"Yes." She gestured helplessly toward the back of the apartment.

The bedroom contained nothing except two beds, one double and one single, jammed together side by side, and a single four-drawer bureau. The windows were covered with butcher paper so the light was dim. An awful smell pervaded the room, a bitter human smell. Lucia lay on the bed with a blanket covering her.

"Lucia," she said. "It's Miss Phillips." She had made Mrs. Pellegrini stay out.

She got no response.

"I don't think your mother knows what has happened. She is very frightened for you, though, Lucia."

That elicited one short sniffle.

"I am anxious to help you, Lucia. Is there anything I can get for you?"

There was a reply, so muffled she had to ask for it to be repeated. "Carlo."

That was the answer Lucy had feared. "Carlo Previtale? You know I cannot bring him into your mother's house."

"Then go away." Lucia's head came up, and she took a long, hateful look, her black eyes surrounded by red, like a beast.

"What has Carlo promised you? He is a liar, you know. I have told you, Lucia."

"He never promised me. He cares about me. He wants me to be happy."

"And how will he make you happy?"

"He will get me out of this dump! He says I should have nice things."

Lucy felt the weightlessness of her words against a man who would promise nice things. Certainly Lucia's parents could not offer any entrée into the glamorous life of an American girl. Lucy also knew that Lucia's father would surely beat her and throw her out. That was why her mother had sent the urgent message this morning.

"Why did you come home this morning, Lucia? Why didn't you stay with Carlo?"

She got no answer again.

"I will tell you why. Carlo sent you home. And I will tell you why. Carlo wants your father to throw you out. He wants him to call you a whore in front of the neighbors."

"Carlo is not like that. You don't know him!"

"Then why did he send you home? Didn't he know what your father would do?"

She waited for an answer, then continued. "Lucia, if you come with me now, I can have you stay in the house for a while. I can try to get you a job. Or you can go to school. Your father will not be happy, but

I think he will leave you alone if he knows that you are in the settlement house."

Lucia's father was a very short dark-skinned man with a twisted arm. Lucy knew him slightly. She would not like facing him.

"Lucia, I feel fearful of your father's reaction if he finds you like this. And I would like you to see a doctor as well."

At that, Lucia began to scream. She made a high-pitched wail, more like a cat than a human, starting in a growl and ascending into a shriek. Lucy tried to put a hand on her, but Lucia jerked away as though she were burned. Mrs. Pellegrini came rushing in, crying, and tried to hold her daughter, but Lucia writhed away and continued screaming. Mrs. Pellegrini became frantic, crying out in Italian, finally falling to her knees and praying. Lucia continued her howl.

Finally Lucy took Mrs. Pellegrini's arm and pulled her from the room. She led Mrs. Pellegrini to the kitchen, where they sat down opposite each other at the kitchen table. The screaming continued, but Lucy thought it had lost some of its energy.

"She wants to be with Carlo," Lucy said. "You know Carlo?"

Mrs. Pellegrini had a small fit of crying. She knew Carlo.

"I don't know what you can do, Mrs. Pellegrini. Carlo wants her father to throw her out on the street, and to tell all the neighbors she has no morals and is not his daughter. Then she will go to Carlo's way. You know what that is?"

Mrs. Pellegrini had taken a handkerchief from somewhere on her person and was dabbing her eyes. "No. I don't know anything in this America."

"Carlo is a pimp. Do you understand? He sells girls. Can you persuade your husband not to throw her out?"

The woman looked up in terror.

"Do you have any influence with Mr. Pellegrini? Or would he listen to me? Or maybe the priest?"

She shook her head urgently. "He will kill her," she said in a whisper.

"Then what can we do? Can we get some of his friends?"

"No. They would do the same to their daughters. They will not interfere."

"Then what can we do, Mrs. Pellegrini? Is there anything that we can do? Do you want me to stay here until your husband comes home?"

Her gaze had become abstract, unpointed. "No," she said. "No, you must not stay. Pray. That is all we can do. There is nothing else that a woman can do."

If I had known how awful I would feel, Susan Konicek thought, *I would never have agreed to do this.* For the entire week she had been wracked by doubts, had hardly slept, had been irritable and dreadful. She had expected the feelings to ease when she entered the church, but no, the tension coiled like a rusty chain in her stomach. She saw a few friends, the lady she taught Sunday school with, her grocer. Though familiar, their faces had no depth to them; they looked like masks. She hoped she was saying appropriate words to greet them, but every syllable required an effort and came out as though she struggled with another language.

Thank God, her mother had not come.

The organ had begun to play. Susan was seated in the front row now, alone. It struck her as odd that she should be so, since she was being baptized to join the church.

Misery had brought her to this point. She had felt so alone, so deserted, that Sundays became her days of relief, not so much for the particular people she met but for the feeling she got by simply sitting in the sanctuary, being in a crowd all facing one direction, feeling her own voice meld with the larger sound, with the organ, with her own children's voices. She had begun to look forward to it all week; Monday through Saturday she hung on through her own spiritual desert.

The pull frightened her. It was all superstition, she had been raised to believe. She leaned on Fred when she felt such fears, not that he could explain anything, but that he was a landmark to trust. One thing she knew: her husband was a good man. If he put his trust in these things, how harmful could they be? Surely there was something true in them. She asked herself whether she was drawn toward church because it represented him. She never got enough of him, it seemed. She couldn't answer that question.

They had a different pastor now, Reverend Smalley, a cheerful, glad-handing man. He did not understand her questions the way Reverend Arkes had. Reverend Smalley was a practical man, not gifted at speculation, who wanted simply to know whether she wanted him to do some religious function: pray with her, explain the Bible to her, baptize her. (Apparently the pastors passed on, like sacred lore, the information that she had never been baptized.)

Do I want him to do something? Perhaps, she thought, *I want him to pray for me.* But she knew right along that she would have no faith in those prayers unless she plunged ahead and became baptized. Why not do so? It would not change one small dotted *i* of her behavior. She was already as faithful a churchgoer as anybody. Yet it represented letting go—to superstition, her mother would say. Her mother had warned her against marriage to Fred so very long ago for this very reason.

Her mother had not approved of anything she had done for years, however, and by now Susan took it as normal. Perversely she found as she sat in the front of the church, waiting for the service to begin, that she actually wished her mother would come. She had invited her, after all. She supposed it was just that your mother is always your mother, even if you are forty. (She was that now, with years to spare.) You want her to approve; you fear she will not.

She had written her plans to her niece, Lucy, and found that she was a little fearful of Lucy's response too. Lucy had been her lifeline, with her interesting letters and her sane, straight mind. Elizabeth had raised Lucy to be a Christian, Susan knew, but she did not know how much of it had taken. Lucy never wrote about religion, except when she mentioned her friend Sarah.

The organ paused and lurched into a more martial tune. The pastor came in, with his swinging gait. (Something was wrong with one of his legs, perhaps some childhood accident.) The choir followed down the center aisle, braying. Susan turned to scan the congregation. Was her mother here? No. But she saw Fred, smiling broadly. All three children sat next to him, scrubbed and neat. George waved to her, just a shy finger wave. He had pulled his shoulders in to himself, his head scrunched into his chest, like a turtle, but he had that rosebud of a smile—his father's mouth—and the happiness that a child can show just meeting his mother's eyes.

When Susan had asked the reverend how much certainty was required, he had waved it off. You had to have faith. Faith in what? she had asked. Faith in Jesus Christ as the Savior, he said, to forgive your sins and take you to heaven. But what if you aren't sure? she had said. Faith isn't the same as rifle-barrel-straight certainty, he said.

Susan was full of doubts. They brimmed up in her thoughts and spilled over like boiling milk. Maybe she thought too much. She knew that she wanted to be in solidarity with the good people here, to believe with them, to be part of them. She hoped that was good enough. She had nothing else to offer.

Lucy Phillips tore her eyes away from the grand vista of the crowd, the street, the tall buildings stretching away into the distance. What a city was New York, how vigorous and full of American freedom. She looked to her right, down the file of marchers, and saw her friend Sarah's pale face looking straight ahead. For a moment that dead-white, dead-serious sight inspired in Lucy a feeling of delirious joy. The pieces of her life were together for this brief parade.

They were marching up Third Avenue, four abreast. Ahead of them and behind were ranks of women from the settlement house, not just the workers but women who came from the neighborhoods. Just in front of her was a huge red banner with yellow letters: WORKINGWOMEN NEED THE VOTE.

The entire parade stretched into the distance as far as she could see: thousands of women, clumps of marchers representing different trades, different organizations, college women, professional women, union women. The rich ladies had been pulled out of their cars and were marching next to workingwomen. Lucy felt the liberty of space: striding across the open pavement as though it were a vast stage, the dark battlements of the office buildings enclosing them, yet opening a broad highway ahead under an open May sky. The sidewalks were crowded with men, dark as a thundercloud in their suits, watching in amazement no doubt that women would parade. Even from balconies above the street men looked down. Some of the women had been hard put to imagine this event. They thought it would be a circus. They feared it would appear unladylike. And that was just the point, as the new suffrage women said. They wanted to do something startling, something to jolt the men. To Lucy, it did not seem undignified; she felt *large,* like Moses and the children of Israel marching through the waters on the way to the promised land.

Sarah had never before been willing to join a suffrage protest, but now, just after the Triangle Fire, she at last grasped that suffrage was not the domain of society matrons. It was a necessity for workingwomen.

The fire had raged through the Triangle Shirtwaist Company, where women had struck for fair conditions just a year before. One hundred forty-six had died—locked in because the fire exits had been chained shut, imprisoning workers like slaves. Could their lives have been so cheap if they had been voters? Suffragists said no, and for once they had an audience.

Lucy could not help thinking back to her earliest suffrage memories. Those meetings she had attended with her mother: large halls stuffed with dignified matrons, long addresses and parliamentary squabblings. How utterly different this: women in the open air, in motion—*the men looking on in astonishment*. Lucy thought she had found the place where she could make a mark.

Chapter 14
1911: California Again

It is an entirely harmless thing I am about to do, Susan told herself. Men of all types spoke on street corners and were treated as a usual part of the landscape. Who noticed? Who cared? In every big city they appeared by the handful.

Another part of her mind, however, was screaming that she was a fool, a fanatic, that no one would listen, that she would embarrass herself. What had drawn her to do this? *My niece,* she thought, *who wrote with such excitement of their marches and outdoor rallies.* Lucy had made her jealous, inspiring her to think that something could be done for suffrage once again. Even more, events had pushed her into hope. Washington State unexpectedly gave women the vote, and in the same election Hiram Johnson was elected governor of California with a mandate for reform. The legislature offered a host of constitutional changes, including woman suffrage, and suddenly, after fifteen years of the doldrums, they found themselves working again for the vote. It was different now, much less orderly and prim. Californians seemed sick of the graft, sick of the Southern Pacific Railroad, sick of the rich, corrupt men who controlled the state. And Susan was different too: free from the labor of small children, free from the fear of her neighbors' opinions.

And yet, not entirely free. At Powell Street she stood watching a cable car turn around. The sidewalk was loosely crowded with dressed-up men and an occasional woman in a tailored suit or a coat with a mink collar. On one corner a street preacher was talking about the book of Revelation: he wore a blue suit with creases like knives, and a gray hat cocked at a slight angle, but he had only a handful of listeners. On the other corner north of Market was a socialist with a set of posters. Every time he said "capitalism" he pronounced the first syllable so it went off with a small explosion—*CAP*. A little crowd of curious people had surrounded his stand-up display, more intent on that than on his speech.

To speak on a street corner had seemed an entirely reasonable activity when she left Santa Rosa this morning. Susan had spoken on the street twice before, and both times found it invigorating. Everyone she knew applauded the new bold day of suffrage activism. Parades, bullhorns, electric signs, billboards, auto caravans, shoe box speakers— they had thought it all made wonderful sense when planning the campaign in May. What had gravitas ever done for them? Susan remembered a letter from Lucy, describing the sensations of their May parade in New York City: the delirious freedom, the space for adventure that seemed to come just with marching down the middle of a broad street.

She did not know whether she had it today. Today, perhaps, was not the day to speak. Some other day. Only she had done it before. Only she would be asked in the headquarters office how it had gone. She thought, *Oh, well.*

Inside a cloth sack Susan carried a clever folded wooden box, hinged so it came together into a small platform. Setting the platform on the sidewalk, she got up on it. Amazing the difference eight inches made—she could now look down on everyone.

Yet no one looked at her! There she perched, exposed to nature on her little foothold, and she was invisible! One passing woman, wearing a fashionable soft silk brown coat, looked at her a little startled, but then frowned, lowered her eyes, and went on. Invisible! Susan had worn her best, her only good dress, but it made no difference at all. She thought, *If I stood in my underwear and sang the "Star-Spangled Banner," I might become even more invisible.*

Very well, she thought, *we will see whether they can hear me. Invisible women make no noise, surely.*

"In October we will have a special election on the most important topic in the history of California. On the ballot will be the question: Woman, slave or citizen? Or as it might well be translated, Woman, human or subhuman?"

A few passersby glanced at her as they walked past, but nobody stopped. Very well, then no harm speaking any way she liked.

"You men, who gave you the right to call a woman your slave? Who made you the master? Do you think you have the right because you are strongest? Do muscles make you the voting member of the family? Then why don't you let your milk cow vote? She's stronger than you and produces something worthwhile to boot!"

A couple of men who had been listening to the preacher wandered her direction. She singled them out. "You two men, I'll bet you have sisters. And I'll bet something else: I'll bet those sisters are smarter than either one of you. Do you know how I know?"

"Women belong at home!" somebody bawled from the other side. The voice startled her. So, somebody was listening. She had stopped being invisible!

"*You* certainly don't belong at home," she said. "You're no gentleman. But you can vote."

She smiled at him, taking her time about it to let everyone see she wasn't mean. Her fear had turned to exhilaration. This was as much fun as she had ever had! This took every cell in her brain!

"Now, people, he raises a point. They say that a woman shouldn't vote because her proper place is at home. I won't argue that a woman should be at home. I have a home of my own, with a husband—a good husband, who wants me here doing this right now—and three children to raise. I know just as well as you do that I am very important in my home. I have a role to play that nobody can take from me.

"I'll tell you what, though, just because I have a place where I am important doesn't mean I have to keep out of every place else. A woman can do some things outside the home."

"She can do tricks!" A heckler. Her small audience couldn't help smiling. They thought such a comment very amusing.

"If you were a decent man, you wouldn't think that was funny," she said, turning on the man. "But since you're not a decent man, I want to talk about that. Everybody in this city knows that there's a problem with female purity. There are houses of ill repute here within a stone's throw. I'm not supposed to know that because I'm a lady. I'm glad I don't know as much as you evidently do!

"I do know that I feel pity for those poor souls who are trapped in that life. Do you know why they are there? They cannot be paid a decent wage for decent work. They can only get woman's work that doesn't pay enough to feed one person, let alone a family. Yes, some of those loose women have families. You would rather not know that, wouldn't you? That's the worst hypocrisy of men who keep the vote from us. They say that men should protect women—that it's a rough world, so women need to be taken care of. Well, are you taking care of those women who need to work to support a child? To support a husband who has broken his back in a mill, with no pension? When women have the vote, we will work with other decent citizens to pass laws that will protect that man and his wife."

She had a good crowd now, fifteen, maybe even twenty men. Some were smiling. Some of them made comments to each other. These were voters, whom she had it in her power to sway. Susan hoped for another heckler. Nothing did more to interest the crowd.

Then she saw Fred, standing at the rear. Her first thought, illogically, was that he was displeased with her, because he wore a doleful expression. She felt embarrassed, turned away from him, and continued to speak.

"Some of you say that women will get the vote, but the time isn't here yet. I want to tell you. My grandfather advocated women's votes when he was just a young man. They told him the time isn't here yet. My mother, who is quite old . . ."

While she spoke, her mind was searching for understanding of Fred's presence. He was supposed to be meeting the children after school. Why was he here? He looked so forlorn.

What was he holding up? His watch. He was swinging it. Time.

Susan quickly wrapped up her talk and got down from her platform. The crowd began to disperse almost immediately. They wandered off without looking at her, as though she had become invisible again.

"Your mother," Fred said. "I didn't want to interrupt, you were doing so nobly. Your mother has had a stroke."

Fred said her mother seemed likely to live. Her left side was paralyzed and her speech slurred, but she was conscious. For Susan, that was enough information. She asked no questions, but silently carried her thoughts up Market Street. Bad news always took her like this: she closed herself around it like an oyster. Fred walked glumly alongside. She glanced at him once, gratefully. He knew enough not to talk. He had his chin on his chest, and his bowler pulled down almost over his eyes.

"What about the children?" she asked.

"I took them to the Dennerts," he said. "I went by and found Russell."

The Dennerts owned a ranch not far from theirs along the slough. They were not close friends, but like most farmers, they presumed on each other freely.

The thought of her children under the care of the large, rough-talking man pierced Susan, however. She could feel it directly while as yet the pain of her mother's illness had not gotten through her defenses. She had left her children for this . . . frivolity.

They pressed through the torrent at the Ferry Building, filed onto the boat, and sat waiting for the voyage to begin. Most of the passengers were outside on the deck, enjoying the brisk sunshine, but Susan preferred the gloomy, echoing interior of the main cabin. She sat with her head in her hands, staring at a golden rectangle on the floorboards where a panel of sunshine broke. Each little nick and mark showed against the dazzling light.

A blast came from the ship's horn. Susan felt the boat lift as though on a pillow. She looked up to see the dock crew pulling away, as smoothly as a cloud blown by a March wind. Then she glanced at Fred and gave him a little wincing smile.

"When did you hear?"

"This morning, not ten minutes after you left. What is that nephew of Charles's named? Eugene. Eugene saw her fall. He got the doctor, and then he sent to find you."

"But you were at the train station."

"I was. I ran into Eugene on my way back home. He had been to the farm and didn't find anybody. It's just lucky that I had to go back home; I'd forgotten to bring my checkbook."

"Lucky?" she said sharply. "I wouldn't consider that lucky."

"No," he said, "I guess not. You know what I mean." Fred never made it easy to pick a fight.

"I should never have started in on this open-air lecturing," she said miserably. "I had no business."

"You couldn't have helped anything if you had been there," Fred said.

That was true, but she felt that somehow she had to pay for her pleasure. "I might as well shoot myself," she said bitterly.

"Don't say that," Fred replied. He rarely contradicted her, but he did not like such talk. "That's the way your mother talks."

"Well, who do you think is going to nurse her? It won't be you, will it? I hate being stuck on that ranch while you go hither and yon, and now what? I'll be stuck with my mother. Can you think of anything worse than that?"

He could not deny the justice of what she said. "It's only for a time," he said.

"For a time," she said. "For a time. Do you have any idea how I hate that phrase? When you have babies, they say, 'It's only for a time.' Every time a woman gets enslaved to some new project it's 'for a time.' When is my time, Fred?"

He looked away from her, out the window where the bay bounced in blue and white. She had hurt him. She could read the grief on his face, but her own was too heavy for her. In time she would work her way through this and be able to carry on. She knew that even while she rebelled against it. For now, she was cut off from Fred. She felt cut off from everyone. She had not even begun to feel pity for her mother, who was surely terrified at life as an invalid.

The campaign had raised Susan out of her stupor. She had doubted she could do it anymore, fifteen years and three children after her last speech, but she found that she loved it more than ever. Just like today, deciding to do something that frightened her, something nobody she knew had ever done. She could talk better and think faster than the hecklers. She could draw a crowd on the street; she could make herself visible. They were going to win this election. Washington State had, just last year, and now California would join them, the first big state to give women the vote.

She thought of this all the way back home on the train—rather, she felt it, like a bruise. She was ready to argue with anybody who said a modern woman could not be simultaneously a mother and a citizen of the world. Yet she herself had never managed the combination.

She fully expected that Fred would say nothing more. That was his pattern: he would not fight back. To her surprise, however, he pulled his gaze back from the window and looked at her squarely. "You go on feeling sorry for yourself while we're on our way home," he said, "but when we get there, you have to quit it. Too many people are counting on you."

———

Her mother lay in her bed in the old house. Entering the darkened room, Susan was surprised by the smell—a combination of dust, violet water, and mothballs that triggered memories of entering her mother's bedroom during childhood.

Rebecca Netherton glared fiercely at her. The look was almost comical because Rebecca's face had become unbalanced, sagging on the left as though she were trying to hold a toothpick in the corner of her mouth. Her left eye tipped. At first Susan thought the glare was an accident of the stroke, but no, her mother was trying with all her might to focus her ferocity on her daughter. The effect was skewed, however, because she could not control her face.

"Go away," she said to Susan, although the words came out in a slushy explosion through the paralysis.

Susan could not immediately understand her mother's mind. "Charles is taking care of everything, Mother," she said. "I can sit with you."

A word came out like a roar; she could not immediately understand it. "Ssshpaygg!" Susan pondered a moment, watching her mother's face, and then grasped her meaning. "Speak!" She wanted Susan not to abandon the cause; she wanted her to continue speaking for suffrage.

Susan was so touched that tears started. While she was resenting her mother's weakness, her mother was concerned for her. In a moment, however, secondary reflections came. Her mother would have other motives. She cared so fiercely about suffrage that she would resent the loss of a single soldier. It was not pity for her daughter but allegiance to the cause that moved her. Another thought cut off Susan's legs even more—that it did not matter her mother's solicitude, there was nothing personal in the force that would pin her down.

"Who would care for you, Mother? Unless you have some secret store of cash, we can't afford a nurse. I'm the only free help you have."

Chapter 15
1911: The Prodigal

September came in with a heavy fog off the ocean, so thick that the moisture collected on the eaves and dripped into the line of splash puddles along the side wall of the house. Susan always thought that the first day of school should be bright and cheerful, but this day could not be drearier. Thomas drove off with his father to begin high school in town. He was a quiet and almost serene child, and he went off calmly, though Susan knew he must be fearful, a country boy approaching the sophisticated town. The younger two walked off to their grade school—no, ran or romped. When they were gone, Susan had nothing left. Hardly anything could seem so bleak as the thought of the children gone to school, and she left alone with her mother to line out the day.

She stayed on the porch, partly because her mother was inside. The trees by the creek showed dim, feathery gray-green piles of boughs, while along the lane a line of fence posts faded into oblivion. Looking into the dimness of the fog, she almost hoped to see one of her children returning for some forgotten object.

Susan heard the bicycle before she saw it. She could not make out the sound: a rattle of loose tin, the popping *whush* that a rubber tire makes on gravel. A figure came out of the fog just where the fence posts disappeared. She could not imagine who it could be. No one she knew rode a bicycle. Her curiosity was increased by the way the rider weaved as he leaned back, not holding the handlebars but directing the bicycle purely by shifting his weight. He had crossed his arms on his chest, and he sat as though expecting to be admired, his face tilted into the air. Susan laughed in spite of herself.

The bicyclist saw her, raised a hand in a broad salute, and called her name. "Susan! Is that my Susan?" She did not recognize the voice. The head was covered with a cap, and a wide handlebar mustache spread across the face. The man was elderly, at least his hair was bright silver, but he did not ride his bicycle like an old man. He spun up to the front of the porch, did a broad circle with his arms outstretched on both sides, then neatly tumbled off while still moving. He parked the vehicle against the palm tree.

"Well," he said, smiling broadly as he walked up to the porch steps, "you don't know me, do you, dear? It's your father! The prodigal father has returned once again. And where is my wife?"

Later she would see the younger man in his tanned and creased face, but at this point it was his manner she recognized—the quiet and gracious way he stopped, with all his bustling energy momentarily stilled. "I am glad to see you, darling Susan. You look well."

They had not seen him for more than twenty years, when he took Elizabeth away. Once, when Susan's children were babies, a postcard had arrived at the boardinghouse, written from Chicago and announcing that he was on his way to Santa Rosa. But he never arrived, and they forgot about him.

"But where did you come from?" she managed to say. "We thought you must be dead."

"Oh, no, not dead yet. Where is your mother? I heard she is not well." He was already past her and through the door before she could invite him in. She later wished that she could have seen her mother's face.

"Well, Rebecca, this may be the best-situated bed you have ever had, right in the middle of the parlor. No need to get up at all in order to be the center of attention. How do you do? I heard you weren't well."

Susan got inside and found that he had taken a seat on the bed, with one knee neatly curled onto the cover. They had put the bed here because there was nowhere else in the house. Rebecca looked bleary, washed out, but she had sat up. She had a nightcap askew on her head, and she pulled her gown up around her neck. That struck Susan when she thought it through later: even at the first moment of meeting her husband (for she was still legally married to him), Rebecca had a girlish impulse of modesty.

"Would you like a cup of coffee?" Susan asked. She did not know how to call him. Certainly not Father—he was no father to her.

"I would love some coffee," he said. "In fact, I wonder whether you have some eggs and toast available. And perhaps some bacon. I am famished. I got off the train and came immediately, without stopping for food."

"Wherever did you get that bicycle?" Susan asked. She bristled at his request for food when it had not been offered.

"Isn't that something? I had not ridden a bicycle for forty years, and I found that I could do it easily. You never forget! I had heard that, but now I can prove it. There was no cab available so I had to borrow that. Incidentally, I must return it as soon as possible. Could you run me into town for that purpose a little later?"

Susan said rather coolly that she had no way to run him into town. Fred would not be returning until the evening. She got coffee in a large porcelain cup and took her time about it. She only halfway listened to her father's description of his train trip down from the North—he had come from Oregon apparently. How could this man prance into their lives at their very nadir and expect to be treated like a king?

"I hope you take it black," Susan said. "We don't have a cow either."

Her father took the cup from her hand with a nod of his head. He did not seem to notice Susan's tone; he was completely absorbed in her mother. And did it seem possible that Rebecca's head rode a little higher?

"I'll get you a cup, Mother," Susan said, and Rebecca smiled. Smiled! Since her stroke, she had not lost that slack, lost, empty-eyed expression. The charm, the famous charm, was certainly at work.

———

Her father had been there a week when he invited Susan to go for a walk. "My dear, do you think we could have a little talk?"

He slept in the cowshed where Fred had rigged up a simple cot out of some old lumber and a rope. George went eagerly to call him to breakfast each day and pestered him with projects after coming home from school. All three of the children seemed happy and easy with their grandfather. This was not hard to understand: he talked to them and showed an interest. He was a storyteller.

Most amazing to Susan was the transformation he brought her mother. Rebecca now got up and dressed for breakfast. While he beguiled her with old memories, she would smile, and sometimes she would even speak haltingly. Fred seemed to enjoy his company. He put on no airs; he was very free with himself. They liked to talk about highways and railroads and the changes that were coming with high-speed travel. One afternoon Fred took him and the boys out driving, and they must have covered half the county, coming back muddy and tired and late for supper because they landed in a ditch. Susan could not get out of them where the accident occurred and why.

Susan was left holding a grudge she could not defend. If he was a disreputable old man, so what? Nobody was proposing to make him a saint. Susan told herself these things, but she could not help resenting him and his presumptions.

"Would you care to go for a walk?" he asked. It was midmorning, and the fog had begun to break up overhead. Susan went in to tell her mother that she would be gone for a little while. When she got outside again, he was rolling a cigarette; she watched him neatly twist it closed with a deft, one-handed motion and then lick the seam. This gave another pinprick of annoyance: he made a pretty show of his dirty habit.

"I'd rather you didn't smoke," she said. "Anyway, if we're going on a walk, there's a danger of fire this time of year."

The grass was still wet from the morning fog, but he made no resistance. He slipped the cigarette into his jacket pocket. Her father had put on a suit this morning as he did every morning. He dressed well.

"I thought we might walk down by the creek," he said. "George has shown me a path that's very nice."

"I don't want to get my feet wet," she said. "I'd rather stick to the road."

"All right," he said.

They walked along side by side, their feet picking up the fine brown dust. Her father had his head down and his hands joined behind his back. At the end of the lane the track met another lane and proceeded down a gentle slope where they had once pastured their cow. Now the grass was dry and worn out from the long dry months, its color closer to gray than to brown.

"Now, darling," her father said, "I wish you would tell me what I've done to make you so mad."

"I am not darling to you," she said. "So why don't we start right there. What makes you think that you can waltz in on this family and claim it for your own? You act like it's the most normal thing to be gone for twenty years and then reappear and charm everybody."

He had stopped where the two lanes came together, and now he drew his cigarette out of his pocket, licked the seam again, and put it into his mouth. "I think I need this," he said. "I'll be careful not to set fire." He got out a matchbox and lit up. After a long draw he continued. "It sounds like you don't want me to come home at all."

"It's not home to you. I've gone my whole life without you, and I'm not going to act like it was nothing. I am not some weak woman you can charm. Don't think I am."

"I'd be very disappointed if I thought you were, darling."

"Don't call me darling. I am *not* your darling."

He took another puff on his cigarette and stood looking out into the distance. Across the plain, through the haze, the darker mountains were visible. Susan was glad for the space; she could yell here, and her words would travel nowhere.

"You think I'm a bad man?" Netherton asked. "You don't want me here?"

She let the words hang. *Yes*, she thought, *he is a bad man. Do I want him to go? No, not really.*

She did not like this censorious part of herself. Even Fred, who meant life to her, felt it. It had caused her a lot of trouble, even when she was a little girl, but it was her nature. She had never been able to let things go. She had thought it was her mother's nature. But how could her mother be charmed by this man?

"Why don't we walk on?" her father said, and he tossed his cigarette down on the road. Dutifully she walked alongside him. It was easier when they did not have to look at each other.

"I'll grant you I've been a poor father," he said. "And a poor husband. Your grandfather, Mr. Nichols, who was the finest man I ever knew, would tell me that I needed to stay at home. I knew he was right, but it wasn't easy. Your mother . . ." He glanced at Susan just at the same moment she looked at him; she looked away, embarrassed. "Your mother was not always the easiest companion. I suspect you can understand that. I sometimes wondered whether money would have solved all our problems. But I'll never know because we had no money. I have never been lucky in work."

He seemed to want to express his regrets, but he was unable to bring himself quite to do so. He would never quite reach the point of apologizing. *In that*, Susan thought, *he is exactly like my mother*.

"I made up my mind," he went on, "that I would come at the crucial moments. When I could help you, I have come. That is why I am here now. I came when I learned that your mother was ill. I keep track, you know. I still have friends in this town."

"You come at crucial moments? Every twenty years we have a crucial moment?"

He tilted his head and smiled. "When you were eighteen. I tried to help you and your sister get away. That was a crucial moment in your life, my dear."

"You think that helped? To take my sister away?"

"You should have come too. It would have made a great difference."

"What is wrong with Santa Rosa?"

"Nothing is wrong. Of course nothing is wrong. You forget that I am the one who brought you here."

"And left me here."

"Once your mother was settled. By then it was impossible for me to stay. A man cannot raise two daughters. I left when I had achieved my goal, when I had your mother's attention."

"What do you mean by that? You are the most aggravating man in the world. Everything gets interpreted so that you are doing good. You kidnapped us and took us here. You stole a mother's daughters. I can't think of a worse crime. Yes, I know, under the law your perfect right, but only the laws of men, not surely the laws of women. As far as I am concerned, you come at the crucial moments of life to do me harm. You took away my sister. I cannot help wondering what you might take from me this time. Do you understand? I am watching you for harm."

It had all come out in a rush, so quick and connected that she burned with angry amazement. For the first time she understood her own reaction. She had every right! If her feeling was mean, it was also just.

She saw out of the corner of her eye that he shrugged. After a pause he said, "I am sorry for that, Susan. Everybody has his own interpretation of events. With your sister, for instance, I think I did a world of good. I don't think she would disagree, do you? I'm sure it looked different from your angle. Though I must say, I think your view would be different if you had come along. Now regarding your 'kidnapping,' do you really know what went on? I would not call your mother a liar, but she has her own peculiar interpretation of events. We all do. We all do."

They had come near to Fulton Road, where one of their neighbors was passing by in a wagon. Susan listened to the creak of harness and the steady clop of the mule's hooves, the shudder of the wagon as it rolled along. Did she want to know what her father might say? He was not honest; he saw the world through his own peculiar lens. So did her mother, however, and only from her mother had she received the history.

"I don't know what interpretation you can possibly put on what you did," she said. "You came and took us from our mother. What were you planning on doing with us?"

"I was only planning exactly what I did do. I knew that your mother would follow and begin to care for you again. I wasn't trying to hide, you realize. If I had wanted to keep you from her, she would never have found us."

"So tell me," Susan said. "Why? Why did you take us away?"

He sighed. "Oh, that was so long ago I can hardly bear to remember. Here it is, my dear. Your mother was in a very bad situation. I didn't have the money to support a family, so she had to move back with her parents until I could get on my feet. That was a terrible time for a man who needed a position. I had worked for the Port Authority, but the commissioner's son wanted my job and so I was accused of some shenanigans. They dismissed me and spread reports. Of course there wasn't any truth to the accusations, but times were tough and rumors were enough to keep people off me.

"Your mother and your grandparents couldn't get along living together. Your grandmother was a fine woman—I think she liked me, at any rate—but she was very tough. And so is your mother, as I suppose you know. Rebecca moved out and left you there. Your grandmother was raising you, while Rebecca went off to live with Miss Anthony and that whole committee of radicals. She was so happy. You cannot imagine how happy it made her. They didn't care about you—they were all spinsters like Aunt Susan, or rich women who had servants and governesses. Rebecca was very satisfied to be busy with the newspaper they put out and to sit in philosophical discussions.

"Maybe from your view that was a fine setup. But I didn't like it. Your grandmother Ruth was getting old, and she couldn't handle you. Nobody was going to do anything about it. Your mother told me that I should mind my own business if I couldn't provide. Your grandmother was quite stubborn, and she wasn't about to hire a governess. She thought the way I did, that your mother ought to come back home, but she wouldn't face the fact that your mother wasn't going to do that.

"That's when I thought of taking you to California, as a way of killing two birds with one stone—three birds, actually. I needed to get away from New York. I needed to get to a place where a man could work, and where no stories would follow him like his shadow. I thought that if I took you with me, it would force your mother's hand. And I thought that once she got here, away from that crowd, she would find a new direction."

Her father smiled happily. "It all worked as I hoped, if I may say so. I found a little work in Santa Rosa. Your mother came and settled down. She has raised you admirably. Or don't you think so?"

Susan thought the story sounded suspicious in every line. However, she could not find a target to attack. She could imagine her mother playing the part, and she could imagine her father too. A moment ago she had been filled with righteous certitude, and suddenly she found herself spun off into the fog.

If her father was telling the truth—and that she did not know—the matter of justice was not simple. If her father was telling the truth or something close to the truth, then the morality tale she had been raised on no longer held sway. Perhaps she and her sister had been merely caught in the complications of imperfect human life.

"I don't know whether to believe you or not," she said to her father.

"I don't know whether it matters if you do," he said. "You could ask your mother. Everybody else is dead."

———

She tried to ask her mother. But whether because the stroke had addled Rebecca, because she could not manage emotions from so long ago, or because Paul Netherton spoke truly, Rebecca did not counter him. She appeared not to understand—one of her traditional approaches to issues she wished to avoid. Susan longed to know the truth of her past in the same way one wants to get rid of a vexing tooth. How to do so, however, she could not see. The truth lay only in the minds of her parents. Perhaps there was no truth at the bottom of it, only more layers of misdirected intentions.

This much was undeniable: her mother, who had expressed lifelong enmity for Paul Netherton, was brightened by his presence. He may have been a bad man, but his way of kicking up the dust cheered the whole family. Susan continued to watch him warily, but she stopped acting mad.

He was helpful too. With him available to watch her mother, Susan was able to make forays into suffrage again. When the Political Equity Association held a rally at the Columbia Theater, at which a former consul to New Zealand held forth on how splendidly woman's suffrage had performed in that place, Susan was able to go to the meeting and report that a large and enthusiastic crowd attended.

Next week when the *Press Democrat* announced that Hiram Johnson would visit Santa Rosa, Rebecca Netherton said that she wanted to attend. They were all around the dinner table when she made this pronouncement, which temporarily stopped all of their talk.

"Why, Grandma?" little Becky asked. To that point, Rebecca had hardly expressed an interest in leaving the parlor.

"Tell me the last time a governor came to Santa Rosa," Rebecca said in a mushy diction. "Hiram Johnson is the best governor we ever had."

"Grandma," George said in surprise, "you can talk."

It was such a great occasion, even the children wanted to attend. They jammed into the Ford, and Fred drove them right up to the front of Rink Pavilion. Susan and her father walked Rebecca inside, one on each arm. The building was so full, George and Becky had to sit on laps, and Thomas stood in the back with two of his high school friends. Rebecca sat grandly on the stage, recognized by several speakers for her path-breaking role in woman suffrage. The governor shook her hand. So did Mr. Finley, the newspaper editor.

Twice in late September, Susan took the train and ferry to San Francisco for mass meetings. She had no role, but she wanted to experience the surge of energy she had heard about. Her father could easily watch her mother—all he had to do was not disappear, as Susan reminded him with a certain fierceness.

The campaign seemed to catch fire. They rallied in Union Square, a huge and energetic crowd that almost filled the block, mostly men, who listened with courtesy and even pressed inward to hear one marvelous speaker after another. Cautiously Susan began to hope that they might really win. They had never felt anything like this in 1896.

In Los Angeles they dropped leaflets from a hot air balloon, like confetti. A corp of women toured the state by automobile. They commandeered special trains for a meeting at the Sacramento fairgrounds and then festooned the trains with yellow ribbons. Some of the younger women in Santa Rosa began to talk—Susan caught them at it—as though they would sweep the field. Susan knew better, knew there were plenty of men to vote against them, even if they kept their opinions to themselves.

Election day Susan spent at the Burbank School, watching the polls. Everyone treated her with slightly exaggerated courtesy, determined to behave as gentlemen. Of course they could not like it, having a woman watch over their work.

By tradition men gathered in front of the newspaper offices for the vote counting. A bonfire was built in the street, and boys on bicycles raced up from the courthouse with the ongoing tally. Susan wanted to stay in town, but Fred said it was not a fit place for a woman, so she sat with her mother after the children were in bed, remembering the election of 1896 and their bitter disappointment. Rebecca was sure they would get even fewer votes this time. She liked to keep a gloomy superiority.

About midnight they heard the Ford from far off. The sound of the motor cut out in the draw about a half mile from them; Susan stood in the window knowing that the sound would reappear at about the same time that the car came in sight. The fields seemed white in the moonlight, the road a dark strip that waggled away until it disappeared like a thread.

"We should have given him a signal," Susan said to her mother. "Honk if we won."

She heard the motor again, a sudden loud purring. The car headlights appeared, bigger and nearer than she had expected. When Fred pulled up in the yard, she stepped outside to greet him. She was simultaneously very excited and very afraid.

He said nothing. He wrapped his arms around her and squeezed her tightly. She thought surely it was a consoling hug, the kind you give a child when you know nothing you say can remove the sting of disappointment.

"Bad news?" she asked.

"Let's get in, and I'll tell you," he said. "I'm cold."

He saw that Rebecca was awake, and he went over to her chair to greet her. "So we lost again," Rebecca said. "I said we would."

"No," he said. "We won in Santa Rosa by a close vote. In Petaluma by a good margin. We lost in Sonoma, however, by quite a lot. It looks to be close in the county, but Mr. Finley said he thought we would probably prevail. None of the north or west county votes are in."

"Did you hear anything from San Francisco?" Susan asked. She had been almost convinced by her mother's gloom, and now she was afraid to hope for a victory.

"We have a small lead there," he said. "But that doesn't mean much, the way the bosses hold out precincts. It looks to be very close."

Before the dawn, Susan got up and made a pot of coffee. She had slept only fitfully, thinking of the election. *And why do I care? It would change not one thing about my life if we lost.*

And yet she was not sure she believed her own skepticism. What if today the election swung their way? Could they grow into a world where women spoke as bravely as men, without thinking how their words might sound coming from a woman? Where a woman's views were listened to, not simply heard as a faint echo behind loud masculine voices? Sitting in judgment at city hall or Sacramento or Washington had no interest to Susan. What she wanted was a different world, where women became solid.

Partly, she cared because she felt the insult in being told, "You are not qualified to vote." The antis pretended respect for motherhood and femininity, but that "No" spoke loudly.

It was more than that, however—more than a matter of wanting to go to the party to which she was not invited.

After she had sat at the kitchen table for half an hour, brooding on these thoughts, she heard the alarm ring. Fred passed through on his way to the outhouse. "You're up early," he said, and when he came back he poured a cup of coffee and sat with her for a few minutes. He had his mind full of business, thinking how he could transport fish on ice from Bodega Bay to Santa Rosa markets. Vegetables and fruits were all but gone, and he had to consider how to fill the slow season.

The house awoke, and Susan was busy cooking breakfast and helping the children prepare for school. When they sat down to porridge, Fred talked to Tom about the football team. Although he was a gangly freshman, Tom said in his understated way that he might get in Saturday's game. The proud pleasure was evident in Fred's face.

Suddenly they were gone, and the house was quiet again. Susan's mother still slept. Her father went out for his morning walk. Susan sat down with her coffee to consider that none of her family had mentioned the election. No doubt that was how it was for thousands of families all over the state. The vote meant a great deal to a few, but for most people it seemed incidental.

When would she find out the results? Probably when Fred came home tonight, he would have a newspaper. Once again, for the thousandth time, Susan wished to live in town.

She tried to keep her mind off it. Her mother awoke; she helped her dress; she fed her breakfast. While Rebecca was eating, Susan's father came back from his walk. He and Rebecca launched into the election, Paul talking cheerfully about hopes for success, Rebecca dolefully predicting that the liquor powers would steal San Francisco again, just as in '96. They often argued these days; it was a daily exercise that seemed to keep them both alert and satisfied. Today Susan found the sound of it as nettlesome as the buzz of a horsefly. She stayed out of the way, cleaning windows in the bedrooms. After she made lunch for them, she took her own outside, on the porch, so she could be alone.

In the midafternoon she decided, very suddenly, she would go to town. If she was unhappy stuck here, she had it in her power to change that.

Her father was napping in the cowshed, and she woke him abruptly and asked him to see to her mother. "And when the children come home from school, see that they remember their chores. I'll be back by suppertime." Then without delay she set out walking.

The trip took her a mile and a half south on dusty Fulton Road, to the juice line where she waited for the trolley. When she arrived at the courthouse, the usual idlers were on the benches in front. They probably knew all about the election, but she could not ask them. She climbed up the broad stone steps and stepped into the cool, echoing chamber. She had a friend in Deeds, so she poked her head in that office. "Good afternoon, Mrs. Konicek," Eva said, smiling. "And how are you?"

"Well, thank you. I was wondering whether you had any news of the election. I don't know where they record the votes."

Eva smiled a little crooked grin and shook her head. "You can't go there. It's only for officials. I know what they are saying, though. They are saying the women have got it."

"Who is saying?"

Eva shrugged. "The men. The ones who are always talking politics."

At first she could not believe it. She wanted to tell someone. She thought she might find Fred, so she walked up and down Fourth Street, and over to the high school where the football team was practicing. The Ford was nowhere to be seen, however. She stopped at a newsstand to buy a *Press Democrat*, then decided she might as well go home. She felt as though the world had come to a temporary halt, that she was walking around in a dream where only she had substance. She wanted to do something, to make some sign that the world had changed forever, but she could not figure out what it would be.

On the way home she had time to scan the headlines. The vote statewide was narrowly against them; at least it had been when the paper was published. Editor Finley, however, was predicting that the strength of the rural districts would overcome the rampant crookedness of San Francisco and Oakland. Finley was probably one of those men Eva had referred to, always talking politics.

A wind had kicked up off the ocean, and the air was cold, fresh, and wet as Susan walked back up Fulton Road. She thought sometimes she could smell the salt. From their lane she looked closely at the square, ordinary shape of the house. Such a nondescript building—how had it become so dear to her?

She stepped in the front door filled with anticipation: for love, for food, for company. It seemed to her that she had been gone a long time. Fred was reading in the parlor, seated in one of the chairs pushed into the corner. From the lump in the bed, Susan could see that her mother was asleep.

"I'm home," she said. "Where are the children?"

"In the kitchen," Fred said, getting to his feet.

She found them around the kitchen table. The light was almost too dim for their homework. They looked up and greeted her as though she had never been gone.

Fred had followed her in. "Welcome home," he said. "I'm sorry I missed you in town."

"That's all right. Have you started supper?"

"I wasn't sure when you would get here."

"I told Grandpa I would be home by supper. I guess that was bound to be true if I'm the only one with the wherewithal to cook." She said it trying to sound irritated, but her heart was not in it. She was simply too glad.

"Where did you go, Mom?" George asked.

"To town," she said. "I wanted to see the election results."

"People I talked to seem to think we won," Fred said.

"That's what they say at the courthouse," she said. "But in the state we are behind by a little over a thousand votes."

"Not much of a margin," Fred said.

They were all looking at her, as though trying to see how to react. They knew the results mattered to her—she could not hide that. "I believe it has happened," she said, and she smiled at them. "I believe we have won."

"Yea!" George said. Susan bent and kissed him.

Her mother shouted from the parlor. "What are you saying? Is that you, Susan? Have we won? Come in here and tell me the news."

She found her mother sitting up in bed, one side of her face waffled red and white from being pressed into the coarse blanket weave. Susan sat on the edge of the bed and told her mother about the votes.

"It is a great day," Rebecca said with dignity.

"We have to wait until all the votes are counted," Susan said. "Everything could change."

"Everything *will* change," her mother said. "We have the vote. I am as confident of it as I can be."

"I thought you were predicting defeat," Susan said.

"I have never thought of it," her mother declared. "Never. I knew our time had come at last. Now that we have the West, the eastern states will quickly come to terms. They cannot evade progress forever."

She sat up straighter in bed and shook her shoulders, exactly like a bird ruffling its feathers. "I will live to see that day," Rebecca said, "when women everywhere will have the vote. I intend to live that long."

"Will you go and vote this next year?" Fred asked.

"Of course," she said. "I will be the first in line. Everyone will have to give me room. I have waited almost forever."

Book IV
Stretched to the Limits

Chapter 16
1916: The Winning Plan

Lucy Phillips still lived in the settlement house, but she no longer worked there. She had struggled long enough with the poor families of the tenements to see that they would not be erecting a Lucy Phillips statue in Washington Square. The never-to-be statue, she mused to herself, would have had little grateful orphaned children spread around her feet, one of them perhaps holding a dog. In bronze they would be delighted with her attentions.

That's a rather bitter thought, she said to herself and tried to come back to the meeting. A blond, clean-shaven male of about her age was reading advertising copy aloud. His name was Stephen Gould. He had a wife and two children—two girls. He often flirted with Lucy, and twice he had invited her out for lunch. Because she turned him down, he accused her of being a cold fish.

Settlement house work could be as interesting as you chose to make it, but she guessed she was not the type to gain endless interest in pushing a stone uphill. Her one great triumph had been a group of Italian and Jewish girls who acted out parts of Shakespeare—a remarkable achievement no doubt. She might help a family here and there, but the tenement smelled the same.

She did not like Stephen Gould. Like many of the advertising executives she worked with, he seemed to expect a bronze statue to be erected in honor of his genius at writing copy for corn flakes. The meeting went on around a large oak conference table, in a room that looked over Manhattan. All the windows were open, for it was a muggy late-summer day. Susan was not listening very much, nor did she need to. She could happily have glided to the window and put her elbows on the sill, looking down at the street far below with its carriages and buggies and automobiles maneuvering like boats without oars. From this height the horses looked like some species of crawling thing. Lucy could see all the way to the East River, where the tall creamy sails of schooners loomed over the tops of buildings.

She had grown a little jaded with the settlement house until, at one of her mother's dinner parties, she was offered a job in advertising. Now she had grown bored with that. Advertising was full of self-important theorizing about scientific motivation. People talked as though, from these Manhattan meetings, they steered America's mind. But it came down to nothing more than selling things.

Lucy knew, and felt, that she was an impossible combination of incompatible impulses. On the one hand, she scorned the drive to make reputations, whether in settlement work or in advertising. She detested the egos. On the other hand, she continued to chafe against the mundane. She still felt, as she had told her aunt so long ago, that she wanted to do something.

Lucy's mind wandered to Mrs. Catt. All along Lucy had kept working at woman suffrage. For last year's New York referendum—which failed badly, after they had thought victory sure—she had overseen press relations for Mrs. Catt. The disappointment had sapped all her energy for the cause, but at lunch hour today a remarkable thing had happened.

Mrs. Carrie Catt, newly elected president of NAWSA, had invited her to headquarters at Thirty-second and Madison, where she asked Lucy to go to Washington. She wanted Lucy to quit her job, to live on charity, so she could work at a final crusade for a national suffrage amendment.

Catt was a tall, silver-haired woman, who sat with perfect posture and gave the impression of impeccable and gracious control. One of the young suffrage workers had told Lucy the gibe that Mrs. Catt was born wearing a corset and a blue hat.

"I have been eagerly seeking information from every state in the Union," Catt told Lucy. "I have sent detailed questionnaires to all our state officers. It is my conviction that we have come to a point of crisis. I want to see a federal amendment to the Constitution within the next presidential administration. I believe we can do it if we move quickly and strongly with absolute organization and complete efficiency."

The woman represented Industrial Suffrage: brilliantly organized, ruthlessly decisive. She had run most of the successful state campaigns and had no use for the old, lazy style, the Ladies' Tea and Debate Society, as some of the younger women called it.

Lucy wondered what her aunt Susan would say to this offer. Aunt Susan had gone to South Dakota when she was Lucy's age. No, younger. Her mother had paid her way, Susan had said. But had it been the right thing? Lucy recalled only a wistful, ironic tone that her aunt maintained whenever she spoke of the trip. She seemed rather proud of her associations with the great Saint Susan, but skeptical of her own motivations. "I thought I was giving my hand in marriage to the association," she wrote to Lucy once. "It wasn't until I married Fred that I realized what a poor husband the association made."

Lucy admired Catt. She believed in the cause. But she had been with a great many idealists and was increasingly unsure about giving her life away to anybody. She had told Mrs. Catt she would have to think about it.

———

Woodrow Wilson was an impeccably dressed slender man, making his way with perfect ease between a gauntlet of suffragists clad in white, each with a golden sash across her chest, each bearing aloft the banner of her state. It was a remarkable moment for those privileged to view Wilson as he proceeded into Atlantic City's New Nixon Theater. They could feel an almost audible rush of air in the room, as though it were a lung expelling oxygen held in for too long.

Many of the women present had never heard in their homes a kind word spoken for a Democrat. Still they felt the power and the titillation of seeing the president. They had all seen his photo in the newspapers, and many of them had been to a nickelodeon where they could witness him as a living creature—a moving creature at least, his life flickering on the screen. But very few had ever heard Wilson's voice or seen him in the flesh.

For four years he had done his best to ignore suffrage. When he was newly elected, he said he had no opinion—he claimed not to have thought of it. Then he said that as the mere head of his party, he must leave the issue to be decided by the party regulars. Then he said that it was a state matter, in which the federal government could not interfere. Like many political men, he was sympathetic, knowledgeable, open-minded, and completely unconcerned that women were discounted in a democracy.

Nevertheless he had come to see them now, in the thick of a presidential election. Never before in sixty years of suffrage conventions had a president addressed them. Once, Taft had greeted them for ten minutes and had said nothing. Wilson asked to listen to the full evening's program, which he surely would not do if he intended to ignore them. As Wilson took his seat on the stage, behind the potted palms, under the gorgeous banners, surrounded by a cordon of Secret Service agents, surrounded also by a vast, attentive host of intelligent women all clad in white, every eye watched him with both hope and fear.

Lucy Phillips had never seen a president either, and what she saw in that hushed room was a distillation of will. *Not power*, Lucy thought. Wilson had nothing brutal or forceful about him, but distilled will, the will of millions of men who had chosen one man to be their will, so that in the most bloodless and intellectual form possible, in the soundless hush of shuffled paper, as though in a library through a single speaking voice instead of a shouting mob, a whole continent of men (and women, too) bent in one direction. It was a glorious and frightening thing to see a man so full of will.

They all wanted to hear from this will, but they all had to listen, with Wilson, to a corps of speakers. "The Call of the Workingwoman for the Protection of the Woman's Vote," Mrs. Raymond Robins. "Mothers in Politics," Miss Julia Lathrop. "A Necessary Safeguard to Public Morals," Dr. Katharine Bement Davis. "Working Children," Dr. Owen R. Lovejoy. They all said, in one way or another, that America's problems demanded that women add their will to the general democracy. Who knew the world better than women?

Then, introduced by Mrs. Catt, Wilson stood to speak. Catt had put Lucy at the correspondents' table, theoretically so she could answer any questions from the press, but really so that she could be close to the heartbeat of the convention. Lucy had still not committed to Mrs. Catt, but she was flattered that Mrs. Catt pursued her. Lucy liked being there among men who looked bored and who frequently pulled out pocket watches, not caring who saw them do it. They seemed a fit with her own skepticism. But even they sat up and paid attention when the president spoke.

Wilson spoke intelligently. He made the point that America had been established as a kind of legal machine, with checks and balances meant to keep the pieces from flying apart. Now, however, the key questions were social ones, Wilson said—more moral and spiritual than legal. He thought that there was no stopping this change and that the suffrage movement was part of it. He didn't commit himself to a thing, but he managed to convey the idea that he was on their side because he thought history was on their side, and therefore, it was just a question of time.

"Almost every other time that I visited Atlantic City I came to fight somebody," he said. "I hardly know how to conduct myself when I have not come to fight anybody but with somebody." He said this last sentence with punctuation, so they knew they were meant to take it in and to applaud it. Then he said that they needed to be patient. Actually he said, "I have not come to ask you to be patient," but he did. "It is all very well to run ahead and beckon," he said, "but after all, you have got to wait for them to follow."

The applause was hearty and sustained, a deep thunder that penetrated Lucy's mind more than the speech had. *So Wilson will not fight against us,* she thought, *but then he never has fought against us. He has done worse; he has patronized us.*

Mrs. Catt asked Anna Shaw to respond. She was quite old, and her bright red hair had dimmed into an indeterminate dull gray that swallowed light. She had suffered a great deal of criticism while president of the association. Now that she was out of the leadership, it was possible to again appreciate her great bitter emotional appeals. The woman could speak. She referred to the president's last words, that they could "afford to wait a little while longer." Then she described the movement and all its frustrations over the generations. "We have waited *so* long, Mr. President! We have dared to hope that our release might come in your administration and that yours would be the voice to pronounce the words to bring our freedom."

She paused then, looking behind her directly at Wilson. Quite spontaneously, with no sound but a vast, muffled rustling from thousands of dresses, the audience began to rise. In a few seconds they were all standing, except the reporters, who twisted their heads to look around them. Not a word was said, but every face said plainly and wordlessly, "Mr. President, we have indeed waited so long."

That was Anna Shaw, Lucy thought while she waited in the stuffy basement room of the Marlborough-Blenheim Hotel. Well-dressed matrons filled the room: the national officers, plus the president of each state delegation. They were all tired from a week of meetings, and it showed. Their faces looked doughy; they hardly spoke.

Miss Shaw, the master of oratory, had magically orchestrated that demonstration of mute female appeal, taking the breath of everyone present. For Shaw that was enough, an event to feast on for days and weeks and months, maybe for years. Shaw favored gestures, while Catt favored results. She was determined to use that moment like a whip, to drive them all forward.

So they were here. The faces looked exhausted, the color of tapioca. There was no elegance in this room with its low ceiling and wooden chairs. It looked like a labor hall. Catt, who always cared about the details, the banners, sashes, plants, costumes, had decorated this room with only one item: a gigantic floor-to-ceiling map of the United States.

Yet when Mrs. Catt stood to speak, everyone would have thought she had recently returned from a holiday in Maine. Her blue dress—she always wore blue—looked fresh, her silver hair impeccable. She had a sheaf of typed papers. (Lucy had typed them herself; like all the older women, Catt assumed any younger woman could type.) Catt stood at the podium straight and precise, making no lighthearted remarks about the convention or references to how tired they must all be. She went straight into her analysis of the situation and into what she called the Winning Plan. What it came down to was: organize on all fronts.

That was her way. Miss Anthony would have spoken to inspire. Mrs. Stanton's speech would have crackled with ideas. Those women were dead and gone. Catt was an organizer. Every state organization would have a job to do. Those westerners who already had the vote would see resolutions passed in their legislatures asking for the federal amendment. States that had a reasonable chance of winning a suffrage referendum—where the machine politicians and the liquor interests were not so strong that they could steal the election—would try to gain the vote on a state level. Other states, particularly in the South, would be better off taking on doable tasks, such as winning the right to vote in primaries. Each state would work to galvanize its locality behind suffrage, thus putting pressure on Washington. No state would decide on its own what to do, for they must all work together. Meanwhile a highly organized effort in Washington would endeavor to convince the Congress. Mrs. Catt's eyes lit on Lucy when she said this, although it would have been impossible to say whether she did so intentionally.

Having typed the speech, Lucy knew exactly what Mrs. Catt would say, and it was dry as dust. No humor, no brilliant language, no memorable phrases, just plans and dates and strategies. Catt hardly looked at her text, but she stuck close to it nonetheless. She went to the map and pointed out states like a schoolteacher. Hadn't she once been a schoolteacher?

It gradually became apparent to Lucy and to the whole room that they were hearing one of the great speeches of their lives. Catt's words were not elegant, but her bearing was. She spoke with a conviction that would drag them all with her to win. The listless, shapeless crowd of women gradually stiffened. They were witnessing a battle queen calling on her army. Catt had brains and organization to impose her will not only on them but also on the entire country. If only they would work, and work together, with a fierceness to match her own.

She swore them all to secrecy. No one outside the room need know anything except what pertained directly to the work. They would stir so much energy and fight in so many places, their enemies would not know where to stand.

And one thing must be absolutely clear. Catt said it as though only a fool could fail to see it. There would be no more independence. Each state, each officer of each state, must do her part. If someone could not do the work because of family inconvenience, she must be quickly replaced. No one would freelance. They would all sign on to the Winning Plan.

She said it pleasantly. She meant it literally. She had a paper she wanted each state to sign: a solemn compact to adhere to the plan. It would take thirty-six states to pass the amendment. She required at least thirty-six states to sign the compact. She would leave no time for deliberations. They must decide now. If they did not begin their work tomorrow, they would be unable to complete it in the necessary time. They must decide.

One by one, women walked up to the table. Soon they had a line of exhausted women, waiting to take up the pen. Lucy was not one of them. She represented no one but herself. All the same, she had made up her mind. She was won over not so much by Mrs. Catt's impeccable logic as by Mrs. Catt herself. Every commitment is personal, in the final analysis, and Lucy knew she could not do other than to follow the magnificent Mrs. Catt.

Chapter 17
1916: The House from Sears

Susan Konicek usually read mail in the kitchen, spreading the pages over the kitchen table. Today, though, the table shook. Tom had brought his girlfriend, Dorothy, home, along with another couple, and they were playing the Victrola and practicing the waltz. They had not learned to do it gracefully. Susan was not sure they wanted to dance gracefully. Susan thought they were closer to what she had called, when Tom was small, "outdoor play."

Her niece, Lucy, had written a long and complicated letter about the convention she had attended in Atlantic City, raising as many questions as she seemed to answer. Susan got up and looked through the doorway into the living room. The furniture and the rug had been pushed out of the way. The two couples laughed and whirled. As any mother would, Susan felt proud to see her son so happy.

About Dorothy, Susan had reservations. *Tommy likes her because she likes him,* Susan thought. She was fun. Reasonably pretty, too, with smooth dark hair around an oval face, an old-fashioned look for a very modern girl. Since Tom had completed high school a year ago, he had helped his father and done odd jobs for the neighbors. Susan wanted him to go to Berkeley and get more education. He needed a challenge, and that was partly the problem with Dorothy. She was smart enough to know that if he went to Berkeley, he would not come back to her.

Susan's mother had bought the Victrola. She saw in the gramophone the greatest cultural innovation since movable type. To hear Caruso in your living room: How could the world carry on unchanged? Even as she passed eighty years, Rebecca continued as the greatest progressive, always hopeful of the next invention. How many gadgets did they have as a result of her mechanical optimism?

Maybe we should have left Grandma in the parlor, Susan thought ruefully, *instead of moving her into the back bedroom with Becky.* She smiled at the thought of the couples waltzing roughly around her mother's bed. Then we'd have no dancing. More Caruso.

I wish we had a gadget to make more space in this house, Susan thought. She gathered up the pale lemon pages of Lucy's letter and went out the kitchen door, heading for the shed. At one time it had held cows and a mule, then chickens; lately it had been converted into a bunkhouse that Tom and George and their grandfather shared.

The shed was dark, lit by only one high window on the north side. Susan paused to let her eyes pick reality out of the bands of light and shadow, the rafters and the bunks. The boys kept a table for schoolwork where she could sit and read.

Then Susan heard the sound of a sleeping body: a soft, repeating, wheezing sigh, languorous as a summer's day. She picked her way through the drifts of boxes and tools and discarded clothes until she could see her father's gray head. Well, his snoring would not disturb her. Her shadow, however, ran over his head, and the change of light woke him, coughing. He smiled before sitting up. "Susan, oh, Susan," he said fondly. "I was taking a little nap. I tire these days. Did you come looking for me?"

She still did not know how to call him, after five years of living together. She could not bear Father, even less Dad, while Paul or Mr. Netherton seemed impossible. So for the most part she called him nothing at all. It was enough that she fed him. He didn't deserve that.

"No," Susan said, "I came looking for some privacy."

He saw the letter in her hands. "To read something?" he asked. "Come along. You won't bother me."

"But you would bother me," she said. "I don't like to have an audience."

"Something close to the heart, then," her father said. She ignored him and stumbled back out the door, blinking in the light, clutching the letter, and looking hopelessly at the house. She was not a lover of the outdoors. Nonetheless she found herself crouched in a hideaway, under a shrub, bare scraped dirt beneath her feet. Becky liked to hide here, Susan knew. In a hollow under the gray-green foliage of the hedge, a refugee from her own house, she found peace to read Lucy's letter.

At six o'clock she heard the car, and then, after the car doors slammed shut, the sound of Fred's and George's voices. She could guarantee they were talking about cars or airplanes. Tom and his friends had stopped dancing, but they still played the Victrola. Its high, crackling energy made it hard to think.

"Biscuits?" Fred asked as he came in the kitchen, smelling the air. "Guess what a Ford car is selling for? Three hundred and sixty dollars. That's half what I paid. Less than half. It looks like if we wait long enough, they'll be giving them out as raffle prizes."

"That's what they're worth, Dad," George said. He loved to talk cars with his father, though he was naturally quieter than Tom, perhaps more like Susan in temperament. "I'd rather have a Packard any day."

"If wishes were Packards, we all would ride," Fred said. "Do you realize what they cost?"

"I don't understand how Henry Ford can pay his workers five dollars a day for just eight hours of work and sell the cars cheaper," Susan said. "How is that, Fred?"

"Oh, Mom, you're so old-fashioned," George said, leaning his lanky body against the windowsill. He had suddenly grown skinny, with legs like a crane's. "With Ford's assembly line they produce twice as many cars with the same number of workers. Everybody will be getting five dollars soon."

"Except the other half who are thrown out of work," Fred said. "It will be a long time before workers in Sonoma County get five dollars for a day of work. Maybe in San Francisco, if the Wobblies get control of the docks. If workingmen got five dollars, George, they wouldn't buy a Ford; they'd want a Packard. And then we'd be back to the beginning all over again."

All of a sudden the noise from the gramophone combined with this rising and predictably pointless discussion to drive Susan toward the edge of madness. The walls seemed too close; they had too many large bodies and loud voices.

"Could we stop talking about that?" she asked. "Who cares what Henry Ford pays his workers? Why should it make the slightest difference to me whether people buy Fords or Packers?"

George and Fred looked at her curiously. The music from the living room continued squalling.

"Fred, you promised when we moved here that we would add on. Instead we have added two grandparents, a Victrola, and a troupe of teenagers who are wearing out my ears. We should never have come here. We could have stayed in town and had room. Other people have plumbing. And electricity."

The Victrola came to the end of its song, but no one replaced the record. She had been louder than she realized. Until the words blurted out, she had not known that the house was what bothered her. Or perhaps it was not the house. Perhaps the house only caught her rampant anger, like a lightning rod.

"You get to go away every day in your Ford," she said to Fred. "I don't have any neighbors or any friends. I'm stuck here with . . ." She did not finish the sentence. She was stuck nursing two old people, but she was not ready to complain publicly about that.

"Susan," Fred said quietly, "anytime you want, you take the juice line into town. Take the whole day."

"I don't want the juice line! I don't want to go on an all-day excursion just to say hello to someone, or have a cup of coffee, or go to a meeting at the church. I'm lonely, can't you see that?"

"You want to move into town, Susan? I thought you said you wanted more space here." Fred looked at her like a dog trying to understand his master's command.

She did want to be in town, but she had spent so many years deferring to his preference, it had become a habit. She had made a truce with the country. Something had to change, something else. "I do. More space. I want us not to be so jammed in together."

"I don't . . . ," Fred began and then thought better of it. He reminded her of the biscuits, and while she took them out of the oven, they all made small talk and pretended that nothing had happened.

The next night he came home with the Sears house catalog, 150 pages of dreams to be ordered by mail, with every piece of lumber precut and every nail accounted for. Each house included an estimate of how many hours were needed to put it together.

At first Susan would not look at it. She said she was sorry for going off and please just ignore her. Fred got her to peruse the book, though, just for curiosity's sake, and the next day she spent much of the day leafing through it. Something in it enchanted her. The plans seemed to pick you up out of your own mess and place you in a clean, uncluttered space. You felt modern and efficient just looking at the pictures. Sears included testimonials from people who had built the houses. They said it was easy because the directions covered every step. They said they had saved hundreds of dollars over what a house would cost built the regular way. They said all you needed was to be able to hammer a nail and to read.

That night they all looked it over around the kitchen table, long after the dishes were dried and put away. The children jerked the book out of each other's hands, comparing favorite models. Their grandfather went off into stories about the house he had lived in once made completely out of portland cement. Rebecca insisted loudly that none of the houses were adequate: they were all too plain and too small.

They settled on a five-room bungalow. The clean lines appealed to Susan, and Fred pointed out that they needed just that amount of space. "That way Becky can raise her geese in the shed, and the boys can move inside."

"You ought to rent this place and live in the new house," Rebecca said, as though it were already built.

At that, Susan's heart took a deep plunge toward the floor. "We might as well all live on the third story of this house," she said. "Which doesn't exist any more than that Sears house does. It costs eight hundred and fifty dollars." She backed her chair out and stood up. "I don't know if it's a good idea to dream."

She wondered what the urgency was anyhow. Was it really so bad that the boys and her father lived in the shed? It was cold, but they did not seem to mind. Becky shared a room with her grandmother, but so did half the girls in Santa Rosa. The house was a little tight, but it was a passing phase. Tom would be gone soon, and so would the other children before they knew it. So, for that matter, would her mother and father. They were both in their eighties. She was the one who had started this, by complaining. What was the matter, truly? She wanted to apologize for bringing it up, but she could not bring herself to that.

That night Fred was quiet as he prepared for bed. He usually chattered about his day, but he completed his ablutions and then sat, in his nightshirt, on the edge of their bed. "What are you waiting for?" Susan said a trifle impatiently. "Blow out the light."

"Susan, your mother has the money. She could lend us enough to buy a house and furnish it too."

"We don't need furniture," Susan said. "We have so many things that came from the boardinghouse."

"All right," he said.

"How do you know what money she has?"

"She sold the boardinghouse. I know she got cash for it."

"Think how many gadgets she has bought. The Victrola."

"Sure, and the washing machine. But I think she has a good bit more, and what is she saving it for?"

"Maybe she wants a large headstone."

Fred laughed. "About the size of the Washington Monument?"

"Maybe."

"Susan, Tom could do the building. It would be good for him, while he waits."

"While he waits for what?" She had been unaware that something lay on Tom's horizon.

"He says he doesn't want to start anything—college or anything—until the war in Europe is over. He wants to join the army if we get in there."

That was a painful revelation for Susan. She did not trust Wilson—could not trust any Democrat—but she gave him credit for keeping them out of that horrible slaughter. Suffrage women were for peace, not officially but quite certainly. Susan did not know how she would bear it if Tom went to war. The thought of it raised in her the angry helplessness of being a woman. They said women should have their influence in their own homes. But what influence could she have, with warmongers in Congress, and her own son hiding his intentions from her? What influence that mattered?

She sometimes thought of that first election day in 1912. Her mother had spent hours dressing in a sober maroon dress, and she herself had despaired of going to vote in a cotton dress. What had they expected, that the earth would move when they marked their ballots? That Prince Charming would leap out of the ballot box and take them away to a glass castle? They had marched to the school to vote, very conscious of being watched, and almost hoping, mother and daughter together, that someone would try to prevent them from using their new right. But everyone treated them decorously. The mayor was there to tip his hat at them. If someone snickered, he did it behind their backs. It had been so simple, to mark the ballots and drop them in, that afterward Susan said to her mother, "What made them think that voting was so difficult a woman could not do it?"

She had expected a sense of power, and instead the vote seemed to underline the insignificance of her life. She dropped her ballot in the box, and it literally disappeared.

"Even if my mother has the money," she said, "how do we get it from her? You know how she operates. She just buys things and presents them to us. God help us if she buys a house like that."

"I thought you could talk to her," Fred said. "I could do it, but it would be better coming from you. She is your mother."

The plans came first, delivered by the rural postman in a large, long package, wrapped in brown paper with thick wads of packing tape. Susan would not open them, so they sat on the kitchen table all day. "It's your house," she told her mother. "You should look." Rebecca, however, did not choose to show an interest. When Susan's father came in for his lunch, he saw the package and asked her why didn't they open it. Susan told him to leave the package alone; it had nothing to do with him.

She felt just slightly afraid of the plans. They represented a liberality and an innovation that they had chosen to seize rather than to wait. It felt risky to Susan—not the house itself but the changes it might bring to their family. They had made do for so long. Now, because of her going off, they were launching into this gigantic project with no idea what good (or bad) might come of it.

Although Tom intended to do the building, Fred and George pored over the sheets, scribbling notes on squares of butcher paper. They had long discussions about how to site it, which rooms to catch the morning sun, how near to their current house to place it. At first this pulled them out of the kitchen and onto the front porch with the plans stretched over the floor, weighed down with the broom and some serving spoons. Soon they had picked up rocks and sticks and placed them in a line where the house could go. Then they had knotted three pieces of string together and used stakes knocked out of an old piece of redwood fencing to mark the perimeter they would follow. Tom and Dorothy came and went without seeming much to notice.

Two weeks later they got notice that the house had arrived. Tom drove the Ford to the station while Fred borrowed a wagon to haul the stuff. The pieces made a substantial pile in the freight yard: long bundles of lumber, wooden boxes of nails and screws and hardware. Fred went clambering over it, inspecting jubilantly. "Look here," he shouted. "Here are the numbers." On the rough side of the lumber, numbers had been branded to match the directions for assembly. "Oh," Fred said, "I think we can do this. I think it definitely can be done."

Rebecca remained in the back of the Ford, surveying the piles. She rapped on the car door until she had Fred's attention. "Are you sure you've got the whole house there?" Rebecca asked. "It doesn't look nearly big enough for eight hundred and fifty dollars."

By the time they had the house piled up next to its site, it was hard to imagine how they could ever make it stretch itself into an honest house. The parts seemed puny next to the space contained by the string and stakes. (Though that, too, seemed tiny to Susan's eye. Fred made her walk off the dimensions of their current domicile and compare them to the new site in order to convince her that the rooms would be ample.) Next morning Fred reluctantly went off to work, George and Becky to the high school, and Tom began to dig. He dug steadily all day—Susan had never seen him work that way—in an unhurried rhythm, trenching out the foundation. At the end of the first day he seemed to have moved not very far.

Just so the second day, and the third. A trench is a trench. They had opted for a stone foundation, and Fred went to barter directly with the stonecutters who lived in boardinghouses in the Mayacama foothills just on the east side of Santa Rosa. They traded—foundation blocks, imperfect, for a year's fresh vegetables. Fred was very proud of the deal. It made him feel substantial, that his reputation was good to purchase stone blocks on a promise. The blocks were loaded on a wagon in small lots and pulled the eight miles into one side of town and out the other. Tom wrestled them into place with a crowbar and a pulley chain. By the end of the second week he had it done, a neat, level rectangle of rough black stone, making a wall a few inches off the ground. Susan saw Becky

walk it like a tightrope and on a whim did the same herself. Very satisfying she found it, to walk the perimeter and think that she had surrounded her domain.

In three days the walls were up. Tom recruited his mother's help to
stand them up until she suggested that his grandfather could do it perfectly well. Paul had been standing around watching and smoking; he
had offered suggestions when Tom was digging the foundation. As
soon as Tom began using his help, he was fully engaged, going for
whatever tool Tom said he needed, searching the hardware boxes for
the correct piece.

It was the most exciting event in the history of their farm. The children came home eagerly from school each day, wanting to see what had
changed. Tom would give an evening tour, tired as he was, and his
grandfather would embellish the story. Together they walked through
the skeletal rooms—they had no floors or siding yet—and talked about
what would go where, how the furniture would fit, what views would
be available from the windows, and how cozy it would be. Tom was
building it tight, he said, so not the slightest breath of fog could find its
way inside.

Susan received several long letters from her niece, Lucy. They were
notable in Susan's life because she did not feel the same fierce need for
solitude to read Lucy's letters and concentrate her thoughts there. The
house building had worked a change, perhaps only temporary but still
remarkable: Susan did not want to be released from her own life. Lucy
asked for advice, but Susan did not know how to give any. Yes, long ago
she had gone off to South Dakota with Susan B. Anthony, but the cases
did not seem parallel. She had left no job, had given up nothing at all.
She was glad she had seen a little of the world, but Lucy's situation was
completely different.

How could Susan evaluate the importance of the campaign? The struggle for the vote seemed far off, not just because Californians already had the vote, but also because voting had come with no revolutionary results. It seemed ridiculous, impossible that California women had been barred from the polls for so long. Once allowed into the secret club, they had found it quite drab inside.

Mrs. Catt wanted Lucy in Washington, at the nerve center of the campaign. It meant living off her mother, Lucy said, because they had no paid positions on the staff. Most of the women had means of their own.

When Susan read that, buried in the second letter, she knew that she would never do it. She rebelled against the idea of appealing to Elizabeth for funds. *My reaction might not be right*, she thought, *but it is surely my reaction.* She wrote as much to Lucy, but she said she could give her no advice. She only pointed out to Lucy that she was young, and whether or not she chose well, she would get other chances.

By late November the house stood unpainted and raw, but real. The piles of lumber were reduced to scraps, and the new facade looked too good to be true, like something in the catalog. Though Tom worked just as much each day, he was now out of Susan's sight inside the house. The family had begun to take for granted the new shape in the yard, to go by it without marveling at its existence. Susan, however, liked to sit on the front porch and admire the neat newness of the place. She felt like a girl who gets her first new dress after a lifetime of hand-me-downs.

Everything else on the farm looked worn out by the long dry season: the blackberry bushes in a dusty coma, the wild grass along the lane dried up in clumps and tatters, ruts in the road worn smooth and filled with tan powdery dust. The first cold fronts blew through, a day of dark clouds interrupting the ordinary rhythm of morning fog and afternoon sunshine. Tom knew that he must get the roof on the new house soon because the rains might come. He was cranky, tired of working, ready to finish. He had never thought that Wilson could win the election. Now that he had, the chances of war seemed remote, and his future strung out into the unknown. Tom ought to have wanted the building to last because he had no activity to replace it, but that is not how it is with waiting.

When he began work the last Monday in November, Tom felt something unusual as he entered the house. His first thought was that a skunk or a porcupine had come in the back door, which still lacked hardware. He found no wild creature, however, but his grandfather bunked out in the back bedroom. Paul Netherton lay fast asleep, a silver gristle across his cheeks, his mouth puckered around the empty space for his false teeth. He had made a bed out of several quilts. One arm cradled his head, holding a bundle of quilt for his pillow.

He did not wake his grandfather, but when the old man wandered into the front room where Tom was nailing the door trim, Tom asked about his bed.

"I got in a fight with the missus," Netherton said and laughed at his own joke. "Of course we got in that fight forty years ago. No, Tom, I thought I would guard the house."

"From what?"

"From intruders."

"We don't have any intruders out here, Pops. We're out in the country. If anybody accidentally happens out here, we set an extra place for dinner."

"But you have a beautiful house now, and you can't be so careless. Don't worry, sonny, I'm going to sleep out here from now on. I don't mind the floor. I've slept on worse, believe me." He was ready to begin reminiscing, but Tom went back to hammering.

When Tom mentioned it to his mother, she asked whether he smelled whiskey.

"Not especially," he said. "No, I guess not. I didn't notice anything."

"Keep your eyes open," she said sardonically. "He wants to drink in there, I'd imagine."

Susan awoke in the darkness, pressed against Fred's solid form. Pale gray light came from the window. She thought it was the first dawn, but then saw a square of dim illumination on the floor. It was moonlight, pouring in the window.

She smelled smoke, which was not unusual. Apple farmers in the hills to the west of the farm burned their prunings, and in still weather the smoke would hang near the ground and creep down toward the laguna. Many times Susan had awakened to the smell and explored the dark kitchen to see whether everything was safe.

No light was necessary for her to go down the stairs and through the living room toward the kitchen. The house was chilly, and she wrapped her arms around herself. Outside she could see silverlit trees, like a photographic negative. The smoke was strong and sharp, and yet it did not worry her. She would sleep soundly once she had eliminated any cause.

Touching the black bulk of the stove, she found it cool to her fingers. Looking into the parlor again, she saw nothing but the shapes of chairs and sofa, the darkened silhouette of picture frames on the wall. Sometimes a wick would smolder, but that left a sootier, oily smell. This scent of smoke must come from outside.

She went to the west window to see whether some glow might be visible on the horizon. The gray sky met the black, rounded shape of the trees: no fire there. Something caught her eye, however, and she leaned closer to the window to look at the new house. It seemed that as she did so, the smell grew sharper—acrid, dry smoke.

Susan walked to the front door, turning open the lock and stepping quickly into the cool night air. The smell of the smoke struck her face. She began to trot, barefooted and hurting her feet on the stones and sticks and rough ground between houses. Then the rough unpainted wood of the new porch rubbed her soles. She slapped the door open, and smoke filled her nostrils. She shouted for Fred, but kept going forward. The place was unfamiliar and invisible. She kicked something, a board? She looked into the kitchen, saw nothing. Then to the bedrooms. In the darkness she could not find the door. Disoriented, she ran her hand along the wall. Her toe throbbed miserably where she had kicked whatever she had kicked. She felt her way ahead gingerly, afraid of locating anything with that swollen toe. She called again for Fred. Then she found the door, which swung open at a push. She sucked in a mouthful of acidic smoke that seared her lungs. Involuntarily she dropped to her knees and coughed violently. The smoke was less intense near the floor, though still bitter and choking.

She crawled across the room. "Fred!" she called out. "Fred!" Susan could still see no fire. Her hand found a living thing, pliable and yielding under her fingers, clothed in soft cotton cloth. It was an arm. She pulled on it and felt a slight tug of life in response. "Come on! Get up!" she cried to whoever it was, but the body gave no further sign. She had her eyes closed because the smoke was stinging and hot; perspiration streamed down her face, and she coughed continuously.

"Get up!" Susan shouted.

She tried to pull but could not budge the form. Then she heard footsteps behind her, and her name called out. "Fred!" she cried, and he found her in the dark. They were both coughing in concert. "Fred, help me," she said.

"What?" he asked. "Where is the fire?"

"I don't know. There's someone here." She put Fred's hand on the arm, and immediately he pulled and made the body roll and slide toward him. Susan found a piece of a shirt to grab, and together they pulled the loose, flopping body out into the hall. Its muscles began to tighten and flex under her hand. It began to groan.

"Keep going," Fred said. "Let's get him into the front room."

Just that moment Tom came in with a lantern. They could suddenly see. The hallway was crowded with their bodies. The form they held was her father's.

Fred got up out of his crouch and took the lantern from Tom's hand. He went into the bedroom again; they heard him coughing and choking. "Oh, my!" he shouted in a voice halfway between anger and despair. They heard dull pounding, as if he was beating on something. "I need help!" he cried. "Come here, Tom!" Tom sprang to his feet and disappeared in the door. Susan heard the double-hung window go up, then the two men shouting. "There!" Fred yelled, as though in anger.

"Fred," Susan cried urgently, "come and help me get Pops out. I can't manage him!"

Fred came slowly back in with the lantern, coughing violently. "Let him lie there," he said when he caught his breath. "It's safe now." He knelt beside her father and with one hand turned the face to look at it. "He breathed a lot of smoke, I imagine."

"What happened to the fire?" Susan asked.

"It was his bedding. It wasn't yet in flames, but smoldering. As soon as I picked it up, it burst into flames. We threw it out the window."

"Do you think it could light a fire outside?" Tom said as he came out.

"I don't know. I guess you better check."

Tom went out, and Susan threw herself into Fred. "Easy," he said. "Don't knock me down. Let's go outside until this smoke clears."

"How did it happen?" Susan asked when they were standing on the porch. Her whole foot was throbbing now, and she could feel the stickiness of blood underneath her toe when she walked. "How did he catch on fire?"

"He fell asleep smoking, I would imagine," Fred said.

When her father awoke, Susan left him to Fred. She was stiff with fury, so she stayed in the distance, getting a cloth and basin so he could wash himself, finding a change of clothes among his few neatly folded possessions in the shed. Tom had gone back to bed, his face thick with the heaviness of sleep. The others never awakened.

Eventually, when she had done everything she could think of, Susan sat down and listened to Fred and her father. Paul had finally stopped his hacking. He was telling Fred about close calls he had known, about fires that had devoured buildings, about a time he had seen a fire roar through a post office but had been powerless to stop it. Fred listened, hardly commenting.

Susan seethed until she could stand it no longer. "Don't you realize what you've done?" she asked her father in a sharp voice. "Are you so stupid, you don't even know it?"

Her father raised his face. He did look stupid.

"What were you doing in there?" she asked. "Did somebody tell you to sleep in there? You're like a child that needs watching."

He still looked stupidly at her, saying nothing for once.

"Do you even know?" she insisted. "Why were you sleeping in the new house? Did you have some reason, besides whiskey?"

"I wasn't drinking, honey."

"I'm not your honey. You don't even know what you did. You nearly burned our house down and killed yourself. Nobody would care about you, but the house is precious to our hearts. You can't take that away from us."

"We're a little upset now," Fred said, apparently to nobody.

"Somebody needs to be," Susan said.

"Susan," Fred said. He used a tone that she rarely heard.

"I'm going back to bed," she said. "Make sure he doesn't have any matches."

When she lay under the covers, she could not relax her body. The silver light still shone through her window, unperturbed by the near destruction or by the cold steel hatred in her heart. She found herself shivering violently from something other than the cold. Maybe she loved that house too much.

Fred came in and slipped into bed beside her. She could feel that he, too, was still and waiting.

"Where is he sleeping now?" she asked.

"He went back to the shed," Fred said.

"Did you make him give you his matches?"

He did not answer immediately. "He's an old man," Fred said eventually.

"So it's all right if he burns down our house?"

"No, I didn't say that. He's too old to change now, Susan. What's the point?"

"What's the point of what?"

"What's the point of shouting at him? He's an old man."

She felt that she could almost see red cones of light flaring out from her eyes as they stared up at the dark ceiling. "Fred," she said, "he was this way as a young man. All my life he's been carelessly destroying. He's taken what is dear to me."

Fred shifted in bed so that he faced her. He dropped his voice lower, into a whisper. "What did he take? What have you done without?"

Susan shifted her fury to him. "What have I done without? Without a father. Without a family life that was normal. I grew up with nothing, Fred. How can you even ask that?"

She reached out her hand and caught his, holding it tight against her neck. "Say something. Please. What are you thinking?"

He spoke haltingly, in the tone of a little boy whose feelings are hurt. "We all grew up without some things," he said. "Nobody is ever going to make up for those missing things, Susan."

She held his fingers so tightly that she knew she hurt him, though Fred did not protest. "I want this house so much, I can dream about it. Do I want it too much? Tell me, because I don't know. Is it wrong? I feel somehow as though it will make up for a lot, not for all the missing pieces, but for a lot. If that old man burns down my house, I'm ready to kill him. I know he didn't mean it, but he's done that all my life. He never meant anything, but he always does it."

Fred put his arms around her and wrapped her tight in the quilt. "The house isn't going to make our lives any different, Sue. We'll fill up those rooms with ourselves. I wish . . ." He trailed off, and though she waited for him to finish, he fell silent.

"You wish what?" she said finally.

He breathed a deep sigh. "I wish I knew how to make you happy. I feel you can't be gentle, Sue, gentle with yourself, let alone your old dad."

She got up out of bed and sat in the kitchen until dawn, telling herself that she had been wronged. How could he say such a thing? In the new light she looked over at the new house, its lumber pale and fresh. She walked across and went through the rooms. The smell of smoke remained, but otherwise she had a hard time placing the dramatic, blind moments of the night. Spots of her blood were on the floor, though, in the regular shape of her big toe.

Susan knew that the intensity of her emotions would diminish if she could simply ride them out through the day, not saying anything unforgivable to anyone. She could manage. She had been managing all her life. That, however, was not the same as forgiveness. She did not see how she could begin to forgive the old man.

Quite without premeditation she found herself remembering Jesus' words when He was being killed. "Father, forgive them; for they know not what they do." How could He say that? How was it ever possible to say something like that?

Chapter 18
1917: Suffrage House

Go ahead," Mrs. Maud Park said with a smile, whereupon Lucy knocked hard on the dense mahogany door and then, after a few seconds' delay, turned the knob and entered.

Representative Stearns did not look up; he was leaning over his desk, running his finger along a document. "Yes," he said tonelessly. The large desktop was covered with papers.

"It's Mrs. Park, from the National American Woman Suffrage Association," Lucy's companion said in a musical way. "I have brought along my newest associate, Miss Lucy Phillips. She hails from your part of New York. I wonder whether this is a good time to apprise you of our cause, or whether you want to suggest another more convenient hour when we can return."

Stearns looked up, annoyance glinting in his eyes despite a fixed smile. He was a middle-aged man, balding in front, his face round and smooth and pale, especially set off against his very black hair.

"Now is as good a time as any," he said after a moment's doubt. "Why don't you ladies sit down?" He stood up reluctantly and gestured toward two straight oak armchairs. "Mrs. Phillips, did you say? What part of New York, Mrs. Phillips?"

"Miss Phillips. I grew up in White Plains, which I believe is your district. My parents are Samuel and Elizabeth Phillips."

He nodded sagely, as though to suggest he knew them well, when in fact he had no idea who they were. "Yes," he said, "and now, the winds have blown you to Washington. What a dreary fate for someone young and pretty like you."

"Thank you," she said. "I suppose like you, I did not come for the scenery."

"No," he said dolefully, "or for the weather." The room was chilly and dark, and outside the sky damp and gray and static.

"I came to Washington," Lucy said, "to take part in the most important battle for democracy our planet has ever known. I came to Washington because I believe in the ideals set forth in our Constitution, that the just powers of government derive from the people. I came because I hope to live to see our great ideal of democracy brought to fruition right here in my own country and in our time."

Mr. Stearns coughed awkwardly. Lucy had used that same little speech for three different appointments so far, and in each case it had managed to stupefy the congressman. She found it amusing to watch their reactions.

Mrs. Park pleasantly picked up the thread. "Mr. Stearns, you have told us in the past that at this time you are not likely to vote in favor of a federal amendment for woman suffrage." She was a middle-aged woman with weak eyes and a mild face, who wore a deep purple suit and a matching purple hat. In going around the Capitol with her, Lucy had been surprised to see how noncombative she was. Mrs. Park said they should avoid argumentation, for it rarely changed minds and more often hardened the position of a man who had given little thought to the issues.

"We know that you believe in fair-mindedness, however," Mrs. Park went on. "We hope that you will support us in our desire to see the amendment brought to a vote in the House of Representatives. As you know, the Rules Committee has refused to allow the matter to reach the floor."

Stearns stared gloomily up into the high ceiling. He had a baby face, and at the moment Lucy thought he looked like a very petulant baby. "Ladies," he said, "the idea of a representative democracy is that each citizen be represented. But only once! Once for each person! And ladies are already represented by their husbands. It wouldn't be fair for you to have another representative, now would it?" Stearns picked up a stack of papers and moved it to another location on the desk, where he tidied it with the flat of his hand.

"But I am unmarried," Lucy protested. "I have no husband to represent me."

"Well, then, your father. Until you marry, your father can represent you."

"My father has no interest in politics. He has not voted in twenty years, he tells me."

Stearns smiled in an attempt at chivalry. "Well, then, *I* will gladly represent you."

"I don't live in your district anymore."

"Never mind!" He said it with a little explosion. "You are determined not to understand, I see. You are not deceiving anyone, I assure you."

"We don't want to deceive anyone, Mr. Stearns." Mrs. Park was calm and musical. "We merely request an honest, up-or-down vote on the floor."

"Didn't you get an up-or-down vote in New York last year? And in Pennsylvania, and in New Jersey, and where else? What was the result? You have lost your bid in state after state, and you know as well as I do that sometimes you have tortured the voters by making them go through your campaign three or four times. Fairness! You've had your fairness, and more than fairness."

Mrs. Park kept her pleasant smile. She stood, and Lucy stood up, too, following her lead. "I hope we haven't taken too much of your time, Mr.

Stearns. Thank you for your willingness to consider these issues. We will keep in touch."

———————

Lucy's feet and calves ached; she seemed to have walked miles of marble corridors. Mrs. Park had led her from one office to the next, up and down unmarked stairways, following labyrinthine corridors until Lucy had no idea where she was. Now Lucy followed Mrs. Park scuttling down a flight of stairs and into a hidden alcove. Several plain wooden chairs were set in a corner there, apparently as a hidden lair.

"Let us sit down for a moment," Mrs. Park said. "I advise all our lobbyists to write down the results of their interviews as soon as they conveniently can. I had better follow my own advice." She took a notebook and a pencil from her purse.

"What is there to write?" Lucy said. "That Mr. Stearns is a rude barbarian?" Her feet hurt more now that she had taken her weight off them. She had enjoyed crossing swords with a congressman—who would have imagined her doing such a thing?—but had just begun to suspect that doing so was futile.

Mrs. Park looked up and smiled, then put a finger to her lips. "We can talk about that later on," she said. "Just now, let me put down my recollections."

When they were riding the trolley up Rhode Island Avenue, Mrs. Park sat close against Lucy and spoke into her ear. "We make it a rule never to talk in the Capitol buildings," she said. "Sound carries in those corridors, and you never know who might overhear. Representatives and senators can be very touchy."

The trolley wheels screeched and rumbled. The car swayed. "Do you encounter such rudeness very often?" Lucy asked.

Mrs. Park considered the question with a half-smile on her lips. "One learns very early on that our representatives are individuals, and they conduct themselves in surprising ways. Sometimes I think that I prefer a man who lets me know frankly where he stands, as Mr. Stearns does. So many of our representatives and senators just put us off.

"I think you can see why we find it so important for the state organizations to bring pressure to bear on their representatives. They listen when they hear from home because that is where their votes come from."

Suffrage House, where Lucy had settled, was a grand and uncomfortable residence on Rhode Island Avenue equipped with sixteen bedrooms and several large public rooms. A secretary of state had once been housed there; so had a European embassy. The mansion had vast and pretentious salons and dining rooms, closets that opened into secret passageways, tiny rooms in inconvenient and hidden locations. It could take days just to learn one's way through the many staircases.

Lucy had a large but bare bedroom on the third floor and a small, grubby room on the ground floor for her office. In both of them she thought she should wear mittens. It seemed impossible to heat the house. What she was meant to do in the office remained unclear, though she had arrived a week before. Catt had said she would serve as her communications officer, but Mrs. Catt remained in New York.

Ten ladies dined each evening in a little alcove off the grand, drafty dining room, and tonight, as every night this week, Alice Paul and her picketers were the main topic of conversation. Paul had headed the NAWSA work in Washington for several years, but now she had split off into something called the Woman's Party and was picketing the

White House. Lucy was taken aback by the venom expressed toward Miss Paul and her friend Lucy Burns.

She had never met either one, though she had seen them both from a distance at NAWSA conventions. Miss Burns, she knew, had preceded her at Vassar by a few years. Miss Paul she had heard of in the settlement house in New York—evidently she had been quite active there while Lucy was still in college. Both Paul and Burns had ended up in England, however, where they were active in the window-smashing, building-burning suffrage movement. Both Burns and Paul had been arrested. They had been force-fed through hunger strikes. Now they seemed determined to bring the same violent approach to America.

"I would like to know just what they expect President Wilson to do," a woman with a lacquered southern accent was saying. "Why target him, who has declared himself in favor of our movement?"

"Today at the Capitol," Mrs. Park said pertly, "we heard repeatedly that the picketers offended. Representative Bosnan said suffrage could go nowhere as long as such suffragists disgraced the nation. We told him that the picketers do not represent suffragists, but we couldn't get him to see. They all seem to know that Alice Paul was once in charge of our congressional work. No one has told them she has left the movement."

"Not the movement," Lucy corrected. "She has left our association." Lucy disliked the pettiness.

"When has anyone from our movement ever done such a thing?" a short woman with a narrow, yellow face asked. "To make such a spectacle against the president!"

"Not only our movement, but any movement. Do they think they are workers, picketing a factory?"

"Aunt Susan went to jail for voting," Lucy said. "That was disgraceful, you know." The table was quiet for a moment. Some of the women looked at Lucy suspiciously.

"I still do not understand why they want to oppose the president," the southern woman said again.

"Their theory," Mrs. Park said, "is drawn from England, where they hold the government in power responsible for the lack of suffrage legislation. According to Alice Paul, the Democrats are in power, so they should be held responsible for passing the suffrage amendment."

"But President Wilson openly favors the amendment. He cannot force men to vote for it, can he?"

"That is the fallacy of the argument," said Mrs. Park. "In the English Parliament, every member must vote with his party. Here in America a party is a much less cohesive organization."

"Even if every Democrat voted for the amendment, it would still not be enough for the two-thirds requirement."

"Totally insensible," a gray-haired woman muttered.

"They make idiots of us all," said another woman. "In the election they campaigned against Senator Steele, one of our staunchest supporters. What are they thinking, that our cause will be advanced if men see that even the friends of suffrage receive no mercy?"

The table laughed at the word *mercy*. As though women possessed enough power to show mercy or severity. As though politicians might fall at their feet begging for their forgiveness. The conversation moved on to the politicians the women had seen that day—for most of them were engaged in lobbying and had, like Lucy, wandered the Capitol hallways. Some of them did quite funny renditions of their interactions. The southern woman described chasing one Texas senator in and out of his office—all under the pretense of cordiality. Mrs. Park described Mr. Stearns's stupefaction when Lucy said her father hadn't voted in twenty years and therefore couldn't represent her. "He was very gallant, of course," Mrs. Park said. "He offered to represent Miss Phillips in place of her father. I didn't tell him that I am a widow and don't have a representative either. He might have offered to replace my husband."

———————

Most of the women at Suffrage House were older than Lucy. They were widows and divorcees and women unaccountably living apart from their husbands; or like Lucy, they had never married and had some source of independent income. No one was paid; in fact, everyone was charged room and board to live in Suffrage House. Most were college-educated, opinionated, capable women who had never before imagined a chance to influence anything outside a home, a church, or a club—certainly not a nation.

They shared an improbable conspiracy: this female band, this group of club women with hats and gloves, plotted to turn America. What was more, they felt a wild hope that they might succeed. Lucy found an unexpected, almost giddy hilarity. They all felt the tide running.

Lucy began her communications work in her third week, handling an unending stream of directives from Mrs. Catt in New York. Lucy produced pamphlets, wrote articles for the *Suffragist*, designed releases to send to the state organizations with directions on contacting the press. Mrs. Catt wanted to create an impression of ceaseless agitation. She wanted local suffrage organizations to create a solid wall of publicity; and she wanted this to interact seamlessly with the Washington lobby. But such a wave did not form itself; it required direction, and Carrie Catt was the soul of direction.

Lucy liked the work, and she liked the women—their intelligence, humor, and maturity. They were the epitome of a style she admired. Nevertheless Lucy felt the absence of Mrs. Catt. It was hard to keep the purpose of their work in mind without that blue-steel woman to embody it. Lucy remembered the advertising agency, where so much energy and pride were devoted to so mundane a process.

Out of curiosity, Lucy sometimes passed by the White House and saw the Woman's Party pickets. She was not the only one. Generally a small crowd huddled near the gate opposite Lafayette Park. Most days there were two picketers, dressed in white, sometimes with a yellow or purple sash. They held banners aloft bearing a message for the president. MR. PRESIDENT, WHAT WILL YOU DO FOR WOMAN SUFFRAGE? Another read, HOW LONG MUST WOMEN WAIT FOR LIBERTY? Nobody had ever picketed the president like this—it was the tactic of labor agitators. Yet the dress and bearing of the women indicated they were not working class. They were from the class of women presumed to be reasonable.

The cleverest banners were quotes from Wilson's book *The New Freedom.* LIBERTY IS A FUNDAMENTAL DEMAND OF THE HUMAN SPIRIT, read one. Who could complain if Alice Paul wanted to display Wilson's own words?

A lot of people expected that the picketers would be driven off by the police. They could hardly believe that the president tolerated them, practically on his front lawn. Evidently he decided it was best to ignore them, in hopes that they would grow discouraged. Alice Paul, however, had no intention of being ignored. After the first publicity died down, she began to designate special days: a day for college women to picket, a day for labor women, days for each of the states. Sometimes the picketers numbered dozens, and then the crowds of hecklers and tourists increased as well.

Lucy was most intrigued by the quietest days, however, when cold rain fell in sheets or a blustery wet wind came off the Potomac. The reflecting sidewalk, the cold bare limbs of trees, the empty expanse of the avenue fronting the black iron fence—sometimes in this bare vista Lucy would be sure that the women had abandoned the chore. But no, as she drew nearer to the gate she would see one and then another. She studied the forlorn, bundled shapes as she approached. She said a cheerful, "Good day," and smiled, but avoided their eyes.

One March afternoon, a gloomy and cold day, Lucy left her desk to go on the long walk down to the White House. She made it a regular routine. She wanted to get out, and the picketers were consistently interesting to her. A fog had descended over Washington streets. Automobile lights cast cloudy halos, and the cars themselves seemed vaguely ominous as they sped past Lucy, their tires sizzling.

By the White House there was little traffic. Official Washington had fled already. The residence seemed far off and dreamy in the gloom, a floating white hulk in the sea fog. When Lucy passed the north gate, she saw that the picketers were preparing to leave.

The woman closest to Lucy was tiny, struggling to hold up her end of a huge banner that had been soaked with the fog. She had on an ankle-length brown coat that did not make it easier for her. She looked up at Lucy. "Will you help me?" she asked.

Lucy went quickly to hold up the end of the banner pole. "Thank you," the woman said. "We're only going a block." Quite unexpectedly Lucy found herself marching alongside, holding up one end of the suffrage banner. She smiled when she thought what Suffrage House women would say if they saw her.

She knew already their destination because she had watched the picketers come and go across Lafayette Park. The Woman's Party had a house there.

The other end of the banner was held by a single tall woman; Lucy wondered how she managed it alone. The tiny woman next to Lucy, half a head shorter, tilted sideways as she struggled with the heavy burden. When they arrived at the house, they entered a large, bright room, full of overstuffed chairs, with a fire roaring in a massive fireplace. They carried the banner through this room into another, smaller chamber, where bolts of cloth and stacks of folded banners ran along the walls.

"We'll just lay this here for now," the small woman said and arranged the banner flat on the floor, letters down. "I'm afraid it will need to dry." She straightened up and looked at Lucy. "Thank you for your helpfulness. Would you come and sit by the fire to dry off a little?"

It took Lucy a moment to recognize the pale, calm features of Alice Paul. Lucy stuck out her hand. "I'm Lucy Phillips," she said. "I work at Suffrage House."

Paul betrayed a slight smile. "Then I should say thank you in double portions." She introduced herself and then the other woman. "This is Lucy Burns," she said, and Lucy got an athletic handshake from a very beautiful, tall, blue-eyed woman who had already thrown her coat off onto a chair.

"Will you come sit by the fire?" Paul asked again. She led into the front room and helped Lucy out of her coat. Burns did not follow, which Lucy regretted. She would have liked to study both of these interesting women, so physically different from each other. Lucy saw that Paul was even tinier than she had appeared in her overcoat. Her hands and arms were thin and delicate, almost doll-like. She sat sideways in her chair and looked at Lucy with the utmost concentration. A thick bolt of dark hair cradled a small, white face. *Her eyes have an unusual stillness to them,* Lucy thought. It was a face that people would either adore or want to escape.

Lucy thought Paul might never say anything, she was so still and concentrated. It was not in Lucy's mind to make small talk, but she spoke because she wanted to see how this tiny woman would respond. She wanted to hear her deep voice again. "I know you've fallen out with Mrs. Catt," Lucy said. "A lot of the NAWSA women have no time for you or your methods, but I myself am more of a distant admirer."

"Why distant?" Paul asked, her face betraying no reaction, only intense absorption. She spoke in the tones of a cello: a dark, velvet pool.

"I prefer logic to . . . to violent tactics. No, not violent, but hectoring. I think men are going to be better persuaded by the power of logic."

"Perhaps, if you get their attention. Why don't you think our tactics are logical?"

Lucy smiled. "You can't get much logic on a banner, even though you make some pretty big ones. But I like your banners, especially when you quote the president to himself. I'm thinking more of the logic of working to defeat representatives who are in favor of suffrage. That is not making much sense to the men I meet."

"They will understand it if they lose. They will understand that they should have worked harder to convince their party to support suffrage."

"What will you do if Wilson declares war?" Lucy asked. "Will you continue to criticize him?" Mrs. Catt had led several informal discussions, whether they would suspend political activities in the event Wilson called the nation to battle.

"Yes, all the more," Paul said. "That would be logical, don't you think? We would only ask him to be consistent, to fight for democracy at home as much as he does overseas."

This comment, stated in a matter-of-fact way, interested Lucy. She had been thinking that the charge of disloyalty would surely come if they kept pursuing suffrage after war was declared.

Lucy had the feeling that this was not just an exchange of views. Paul had no interest in the discussion except to get a glimpse of how Lucy thought. It made her suddenly uneasy. "I had better go," she said, standing up. "It wouldn't do for word to spread that I am in secret talks with Alice Paul."

Chapter 19
1917: Street Fight

On an almost weekly basis Susan Konicek received a letter from her niece, Lucy. The letters generally arrived on Thursday, expensive pale lemon envelopes addressed in a rounded, energetic hand, elegant totems from a world far from the farm. It was a happy moment for Susan whenever she first grasped these distinctive envelopes, not only because she loved to hear from Lucy, but also because her whole world and history seemed, for a moment, to come into focus. Her sister, Elizabeth, gave Lucy the stationery for her birthday each year, and Susan took it as an implicit message aimed at her. Surely Elizabeth knew that Lucy wrote frequently. Surely Elizabeth chose the yellow color in deference to the suffrage movement that had wrapped around everything in their girlhood. Surely, then, her sister's goodwill was under every word that her niece put on paper.

These thoughts were Susan's private pleasure, and until Lucy went to Washington, so were the letters. Now that America was in the Great War, and Tom had joined the army, the whole family liked to hear from someone who might actually see the president as he drove out the White House gates on his way to a meeting. Susan read Lucy's letters aloud over dinner and found it gratifying when the others listened intently.

On the fifth of July Susan read from a yellow packet telling about the Russian visit to the president. Some of this news had appeared in the newspapers, but who else in Santa Rosa could say they knew someone on the spot? The Woman's Party had greeted the Russians—who, having just overthrown the czar, were doubtful allies in the fight against Germany—with a huge banner at the White House gate. Lucy wrote out the entire text because she thought it had not been published in the newspapers:

TO THE RUSSIAN ENVOYS:

PRESIDENT WILSON AND ENVOY ROOT ARE DECEIVING RUSSIA WHEN THEY SAY, "WE ARE A DEMOCRACY. HELP US WIN THE WORLD WAR SO THAT DEMOCRACY MAY SURVIVE."

WE, THE WOMEN OF AMERICA, TELL YOU THAT AMERICA IS NOT A DEMOCRACY. TWENTY MILLION AMERICAN WOMEN ARE DENIED THE RIGHT TO VOTE. PRESIDENT WILSON IS THE CHIEF OPPONENT OF THEIR NATIONAL ENFRANCHISEMENT.

HELP MAKE THIS NATION REALLY FREE. TELL OUR GOVERNMENT IT MUST LIBERATE ITS PEOPLE BEFORE IT CAN CLAIM FREE RUSSIA AS AN ALLY.

Hoodlums had torn the banners to shreds. Lucy said she had arrived just minutes late at the scene to find boys racing up and down the sidewalk waving purple-and-yellow scraps of cloth. From curiosity Lucy had gone by Cameron House, the National Woman's Party headquarters, to ask for the text. She hoped that Susan would find it of interest.

"You can imagine quite easily," Lucy wrote, "that our great defenders of democracy were of one mind that the women were entirely at fault for getting their banners torn and themselves knocked down. Newspapers that depend on the right of free speech for their daily ink find themselves shocked that women would behave so unladylike.

"Next day the picketers went out again, this time with banners quoting the president's words, that we should fight for democracy, 'for the right of those who submit to authority to have a voice in their own governments.' These were words from his war message to Congress. The president ordered them arrested. Some numbers of women have been carted away and given jail sentences, supposedly for obstructing traffic.

"I don't particularly sympathize with the picketers," Lucy wrote, "but I think the administration is giving them legitimacy by arresting them. If they were not illegal in January, how can they be now? And how were a dozen women obstructing traffic on a twenty-foot sidewalk?"

"Good for them," Susan's mother stated, even while Susan read aloud over the dinner table. Bowls and cutlery and napkins lay strewn around—they had finished the meal. "If I had any strength in my legs, I would go there myself." Rebecca was confined to the house, where she staggered down the hall from her bed to a kitchen chair, and back again.

"Grandma!" exclaimed seventeen-year-old Becky. "You can't picket the president during a war!"

"I don't see why not. It's not my war."

"It is if your own flesh and blood is fighting it." Fred spoke with a tight and deadly serious look on his face. Tom had joined the army a week after the declaration on April 6. He was in Oakland for training and expected to be shipped out any day.

"He's not fighting it for me. I tried to talk him out of going. I don't know why you let him, Mr. Konicek. Nobody can tell me why they are fighting this war."

"I don't think that's right," Susan said dryly. "We've been told we are fighting for democracy, Mother."

Rebecca let out an impatient sigh. "Who has democracy? Do I have democracy? Certainly not. Let President Wilson give us the vote, and then we will see about his war. The only fight for democracy I am aware of is the one those poor women are fighting in Washington. More power to them, I say."

"What is wrong, Fred?" Susan asked. His face seemed tense around the mouth.

He stood up slowly and threw his napkin down on his chair. "As long as my boy is fighting, I won't have anybody talking treason in my house," he said.

"This is my house, I believe," Rebecca said. "I paid for it."

"Please sit," Susan said to Fred. "I want us to change the subject."

"You brought it up," George said. "You read the letter."

"Your cousin is not advocating these positions," Susan said. "Nobody is doing more to help the war effort than our suffragists. These picketers are merely a small contingent, a minority."

"If she isn't advocating," Fred said, "why does she write about it? Why did she write out the banner? She's not a newspaper reporter, is she?"

Susan stared at Fred. "Please sit down, Fred. I believe she is trying to write interesting letters to inform us of the events in Washington. I find them quite fascinating. Would you rather that I not read them aloud?"

She said this in defense of her niece. If she were entirely truthful, however, Susan would have to admit that she felt Lucy teetering between the two organizations. She had written about Alice Paul and her fascinating confidence. Sometimes Susan skipped over sentences that showed a growing sympathy for the picketers.

Susan could not say which side she was rooting for. She did want, as though she wanted it for herself, her niece to find a way to satisfy her craving for consequence. Fred's resistance to the letters underlined how difficult that was for a woman. He expected Lucy would stop whatever she was doing because men had declared war. A woman's mind would be erased and her ambitions sent to the barn until the important business of fighting was completed. Susan felt the injustice in Fred's point of view, though she said nothing.

––––––––––

All through the ripe, hot summer the women at Suffrage House glistened, fanned themselves, and complained about their corsets. They made no effort to be ladylike among themselves, which reminded Lucy of her college days when the girls first discovered the delicious freedom of acting coarse in the privacy of female company. She liked this atmosphere, she was comfortable in it, and she admired the steadiness and grit of some of the women older than she. It was hard to see anything great in what they did, however, and sometimes she thought that they sniped at the Woman's Party out of jealousy. To show support for the war effort, Mrs. Catt had suspended Washington lobbying.

The picketers had stirred the hornet's nest. When Suffrage House women did meet with congressmen, they had to keep explaining that they were not the same as the Woman's Party and had no sympathy with them. The picketers made government men so angry, they would not listen. When Lucy saw that red light in their eyes, she wondered what caused this feeling.

Some days when Lucy passed the White House, she found the picketers unmolested. They stood in peace with their banners and their colors of white, yellow, and purple extended into the dull summer sky. Other days a raffish crowd assembled, staring tourists and loquacious soldiers and dull government workers drawn to any possibility of entertainment. Sometimes Lucy watched the police come to arrest the picketers and take them off in a black wagon. She could never understand why they arrested the picketers some days and left them alone on others.

Invariably the protesters refused to pay fines and got three days in jail or at the Occoquan workhouse in Virginia. There were irate complaints written to the newspapers that the women were mistreated, a concern that Lucy thought misplaced. What did they think, that jail would be like a hotel on Pennsylvania Avenue? The picture of these well-off women behind bars, mixed with drunkards and women of the street, added bitter humor to the commentary over dinner at Suffrage House.

Lucy half agreed with Mrs. Railsward, who repeated almost every night at dinner that if men tried to picket the president, they would be in prison before they got their banners unfurled. At the same time Lucy felt a grudging admiration for the picketers. They were engaged in something much more interesting than her work. Also, Lucy often found herself thinking about Alice Paul and her interesting face, with those quiet, intent eyes.

On August 13, when she went for her walk, Lucy came unexpectedly upon a massive, sweaty crowd jostling along the sidewalk in front of the White House and filling it for half a block. It took considerable persistence for her to work her way through the pressing mob, holding her breath as she passed through clouds of sour man-smell. She actually walked into the street, where she was in danger from passing traffic, in order to read the banner. The picketers were barely visible through the crowd, but the banner stood above them on two poles. It was a long message in block gold letters, addressed to America's special envoy to Russia, who had recently returned to Washington.

TO ENVOY ROOT:

YOU SAY THAT AMERICA MUST THROW ITS MANHOOD IN THE SUPPORT OF LIBERTY. WHOSE LIBERTY?

THIS NATION IS NOT FREE. TWENTY MILLION WOMEN ARE DENIED BY THE PRESIDENT OF THE UNITED STATES THE RIGHT TO REPRESENTATION IN THEIR OWN GOVERNMENT.

TELL THE PRESIDENT THAT HE CANNOT FIGHT AGAINST LIBERTY AT HOME WHILE HE TELLS US TO FIGHT FOR LIBERTY ABROAD.

TELL HIM TO MAKE AMERICA FREE FOR DEMOCRACY BEFORE HE ASKS THE MOTHERS OF AMERICA TO THROW THEIR SONS TO THE SUPPORT OF DEMOCRACY IN EUROPE.

ASK HIM HOW HE COULD REFUSE LIBERTY TO AMERICAN CITIZENS WHEN HE HAS FORCED MILLIONS OF AMERICAN BOYS OUT OF THEIR COUNTRY TO DIE FOR LIBERTY.

Lucy stood on the curb, her back to traffic while facing a bobbing sea of hats. On her left stood a pack of sailors, grinning and poking each other as though they walked a county fair midway. On her right an elderly man, shorter than she, wore a grubby gray suit and stared ahead as though looking uncomprehendingly into the apocalypse. The thick crowd made an uneasy sound, a chorus of unintelligible shouts. Lucy stared blankly for several minutes, absorbing the growing tension.

She understood why the banner's words disturbed her and the crowd. She had never heard a woman speak so: harsh, demanding, bombastic. Ladies spoke gently, persuasively, humorously, but this message grated like a sheet of iron dragged over pavement.

That night at dinner the conversation was all about the banner. They said it insulted the president. Lucy said nothing. She did not want to say that she had seen it, for then she would be required to describe the scene. She wanted to think, without having to explain her thoughts.

The picketers were rude. Lucy recognized it as the end point of a mentality she had first experienced in college, when they marched out behind Mrs. Blatch and listened to a trades union leader. They were going to say what they meant and insist on it. They refused to simper and smile and flatter. And what was wrong with that?

Something warned her that it was an important change, however, not just a change of tactics but almost a change in the way they thought about being women. Lucy's friends at Suffrage House complained that the picketers abused their female privilege. They picketed like men, but they expected to be treated like ladies. It was obvious to Lucy that such a double standard, if it even existed anymore, could not last. Which meant that the picketers would find their rudeness met by something more than rudeness.

The next day Lucy woke with this anxiety still hanging over her, and she could not shake it. Staring at the wall behind her desk was not accomplishing any work for suffrage, so in the afternoon, a little earlier than usual, she went out on her walk.

Long before she reached the picketers Lucy could see that the crowd was large. She had to cross the street to view the scene from Lafayette Park because the sidewalk in front of the White House was jammed. An intermittent rain of boys and men pelted across the street to a mob spilling out into the street. The crowd was so large, the banners seemed small, especially the colors that bloomed over the dark men's hats like large tropical flowers. Lucy could not immediately locate the banner with text, and then, when she did, found it difficult to read from across the street. When she made it out, she knew immediately there would be trouble. They were hard, metallic words that men might use to insult.

KAISER WILSON—

HAVE YOU FORGOTTEN HOW YOU SYMPATHIZED WITH THE POOR GERMANS BECAUSE THEY WERE NOT SELF-GOVERNED?

TWENTY MILLION AMERICAN WOMEN ARE NOT SELF-GOVERNED.

TAKE THE BEAM OUT OF YOUR OWN EYE.

Lucy went across the street and worked her way into the crowd. A small strip of open space separated the throng from the picketers. The men at the front were constantly heaving their backs into the mass behind to prevent being pushed forward. A skinny blond sailor, with his hat cocked sideways over white eyebrows, his navy uniform loose around his shoulders, was shouting words Lucy could not get. Sometimes the men around him would laugh or would erupt in a clamor like barking dogs. The picketing women looked straight ahead. How misplaced they seemed in their soft dresses and showy hats.

Suddenly the barking sailor jogged toward one of the women bearing KAISER WILSON. She feinted away in fear, raising her arms so the banner jigged backward, but the sailor leaped into the air, seized the cloth with one fist, and dragged it down. Holding with both hands, he ran toward the crowd, jerking the woman off her feet as she tried to keep a grip on her pole. The cry from the crowd was instant and elated, a sound Lucy had once heard at a baseball game in the Bronx when a young pitcher from Boston hit a ball in one smooth, sudden arc over the wall.

All along the White House fence other men leaped and tore at the colors. The crowd closed in, obliterating all space, shoving Lucy ahead until she was flattened against the iron fence of the White House grounds. She could not see, except to know that men were running and shouting and pushing, that the crowd tossed like a surging sea, and that only one tricolored banner still stood above them. Then that was gone as well.

Near Lucy a wide black man had climbed on the low stone wall supporting the White House fence. Imitating him, Lucy boosted herself up to see. A tall white plume, the kind used in a woman's hat, was making its way through the crowd. She could not see what head it was on, but she could see men laughing, their faces bright and plastic, as they followed the plume. Several women crossed the street behind it, moving slowly but surrounded by, followed by, a happy, shouting pack. They went into Lafayette Park, then were lost to sight. Lucy supposed she had seen the picketers, returning to Cameron House with what little dignity they had left.

A bored peace descended over the dwindling crowd, now no longer a unit of madness but a collection of curious individuals. For ten minutes they mingled pointlessly. Then suddenly from the park Lucy heard a loud, swelling cry. She climbed up again on the stone wall to see the tricolor banners blooming in the park, swinging along in a line of five, with a printed banner at the rear. They marched across the street, surrounded by a dashing crowd of boys and sailors and men in suits and fedoras prancing backward in front of them. Yes, the picketers had returned.

One tricolor banner marched directly to the spot where Lucy stood clutching the iron pale. The picketer was a dark, thin creature. For a moment Lucy thought she looked at Alice Paul, but this was another woman with a wide, cream-colored straw hat, a periwinkle ribbon around its brim. She turned just by Lucy and stood to face the mob. Now Lucy saw only her hat, a cream disk. Immediately a little boy in overalls and brown boots came running, grinning, and trying to seize the banner, but he was too small to reach it. He stood leaping as though the picketer was not even there. "Give it! Give it!" he cried.

The crowd was roaring, whether at the boy or for his cause, Lucy could not say. She herself was shouting. A man in suspenders and a cap stood behind the boy for an instant, his hands on his hips, and then stepped forward, reached, and pulled the banner down. He held to one end, the boy grasped the other, and together they pulled apart until the banner ripped down a seam, the purple separating from yellow and white. The man tossed the yellow and white into the air, where a dozen hands pulled it and ripped it.

Within a few moments, all the banners were down again, ripped to shreds. The mob jubilated as though for a great victory. The picketer in front of Lucy had been thrown to her knees, but now she found her feet again and stood with her pole, as though not sure where to go or what to do. Lucy went to her, not wanting to startle her. "Are you hurt?" Lucy asked. A glimmer of contempt seemed to fly through the woman's dark eyes. She shook her head abruptly and looked away from Lucy.

The woman acted as though Lucy did not exist, as though she was merely part of the mob. Lucy thought, *How could she think anything else? She seems to have no friends here.*

Walking single file, the picketers made their way back across the street, and this time the entire crowd followed them, shouting, jeering, trotting, celebrating. Lucy went along, staying to the rear. They traipsed through Lafayette Park and onto Madison Place, where the picketers disappeared through the front door of Cameron House. As Lucy wedged herself closer between spectators, she was able to see a sailor standing on the front steps of the house, the same blond sailor with the white eyebrows, haranguing the crowd that filled the street and jammed the front garden.

The front door opened behind him, and another group of suffragists emerged from the house, bearing banners. The sailor shouted, lifting his arms. A cry arose. The women were surrounded by the mob, the banners torn from their poles. Lucy saw one of the women cower, holding her hands over her head in fear of being beaten.

Looking behind her, Lucy saw two policemen watching from Lafayette Park. Both stood with arms crossed, identical models of relaxed indifference.

Lucy marched to them. "Don't you see that those women are being attacked? Why don't you protect them?" she demanded.

One smiled at her; the other put up his hands as though to keep her at a distance. The one who smiled, a thin young man with a handlebar mustache, said, "Those aren't our orders."

"You need orders to protect an innocent lady?"

The other, older man said, "I don't see any ladies. Those girls are insulting our president."

"And who made you the man to judge?"

The older policeman shrugged. The mustached one said apologetically, "Ma'am, we have our orders."

Lucy could hear the ranting of the sailor—he had a high, clear voice that carried. "Tear them down," he was crying. "Tear them down! We won't take insults!" More women had emerged bearing banners. Lucy saw one tricolor aloft for just a moment before it was ripped down.

"Tear them down!" the high voice sounded. "Tear them down!"

From one side of the crowd Lucy saw that a large object was moving overhead, a large, long package making way through the mob. It reached the front door and was stood on end: a ladder. A cheer arose as a sailor tripped up the rungs, followed by a little boy wearing short pants and no hat to cover his dark hair. The sailor quickly reached the second story and seized a tricolor banner that hung over the door. He pulled on it with both hands. The crowd cried out, for he swayed with the effort and seemed about to fall.

"Take it down!" shouted the sailor below.

The man on the ladder gathered himself and pulled again. He managed to rip the banner off its pole. Just as he did, the window next to him opened, and two women appeared on the balcony. They reached down to the top of the ladder and tried to push it away from the building, to tip the sailor and boy off into the crowd. The sailor held on to the pole from which he had just removed the banner. Arms appeared from behind the two women to pull them away.

Another sailor had scaled the wisteria vine that covered the front of the house. Clambering up to the balcony, he jerked down the American flag. On the balcony a door opened, and two young women emerged. One carried a tricolor; the other—Lucy saw that it was Lucy Burns—carried another KAISER WILSON banner. They stood defiantly above the reach of the mob, one pale as death, the other flushed and strong, and Lucy could not help herself—she was ravished. Her heart beat faster than her mind could compute. Something flew up from the crowd and smashed softly against the house just over Burns's head. More objects: eggs, making a cracking smash; apples, bounding with a harder, rounder thunk off the walls; tomatoes that squished on impact. The women did not move or even look down to see what might fly next.

Suddenly a shot rang out. A window above the women's heads shattered. Screams were heard. A sailor ran past Lucy so fast that his hat fell off his head. Lucy watched his escape and saw, in his right hand, a black revolver. Another woman bearing a banner had joined the two on the balcony now, and three sailors were going hand over hand up the wisteria toward them.

Lucy made up her mind. Walking fast, she dodged her way through the crowd and to the front door. The spectators were so intent on the balcony that they let her pass: a touch on the shoulder and men would move to let her go by. She tried the door, found it locked, and knocked loudly. Perhaps by coincidence the door opened and a group of women, four or five in number, went out, while she slipped in. (She later learned that these women carried banners under their clothes, which they unfurled at the White House gates while the mob was distracted at the house.)

Inside the great room with its fireplace, ten or fifteen women were sewing banners, some hanging across tables, some looped over furniture. Strangely, ironically, Lucy was struck by the similarity to sweatshops she had seen in New York, where rows of women could not glance up lest they dent their tiny earnings.

She ran up the grand staircase and found her way through a paneled hallway to the balcony door. A woman in a light pink dress, a summer creation, stood behind the door peering out, for the door was made of glass. In her arms were tricolored banners. Out the window Lucy saw a struggle: a sailor seemed to have someone by the throat and was pushing her backward while pulling at her cloth banner, which she refused to relinquish.

"Here," Lucy said to the woman in pink and took a tricolor from her arms. Lucy opened the balcony door and stepped out. For a moment she was confused. Two women were struggling with sailors, and one, Lucy Burns, seemed likely to be thrust over the balcony, for she would not let go of her banner. A third woman was on hands and knees, her hair hanging down over her eyes. Not knowing what to do, where to turn, whether to comfort the weeping or struggle with the combatants, Lucy lifted her arms and held her own banner high. Instantly she was set on by a sailor. She wrapped a corner of cloth around her arm and held on, twisting her body to pull the tricolor from the sailor's grip. He pulled back savagely, and she felt the cloth brace and scream through her fingers. She lost her grip, and the sailor tore the whole thing from her, whipped it into the air, and let it fly over the edge of the balcony. The colors caught the air and fell loosely, swirling downward, into the mob.

———

Carrie Catt sat on a blue chenille bedspread in her room in Suffrage House, her legs curled under with a casualness that was deceptively inviting. In contrast to this supple pose, her eyes appeared like two chips of blue stone. Her words were precise as a drill. "We have every reason to be supportive of President Wilson," she said. "Never since our last convention have I requested his ear or his aid without receiving it promptly. The president favors suffrage. He has spoken for our cause, even though he carries an immense weight of responsibility for our troops in Europe and for the future of a peaceful world. I don't understand your action."

Lucy was the kind of quiet person who feels no particular obligation to speak. She had taken a desk chair where she sat calmly, her own blue eyes seeming to smile at Mrs. Catt's, her gorgeous blonde curls spilling down her head.

Catt had arrived last night from New York and had asked Lucy to come to her room immediately after breakfast. "Will you explain your action to me?" she asked. *It is inevitable,* Catt thought, *that the younger women will be impatient.* But she believed that Alice Paul could not be permitted to fracture the united front of NAWSA.

"I don't think there is anything to explain," Lucy said. "I could not sit by and let the mob attack my fellow suffragists. I thought they were very noble and brave, however misguided their tactics. I was afraid that someone might be hurt or killed. Miss Burns very nearly was."

"A state of affairs that she brought on herself," Catt replied.

"Well, perhaps so," Lucy said and dropped her eyes for the first time. "I could not stand by and watch, nonetheless."

Catt slowly stroked her skirt, smoothing the cloth. "I suppose your sympathy is very commendable," she said. "Even so I want you to realize that Miss Paul and Miss Burns have set back suffrage a great deal by their antics, and furthermore they are in danger of annoying the most powerful man in the world, who up to this minute supports our cause. You know yourself how ceaselessly we have had to tell the Congress that we have nothing to do with the Woman's Party." Catt raised her eyes and looked straight into Lucy's, which seemed a little cowed. "I cannot have one of my most valuable associates recognized as holding up a banner for the Woman's Party. I will lose all credibility. Our organization will lose all credibility. Do you see that?"

"Yes, I think so," Lucy said.

"Then you won't do it again? Not even if they are firing cannons at Cameron House?"

Lucy was silent.

"I want to hear you promise that you will not again carry a banner or make a public display for Alice Paul. I don't care if you become fast friends in private. They are marvelous, interesting women. I know that. In public, however, we must keep a separation."

"Mrs. Catt, why do you think the president makes it so hard for the picketers? I asked the police why they wouldn't stop the men from attacking them, and they said those weren't their orders."

"Goodness, would you like somebody picketing on your house? Would you like to be called kaiser when you drove out for a dinner? I think those women invite their persecution. I imagine President Wilson is quite sore at them. I would be."

Lucy's lips tightened perceptibly, but Catt did not see it. "Well, Miss Phillips," she said, "will you just promise me?"

Lucy gave her head a quick shake. "I don't know," she said. "I can't promise."

———————

August 26, 1917

Dear Aunt Susan,

I am sorry I did not write last week. I had you very much in mind, but felt so confused, I did not know where to begin. I wish that I knew what has reached you through the papers because I can't manage much of an eyewitness account at the moment. I have observed scenes these two weeks that I never dreamed of seeing. It is too long and too upsetting to write in full, and other matters feel more urgent to me at the moment.

Suffice it to say that I have watched the Woman's Party picketers at the White House. When the president gave orders to have the police stand by while various hoodlums attacked, destroying banners, knocking down women, even firing shots, and threatening the women in their own house, I could not stand by, so I went to the women's aid. Nothing was premeditated on my part, but I ended up standing on the balcony of their house, holding up their tricolored banner until a trespassing sailor tore it from my grip. I was pelted with eggs, apples, tomatoes, and I don't want to think what else.

Unfortunately this was reported to Mrs. Catt, who happened to be coming to the capital and called me in to scold me. She asked me to promise I would never do anything like that again, and I couldn't. You can imagine how furious she was, though of course she did not show it except through her eyes. She has remarkable eyes. My point was that I could not promise to stand by if I saw women assaulted. Her point was that the picketers have made so many enemies that we have to keep clear of them absolutely, at least in public. I told her I would do my best, but I could not absolutely promise. I can tell you that she was not happy. I suppose you can imagine. Did you ever know her?

Since that time I have gone to watch while the attacks continued day after day. I have seen dozens and dozens of beautiful banners ripped from the picketers' hands and destroyed. Often enough the women were hurt or knocked down in the process. The police always stood by, until their orders changed and they began to attack the picketers themselves. They were more savage than the hoodlums, and all for carrying mere signs, many bearing the president's own words. Recently they have begun to arrest the picketers again and sentence them to long periods in the workhouse. I suppose you read all this, and there is no need for me to repeat it. But here is where I need your advice desperately, or perhaps even more your prayers, because a prayer I imagine, if it has any effect, has it immediately and does not have to wait for a letter to cross America. I have a strong impulse to offer myself to the picketers. They are going into prison by the score, and so Miss Paul appeals for more women willing to make this sacrifice. Of course not everyone is able to do it because of personal responsibilities, but the truth is that I am responsible to no one at all. I have no attachments and can do it without afflicting anyone but myself with the folly of it.

I say folly, and I do mean that. I am greatly confused and wish I could see you to discuss it. You ask why I would want to do it, and I say that I have a sense that by acting directly and asserting our rights, we act like citizens ought to act. Do we not have a right to object firmly that we are governed without our consent? Perhaps— as Mrs. Catt would argue—it is impolitic to picket, but if we are refused our right and then attacked for asserting it, should we not stand firm, whether it is politic to do so or not? Perhaps I mean to say, is it finally good politics to stand mutely while we are treated as chattel? Will not those who act as chattel demonstrate that they might as well be chattel?

I don't mean to suggest for a moment that the thought of picketing and arrest and prison does not fill me with horror. Can you imagine what my mother would say to it? That does not really matter, however. Mrs. Catt is a more serious objector. She says that the picketers will delay our suffrage rights yet more because they act intemperately and make our officials angry. Would she have told the Boston patriots the same thing when they unloaded tea? Yet she may be correct. It is very hard to watch women abused for exercising what everyone, even President Wilson, publicly states to be their right. I fear fanaticism, and also I fear quietism. I would far prefer to be in peaceful Santa Rosa just now. Yet once here I cannot flee and maintain my own dignity.

I mean it when I say that I wish you would pray for me. If you have any advice, please give it. I would value it highly. You know that I am not much of a Christian. I had a friend in college who manifested real faith, and I knew then that comparatively I had none at all. Dear Aunt Susan, it is an advantage to be alone in this situation because I do not have to worry myself about what somebody else might think or how someone else might be affected. With you, however, I do ask that you make your prayers on my behalf, and knowing that you will, I do not feel quite so alone.

Your niece and your sister,

Lucy

Chapter 20
1917: Jailed for Freedom

Lucy Phillips came in out of the November drizzle and stood gathering herself in the somber and elegant seclusion of the Cameron House entrance hall. She stared doubtfully at coatracks overburdened by piles of damp coats and rubbers. If she once put her rubbers into that dull, black, floppy heap, would she ever find them again? For an instant the decision seemed too much for her. Then with a gesture like a shrug, she put her rubbers into her purse and carried her umbrella and her coat with her.

In the grand room of Cameron House a chesty fire blazed, and the chandelier gleamed with reflected flames. It seemed a long time ago, much more than two months, that she had walked into this room to join the Woman's Party. She had come in almost trembling, prepared to encounter radicals and Reds and all kinds of bent females. The room's elegance had exaggerated her fears. It had seemed so out of keeping with the organization's reputation that she half expected to encounter a misshapen beast, something out of a tragic fairy tale.

Now the room was just a room to Lucy. She was used to it; she had settled into the business of the Woman's Party. Dozens of bentback chairs set in fractured rows had spoiled the room's elegance anyway. A scattering of well-dressed women sat quietly in the chairs today, as though they concentrated on something happening elsewhere, some inaudible conversation.

Among the wooden chairs were some pieces of soft, upholstered furniture, but most of the women had taken the stiff seats, as though they expected somebody better to come for the comfortable chairs. Lucy might have done the same two months ago, but experience had taught her that the meetings could be interminable. One might as well be comfortable. She sat down quietly on one of the sofas. A plain slip of a girl, seated at the other end, leaned over conspiratorially. "Dorothy Day," she said. "I write for the *Masses.* I decided it is time I got arrested."

"Lucy Phillips," Lucy responded. Then because she was learning to say what came to mind, she asked, "Could I ask how old you are?"

"I am twenty," the girl said in a tone that made it clear it seemed to her very old. "How old are you?"

"I just turned thirty. There is a lady here, Mrs. Nolan, who is over seventy. That little white-haired lady over there."

"Are you going to get arrested?"

"I don't know. Probably I will."

"Why aren't you sure?" the girl asked.

"Alice Paul said I wasn't to. I do the press communications for the Woman's Party, and Miss Paul said I would be difficult to replace. But then she went out to get arrested two weeks ago, and I assume that means nobody is irreplaceable now."

Lucy noted her own pleasure in quoting Miss Paul. She drew strength from Alice Paul's calmness and certitude. She adored watching Paul's luminous eyes as she listened, listened, listened in utter stillness. Going against Mrs. Catt had been emotionally wrenching for Lucy. Her aunt Susan, whose thoughts she relied on, had been curiously oblique in answering Lucy's request for advice. Even now Lucy did not capture any clear feeling from Aunt Susan's letters; she said nothing direct about

Lucy's decision, either to approve it or to argue that she made a mistake. Lucy thought perhaps her aunt was afraid for her, though she had not a word of evidence for that.

Lucy's mother and father had commanded her to come home and stop this nonsense, but she had expected that response. She was used to feeling adrift from them.

Standing near the fireplace, Lucy Burns talked with Doris Stevens, another of the Woman's Party leaders. Burns had just been let out of jail, after two months of confinement. Her hair was the same full, brilliant bonfire, but even from across the room Lucy could see that Burns was thin, and her complexion sallow. The food in the Occoquan workhouse was almost inedible, all the women said, spoiled, infested with maggots. One woman had filled up her spoon with little white worms and tried to deliver it to Mr. Whittaker, the workhouse superintendent.

Jail sentences were growing steadily longer. The picketers of the summer had been given three days. In September, they were sentenced to thirty days or sixty days. Paul had been sentenced to seven months. There were fifty women in prison, living in filthy, abusive conditions for the crime of obstructing traffic. Apparently the administration thought it could put them all away.

Lucy Burns rapped on a table in order to quiet the room. *She does not look well,* Lucy Phillips thought. But when she spoke, her dimples showed, and her face came alive.

"I want to mention the victory in New York," Burns said, without bothering to make welcoming flourishes. That was part of what Lucy favored in the Woman's Party—the lack of rhetorical show, the straightness. "Our opponents have said that no state east of the Mississippi would ever give woman the vote. They are proved wrong. It is by far the largest state so far where women have the vote."

With a little shock Lucy realized for the first time that she could vote. The New York election had occurred three days before, but until now she had not personalized the result. Her aunt Susan and she could vote, at opposite ends of the nation. So could her mother, for that matter, and her grandmother.

"Some of us might be tempted," Burns continued, "to think that we will all get the vote by the state method. It looks like an inevitable trend. It would be easy to overlook those states, especially in the South, where that inevitable trend appears likely to reach its goal in about a hundred years, if then. Some of us are already voters; we dare not abandon the rest to the whims and peculiarities of their state governments. Voting must be available to every citizen. Now is the time, when momentum is on our side, to push to a complete victory."

Burns went on to summarize the arrests, Alice Paul's long sentence, her detention in solitary confinement. She spoke in a matter-of-fact way, but unexpectedly Lucy Phillips felt a wave of panic. She had come knowing full well the purpose of the meeting: to recruit a large corps of picketers to be arrested, showing Wilson and his administration that imprisoning Alice Paul was not enough to stop them.

"I want each one of you to think seriously about this before you commit," Burns went on. "We cannot afford to have anyone falter."

In New York Lucy had visited in the jails; she had some idea what prison would be like. Inadvertently she glanced at the slender girl sitting near her on the sofa. The girl leaned forward, her face intent on Lucy Burns.

It is not physical fear, Lucy thought. She was not afraid to suffer if it came to that. (Of course she knew nothing at all about suffering, but that was the point. She could not fear it because she felt no connection to it.) Her fear was more prosaic, muddy, and shadowed: that she would become lost and forgotten. What if all this came to nothing? Something in the memory of the New York tenements and the jails that had seemed to be an extension of them, of their dim light, their noise and confusion, their lack of any beauty, was the essence of her anxiety. She had spent years in that dimness and had made no trace; it depressed her to think how her love and intelligence were poured out to disappear, as a deep pool shows no sign of the rain that showers from above. She wanted to do something to last.

———————————

On the day of the picketing the sky had a thin scud of overcast, through which a weak sun shone on their banners. The trees had already dropped their leaves, and they all wore coats, for the thin light had not warmed the day. Lucy carried a sign quoting President Wilson, words she had selected herself, words stitched on in golden letters:

I TELL YOU SOLEMNLY, LADIES AND GENTLEMEN, WE CANNOT
POSTPONE JUSTICE ANY LONGER IN THESE UNITED STATES, AND
I DON'T WISH TO SIT DOWN AND LET ANY MAN TAKE CARE OF
ME WITHOUT MY HAVING AT LEAST A VOICE IN IT; AND IF HE
DOESN'T LISTEN TO MY ADVICE I AM GOING TO MAKE IT AS
UNPLEASANT FOR HIM AS I CAN.

Women circled Lucy, reading it, grinning, saying, "We will make it unpleasant for *him*." Lucy met two schoolteachers, a nurse, the wife of an Illinois banker, and an architect. Some had come from considerable distance because of appeals sent out to the state organizations. They lined up outside to have their picture taken. How should they look at the camera? Was it right to smile? Some of the women acted positively giddy, as though they were contesting for Dairy Queen at a local fair.

They became sober when they marched out of Cameron House and found hundreds of people waiting. Something about carrying a banner into a crowd filled them with a sense of grandeur and battle. They went slowly in single file, parading their suffrage colors. As they had been instructed, they did not look at the staring faces. Lucy could hardly believe what she was doing, after months of watching and hesitating. It felt grand.

They marched right to the battlements—to the black metal pales of the White House fence. The police were there already, but the women paid no mind. They took up positions by the east and west gates, standing tall, looking straight ahead. Lucy came in the fourth rank of marchers, and by the time she reached her position, the advance ranks were already herded toward the black patrol wagons that waited in line. She found her position, extended her banner at the end of its long pole, and focused her eyes into the medium distance. She heard the spectators' snickers and remarks as they read the banner out loud and understood eventually—some of them were slow to realize it—that it quoted the president.

She had no time to be afraid. A police officer approached her and said politely, "Come along. I'm ready to arrest you."

"What is the charge?" she asked loudly. Her voice sounded rude and challenging, not at all ladylike.

"You'll find out the charge at the station," the policeman snapped and held out one arm pointed in the direction of the paddy wagon.

November 14, 1917

Dear Aunt Susan,

I write from the District of Columbia courtroom where I expect to be put in prison within a short time. Forgive my scribbles. I am balancing this notebook on my lap in a most uncomfortable seat. You will not hear from me again for at least a month, I expect. We have about fifty women in jail or at the workhouse, and they are not allowed to see their lawyers, to have visitors, or to send or receive letters. I expect that I will join them. People say the conditions are awful, although I must say that many of our women have never walked a mean street in their lives and so might consider it a privation to do without silver service. I do not mean to belittle what they go through, only to suggest that I am not sure I will find the deprivations as serious as they do.

Let me describe this scene for you. We are thirty-one women waiting for sentencing in a courtroom far too small for our numbers. Last Saturday we began with forty-one picketers, who were promptly arrested and ordered to trial on Monday. I have been carried in a paddy wagon and booked at a police station. Imagine that. It was a very stirring experience to march out with our banners, but since then we seem to do nothing but wait. After we testified and the police testified and the judge gave a long, stirring talk about the dangers of restricting traffic in the nation's capital, plus the temptations of revolution that have afflicted Russia, we were pronounced guilty and released without sentence. Most of us went immediately back to the White House to picket again. The police were unprepared for this and had to commandeer private cars to take us to the station house. We were told to come for trial on Wednesday. On Tuesday we went out to picket and were arrested for the third time. The crowds have been very friendly, but one of our sailor friends—the same man who dragged Alice Paul thirty feet along the sidewalk in August— ripped up our banners. There was a little old man handing out pieces as souvenirs—I wish I had got some to send you. Because we would not post bail, having done it already (the money was not refunded), they kept us all in the holding cells. Some of us slept on the floor and are decidedly grumpy this morning. (I shared a bed but did not sleep.)

In fact I am not irritable. I do not know how to describe my state of mind. I am, I suppose, a little frightened. Mostly I feel impatient. This week has seemed to last forever, and I want to go on and see where it may lead me. We have conferred and agreed to demand that we be treated as political prisoners. If they will not, then we will refuse food or work. They call this hunger striking. We do not know how the authorities will react. We understand that Alice Paul has already been hunger striking for several weeks.

I wish that you were here with me. I feel quite alone. I believe the trial will come to a close within the next few minutes, so I will end this letter here. I give this to our lawyer to mail. Don't forget me.

Lucy

How dark the gentle Virginia farms and woods became when the sun disappeared! The train had taken them only a few miles out of the District of Columbia, yet they seemed to have entered an uninhabited country. The Occoquan station appeared like a glowing haven in the pure emptiness of space.

At Union Station crowds of travelers had stared at them as guards led them to the cars, but here the train pulled into a dimly lit and deserted station, where they disembarked in complete anonymity. The guards spoke softly with their instructions; the women moved quietly onto the platform. Lucy felt strangely disembodied, as though she watched herself from above. Her mental acuity was such that every bolt on every stanchion for the station roof stood out as sharply as a diamond. She was not afraid. She was extraordinarily keyed to the moment. She wondered if this was how it felt to do something with your life.

Behind the station house three prison vehicles waited for them, headlights making long streaks of shadow from stones in the road. The engines had been turned off, but they made ticking noises as the hot metal contracted in the sharp night air. Lucy caught a scent of hot oil as she was herded into the windowless maw of the first truck. She had barely sat down next to another woman, almost invisible in the dark, before the engine kicked over into rattling life. The door slammed, and the vehicle started up before the last women were seated. They cried out and grabbed for handholds.

It was a short trip, only a matter of minutes bucking over a rough road, before the truck rocked to a halt and the door was opened from the outside. Guards led them toward a white frame building. Lucy caught glimpses of other scattered buildings, dimly illuminated.

Thirty-one women crowded into an office, the front room of a small cottage. A middle-aged woman in a smock stood behind a heavy government desk, watching balefully. "Please come to the desk one at a time," the woman said when they were all inside. "We will need to register you." When no one moved forward, she repeated her request. "I am Mrs. Herndon, the matron here. You need to register so that you can be shown to your quarters. Could you just line up here? Why don't you go first?" She spoke to one of the women in front of the huddle.

It suddenly struck Lucy as funny, in an ironical way, that this group of women in their tailored dresses and well-made, warm coats, women who might be on the prison commission, inspecting conditions of indigent prisoners, were themselves the guilty, huddled here in this little mob.

Mrs. Lewis extracted herself and approached the matron. She was a fine-looking, upright woman in her fifties, with high cheekbones and a naturally imperial manner. "We want you to understand," she said in a clear, melodious voice, "that we are here as political prisoners. As such we expect to be treated in accordance with international law. We want to speak to Superintendent Whittaker."

"He's not available. I'm in charge, and I need to ask each one of you a few questions before you can be assigned."

"We will wait for Mr. Whittaker," Mrs. Lewis said.

"Then you will wait all night," the matron said.

Mrs. Lewis turned to address the women. "Since it may be a long wait, we ought to make ourselves as comfortable as we can," she said. Taking a handkerchief from her pocket, she knelt down and dusted a square of the wooden floor. When she had it clean to her satisfaction, she carefully lowered herself to a sitting position.

The others followed suit. Soon some of them folded coats into pillows and stretched out. The matron tried to bully them into coming forward to register. She said they would be disciplined. They all ignored her.

They had waited at least an hour when a sound caught Lucy's attention. Half a dozen men in uniform had quietly come in behind the matron, she saw. Out of the silence Mrs. Herndon suddenly announced quite loudly, "I want you women to line up and register yourselves right now. Come now, and you can be shown to your rooms."

Lucy sat up. So did Mrs. Lewis.

"You had better answer up," one of the guards growled. "It will be the worse for you if you don't."

Two more guards slipped in behind Mrs. Herndon from an entrance behind the desk. They spoke to no one, Lucy noticed, but took up positions in the corner of the room, their hands behind their backs.

She heard the sound of a car pull up outside, grinding gravel under its wheels. A door slammed, and just seconds later the door to the office was flung open. "Mr. Whittaker!" someone said loudly. A white-haired man, thin and long-legged, raced in.

Lucy saw Mrs. Lewis struggle to her feet. "We demand to be treated as political pris—" she began.

"You shut up! I have men here to handle you!" Whittaker turned back toward the door, where half a dozen men were filing in behind him. Whittaker had a dark birthmark on one temple, a kind of ink blotch. "Seize her!" he cried, pointing a long finger toward Mrs. Lewis.

Two men in plain clothes trotted to Mrs. Lewis and, grabbing her roughly, began to pull her toward the door. She struggled. Her feet dragged behind her as she drooped in their arms. In a moment Mrs. Lewis was out the door, but Whittaker was whirling, pointing, shouting. His guards hustled forward and seized others. A dozen cries went up. The men shouted.

Lucy saw Mrs. Nolan's tiny figure lifted straight up in the air, like a doll waggling in the arms of the guards. "Be careful of my foot! I have a crippled foot!" she cried in a high falsetto. Lucy Burns had her arms pinned behind her by two men, but she struggled furiously. Her captors bayed for more help. "I'll walk. Don't hurt me!" someone screeched.

Thick muscular arms covered with black hair wrapped around Lucy from behind. She screamed and tore at the arms with her fingers, then her nails. The arms wore a dark blue cotton shirt, sleeves rolled up, and one cuff frayed. Another man with a face like a basset hound was on her suddenly, soundlessly. She felt the secure, overwhelming force of two men, and she cried, "I'll go! I'll go!" They did not listen, but spun her around and began to march her to the door with her arms clamped in their grips.

Lucy was dragged through the door and down the outside stairs. She threw back her head and looked into the sky—no stars, only the vacuum of space. The cold wet grass battered her feet. In the distance, across a darkened field, she saw the dim light of another building. A bulb inside one window illuminated the top half of an American flag. She was carried that way.

She banged a knee hard against the edge of the door. "You shut up!" the man on her left side snarled when she cried in pain. He gave her one savage shake, like a dog with a stick. The large room was lined with metal benches. Lucy's first glance took in fifteen or twenty people, huddled like factory workers. She saw Mrs. Lewis lifted up and slammed down on a bench, then lifted up and slammed again. The sleeve was torn from the dress of one dark-haired woman; Lucy heard the fabric give up its hold in a long, loud rip.

Her captors hurried her through the room and down a corridor. A door opened, and she was launched through it. For a moment she was wobbling forward, her arms reaching for some support. Her shin hit something hard; she fell forward; she thumped down and found the padded toughness of a mattress on her cheek.

No hands were on her. No sounds were near. If she did not move, if she did not make a sound, they might leave her alone.

She heard more footsteps outside, and scuffling, struggling, grunting. Lucy opened her eyes and saw they had Dorothy Day, her arms twisted together up over her head. Three men escorted her. They gave the girl a shove from the doorway. She staggered, but did not move until a second guard raised his boot and gave her a hard shove with his foot. The girl came spinning toward Lucy and hit the edge of the bed as Lucy had. Their heads collided.

———

They talked in low tones about what they had seen, sharing the information for some possible future use. Whittaker came down the corridor and shouted at them to be quiet. "I'll put a buckle gag in your mouth if you don't shut up," he yelled. "It must be quiet!"

The cell had a barred door, a toilet, a single bed. The walls and floor were cement, clammy to the touch. Every inch of the cell, every move-ment was exposed to the guards who passed by. Lucy had seen jails, but she had never thought of the indecency. The toilet could not even be flushed except by the guards. Lucy heard a woman down the row of cells ask the guard in a low voice if he would please deal with their commode. "You want it flushed, do you?" he said loudly, jeeringly.

In the cell to their right a Mrs. Cosu had been thrown against a wall. Lucy remembered her as a short, plump, pleasant woman of middle age. She was unconscious and vomiting. The two women who shared her cell thought she was dying and called out for a doctor. The guards shouted at them to be quiet. Again and again the women made the cry for help, but after a time even the threats died out. The guards made no answer, and so eventually the women fell silent.

Lucy remembered the arm with its frayed blue shirt, the strength of a grip that shook her whole body, the sight of Mrs. Lewis seized and dragged. Why would men treat them so? What moved them?

By the third day of the hunger strike, pangs had subsided. A headache rode on Lucy's skull like a helmet, and all her movements became pre-meditated. Rising from her bed was a series of studied motions rather than a single, fluid, unthought action. Her joints were weak.

Whittaker called her in to his office, and she walked limply, loosely. "You have not eaten," he said.

"No."

"Why not? Are you ill?" He did not seem like a bad man at that moment, only a man trying to do his job.

"I am not ill. I am on a hunger strike until you recognize us as polit-ical prisoners and treat us accordingly."

"Why do you think you are political prisoners? You are not here for being Republicans, are you?" He tried to get her to smile.

"A sentence of six months for blocking traffic is a political sentence," Lucy said.

"Why a hunger strike? Did you think of that yourself? Everyone else is eating well."

She did not answer. He did not know that they passed notes between the cells via the conduit for a steam pipe. Twelve of the women were on a hunger strike.

"If you don't answer me, how can I make sense of what you want?"

"I want us all to be treated as political prisoners. Shall I repeat the terms of that?"

Whittaker stood up. "Guard!" he shouted. "Take this woman away." Lucy stood up and felt the blood rush away from her head. She caught the arm of the chair.

"You'll starve to death," he said. "You can't live for six months without food."

Lucy had heard tales of the inedible food at Occoquan, of uncooked split peas and cereal teeming with weevils, but the trays she was brought every day had toast and butter, eggs, coffee, and once even fried chicken. It was no use refusing them; the grim ladies in their heavy smocks and cloth caps would leave the food until the next meal came. Strangely, however, Lucy did not find it tempting. Her appetite had disappeared.

By the fifth day Lucy could not rise out of bed. Her headache had disappeared, but her eyes seemed to malfunction, producing shifting colors in blues and yellows whenever she stared at any object for long. Since she stayed in bed, she lost communication with the other women, and she lost the memory of her situation too. She seemed to hear her own thoughts echoing in the room. Sometimes she could not understand why she was in this hospital or why she was forbidden to eat. At times her mind was clear and the whole situation seemed obvious, but her mind wandered like a small animal in a maze.

When she could think clearly, she would stare at the ceiling and recall quite vividly the day she was arrested. It seemed to come from some other age of the universe. How noble she had been, marching in parade with her banner! The gawking faces she remembered quite well. Now she had become invisible, forgotten. It was hard to believe that she did anything significant for anybody.

Whittaker came in on the seventh day. He stood by her bedside for a moment, studying her. A weak attempt at a smile lifted his lip, but to her, it seemed to accentuate a demonic appearance. His eyebrows peaked upward, like tents, making his gray eyes more prominent.

"How are you, Miss Phillips?" he asked. "You don't look well."

"I don't feel well," she said.

"The doctors are worried about you," he said. "You are weak and need to eat."

"Will you treat us as political prisoners then?"

"I'm afraid I can't do that. Such a decision is not in my hands."

"Then I can't eat."

"Do you think you will accomplish anything this way? By now you should know how serious we are. We cannot allow you to run the work-house."

"Why not?"

"That would be like letting the insane run the asylum."

"They already do."

A vector of annoyance twitched over Whittaker's face. He looked at her for another minute, quite coldly. Then he squeezed his hands together and left.

She felt a twinge of fear and wondered why she should not give up. Did she accomplish anything? Only her habitual stubbornness, her reluctance to change course, kept her from calling out for the matron. She thought of Alice Paul.

Within the hour she heard the rattle of a cart in the corridor outside. It was not the usual cart they used to carry meals—that had a squeak. This was a heavier, smoother sound. Lucy listened carefully, feeling that something important might happen. She remembered Whittaker's look. Why had he come at all?

Many footsteps were moving in the corridor. There were whispered conversations. Then without a knock the door was opened, and a man in a white doctor's coat came in. He stood in the door looking at her with cool blue eyes. He had his hair cut short as a brush, and he blinked rapidly. His smile never got beyond his mouth, but he kept trying to work it.

"I'm afraid," he said, "I'm afraid, Miss Phillips, I'm afraid that we are going to feed you. This is to prevent damage, to prevent any health accident." He stopped abruptly and seemed to think back over his words to make sure of what he had said.

"I won't eat," Lucy said.

He blinked. "That's what I understand," he said. "That's what I understand." He went back to the door and with a wave of his hand summoned his helpers.

Lucy knew about force-feedings. The stupid English had done it to the suffragettes too. She had made up her mind to fight, but she was already weak. They had two matrons hold her feet and two men hold her shoulders and arms. The doctor clamped down on her jaw and squeezed until the pain made her open. He thrust in a rubber mouthpiece and proceeded to snake a rubber tube down her throat. "Swallow," he said, "swallow. It makes it easier." He had her head in a strong grip. She tried to rip her head back and forth, but the grip grew tighter, like a vise. All she could do was thump her torso up and down on the bed, which made the tube press sharply into her stomach. It hurt so that she had to stop. She was gagging, struggling to breathe. They poured a liquid down the tube, and it landed painfully cold on her empty stomach, as though a ball of iron had thumped there.

"Good, good, good," the doctor said, and he tried to pull the tube. Instead the rubber mouth guard came out, and Lucy took advantage of the confusion to break the doctor's grip on her head and roll it back and forth, side to side. The tube thrashed inside her. She tasted blood. The doctor got his grip again and pulled the tube out safely. She did not fight too hard, for the pain was too great. As soon as the tube was out the hands released her. She thrashed for a moment and then lay still, gagging whenever she remembered the taste of the mouthpiece. Then she broke out crying.

———————————

She could identify the cart by the heavy sound of its wheels. Sometimes it did not come directly to her, but disappeared in another room. She realized that others were force-fed as well. When she heard the sound of breaking eggs outside her door, she knew that her turn had come.

It did not seem to her that she digested the food. Certainly she did not gain strength. On the contrary, she became increasingly lethargic. Her lips were swollen from the beating they received each day. She tried to resist, but the futility sapped her energy. She recognized that she made only token efforts, but she wanted to maintain them nevertheless. Why, she could not so clearly remember. She was living on will.

Never before had Lucy understood what it meant to be alone. Because of her beauty, she had always attracted others to her, without effort. Now she began to long for anyone to help her, anyone who was on her side.

On the tenth day—she did not know it was the tenth day, for she had lost track of time—she heard a commotion in the hall. Many footfalls scuffed along, but Lucy heard no cart. The sounds grew, diminished, crescendoed again, all but stopped. None were familiar. Finally she gave up caring, closed her eyes, and tried to rest. *I have a fever,* she thought.

Lucy opened her eyes when the door burst open and was mildly surprised to find someone other than the blue-eyed doctor. Two men in dark blue uniforms unrolled a stretcher next to her bed. One stood at her head, the other at her feet, and together they lifted her off the bed and onto the stretcher. Moving quickly and wordlessly, they began to swing her out the door.

"Where am I going?" she asked hoarsely, but they did not answer.

The corridor seemed crowded with women in heavy, coarse garments. She did not recognize them at first: it seemed as though she had come upon some East European pilgrims or a Gypsy caravan. Then she glimpsed a familiar face and another. These were the picketers she had come with, dressed in workhouse uniforms. She remembered hearing others complain about the ugliness of the uniforms.

"Where am I going?" she asked again. "Where are we all going?"

"To the court in Alexandria," someone said and reached out to caress her arm. "They've given a habeas corpus on us."

In the van some of the women told her about their own experiences in the workhouse, about the denial of counsel, about the habeas corpus motion that demanded the government account for their presence in Virginia when they had been sentenced to jail in the District. Lucy could not focus on the legal issues. She saw so many faces. She held to herself the sense that she had come in from isolation. It was as though the sun rose on a June morning. She did not want to be alone again.

The passage into the old courthouse was lined with spectators, whom Lucy looked over with distant curiosity from her odd, prone angle. She sensed no hostility or friendliness in the crowd. She could not care. She had begun to tremble from the inner fire. Let them carry her wherever they wanted.

A cot had been provided her in the very front of the courtroom, under the nose of the judge. She looked up to see him from a strange angle. The lawyers moved back and forth as though walking on the ceiling. It made her dizzy. She could not understand what was said.

She was too low to see past the front row of spectators, but she could see up into the balcony. There were many women in hats. Men were holding their hats.

One woman watched the proceedings closely. Wearing a wide yellow hat, she leaned forward over the balustrade. In fact, she seemed directly interested in Lucy. Lucy studied the weathered, middle-aged face with rising interest. The woman looked at her, smiled, and gave a small wave with her fingers. She was Lucy's aunt Susan.

Chapter 21
1918: Recovery

Lucy understood only vaguely when the judge ordered the prisoners released. There came a period of commotion, with bold-patterned women's dresses pressed next to Lucy's cot, and shrieks of congratulations puncturing the air over Lucy's head. Then Susan's face appeared at Lucy's eye level. "Can I take you home?" she murmured. Always practical and never panicked, Susan led the stretcher-bearers through the crowds and onto the street, where she had a taxi waiting. She tucked Lucy under a shawl on the soft gray cushioned seat of the car, and Lucy lay with her head low and dizzy, feeling the sway of turns right and left, but neither knowing nor caring what direction they took or what destination they pursued. Susan sat opposite her on the jump seat, one hand on her arm, and Lucy was content to watch her face.

They went to a simply furnished room in a boardinghouse. Lucy went to bed and slept, waking to eat and then sleeping again. Only after several days could she think clearly about where she was and what had occurred. She dictated a letter to her parents, to which Susan added a note. Soon Lucy was able to get up and move about, to read a newspaper, to write a note to Cameron House. And she began to ask questions of Susan. How had it happened that she had come from California? Aunt Susan answered softly, as though explaining to a child how the rain came.

Lucy could not take her eyes away from her aunt's face; she followed Susan like a weather vane pointing the wind. Susan's hair no longer flamed, but had dulled toward the color of pepper. Her white skin gathered into wrinkles, like linen washed in hot water and left to dry in the sun: fine, tight lines cascading through the folds of her face. And yet—or perhaps it was because of this aging—Susan's face appeared to Lucy as a comfort and a safety, a place to cling.

"You haven't left Uncle Fred?" Lucy asked, and she noticed that Susan hesitated for a heartbeat before she answered in the negative, shushing the question aside and saying not to worry, there was nothing the matter. But Lucy did worry as her eyes watched her aunt. Aunt Susan admitted that Fred had not been happy that she left.

Susan had the warmth and calmness of a mother, almost a Madonna, to fill a niche in Lucy that she could not begin to imagine her own mother fitting. She felt no barriers of propriety with this aunt—barriers that, with her own mother, always rose up, almost filling the room. Yet there was a kittenish sisterhood between them, too, a playful, frank factuality. It was all right to say anything.

That was exactly what alarmed her, though, so that her pleasure was uneasy. She thought about it very often in the long silences as she regained her strength, for she was lazy and empty enough to stare and think quietly for long periods. She recognized her fear as the old familiar charge of their opponents. The rights of woman had beguiled them, so they could no longer abide a man. They were home wreckers. They had lost, no, thrown away, the feminine instincts. They neglected their families. They thought it was their right to do and say anything. They insisted on being lords of their own destiny. The very thought of modesty and servitude revolted them; they must be independent.

Because Lucy was unmarried, she had never felt the fully angry thrust of these charges. Now, feeling the warmth of her aunt's face while yet sensing that something was wrong, she feared that she was participating in some terrible wreck.

That was nothing to what Susan felt. She wrote to her family every day, feeling nervous and afraid when she dropped the letter in the mailbox, as though the mail slot might jump out and bite her. Her family were so far from her reach, and she had no clear sense of how her letter would be received. Further, she was confused in herself. She did not feel at all that she had done the right thing, only that the aches and sorrows had grown in her to the point of blind wretchedness, and she had broken this way.

All my life, she thought, *has been a balancing act.* No wonder she had been so happy a girl, for her twin sister had counterbalanced her like another child on a seesaw. It had never been so easy after that. Susan had struggled to stay in balance with her mother's fanatical eccentricity, trying to maintain normalcy almost by disappearing. And then, in married life, she had balanced her family's needs with the spikes and valleys of the woman's cause. She had been pulled in all directions, so it took her utmost exertion to maintain faith in her own life, her own purpose and individuality. *Sometimes,* she thought, *you balance so strenuously that no center is left.*

Every day she thought of her children. They were nearly grown, and they did not need her the way they once had. It seemed to her sometimes that they were retreating from her in silence, as though the air would no longer conduct their sounds and they were gliding away, like figures on a receding ship. But though they were grown, they remained her children.

Mainly Fred came to her mind. Sometimes she would hear a sound on the stairs or a car stopping on the street below, and for a ghostly second she would think he had come. Fred had always helped her balance. He had lent his confidence to her when she felt pulled apart. Yet for the past eighteen months, since Tom went into the army, Fred had been upset. He must fear for Tom, as she did herself, but he brooded so that his anger rose up in unpredictable ways. She did not understand what was happening to him. Had his calmness and confidence always been a struggle for balance, like hers? If so, she never realized it; she thought it came naturally to him.

Susan had come to rely more and more on the letters from Lucy, as though she were a starving prisoner fed once a week. Then she received Lucy's letter from the courtroom, with a strange return address on the envelope, written by a strange hand. She knew from the newspapers what had happened: that Lucy must have been sentenced, that there were reports of mistreatment, that some of the prisoners had gone on a hunger strike.

She had felt instantly, in her unhappiness, that she must go. No, not only *must* go, but wanted to go. It was as delicious a prospect as a feather-bed: to go on the long journey and help this girl, her sister's child, who seemed as close as she had ever had to a sister herself.

Fred, in his unhappiness, had been unyielding; he had refused to understand her reasons and refused to bless her going. She had received the letter on Friday, they had fought all the evening, and she had left the next morning. Yes, he had driven her to the station, saying not a word. He had not looked at her, let alone kissed her on the platform. Leaving him had been for her like the ripping of fabric, intentionally seized and pulled until the loud shriek of cloth cried out its separation of fiber. She did not know what it had been for him. That was the most fearful and sickening thing of all: she could not feel him. She seemed to have made him a stranger to her own mind. Yet still she thought of him every day, every hour.

———————

Susan rented a tiny efficiency above a drugstore on Key Street, with a gas fire that she lit every morning while she made coffee on the hot plate. By the time coffee had perked, Lucy could raise herself from the covers and feel a pool of warm air hanging over the bed. Susan would bring the tray, and they would sit parallel to each other in the bed, reading the newspaper. Susan set the toaster on a little round table next to the bed, so they could make toast and jam without getting up. It was delicious and peaceful, though Susan felt that they lived in a tiny soap bubble clinging to a blade of grass.

During the day Susan went to headquarters, which in the new year had moved across Lafayette Park to Jackson Place. Those were the hard hours for Lucy, when she was alone, too dizzy to read and too apt to remember. The toast and jam that had tasted so delectable in the morning invariably made her gassy and uncomfortable. She thought something might be permanently damaged in her digestive tract; she still tasted the rubber hose the doctors had pushed down her throat. Vivid dreams of the feedings would come when she shut her eyes to sleep.

Late afternoon Susan would return to change into her working clothes. Inevitably she had interesting news, of some organizer she had met telling tales of lobbying in far-off state capitals, or of the jokes that exploded like firecrackers in the busy offices. Susan never had time enough to rest before she was gone again. She worked in the kitchen at the Saint Bernard. The job enabled them to survive while Lucy recovered.

Every evening Lucy went downstairs to eat a meal in the diner next door to the drugstore. Originally Susan had proposed that Lucy heat up soup on the hot plate, but the hours were so long for Lucy that she needed some diversion. A trip down the stairs, twenty feet along the sidewalk, and into a booth at Pete's was all that Lucy could manage. Getting back up the stairs was the hard part. Fortunately she met a man who also ate dinner at Pete's, and he courteously helped her to her door. She usually fell asleep until Susan came home at eleven.

On January 10, seven weeks after this living situation began, Susan handed Lucy her morning's first cup of coffee but did not join her on the bed. Instead she began a sponge bath, grimacing from the cold water on her torso. The room had a sink but no bath.

"I've decided," she announced while lifting her shift to reach under her arms, "that I want to see the vote in the House. I'm sure the gallery will be full, so I need to get there early. If I'm not home this afternoon, you're not to worry."

"What about your uniform?"

"Oh, I'll have to come for that if the vote is finished on time. What I'm saying is that it might go into the night."

"Then what will happen to your job?"

Susan paused in her washing. Lucy did not usually think of her aunt as an older person, for they talked more like peers. But now, in the unhappy, vulnerable look she wore, Aunt Susan seemed quite outside Lucy's sphere, as though life had hurt her in unknowable ways. She looked her age, which was fifty-two.

"If they fire me, they fire me," Susan said with a peculiar stress.

"You've thought about this," Lucy said with quiet surprise. "Why didn't you tell me? You haven't been telling me your plans."

"It wasn't worth worrying about. I didn't come here to fret about whether I would please a cook at the Saint Bernard."

"It's not necessary that you work anyway. I could ask my parents for money. I'm sure they would give it."

Susan shook her head. "You could do that, but then you would deprive me. Lucy, I want to do this. If your mother wanted to, she wouldn't need to be asked."

That evening the young man who helped Lucy up the stairs invited her to share his table at Pete's. He had introduced himself as Daniel Fuller. He had an ageless, round face, with dark pink skin and two moles under his left eye. His hair he wore combed straight back so that his forehead seemed as large and round as a muskmelon. He did something with the State Department. He had studied Egyptology, which, he said with a grin that made him look like a man imitating a jack-o'-lantern, meant that he knew more about the Egyptian belief in the afterlife than any other man in the government.

He was easy to talk to, and Lucy told him what had brought her to Washington. She was glad he did not, like so many men, take a mention of suffrage as an invitation to explain how he viewed woman in the modern world. He did say that when he left the State Department at 4:30, he had heard that the House of Representatives was debating the suffrage amendment. "I passed by the Capitol thinking to listen, but the galleries were jammed and there were long lines outside. So I gave it up."

"My aunt is there," Lucy said. "She went out early this morning to get a seat."

"She's the one who shares your apartment? I think I've seen her coming and going."

"She came all the way from California just to help me when I got out of prison."

"You must be very close," Fuller said.

The implausibility of Aunt Susan's arrival struck Lucy all over again.

"The truth is, I had hardly seen her before. Never since I started college. Yet we are close. I don't know why. We write a lot."

"It sounds as though she is as committed to suffrage as you are."

"Yes. Maybe that's it. Suffrage runs in our family. My great-grandfather favored it, back in the days when it was a very radical thing to believe."

"What about your great-grandmother? Was she a suffragist?"

The sickness had left Lucy's face haggard, but a smile lit it up in a way that showed her still beautiful. "I don't actually know what my great-grandmother thought about anything. That's a funny thing, isn't it?"

"Not so funny," Fuller said. "I don't know what Egyptian great-grandmothers thought either. Women's opinions weren't always considered noteworthy."

Susan came in late and hungry. Somebody had surreptitiously passed her half of an egg sandwich in the House gallery. Otherwise she had eaten nothing all day, and now that the crisis was over, a great galloping hunger consumed her. She tried in the dark to open a can of soup and put it on the hot plate, but could not find the hot plate switch. After rattling around she located a match, but the flare of the light awakened Lucy, who stirred and spoke.

"It's me," Susan said. "I'm trying to switch on the hot plate."

"Turn on the light," Lucy said. "I want to talk with you anyway."

The light revealed a tiny, crowded room, with a young blonde woman blinking and sitting up in a foldout bed. Books and piles of newspaper surrounded her everywhere, for they had no bookcase. Without daylight the room seemed smaller and dingier, and the contrast with Lucy's penetrating and beautiful gaze more striking to Susan.

"It is a great night," Susan announced, with happiness filling her lungs. "The Susan B. Anthony Amendment has passed the House of Representatives."

"Was it very close?" Lucy asked.

"Not very close. We had one vote to spare." Susan laughed.

"Ah," Lucy said wistfully, "I wish I had been there. Was it great fun?"

"I wouldn't have called it fun for most of the time. We dared not leave our seats because there was such a crowd outside. I spent a very long time in some very uncomfortable seats listening to some very stupid speeches. The House guards would not allow us even to whisper." Susan put a hand on each side of her neck and stretched her head upward. "I'm all stiff from leaning over to see."

"And you had no certainty who would win."

"No, none."

"Did anybody mention the picketers?"

Susan paused a moment to think. "I can't remember any mention. Most of the talk had nothing to do with suffrage at all, but with states' rights. The antis have all but abandoned telling women that they ought not to bother their pretty sentimental heads with politics. Now they tell the representatives for the federal government that they ought not to bother their heads with such a local matter as who can vote. As though citizenship is a very local matter." Susan had an expansive feeling that she might well go on talking if given half a chance. There was such a pleasure in the occasion, not only of the vote but of being able to tell her niece in the privacy of this place of their own. Here at least she was fully understood, for once in her life.

"I wish they had talked about the picketers," Lucy said. "I want to believe that I did something important."

"It was a long day, with a lot of hot air," Susan said to discourage her niece from making too much of what was said or not said. "The roll call went on and on. They had quite a controversy when several members claimed that their votes had not been recorded. After a great argument they had to take the vote all over again. From the way they were fighting you could infer that the vote was extremely close, that one vote might make all the difference.

"Only when the total was announced did we know that we had won. There was cheering, and then the part I loved. When the noise died down, outside the gallery doors a woman's voice began to sing the doxology. *'Praise God, from whom all blessings flow.'* The whole gallery took it up, mostly women's voices, as sweet and melodious a choir as you ever heard. Very slow and elegant, and it filled that great room to the top. *'Praise God, from whom all blessings flow. Praise Him, all creatures here below. Praise Him above, ye heavenly host. Praise Father, Son, and Holy Ghost.'"* Susan sang this in a rusty contralto.

"You liked that," Lucy said.

"I *loved* that."

"Why?"

Susan had put her soup on the hot plate while she talked, and now she tested the temperature with her finger. It was hot enough. She used the time it took to pour the soup into a bowl to think about her reaction. She sat down on the edge of the bed with the bowl on a tray in her lap.

"I suppose I always fear in the back of my mind that we are just doing a woman's club kind of thing—agitating for another privilege. You know, the elite women of America asking that they be treated with proper respect. Not that it would be wrong to do that, but it would seem rather narrow to me. I wouldn't care to make it my cause. I like to think that we are part of something larger, something even God and the angels would embrace. That broadens it out for me. And also, I like thinking of joining such a chorus, of all the creatures in heaven and earth, along with the Holy Trinity. I love to think of all those women at the Capitol, and men, too, singing together with the heavenly host. I like it when the cause brings us together. Sometimes I fear it divides—and along narrow lines." Susan stopped and sighed. She suddenly thought of Fred and her children at home, and it took the breath out of her. But she did not want to say so to her niece and spoil the evening.

Susan ate her soup while Lucy pondered in turn. She had no emotive response to hymn singing.

"I had dinner with that man this evening," Lucy said. "Daniel Fuller is his name. He's at the State Department."

Susan asked what had brought them together.

"He said, 'Do you mind if I join you?' He had been so nice helping me go up the stairs, I couldn't say no. I enjoyed talking to him."

"What did you talk about?"

"Oh, what we were doing in Washington, that sort of thing. He asked me about you, and I realized again what an amazing thing it was that you came to help me. He asked if we were very close, and it was a shock to realize I hadn't seen you since before college."

"But we have written a great deal."

"Yes, we have. But still it's quite extraordinary that you came. I'm very grateful. I don't know what I would have done."

"You would have managed," Susan said calmly. She finished the last dollops of soup and wondered whether she ought to open another can. She was still hungry.

"Do you want to know how it happened?" Susan asked. "I had been following the case in the newspapers, and I knew that the sentences had been severe. Fred was extremely angry with you because Tom is in France, and I think he feels that the only thing he can do for him is to keep anybody from saying anything that might be negative about the cause there. He's like a librarian trying to shush up everybody in the library. I suppose that fed into my reaction because I'm not very happy that Tom is there, and I feel that I can't do a thing for him either. What can I do, knit bandages? I hate to knit. So when your letter came, I wasn't very happy. I thought, *Here's somebody I love whom I can help*. I just came. It worked out that I got here just before the habeas corpus trial."

"Was Fred very unhappy?"

Susan swallowed. "Yes, he was. I think he expected me to shun you because you weren't supporting the president. And he talked about the children. How could I desert the children? But Becky is seventeen. She's better at keeping house than I am. George is fifteen, almost sixteen, and he's never home. They don't really need me right now. I got the money for the ticket from my mother. She thinks you're a hero, by the way. She would have loved to do what you've done."

"I'm sorry that it caused a fight," Lucy said quietly. "I don't like to be a cause of that."

Susan had received just one terse letter from Fred, asking her to come home. She had gone out and walked alone for an hour because she had not wanted Lucy to see her tears. They were angry tears. How could he be so unforgiving? Men left their families to go to war, and nobody blamed them. Men went off to be missionaries and sometimes their families did not see them for months, but that was considered noble. David Livingstone was gone for *years*. Why couldn't a woman have the same freedom to decide what she had to do? Why had it always to be her family that decided it for her?

"I'm very glad you came," Lucy said when she saw that Susan was lost in thought. "I want you to go back as soon as you can. I think I'm all right now."

Then Susan's tears fell, and she turned her head away from Lucy. She remembered her father. She did not want to recapitulate his glib abandonment, or for that matter her mother's tilting after causes in such a way that she neglected those who needed her close at hand. Susan had suffered at the hands of those two, and she could hardly consider that she made her own family suffer.

And yet when she had control of herself, she shook her head at Lucy. "I'll go back when I can, Lucy. Not yet, though. I don't want to leave you when you're still so weak. And it's more than that. Now that I'm here I want to see what it's like."

"You have to admit that it's an unusual thing, coming so far for a niece you haven't seen for twelve or thirteen years."

"I admit that," Susan said slowly. "It seems strange to me too. And yet I feel I've been longing for this forever. I didn't just come. I plunged. I feel that I am reclaiming something I lost long, long ago. I was very close to your mother when we were growing up. I suppose I am doing it for her, in a way. Or doing for her daughter what she ought to do herself. I'm not sure I can define that part. I have found that I care for you very much. Even though I feel very guilty about Fred."

Susan sat quite still for a minute, rubbing her spoon around the bottom of her soup bowl. The scraping made a diversion from the silence of their room. The night was very late. They ought to sleep. It was a night to celebrate their victory, and instead they were discussing these sorry topics. She made up her mind to open another can of soup and asked Lucy whether she would care for any.

"You've always written of Fred with great fondness," Lucy said tentatively, ignoring the offer of soup.

"Yes. He is incredibly good for me. He is the best man I have ever known. But there is something that women share."

"Such as you and your mother," Lucy said with a mischievous grin.

Susan sighed. "Let me change my statement. Some women share. Or maybe I have to amend even that. I've been around a lot of women whom I didn't particularly care for. You stand apart, very dear to me.

Every morning I say a prayer of thanks that I have been given this chance to be with you. Praise God, from whom all blessings flow."

"There's that song again," said Lucy, faintly embarrassed by the intimacy of the conversation.

Susan got out another can of soup and opened it. "You've asked me about my decision," she said in a low, even voice. "Now I'd like to know about your decision. How you came to picket, that is. One minute you're working for Mrs. Catt, and the next you're carrying banners and getting arrested. And hunger striking."

Lucy lay back down and pulled the covers up to her neck. Her golden hair rayed over the pillow, while on her face she wore a sleepy smile. "I don't know if I understand my decision any better than you understand yours. I thought about it a great deal, starting when I saw the mobs tearing up banners and attacking Cameron House. I could not stand by and, so to speak, hold the cloak of the attackers. I took up a banner. Which upset Mrs. Catt mightily. She said that the president had allied himself with our cause, and that to have a woman from NAWSA picketing him at the White House would be completely detrimental to his cooperation. I knew she had a point, but I thought Alice Paul had a point too. To this day I don't know who is right. Maybe they both are. Maybe it takes both politicians and revolutionaries to make a change."

"But if you don't know," Susan asked, "how could you take such action? To go to prison, to hunger strike."

Lucy laughed dryly. "It doesn't sound like something an undecided woman would do, does it? In my mind I was undecided, Aunt Susan, but perhaps not so much in my heart. In the end I felt very clear about my own course. It was personal, what I thought *I* should do. I don't think I would argue with Mrs. Catt that her way is wrong. Even if I *could* argue with that woman. I love NAWSA, and in some ways it is the image of me. It is reasonable above all. Mrs. Catt is a reasonable woman. Just as

President Wilson is a reasonable man. I thought to myself, *I am tired of being reasonable*. I have never seen anything change by reasonable measures. Lucy Burns and Alice Paul are the most exciting people I have ever met. I liked them instinctively, and I said, 'Why not? I could hurt nobody but myself, and I don't count. Why not?'"

Susan thought that as a mother she could not let this pass. "I don't like you to say you don't count."

Lucy considered that. "I don't mean that I'm worthless, just that I don't stand for anybody or anything beyond myself. I don't have any followers. I don't have any family. Nobody cares what Lucy Phillips does." She saw that her aunt was about to remonstrate again and stopped her. "I don't mean that nobody loves me. My parents love me in their own way. And you certainly do. I mean that I'm single and free in a way that allowed me to try on something to see if it fit."

"And did it?"

"I don't know. I have asked myself that, and I don't know. I can't imagine hunger striking again. To be force-fed is terrible." Lucy shut her eyes and gave her head a shake, as if to drive the experience away. "I'll tell you what, though, it was very exciting. I will never forget the excitement. To be at the heart of the action. To do something. To think that a woman can actually do something in the world." Her words trailed off.

Susan said, "And now we have the House. All my life, from the day I was born, I have heard suffrage, suffrage, suffrage. All my life." She suddenly smiled. "I wonder what my mother will find to talk about."

Chapter 22
1918: The Last Campaign

Susan was ready to go out to headquarters. She had her purse in her hand when she heard a door slam on the street and looked out the apartment window to see Fred paying the taxi driver. He was standing in a pose she would know anywhere as his, with one hand on his hip, the other hand stretched out for change. His shape was so familiar, and yet so unexpected and out of context here, he seemed to be seen in a dream. She watched in silence and shock as the driver counted out bills into his palm. Fear made her weak because she thought Fred surely came in anger. At the same time his dapper, straight figure made Susan experience something she had almost forgotten, a readiness to rush and bury herself into his arms.

She found him at the bottom of the stairs and gave in to that emotion of abandon, kissing him and crying she was glad to see him. "Why didn't you tell me? I had no idea. I might have been gone."

He could feel her fear, and he sought to reassure her with his body, holding her tightly for a long time before he answered. "I came spur of the moment. There wasn't time to even cable."

"Where are the children? You didn't bring them?" She thought of them all the time; she prayed for them.

He stiffened; she felt it through his coat. "No, they're at home. Becky is taking care of the farm and the old folks."

"George is in school?"

Fred paused and backed off to look at her. "George wanted to take on the business while I was gone."

"What about his education?"

"He doesn't want to go back to school." He paused. "I argued with him, but he knew his mind."

She felt it as a reproach: her family reclaiming her, pulling her into their lives. If she had been there, it might have been different. George had the brains for college. The problem was that the high school was too easy for him. The vegetable route was more challenging. Now, that is. It would not be for long.

What could she say, however? She had not been there. Fred had written, asking her to come home, but she had said not yet. She *would* come home, but not yet. She had been amazingly happy here. Lucy had needed her.

She sensed his nervousness. He had come a long way without knowing whether he would be welcomed. She was so relieved because he came in love. Whatever bitterness he held lay buried, at least for the moment. He was a strong, good man. She took him in her arms again and pressed the hard frame, the compact rib cage, until her hands felt the strain.

"I want you to come up and see Lucy," she said. "Do you have any place to stay?" Then she realized how wrong that sounded and amended her words. "Of course you'll stay here, but we'll have to do some rearranging."

———

They all three shared the efficiency that night, Fred making a pallet on the floor with some blankets they borrowed from the neighbor across the hall. Lucy made him turn his back while she changed into night-clothes. Susan quietly laughed at herself, realizing that she watched Fred watching Lucy with a touch of jealousy. It reassured her in a way. *After all, he is my man*, she told herself. She dreaded the talk they would have, which she knew to be unavoidable, but she took some encouragement from feeling the attraction that still drew her to him.

The next day she took him to see the capital monuments. Fred was interested but mainly quiet as they went through the Capitol and the White House. She led him to her favorite spot, the new memorial to Lincoln. It had been under construction ever since she arrived in Washington, so she felt a kind of kinship with the building. They both had looked over Washington for the same amount of time. It was a building under construction, just pillars as yet. The statue of Lincoln had not yet been installed. Sometimes she left headquarters and ate lunch there, all alone. Now she led Fred to sit on the steps with their long view over the Mall.

Fred ate the egg salad sandwiches without saying a word. He neatly folded the waxed paper into a square, licked his fingers, and then leaned back on his elbows. "Is this a good time to talk?" he asked.

"Yes," Susan said, though she felt clumsy with nervousness. "Why not?"

"I came hoping I could bring you back home," Fred said. He couldn't see any other way than to plunge into it. "I don't think it's right for a woman to leave her family."

"I don't either," Susan said quickly. "You know that. I came on an errand of mercy. Lucy was in trouble. She really was, far more than I realized. When she came out of prison, she was very, very sick."

He nodded. "But she's not sick anymore."

"She's not completely well either. I'm not sure she could hold a job. I know she looks well, but she is still weak."

"That doesn't mean she needs a full-time nurse."

"I'm not her nurse anymore. She takes care of herself. I'm just saying I don't think she's quite ready to make a living."

"Doesn't she have some money saved up?"

"No, I don't think so."

"You've been working to support her?"

"Yes, Fred. She could have gone to her parents for help, but you know how that is. She feels closer to me."

"And you obviously feel closer to her than to your own family."

That stung—as he had obviously meant it to. Susan took the remark quietly, wrestling with its truth in her mind.

"Fred, I don't think you do me justice. If you or George or Becky had been in need, I would have cared for you just the same. I have, in fact. Even my mother. Even, God forgive me, my father. I have spent my life putting my family first. Lucy was in need in a way that you weren't."

"All right," he said. "That's fair. But I don't think I want to be on a charity basis."

"What do you mean?"

"I mean that I don't want to have to break my leg to get your attention. I'd like to have you all the time."

The yellowing haze of the afternoon filled the sky in front of them, vast banks of filmy air far out over the city with its monuments. At their backs Susan could sense the cavern where Lincoln would someday brood behind his pillars. *I have to be truthful,* she thought, *if I know what is truthful.*

"I take my vows seriously, Fred." She stopped, took a deep breath, and let it out again. Suddenly she felt trembly and weak, and her voice wanted to quaver. "I belong to you, and you do have me all the time, though I admit it must not always seem to be that way. But that is not all of me. That is not the whole story. I have been looking for something all my life, something I am not sure you have to give." She could hardly talk for emotion, but she made herself go on because she did not want to leave Fred with that as a final word, even for a moment. "I don't know what it is. Sisterhood, maybe. A sense of complete and easy sympathy, a matching of minds and hearts. Something I had with Elizabeth when we were girls and then lost completely. I don't know whether I can explain it. Probably I don't understand it myself."

She shook her head and took a handkerchief from her purse, but let it sit unused in her lap. "When I saw you get out of the taxi, I realized that I had missed something else. I missed you, Fred. Very much. I have been missing you all these weeks. I feel guilty, too, but missing you is something more than that. Perhaps I didn't realize it because I was so full of the other thing."

"And I can't be a part of this other thing?" Fred asked. "The matching of heart and mind?"

"I don't know," Susan said. "I don't know whether it's a passing thing or whether it can last. I don't know whether I can share it. Most of my life I've missed it; I've never found it before."

She paused and gulped. Remembering her handkerchief, she lifted that flimsy square of white to her eyes. It seemed pointless: to dab them seemed to make them flow faster. After a few moments she gave up and put the handkerchief down.

"Do you think Lucy would come west?" Fred asked. He did his best to suppress his feeling, thinking it would not do for both of them to be overwrought. He had started on this trip full of fury, and he had needed hundreds of miles of sagebrush and rock, hours to breathe and remember, before he had realized that he could not drag her back home. Fury was pointless. He had to discover how to reattach himself.

"It's more than Lucy," Susan said. She stood up. "Come on, I want to show you. Let's go to headquarters."

———————

Headquarters had moved to a vast mansion fronting Lafayette Park. Susan led Fred through the grand white entrance, festooned with gold, purple, and white. In the entrance hall a young woman with a headset smiled in their direction but stayed steadily occupied operating the switchboard.

"Here is the press office," Susan said, indicating a door to their left. Fred peeked in and saw a very crowded room, with young women walking very fast, hips waggling, or conversing together, or huddled over their desks. "That's where Lucy worked," Susan said. "Sometimes I do something useful there."

Halfway up the stairs Susan was greeted by a party of three women descending. She stopped and introduced Fred. "Oh, so this is the *husband*," said a brunette wearing a wide purple hat. "It's about time you got here." She smiled coquettishly at Susan. "See if Alice can't put him to work," she said. "We definitely need some men in this place." The other women burst into laughter.

They entered a very large and elegantly decorated ballroom, with antique tables and chairs clustered under high casement windows. "We can seat three hundred here," Susan said. "But every day you can find women reading or talking. Isn't this marvelous?"

"Where did they get the furniture?" Fred said. He had an eye for good things.

"A Mrs. Pflaster gave most of it," Susan said. "It's funny about Miss Paul. She wouldn't complain if she slept in a tent pitched on the Mall, but somehow she ends up with this stuff. It's priceless, I'm told. I like that painting." She indicated a large canvas that hung near the fireplace, showing a cluster of women working in a hayfield. The pitched hay seemed to shine like gold.

"Come see Miss Paul's office," Susan said and led Fred out of the ballroom and into a corridor. From every doorway they heard the chatter of typewriting. Occasionally a burst of laughter was flung out, and more young women strutted jauntily between the office doors. Some of them stopped and let Susan introduce them to Fred. They all seemed to know her.

The door to Paul's office was closed, but Susan went to an anteroom where a secretary was busy typing. "I was just wondering whether I could show my husband Miss Paul's office," Susan said.

The secretary said that they would have to wait, Miss Paul was occupied, but just as she finished saying it, the door opened and a tiny, pale creature, all eyes and mouth and thick black hair, appeared. She looked them over with the curious attention of a cat, but no smile. "Mrs. Konicek," she said gravely.

"I didn't mean to bother you, Miss Paul," Susan said. "This is my husband, Mr. Konicek. Fred, this is Miss Paul, our president." Susan asked whether Miss Paul would mind if they looked into her office. It was a showpiece: wooden furniture done in golden oak, upholstery in purple velvet.

Paul came in behind them and asked Fred what he did.

"I'm in fruits and vegetables," he said. "Wholesale. In California. But truth to tell, I don't know what I'm doing right now. That's what my wife and I are trying to discuss."

Paul looked at him steadily, as though her deep eyes might suck him in and absorb him. "Mr. Konicek, we are at the most critical period in our fight for democracy at home. Most of our women are very young, as you may have seen. Susan's experience in life is invaluable. She is one of the people I rely on."

Paul's eyes switched off him, as though a plug on the switchboard had been pulled. She shook hands again, but she was already gone. Fred looked at Susan. "That's quite a woman," he said after Paul was out the door. "She makes an impression."

"I wish you could meet Lucy Burns," Susan said.

They descended to the tearoom, where even at two o'clock women sat in an expanded circle, talking intensively like surgeons discussing a case. The brick walls had been painted suffrage yellow; the tables and chairs in a sleek black. Light fixtures hung swathed in yellow silk. The room was as chic as the rest of the mansion was elegant. "This is the place," Susan said with an almost romantic warmth. "I love this tearoom."

They drank coffee in pregnant silence. The room's cheery space vibrated with young life coming and going, chatting and laughing. Finally Fred cleared his throat. "All right. I can see you're not ready to leave this place."

Susan did not respond, but merely waited in fear to hear what he might say.

"Here's what I will do," Fred went on while staring away from her into the glare from one of the windows. "I will see about a job so that we can get a bigger place."

She looked up at him sharply, questioningly. She did not understand.

"We've got no choice," Fred said truculently, and then his face eased into a smile. He was going to make a joke, she saw. "You've got no room for another bed, and I'm not sharing my bed with a second woman."

Susan laughed. The joke was not funny, but she felt the tension diminishing. "You had better not."

"Absolutely not."

"Fred," she said, "you are willing to stay here with me?"

"Sure," he said. "That's what I've decided to do."

"What about the children?"

Fred looked at her with a crooked smile. She could tell the children got his dander the most, and it was still for her, too, the sorest spot. But he had decided not to make an issue of the children. "I've got them covered," he said. "It's the old folks I worry about the most."

"That they might murder each other?"

"Really, Susan, it might be the best thing. For me to be gone, not for those two to murder each other. Though that is not a bad idea either. I'm thinking of George. If George is going to get anything out of the vegetable business, he needs to do it on his own. He doesn't need me anywhere nearby. And Becky is like the woman she was named for. She is a strong young woman. She doesn't want either one of us bothering her. Who knows? If we give her enough time, she might get those two old folks in hand."

They returned to silence for a few minutes, sipping at their coffee and listening to the noise reverberating in the room. Susan had shed her fear, but she felt a sense of sadness replacing it. It took her a moment's thought to locate its cause. She would miss out on her children. That was the cost she must pay: she was far from them as they stepped out into the world. It tore at her to think so. Was it right? Was it what she truly wanted?

Fred would miss out, just as she would. And why? For her. All of a sudden the magnitude of his care filled the air, as with a thousand July Fourth sparklers. "You will really do this for me?" she asked.

"What?" he said.

"You will leave everything and come here to indulge me?"

He twisted one corner of his mouth, showing that he did not care for the way she put it. "I've never lived in this part of the world. I'll give it a try. I'll miss the kids, just like you do, but they're practically grown up anyway. If I had to give up everything, I don't know that I would, but most of what I have is portable. To tell you the truth, I'd rather be with you here than to try to make sense of life out there while you're gone."

"Fred," she said, and she was crying again, "how do you forgive me? Time and again."

"I guess the same way you forgive me," he said.

———————————

Fred took just two days to find work. He was employed by a Portuguese fishmonger to hustle crabs and oysters and fish in season on a regular delivery route. He smelled of fish, but he said he was happy enough with the job. They were able to get an apartment from a Department of Agriculture employee who had been posted with his family to France and claimed to have information that the war would end shortly.

The apartment, a walk-up in a building opposite the efficiency, had two small bedrooms and a tiny kitchen with a hot plate. The walls had been painted orange by some previous tenant, and they left them that way. It was a temporary accommodation. Everything was conditional: the war, the suffrage campaign, their stay in Washington.

They were seldom all together. Fred left very early for his route. Lucy was well enough to go to headquarters with Susan, coming home with her in the afternoon and eating in the diner while Susan went to work. Fred seldom came home before Susan. Sometimes he worked extra hours, but more often he used his evenings to visit automobile workshops. He had found some racing mechanics who worked on their vehicles in the after-dinner hours, and Fred said he liked to listen to them talk.

It could not last, Susan knew. Lucy was a young woman and must move on. The campaign could not go on forever. Fred would want to go home again—and so would she.

They had expected in January that the Senate would soon follow the House in passing the Anthony Amendment. Not so. The spring turned into the soupy heat of summer. Lucy said it was the history of suffrage all over again: great expectations, followed by the most astounding display of patronizing effrontery. President Wilson made fine-sounding signals to Mrs. Catt's delegations about his support of this significant reform, but he never put any weight on it. The war was more important. The terms of the coming peace were more important. How, the women wanted to know, could he continue to believe that the disenfranchisement of half the population was a minor affair?

In August, Alice Paul led a large contingent from headquarters to Lafayette Park. They lit a fire in a large urn and burned the president's latest speeches. After that they started watch fires every day in front of the White House. Sometimes the police tried to extinguish the fires, but more often they stood by and let the sailors and soldiers do the job for them. When Susan and Lucy entered headquarters each morning, they could smell the strong kerosene solution the logs were soaked in. The smell penetrated their clothes and their hair; Lucy said cheerfully that it blotted out the smell of fish. Soaked in this solution, the logs would not go out. Kicked halfway across the street, they would continue to burn.

Every day a substantial crowd lined up to see the confrontation. Susan typically went out to watch at least a few minutes. (Lucy, she noticed, made excuses to stay in.) Sometimes the police arrested the picketers (who now got five days' sentence), but many times they stood back to let the sailors assault the women, tear up their banners, and turn their fiery urns upside down.

At the end of September, President Wilson took the unprecedented step of going to the Capitol to address the Senate, urging them to pass the Anthony Amendment as a war measure. The senators were uninfluenced. They turned it down by two votes.

So Alice Paul led them to picket the Senate. Susan, who had hung back from picketing, decided that she was finally ready. She told Fred, expecting him to disapprove.

"What kind of banner are you going to carry?" he asked.

She looked at him as if he were crazy. "It's going to say, 'Democracy begins at home.'"

"What about you, Lucy?" They were drinking chamomile tea around a drop-leaf table that Susan had bought at an estate sale.

"No," she said. "I can't." Her pale eyes looked away, out their double window.

Susan put a hand on Lucy's arm. "It's all right," she said. "You have done your part."

"I don't know how Alice Paul manages it," Lucy said angrily. "She never flinches. I wish I could be like that." She squeezed Susan's hand.

"Go ahead and picket, Susan," Fred said, changing the subject. "It's all right with me. If you are going to be here in Washington, you may as well do it right."

A month after Susan was first arrested—but not jailed, only detained and released—the war ended. Susan thought she had never seen Fred so happy, at least not since their children were born. He kissed her on the mouth; he kissed Lucy on the mouth; he tried to kiss other women at headquarters. He bought a huge piece of meat for their supper. It would not fit into the frying pan, so Susan cut it in half and fried the two pieces separately. She did it before leaving for work; she was fairly sure that Lucy did not know how to cook, and she could state for a fact that Fred did not. Who was going to eat so much beef? she wanted to know. It turned out that Fred gave half of it to a neighbor.

War or no war, they had not heard from Tom. Fred said not to worry; there was no reason to worry now that the war was over. But he seemed uneasy. For the first time Susan felt impatient that the crusade went on so long. She would not depart Washington before they had won victory, not after all they had invested, but thinking of Tom gave her an inkling that she would have a life beyond, a life at home with her family.

The Senate picketing had taken a rhythm. They marched from different locations, at different times, but the result was always the same. The Capitol police would take their banners and detain them, but never charge them. Sometimes they were held for hours, until (by someone's calculation) it was too late for them to picket again. Susan took to carrying a book of Browning with her to read while they waited for their release in the Capitol basement. At Fred's suggestion she switched to a small black Bible. She always found something there to read. It was in the Capitol basement that she read, for the first time as far as she could remember, the riveting story of Jesus' crucifixion. She had been looking for that phrase, "Father, forgive them" (which she never found), and had caught on to the whole passage in Matthew.

It helped her to understand Fred, to think of his life as a coherent whole. She had known, of course, what the cross stood for, and she knew in general terms the Christian formula that Jesus Christ had given His life on the cross to forgive us for our sins. Before reading the gospel account, however, she had not grasped that formula's roots in biography. It was one very vivid man's conscious, stubborn willingness to die at the hands of misguided people, to die *for* misguided people who put their lives in opposition to His. It was a decision to sacrifice a life in hopes of winning through to a better day in company with the very people who were so wretchedly wrong. Fred could not or would not articulate his thinking this way, Susan knew, but she saw that his life had been formed in the shadow of this biography. Not that he was perfect, or his motives unmixed. But it was not entirely an accident of character that he was the kind of husband that he was. Susan pondered that at length. She knew that she still had him, that she still had her family and her future, because he had made the long journey here to join her and to forgive her.

In December, Alice Paul led them back to the White House to burn Wilson's words. They did that all through January, not every day, but on many days. In February they burned Wilson in effigy—a paper figure, that is, that they dumped in their pot of flames.

———

"What will you do when this campaign ends?" Susan asked Lucy one day when Fred was gone on his route, and the two of them had been left to fill the morning together. Lucy lay stretched on the yellow sofa, which clashed awfully with the orange-painted walls. Susan had a cup of coffee that she held out toward the window, as though offering it to the gods. She did not drink at it, but she said it felt good to hold something warm in her hands. The day was brilliant blue, cold February weather, and she could not get enough of its brightness and color. *That is another sign,* she thought, *that I will be happy to go home, though probably it has more to do with five days in the absolute gloom of the old workhouse.*

She had been arrested in front of the White House, and this time she was sentenced. She could not exactly compare notes with Lucy because the authorities had stopped sending women to the Occoquan workhouse. Instead they had reopened the District's long-closed workhouse, full of vermin and fumes from a sewer. She and the other protesters had been put in barred cells far below the high, dirty windows. Like all the women, she had hunger struck while there—a gesture she had doubts about, since five days was not enough for starvation, only misery.

"What makes you think it will end?" Lucy asked. Two days earlier, the Senate had turned down the suffrage amendment again, this time by one vote. She did not name, nor did she need to, the history of discouragement that had dogged woman suffrage. That was a fundamental fact of the movement—that they had waited so long.

"Fred says we are going to win. He says he can smell it."

"How can he smell anything with all those fish?"

"He's usually a good prognosticator. Myself, I think the prohibition amendment has almost guaranteed ours. The liquor interests don't have any reason to fight us anymore, so we've lost enemies. And the politicians will conclude that the wind is blowing for progress, so they'll give in to us."

Lucy stretched lazily. "I don't know what I will do. Go back to advertising, I suppose, if I can get a job. I'll always be able to tell my grandchildren that I got arrested and was force-fed fighting for the great cause." She looked at Susan and smiled shyly. "Seriously I'm very glad for that. I wanted to do something important, and I feel that I have."

"Seriously, when did you decide about the grandchildren? I wasn't aware you were taking steps in that direction."

Lucy laughed and put her head down into the cushions. A moment later, however, she popped up again. "What do you think Lucy Burns will do? Or, for that matter, Mrs. Catt? I can't imagine any of them retiring to have grandchildren."

"Mrs. Catt has her plans already laid out. She will head a League of Women Voters to channel all women's energies toward reform."

"Really?" Lucy said. "Miss Paul has political plans, too, from what I gather. She wants an amendment guaranteeing equal rights for women—not just in votes, but in everything."

"Those two women are not as different as they seem," Susan said. "Women and politics, politics and women."

"You sound skeptical."

"No, not skeptical. I wouldn't be here if I were skeptical."

"So being in prison didn't make you lose your faith in the movement?" Lucy said.

"No, I certainly believe in the cause. I would do again what I have done. But I can't imagine myself pursuing the same political logic for the rest of my life. Not like Mrs. Catt or Alice Paul. For me, the logic of this movement ends when we get the vote. The vision is too narrow to carry any farther."

Lucy sat up. "In a way Mrs. Stanton, my mother's namesake, thought like that. Her daughter, Mrs. Blatch, told me that Mrs. Stanton thought suffrage was too small an issue to carry the kind of movement she wanted. She thought we should talk about religion, you know. And many subjects. The movement shut her up. It was too controversial."

"Yes, I know, I was there for some of that discussion. Lucy, do you know I even spoke in Mrs. Stanton's defense at the convention that censured her? Miss Anthony asked me to. That's how ancient I am. Not that I was so important really, but I did have a small role.

"I think now that perhaps Mrs. Stanton was right, though not right in a way I would follow. She scandalized the women by blaming religion for our troubles. I think she was right to take up such fundamental issues, but wrong in her analysis. Probably we need more religion, not less, I believe. I think back to my grandfather, your great-grandfather. You know that all the earliest suffragists were abolitionists. That is where they got their beginnings—not simply in activism, but also in the way they came to think about human life. They believed in God's gift of dignity to every person and His concern for the sufferings of the unprotected. Those were abolitionist ideas that carried on to the woman's cause. It is not just a matter of politics and voting rights. Something has to stand before that."

Lucy smiled at her aunt. "You haven't told me what you plan to do when this is over," she said.

"I'll go home," Susan said. "I'll go home and see what there is to do."

Chapter 23
1919: Victory

Lucy came back from dinner one May evening to find Tom and Sylvie, his French bride, on the curb with their suitcases. Lucy invited them both up to the apartment and made them comfortable, then rushed to a pay phone to call Susan at the hotel. It was a wonder to see Susan's face when she first looked at her grown son, home from the war. She was just so terribly happy to see him alive.

So was Fred, when he eventually arrived late that night. He took it more coolly, but his face would not stop grinning. The corners of his mouth were like twin springs: however they were forced down, they came popping up again. Lucy noticed how Tom and Fred fell into a private conversation, as though taking up where they had left off two years before.

When Susan saw the wife Tom had in tow, a complete surprise to them all, she squelched any questions about why he had not written. *Sylvie is enough explanation*, she thought. *He has surely been occupied.*

Now, two weeks later, Susan still joyfully searched Tom's dark features, as though seeking to confirm his real existence. He looked too young to be wearing a uniform, to have fought in a war. His face seemed thinner, but his shoulders, neck, and arms had added ropy strength. And did he carry himself differently?

"I'm still surprised you aren't more excited," Tom said to his mother. "I thought you'd be turning cartwheels. You've been talking about this all my life." He referred to the Susan B. Anthony Amendment to the Constitution, passed by the Senate four days ago, June 4.

Lucy overheard Tom's comment as she came out of the back of the apartment bearing a wooden crate filled with books. "I think it surprised all of us," she said to her cousin as she put the crate down next to a neat line of suitcases and boxes. "It wasn't just your mother. I heard several women comment on how depressed they felt." She and Susan had sat in the gallery. They had listened to the long speeches against the amendment, senators thundering about states' rights, warning about the enfranchisement of colored women. Yet everyone knew the result. The amendment had the votes.

"Don't you remember feeling that way at Christmas sometimes?" Susan said. "You wait and you wait, and then when you open the presents, it's a little disappointing."

"Yes," Lucy said, sitting down. "We waited so long, and we worked so hard, it seemed that if we could only win the vote, it would mean everything. Now it turns out that we have to go on with our lives."

"Where do you suppose Dad is?" Tom asked. "He should have been back an hour ago."

Susan glanced at Lucy and gave a private smile. They could talk for hours about the suffrage campaign, but for Tom, it held only a passing interest.

He went over to the window, where his bride sat drinking a cup of tea and looking sadly out the window. Since Sylvie spoke hardly any English, they worked around her like an odd piece of furniture. She had black hair cut short around a small face. Just above the corner of her mouth, a tiny birthmark in the shape of an hourglass gave her the semblance of a lopsided smile. Sylvie always seemed about to wink, which made Susan want to talk to her, to find out what she was thinking. Susan wondered how they would communicate on their long journey home. She supposed Tom would interpret.

How had he learned so much French? He had two years at Santa Rosa High School. When Susan asked, he brushed the question aside— he said he really didn't speak well at all. *He spoke it well enough to get Sylvie to come with him,* Susan thought.

For her, the Anthony Amendment had been reduced in its importance just by the presence of her son and her daughter-in-law. Plenty of work remained. The amendment had to be ratified by the states, which would require campaigns in forty different capitals. She could have stayed and worked. She might even have been paid. That possibility did not seem serious to Susan, however. After eighteen months in Washington, she was glad to be going home.

With Tom's army pay and Fred's connections they bought a Packard automobile, which they planned to drive all the way west. Susan would never have chosen that course—she much preferred the security of the train—but she saw that the two men had their wind up, so she let them organize it. If and when they broke down or got lost, that would be their problem to solve.

Three times Tom had walked to the window and looked out on the street. "I don't know why he is taking so long," he said. "We ought to be gone by now. Is everything packed up?"

Lucy came in with a cloth bag spilling over with rags. "I think this is it," she said. "Look, Tom, you aren't doing any good fretting. Is there anything in Washington that you want to see? Your dad will need to eat when he gets here anyway, so why don't you go over to the Mall and take in some sights?"

Tom whispered to Sylvie. Her small features narrowed in concentration, and then she turned to put her mouth near to Tom's ear and whispered in voluble French. Watching, Susan wondered whether

Lucy's gorgeous blonde beauty troubled Tom at all, whether he had any second thoughts about marrying a dark French girl. If so, he did not show it. The two seemed to exist in a private car of their own.

"Sylvie would like to see Lafayette's statue," Tom said with a pleased smile. "She says she learned about it in school. Do either of you know where it is?"

Susan exchanged a smile with Lucy. "Oh, yes," she said. "That is one monument we can locate." They both laughed conspiratorially.

When they had gone, Lucy asked Susan whether she cared for some tea. Susan sat on the sofa, and Lucy came next to her, sitting so close that they almost touched. For some time they were silent. They would part within an hour or two. After eighteen months on the closest terms, they might never be so near again. Susan thought that was the reason for the poignant silence. She noticed that Lucy was hunched over her cup in a most vulnerable way, almost as though she were wounded.

"Don't take it so hard," Susan said. "We will see each other again. If you want to come out to California, you are welcome."

"Aunt Susan, I would love to come, but that isn't it. I have been waiting for a chance to talk with you. Daniel Fuller—you remember him?"

Susan remembered the name, though they had never met. He was the young man at the State Department with whom Lucy shared dinner each evening.

"He has been posted to Argentina, in the embassy. He wants me to go with him."

Lucy had turned a deep, confused red. Susan could not think that she had ever seen her blush before.

"'To go with him'?" Susan asked.

"To marry him. I never thought of him that way, Aunt Susan. I liked him, I liked talking to him, but I did not realize that he had fallen in love with me."

"Of course not. How would you know?"

Lucy gulped in a huge breath and held it. She blinked her eyes several times. "Aunt Susan, what should I do? He has to go at the end of June."

Susan did not answer. She felt suddenly alert and alarmed, understanding as she did the risks of marriage.

"Daniel says I need to apply for a passport. I don't want to go to Argentina. I don't have any idea what I could do there. Aunt Susan, don't you think it is important that I know what I could do?"

Susan still kept quiet. She was trying to interpret the meaning of Lucy's agitation. She looked down at her tea, which she had barely sipped. It was in an unfamiliar blue china cup.

"We need to pack these cups," Susan said. "Where did they come from?"

"It's my mother's. I mean, she sent them."

"You heard from your mother?"

"Some time ago. Just a note. You know she doesn't write."

Susan put her left hand out to Lucy's right and held it, massaging the knuckles while she thought. "What do you think of this Daniel Fuller?" she asked.

"I like him very much, Aunt Susan. He's somewhat strange, but I don't mind that. In fact, I like the way he looks. I like talking to him because he is very well educated, and he acts as though he thinks I am too. He's a very interesting man. I want you to meet him."

"It's late for that, I think. So, Lucy, do you like him well enough to marry him?"

Lucy pulled her hand away. "I don't know. I think I would if I had more time, and he weren't going to Argentina. I don't want to go there."

"Why not? I hear it's a very beautiful country."

"Yes, I've heard that too."

Susan thought she had heard enough. "Lucy, I wish I had more time to meet Mr. Fuller and make a careful study of his intentions. I assume he is for suffrage?"

"Oh, of course."

"I wouldn't like to see you married to someone who held very different views from yours. I suppose eating dinner with him every night, you've had a chance to talk over all kinds of things."

"Yes. He's very intellectual. I like that he has surprising views. I would say we get along well on most subjects."

"Lucy, years ago when I was about your age, Fred asked me to marry him. I was completely unprepared for it. I hadn't expected I would ever marry. I didn't know how it would work out. We didn't have any money, either one of us. I suppose just the institution of marriage seemed like a strange country to me, not having grown up with it. As strange as Argentina or stranger.

"I reached a point, however, where I wanted to marry him, even though I was afraid. It hasn't been altogether easy, but I am glad I did. Very glad. If you want to marry this Daniel Fuller, I wouldn't let a little thing like Argentina scare you off. That's my advice if you want it."

Lucy put her hand back over Susan's and squeezed it. "That's exactly what my mother said."

Susan looked at her. "I thought you said she didn't write."

"I telephoned. She said marriage would do me good. But she recommended I ask you. She said we are very much alike, and I would do well to do what you say."

Before Susan could respond, they heard a loud shout from outside the apartment. Fred's voice was halloing and bellowing as though the rain had turned to pearls and he needed somebody to help him pick them up.

"Somebody's happy," Lucy said and got up to look out.

There stood Fred on the damp pavement, looking up at them with a grin all over his face. The Packard was at the curb. Rain had formed tiny silver beads on its shiny hood.

"Aren't we ready to go?" he shouted. "Guess what I got to do. I flew in an airplane."

"Really?" Susan said. He had wanted to fly for years. The day they went to the Pan-Pacific Exposition in San Francisco, the weather had been too windy, and the planes had not been going up. Somehow, every time an airplane offered rides at the fair, Fred missed it.

"It was fabulous. Susan, I've made up my mind that I want to learn to pilot."

"That's for young men," Susan said.

"Who says I'm not young?" he shouted. "You'll see. Where's Tom? Come on, start carrying the luggage down. We need to go. I'm sorry I'm late, but I couldn't pass up that chance." He disappeared from sight as he headed for the stairs.

Susan looked at Lucy. "It's not to be done lightly," she said. "But they can make life very exciting."

"I think life has been exciting already," Lucy said. "Don't you?"

"I would not trade this year for anything. Can you believe it, Lucy? We have the vote. What Mrs. Stanton and Aunt Susan and the original Lucy herself wanted but didn't get. Every woman from this time forward will have the same rights as men. We have done something."

"Yes. I will remember it all my life. I am glad that I could do it with you. You have been like a mother to me."

"More like sisters, I think," Susan said.

For Further Reading

Barry, Kathleen. *Susan B. Anthony: A Biography of a Singular Feminist.* New York: New York University Press, 1988.

Coolidge, Olivia. *Women's Rights: The Suffrage Movement in America, 1848–1920.* New York: E. P. Dutton, 1966.

Dubois, Ellen Carol. *Harriot Stanton Blatch and the Winning of Woman Suffrage.* New Haven: Yale University Press, 1997.

Flexner, Eleanor. *Century of Struggle: The Woman's Rights Movement in the United States.* Cambridge: Harvard University Press, 1959.

Griffith, Elisabeth. *In Her Own Right: The Life of Elizabeth Cady Stanton.* New York: Oxford University Press, 1984.

Hays, Elinor Rice. *Morning Star: A Biography of Lucy Stone, 1818–1893.* San Diego: Harcourt, Brace & World, 1961.

Kraditor, Aileen. *The Ideas of the Woman Suffrage Movement, 1890–1920.* New York: W. W. Norton, 1965.

Shaw, Anna. *The Story of a Pioneer.* New York: Harper and Bros., 1915.

Stevens, Doris. Edited by Carol O'Hare. *Jailed for Freedom: American Women Win the Vote.* Salt Lake City: New Sage Press, 1920.

Van Voris, Jacqueline. *Carrie Chapman Catt: A Public Life.* New York: The Feminist Press, 1987.

Ward, Geoffrey C., and Ken Burns. *Not for Ourselves Alone: The Story of Elizabeth Cady Stanton and Susan B. Anthony.* New York: Alfred A. Knopf, 1999.

Wheeler, Leslie, ed. *Loving Warriors: Selected Letters of Lucy Stone and Henry B. Blackwell, 1853–1893.* New York: Dial Press, 1981.

About the Author

Tim Stafford is Senior Writer for *Christianity Today* magazine. He has written many books, including *Knowing the Face of God; That's Not What I Meant; Love, Sex, and the Whole Person;* and *A Thorn in the Heart,* a novel. *Sisters* is the second book in a four-part series that began with *The Stamp of Glory.* Stafford has served on the editorial staff of *Campus Life* magazine and helped found *Step* magazine in Nairobi, Kenya, and Accra, Ghana.

Stafford lives in Santa Rosa, California, with his wife and three children. He enjoys backpacking, running, and baseball.